SUSPICIOUS ACTIVITY

Also by Mike Papantonio

Novels

Inhuman Trafficking – A Legal Thriller (2021; with Alan Russell)
Law and Addiction – A Legal Thriller (2019)
Law and Vengeance – A Legal Thriller (2017)
Law and Disorder – A Legal Thriller (2016)

Nonfiction

Closing Arguments – The Last Battle (2003; with Fred Levin)
Resurrecting AESOP – Fables Lawyers Should Remember (2000)
Clarence Darrow, the Journeyman – Lessons for the Modern Lawyer (1997)
In Search of Atticus Finch – A Motivational Book for Lawyers (1996)

SUSPICIOUS ACTIVITY

MIKE PAPANTONIO
WITH CHRISTOPHER PAULOS

Arcade Publishing • New York

Arcade Publishing books may be purchased in bulk at special discounts for
sales promotion, corporate gifts, fund-raising, or educational purposes. Special
editions can also be created to specifications. For details, contact the Special
Sales Department, Arcade Publishing, 307 West 36th Street, 11th Floor,
New York, NY 10018 or arcade@skyhorsepublishing.com.

Arcade Publishing® is a registered trademark of Skyhorse Publishing, Inc.®,
a Delaware corporation.

Visit our website at www.arcadepub.com
Please follow our publisher Tony Lyons on Instagram @tonylyonsisuncertain

10 9 8 7 6 5 4 3 2 1

Library of Congress Cataloging-in-Publication Data is available on file.

Cover design by Erin Seaward-Hiatt
Cover image from Getty Images

Print ISBN: 978-1-956763-89-8
Ebook ISBN: 978-1-956763-90-4

Printed in the United States of America

ACKNOWLEDGMENTS

The authors wish to thank the following individuals for their help in the preparation of this novel: Raymond Benson, Mark Gompertz, Kim Lim, Tony Lyons, Cynthia Manson, Patrick Nichols, and our colleagues at Levin Papantonio Rafferty Law Firm.

This is a work of fiction, but it is inspired by true events. While most locations in the book are real places, "Plainsburg, Kentucky" is completely fictional. Likewise, entities such as Gold Star Plus, the Mohawk Warriors (MWs), and Bank Antriol are creations of the authors' imaginations.

PROLOGUE

Iraq

It was during the second week of November 2007 that Death came to visit a godforsaken bridge in Kirkuk, a town approximately 220 kilometers north of Balad Air Base.

Joel Hartbeck had arrived in Iraq in August as an E-2 Airman—an "apprentice," really—after undergoing the required training stateside. Now, here he was, in the thick of it.

He and his teammates assigned to the 332nd Expeditionary Civil Engineer Squadron Explosive Ordnance Disposal (EOD) flight had received an assignment to go to Kirkuk because five US servicemen had been killed a few days earlier by a roadside bomb, and more hidden IEDs—improvised explosive devices—were suspected in the area of the bridge where the tragedy occurred. Usually three-man teams and a team leader in a Humvee worked missions from Balad, and they were among the thirty-four men assigned to the 332nd.

Kirkuk has a diverse population of nearly a million people that consists of Arabs, Kurds, and Turkmen. It played a key role in Iraq's oil industry and had long been a disputed territory within Iraq; hence it was a hotbed for trouble even before Operation Iraqi Freedom. One of the central "attractions" of the city is an ancient citadel, the Castle of Kirkuk, dating back to the seventh century. The citadel overlooks the Khasa River, which runs north-south through the city. The Khabat

Bridge spans east-west over the barely trickling Khasa River from a dense metropolitan, commercial area of Kirkuk to the citadel.

This major thoroughfare was the target of the EOD unit.

When the Humvee, the EOD team, and a platoon of infantrymen arrived at the site, they found the bridge teeming with pedestrian and civilian traffic. Eyeing the onlookers from his seat in the Humvee, team leader Derek Bolt was trained to spot anyone behaving suspiciously. A man or woman covered up by more clothing than usual could possibly be hiding a suicide vest of explosives. Or a child or woman standing innocently with a head bowed over a cell phone might trigger an IED. Of course, many Iraqi citizens had cell phones, and the voyeurs on the road were no exception. Some were holding up their phones to take photos of the troops, which was often done as a distraction to the soldiers.

The infantrymen immediately set up road blocks and attempted to work together with wary and uncooperative Kirkuk police. Joel found the locals' mistrust understandable. Who, after all, were the invaders in Iraq? Nevertheless, townspeople and city workers tended to comply with what the US military ordered. They had seen firsthand the arbitrary death and destruction of the foreign insurgents that used terror and intimidation to strong-arm local obedience.

Joel was equipped with a Warlock Duke V3, a frequency jammer that its makers were improving every year. The indicators on it were going haywire. IEDs were frequently triggered by cell phones or walkie talkies, and the Duke jammed the radio frequency that "talked" to the explosive device. The sophisticated tool would also alert users that a signal had been jammed. That way, servicemen would know that an IED was nearby. Usually the terrorist wanted to explode the device when US or allied troops were in a position to take maximum damage, so the bomber had to be able to see what was going on. That meant that wherever an IED was placed, the triggerman was usually in the immediate area.

This time, though, Joel was unable to pinpoint locations of IEDs because it seemed that the entire area was setting off the Duke. The counter-IED systems were not perfect. The enemy had quickly learned that they could "confuse" the signal jamming devices by bombarding the target with all kinds of radio signals—doorbells, garage door openers, walkie talkies, and shortwave radios.

"I think we need to break out the Thor and do a manual check," Joel suggested.

Derek was skeptical. The Thor device was like a Duke, except it was carried on the back of an EOD tech while he walked around a dangerous site. While a Thor allowed an EOD tech to get closer to an IED in order to pinpoint its location, therein also lay the danger—getting closer to an IED and leaving the relative safety of an armored vehicle. And if the IED happened to be an EFP, everyone in the vicinity was in trouble.

An EFP—explosively formed penetrator—was a particularly deadly type of IED. It was comprised of a steel cylinder filled with high energy plastic explosives and sealed on top with a precision-milled concave plate of high-grade copper. The blast of an EFP created so much kinetic energy that it turned the plate into a molten metal slug capable of penetrating several layers of hard steel. The insurgents who built it were counting on the fact that it was most effective at shredding human bodies into unrecognizable piles of partially vaporized flesh.

Team member Kenny Charles said to Derek, "There's a bus coming on the bridge from the other side!"

"What the hell?"

The citadel side of the bridge had not yet been blocked off. The bus was full of what appeared to be civilians. The driver, likely used to seeing American military men all the time, was simply minding his own business. He pulled on to the bridge on his way to deliver his passengers to their destinations.

The infantrymen had seen it, too. Some of the men waved flags and shouted at the driver as the bus slowly rumbled toward them on the other end of the bridge. The driver must have reconsidered his actions, as the vehicle began to slow down.

"Tell him to back up!" Derek shouted into his radio communicator. His infantry counterpart at the west end of the bridge acknowledged, but it was too late.

The massive explosion of an EFP on the overpass sent a concentric shock wave over the structure, propelling debris and flames toward the infantry. The scalding copper fist cut through the bus as if it were but-ter. The vehicle tore in half in a horrific retching, and it careened to the collapsing side of the bridge. A chunk of the crossing and the halves of the bus seemed to plummet in slow motion into the shallow river, some fifty yards below.

"Oh, my God," Joel muttered. There were women and children on that bus.

Three infantrymen then instinctively—and recklessly—rushed onto the west end of the bridge to gaze at the wreckage below, and another blast enveloped them in a shocking second blow from another bomb. Tiny droplets of hot, molten copper that had invariably separated from that EFP's main slug pierced all three. One man was severed into two—an upper body and two legs connected to a lower torso.

Chaos dominated the next several minutes as the situation turned into a near riot. US personnel attempted to control the scene as civil-ians ran and screamed and belligerently berated the soldiers as if the Americans had caused the disaster. Gunshots were heard within the thick, billowing smoke that enveloped the bridge. Who was shooting whom? No one seemed to know.

Joel watched with trepidation behind the cover of the Humvee as the infantrymen eventually managed to round up the Kirkuk citizens, get them away from the bridge, and restore some kind of order at the site. The shooters were never identified, but several men wearing caf-tans and headcloths had ended up on their knees with hands above their heads.

It wasn't long before two Pave Hawk helicopters arrived with other aerial reinforcements. The pararescue team from the 64th Expeditionary Rescue Squadron had arrived, and more ground support units were on the way. The easiest way down to the ravine to search for and rescue sur-vivors was lowering by tether a pararescueman—known as a "PJ"—in a harness as a Pave Hawk hovered over the disaster site. The death toll was tragic, but miraculously, a few people had survived the blast and fall and were trapped in the wreckage. One of the more gruesome tasks, though, was also to pull up the dead. They couldn't very well leave corpses in the river. By spring, when the water completely dried up, the ravine would be littered with the bodies of all the men, women, and children the insurgents had massacred.

As for the infantrymen that had caught the second explosion, one was still alive. He and his two deceased colleagues were medivacked to Balad's Air Force Theater Hospital in US Army Blackhawks.

While the pararescue teams worked, Joel conferred with his team and determined that the IEDs were likely made to counter the radio signal jammers. Instead of detonating an explosive with a cell phone or other signal, these were more victim-operated devices. These bombs were indiscriminately ignited by simple pressure plates—two metal strips that completed an electrical firing circuit when pressed together by a tire or an unsuspecting footstep. Insurgents also repurposed automatic garage door and motion sensing technologies using passive infrared triggers tripped by a passing victim. This random system was as likely to kill the insurgents' own friends and neighbors as it was military targets.

Obviously, the Duke and Thor equipment were not going to help in these cases. In the ensuing IED countermeasures race, Joel's squadron had been testing in the field all kinds of technology being developed. Some worked; many didn't. A high-powered "microwave emitter" was currently in the testing stage. It was intended to defeat the electronic circuitry in EFPs, but the jury on it was still out.

Joel was fingering the new microwave emitter in the back of the Humvee when Derek sidled up to him. "You really want to try that thing? Reports are coming in that it doesn't work."

"I'm willing to give it a shot," Joel replied. He pointed to the many civilian onlookers that had gathered behind the perimeter barricades set up by the infantry. "Doesn't anyone have anything to say? Are we questioning those people? Weren't the bombers seen rigging the EFPs? Somebody must have seen them. We need more intel."

"Hey, Hartbeck!"

Joel turned to see none other than Michael Carey, his buddy he'd met a year and a half ago during the Assessment and Selection course at Lackland Air Force Base in San Antonio, Texas. Joel had originally thought he wanted to become a PJ along with Michael, but an injury had curtailed that career path. After some months passed, Joel changed tracks and went the way of the EOD unit. Michael, however, had made it to be a full-blown successful PJ.

Michael was decked out in his gear and was sweating waterfalls. He had come over from one of the Pave Hawks that sat in the parking lot nearby. Victims he had rescued from the bus wreckage were being loaded into ambulances for transport to the nearby hospital that was inaccessible to the chopper.

"Geez, Michael! Good to see you. Was that you playing superhero up there?"

"I was one of them, and I'm about to go back up again. It's a mess down there. It's a bloodbath."

"I know. We're trying to figure out what to do about the bridge. We think it's loaded with more EFPs."

"Then I'll let you get to it." He nodded at Joel's team leader. "Sorry to interrupt."

Derek shook his head. "Not a problem, airman. You're doing great work."

Michael shook Joel's hand. "I saw you over here and just wanted to say 'hey' while I caught my breath. Good luck."

"You, too." He watched Michael run toward the waiting helicopter, and then turned back to the problem at hand. He took the microwave emitter and switched it on. He turned to the team leader and said, "I'm just going to take a few steps toward the bridge."

"Carry on, Hartbeck, but don't go too far. Keep to the edge and stay off the bridge."

Joel walked cautiously in front of the Humvee. He was thirty feet from the roadblocks that the infantry had set up. The second EFP detonation had created a huge crevice that dominated the western end of the bridge. He wanted to make sure there was nothing else preventing the team from getting closer.

The trickling sound of the Khasa River below was surprisingly loud in Joel's ears. He knew the shallow water was flowing with blood.

He slapped the microwave emitter on its side. *This damned thing doesn't work!*

Trickle... trickle...

Joel turned to see several more men in the infantry watching him. "Is it safe to grab that?" one of them asked him. He was pointing to a fallen infantryman's backpack that still lay about fifteen feet away on the concrete next to the crater on the bridge. No one had picked it up.

Joel thought it should be all right. No use letting the poor guy's personal things and equipment fall into the wrong hands. The EOD team would need to powwow to pinpoint explosives farther east on the bridge.

"Sure, go ahead," he said.

The infantryman moved past Joel, bent to reach for the backpack... and a deafening *crack* in the air became a flash of bright, hot light and searing pain.

Then there was darkness and silence.

Chicago, Illinois

Seventeen years later, and thirteen years after the US military "officially" declared in 2011 that the Iraq War was over, Army veteran-turned-attorney Bernie Serling stopped a video presentation that illustrated in explicit detail the effects of EFP explosions on tanks, vehicles, and people. The frozen image of horrifying destruction remained on the meeting room's big screen. The footage, shot in Iraq between the years 2004 and 2010, would never be broadcast on CNN, Fox News, or any other major news network. It was far too honest for an American corporate media that had become a mere extension of the vast US military-industrial complex. Such bloodshed and terror was still too hideous to comprehend, nearly two decades after the fateful events.

Serling acknowledged the gasps from the audience of approximately fifty people. "I'm sorry," he said. "I might not have been clear enough about how graphic this would be." He gestured toward the volunteer helper at the back of the space. "Lights, please."

The sudden brightness was a shock to the senses for both Nick "Deke" Deketomis and Michael Carey, who sat in the second row of seats. Deke blinked and rubbed his eyes. He also felt a little queasy. Deke was struggling to process the footage he had just witnessed. He couldn't imagine the fear that soldier-victims must have felt and the suffering their families inevitably had to experience.

Michael quietly asked, "You okay, boss?"

"Yeah. I don't know that I was ready for that," Deke whispered.

"Well, I got to see a lot of that and even worse in my tour over there."

"Did you have a question, Mr. Carey?" Serling asked.

Michael cleared his throat and spoke up. "Oh, no, sorry, Bernie. I was just telling Deke that I saw a lot of that over there when I was in the Air Force."

"You were a PJ, isn't that right?"

"Yes, sir."

Bernie enlightened the rest of the crowd in the room. "A PJ—that's a pararescueman. Our distinguished guest, Mr. Carey, here, is a fellow veteran." He pointed out the handsome, broad-shouldered man in his late thirties with the reddish-blond hair and green eyes. That elicited a little applause, but then, just about everyone in attendance was a veteran or related to one. Bernie, a tall, charismatic black man in his fifties who walked with a limp, went to the laptop at the podium and shut off the video.

"Yes, folks, what you just saw is disturbing, but it is reality and I'm afraid it's still going on. Terrorists are still active in the Middle East. Not just in Iraq and Afghanistan, but other hot spots like Syria, Yemen, Egypt, and Israel. I'm sorry, but as long as terrorists keep getting funded, then we're always going to have IEDs. The legacy of EFPs, an invention of Hezbollah, the notoriously violent terrorist organization, has devastated the lives of Americans. The Gold Star families and wounded veterans who are with us at the conference this weekend can attest to that. Are there any questions about what you've seen?"

A woman with WGN News in Chicago held up her hand.

"Yes, Nancy?"

"Just how are these terrorists being funded? Does the money come from overseas? Europe and the Middle East? It's my understanding that the US government has sanctions in place to prevent American companies and individuals from sending money to known terrorist organizations."

"Nancy, you are correct that there are sanctions in place," Bernie answered, "but unfortunately, the sanctions are pretty much a joke. Money still gets through. We believe there are banks right here in the

US of A that allow illegal money transfers. But we don't have the proof yet, and that's going to be the subject of two panels this afternoon. I hope you'll attend them, and I think you'll get some pretty painful answers to your questions."

The meeting ended. Deke and Michael stood and approached Bernie. "That was a powerful reality check, and I want to thank you again for asking us to attend the conference," Deke said. He made a show of wiping his forehead. "Forgive me, but I'm still a bit shaken by it. You say it's still going on? Even though we're out of Iraq and Afghanistan?"

"Yes, sir. And just because we're supposedly *out* of those places doesn't mean we're *really* out of them. And victims of EFPs don't necessarily have to be Americans. Victims can be innocent women and children or citizens who don't agree with their local terror cells. Come on, let's go downstairs. We have time for a drink before the next presentation."

The three men left the conference room and descended to the hotel's ground floor and the Lockwood Bar, one of Chicago's landmark destinations inside the historic Palmer House. Deke and Michael had agreed to attend the "Let's Do Something About It" conference hosted by the nonprofit organization, Gold Star Plus. GSP's members consisted of Gold Star families from around the country; the "Plus" indicated the inclusion of wounded and disabled veterans. The Midwest location of Chicago was chosen for its centrality and convenience. The Palmer House management had generously donated the space and its catering services to the group, probably foregoing significant income from the usual swanky wedding.

"As in-house counsel for Gold Star Plus, please let me say again how pleased I am that you both agreed to accept my invitation to attend," Bernie said as they sat around one of the ornate tables in the cavernous, decorative room.

"It's our pleasure," Deke said. "Although I'm not sure exactly *why* you wanted us to come."

Michael shrugged. "I have a vested interest in the topic. I'm a veteran, but I wasn't wounded in battle. I was injured in a chopper accident." He knocked on the tabletop. "My injuries didn't disable me for life, thank God. They just prevented any further advancement of a career in the Air Force."

"So you became a lawyer!" Bernie noted with a laugh. "You *are* going to thank God for that! Ask any lifer."

"Yeah, I guess so!" All three men chuckled, but then Michael grew serious. "I knew a lot of guys who were injured by roadside bombs, and I knew a lot who were killed by them, too. So, Bernie, I'm supportive of what you're trying to do here."

"I just want to get the media to focus on the message," Bernie said. He looked at Deke. "As for why I asked you to attend, Deke, I'm hoping that, with your semi-celebrity status, maybe we'll get some national television coverage. I see your talking head appearances on a pretty regular basis. Plus what is obvious to all of us is that you don't hold back when it comes to saying what's on your mind. My clients desperately need that right now."

Deke, a good-looking, tall man in his mid-fifties with sandy brown hair and blue-green eyes, shook his head. He spoke with a peculiar Southern accent that was more Texas than Florida. "I think maybe you place too much stock in my so-called celebrity status. I'm just a guy in a law firm in Florida who has gotten lucky a few times with some high profile cases."

"Whatever," Bernie said. "But I need your attention on the fact that the government doesn't do enough for these veterans and their families."

Deke nodded. "Maybe it would help if you forced that latte drinking crowd of do-nothing politicians in DC to quit just running their mouths and maybe sit down and watch what you just showed us."

A voice behind Deke spoke. "Not if American banks keep getting away with funding the terrorists who make and use those bombs you just saw."

Deke turned his head to see a man who was missing a left arm. The sleeve of his shirt was folded and pinned to the shoulder. The same side of his face was a mass of grafted skin, and he wore an eye patch. Standing beside him was Nancy, the newswoman from WGN, and a man hoisting a camera. It was trained on the trio at the table.

The veteran continued, "And if American banks *are* doing that—and I believe they are—then I would say Gold Star families and disabled veterans deserve to have that story told."

"Scotty," Bernie said. "Let me introduce you. Deke, Michael, this is Silver Star recipient Scotty Weiss. He's vice president of Gold Star Plus. Scotty, meet Nick Deketomis and Michael Carey, from Bergman-Deketomis, a law firm in Spanish Trace, Florida."

"Do you mind if I get a little footage for our television audience?" Nancy asked, but the camera was already rolling.

"I don't mind," Deke said. He shook hands with Scotty, and Michael did the same. "So very glad to meet you, Scotty. You are only the second person I've ever met who had a Silver Star pinned on them. I can't even imagine the story attached to that star."

"Glad to meet you, too, sir. Maybe over drinks you can tell me a few courtroom stories, and I can tell you a couple of soldier stories," Scotty said.

Deke modestly waved the comment away. "I'm pretty sure you would win when it comes to war stories, but I'll look forward to it anyway. Would you care to join us? We're just waiting on someone to take our order for some drinks."

"I don't want to bother you right now cause I hope I can bother you plenty in the future if you would please help us go after some of these US banks that are funding terrorists," Scotty replied. "They know damn well that they are helping to kill American soldiers and nobody seems to care right now."

Deke displayed his empty hands. "I'm afraid you have me at a disadvantage. I don't know much about what you're saying, but I suppose that's why I'm here at the conference. To learn more and educate myself."

"Mr. Deketomis," Scotty said, as he glanced at the camera and back at Deke, "we at Gold Star Plus want an attorney of your caliber to represent the thousands of Gold Star families and wounded servicemen and women who have been injured by roadside bombs bought and paid for by a bunch of miserable bankers. We want an investigation and possible lawsuit against banks that still work with terrorist organizations overseas. We *think* it's happening. Actually, we *know* it's happening, but we can't prove it. And right now they have a free ride to do it. We need to end that free ride!"

"I'll be listening, Scotty," Deke answered, knowing full well he was on camera. "You have my word. My associate and I are definitely here to learn more about what's going on. I appreciate your bringing this to my attention."

Scotty gave him a salute and a slight nod, and said, "That's all I can ask. Thank you, sir." He nodded at Michael, too. "Thank you. Enjoy the conference, gentlemen. I'll be seeing you around." He turned and walked away.

Nancy gave her cameraman a signal and cut. "Thank you. Maybe you'll see yourselves on the Friday night news at ten o'clock tonight. I'm Nancy Berk, by the way." She held out a hand, and Deke and Michael both formally introduced themselves.

"Thanks, Nancy," Bernie said as she went away with the cameraman. He turned back to Deke and Michael. "Sorry about that. I didn't mean for you to be ambushed."

"It's okay. That man has earned his right to say and do most anything he wants," Deke said. "Is it true what Scotty said? Are banks in America still actually funding terrorists?"

"We know, of course, that banks like HSBC and Standard Charter signed documents with the DOJ admitting that, yes, they did wash money and, yes, they knew the money was being used to fund terrorism, and, yes, they knew it was resulting in the deaths of American soldiers, and, yes, they made billions of dollars doing that. And you will really love this ... no one was prosecuted. Does that maybe grab your attention? Because most Americans have never even heard that story."

A waiter appeared with a friendly greeting and asked what they'd like to have. Michael and Bernie ordered beers, but Deke simply stared at the floor, seemingly unaware that anyone else was around him.

Bernie cocked his head. "Deke, I would be lying if I told you I had no intention of rocking your world with the facts of this potential case. Truth be told, friend, I need your help."

Deke shrugged. "Well, you damn sure rocked me into attention. And I'm grateful for that."

* * *

That evening in his hotel room, Deke turned on the television to watch the ten o'clock news on Chicago's independent WGN station. Sure enough, there was a short piece hosted by Nancy Berk on the "Let's Do Something About It" conference. She highlighted the concerns of the Gold Star family members and disabled veterans with short sound bites from various attendees, and then ended the piece with the footage from the Lockwood Bar.

"Also attending the conference was celebrated attorney Nick Deketomis of the Bergman-Deketomis law firm in Florida. He and his associate, Michael Carey, were at the conference on a factfinding mission," she announced.

The footage plainly displayed both Deke and Michael as Scotty Weiss approached the table. The complete conversation aired, unedited, after which Berk reappeared on the screen. "Will Mr. Deketomis take on a new high profile case against big US banks on behalf of Gold Star families and disabled veterans? At the moment, as you heard, the attorney is 'listening,' so we presume that he's taking it under advisement. This is Nancy Berk at the Palmer House in Chicago."

Deke let the television drone on as he prepared for bed, and then his cell phone rang. It was his associate.

"Yes, Michael?"

"You're still up, I hope?"

"I am. Just winding down."

"Did you see the news?"

"I did."

"I think this is good for the firm," Michael said. "How do you feel about it?"

"I don't know yet."

"Well, I think the footage is being picked up by national networks. I just saw it on CNN."

"You're kidding. Really?"

"And there are links on Twitter. It's going to get some notice, Deke."

Deke sighed. "You know what, Michael? In the words of Forrest Gump, 'sometimes there just aren't enough rocks,' and I get that. But aren't you just a little worn out from the six-year opioid case we are still trying to land?"

"You're just tired, old man," Michael said with a friendly laugh. "Let's talk more in the morning."

"Okay, I'll see you then."

* * *

They met in the conference meeting room where a modest breakfast was laid out for attendees of the event. Deke and Michael gathered their plates with pastries and fruit and then sat together at a table in the back. The coffee was a welcome component.

Deke pulled out his phone. "If you don't mind, I need to call Diana and check for messages. She's apparently in the office this morning."

"Go ahead."

Deke phoned the office in Florida, and Diana Fernandez, the office administrator at Bergman-Deketomis, picked up.

"Good morning, Deke. How's it going in the Windy City?"

"Big winds are blowing up here, Diana; how are things there?"

"Well, it's not a quiet Saturday morning. The phone is ringing off the hook from journalists wanting a statement from you about the Gold Star families and if you're going to file a suit against any banks."

"Oh, gee." Deke rolled his eyes at Michael, who could guess what it was about. "As it's the weekend, they can surely wait until Monday because nothing's happening right now. As far as *I'm* concerned, anyway. Just ignore them for now."

"Okay."

"Anything else?"

"Yes. Michael got a call from someone who says he's an old friend from the Air Force. Is Michael with you?"

"He's right here. I'll hand the phone over."

Michael took the phone. "Hi, Diana, what's up?"

"Michael, a gentleman named Joel Hartbeck called a couple of times and says he needs to speak with you. He said it was urgent."

Michael's brow wrinkled. *Joel Hartbeck ... Joel Hartbeck ... WAIT! Joel Hartbeck?*

"Do you know him?" Diana asked.

"Yes. Yes, I do. We go back a ways, and I haven't spoken to him since, gosh, when was it? Probably not since 2007. Did he say what it was about?"

"No. But he left a number and said to call anytime, but as soon as possible."

"Give me the number." Michael pulled a pen out of his jacket pocket and wrote the number on a napkin. "Okay, I guess I'll give him a call. Thanks. Do you need to talk to Deke again?"

"Not unless he needs to."

Michael raised his eyebrows at Deke, who shook his head. "Nope, that's it. Thanks, Diana, have a nice rest of the weekend." He handed the phone back to Deke.

"What was that about?"

"A guy I knew when I was in the Air Force, Joel Hartbeck, called. Wants me to call him. This is a 'blast from the past' moment. We were both in the Special Warfare Assessment and Selection course to become PJs. I remember he got injured during a training exercise and dropped out. But he showed up later in Iraq as a member of a bomb disposal unit. We were friends. Good guy. He got badly hurt, though—from an EFP! He was discharged and went home. I never spoke to him after that. I suppose I should've kept in touch."

"Is this a coincidence that he called?"

"I don't know. I'm going to step out into the hall."

Michael took the napkin with him and pulled his own cell phone from his pocket. He recognized the area code as one in Kentucky. He dialed.

The man who answered was out of breath. "Yeah?"

"Joel?"

"Who's this?"

"Joel, it's Michael Carey."

There was a beat of a couple of seconds. "My God, Michael! You returned my call!"

"Of course I did. How are you, brother?"

"I'm ... ha, I'm running for my life!"

"You're *what?*"

"Never mind that. Hey, listen, I can't talk long, but I'll get right to the point. I saw you on the news last night with your lawyer boss, the famous guy. Man, was I surprised and happy to see you. You really *did* become a lawyer like you said you would!"

Michael laughed. "I did indeed!"

"Michael, anyway, I heard your boss talk to that veteran, and what the veteran said is absolutely true."

"What's true?"

"About banks funding terrorism. I work for one of them—well, I did until recently. That soldier is a hundred percent accurate. Banks have been and still are laundering money that's being used to kill our guys in the Middle East. And I can prove it!"

PART ONE

1

San Antonio, Texas

Joel Hartbeck had been told when he enlisted that becoming an Air Force
Special Warfare (AFSPECWAR) operator wasn't easy. Airmen who under-
took the challenge had to endure unique and intense training. Among the
various career fields offered by the Air Force was the one that most interested Joel—becoming a pararescueman. He had always been fascinated by
jumping and had done some for fun prior to joining the military. When
Joel was told what he would need to accomplish before he was awarded
the opportunity to be a PJ, he was at first shocked. It sounded daunting.

The basic physical requirements were not a problem. He was between
eighteen and thirty-nine years of age, his height was between sixty-
two and eighty inches, he was a high school graduate, a US citizen, he
had passed the Armed Services Vocational Aptitude Battery (ASVAB)
exam that covered all manner of subjects in order to assess his general
knowledge and ability to learn new things, and also the PAST (Physical
Ability and Stamina Test), which was a physical endurance assessment.
He could do the eight pull-ups, the forty-eight sit-ups in two minutes,
the forty push-ups in two minutes, and the 1.5 mile run in less than
eleven minutes.

It had begun with the eight weeks of BMT (Basic Military Training)
that everyone went through. No problem. The next eight weeks of SW
Prep (Special Warfare preparatory course) were grueling, certainly a step

up in intensity from BMT. This consisted of a lot of strength condition-
ing as well as classroom learning of Special Warfare's history.

In May 2006, he was in the second week of AFSPECWAR's four-
week Assessment and Selection course at Lackland Air Force Base in
San Antonio, Texas, and he was struggling. This was the step in the
training in which the men were separated from the boys, so to speak.
Candidates had to prove they were truly worthy to be selected by the
Air Force to continue in Special Warfare training or else find another
kinder and gentler career field within the military. If Joel were selected
at the end of the initial four week course, he would then undergo *eighty
more weeks* of specialized training. The goal was to identify the very best
recruits the military had to offer.

Without question, the PJs and other Special Warfare operators were
the elite of the elite … and Joel was beginning to wonder if he truly had
what it takes to succeed. It was hard. *Damn* hard.

Joel was done for the day and went for dinner at the Special Training
DFAC, Building 5570, a dining facility separated from others on the
base. Food was served strictly between 5:00 p.m. and 6:30 p.m., so one
had to be prompt. Like every other part of the grueling training, there
was no compromise. He picked up his tray of food and joined his friend,
who was already at a table.

Unlike the struggle Joel was experiencing in the course, Michael
Carey seemed to be breezing through it. The guy was a dynamo.
Michael was also friendly, didn't put on airs like so many of the other
trainees who thought they were John Rambo incarnate, and seemed to
be extremely independently minded. The two men had hit it off on the
first day of SW Prep. They bunked together in basic and had become
like brothers in the relatively short time they'd been in Texas. Further
bonding ensued when they learned that they had both been orphaned at
a young age and shared a common thread of developing the attitude of
"nobody cares, work harder."

"Hey, Joel, what's it all about?" It was Michael's standard greeting.

"It's about dinner, that's what's it about," Joel replied, ready to dig
into his pork chops, potatoes, and vegetable slop. "Are the portions too
small here? I'm always still hungry after a meal."

Michael shrugged. "Maybe it's intentional. They don't want us to get fat. They want us to be lean, mean, fighting machines."

"I guess. It's not bad food, though, I must say. Better than what we got in basic."

"I suppose it's not Kentucky bar-b-que."

"No. It isn't. Not by a mile." Joel, being from Kentucky, had often waxed poetic about how he missed his home state's distinct style of slow-smoked meats.

They ate in silence for a couple of minutes as more men piled into the DFAC. Michael, however, was watching Joel intently.

"What?" Joel asked.

"Nothing. I was just going to say ... well, you look a little stressed. Are you okay?"

Joel nodded. "Yeah, I'm all right. I just ... hey, just between you and me, okay?"

"Sure."

"I'm not really hacking it. At least I don't feel like I am."

Michael wrinkled his brow. "What are you talking about? Of course you are."

"Nah. You've seen the way Sergeant Miller rags on me? He treats me worse than the guys you can really tell aren't going to make it."

"Maybe it's because he sees in you the potential to be one of the best, and he just wants you to work harder."

"I don't know ... I think he's a prick."

Their Military Training Instructor (MTI), James Miller, was indeed as hard as nails. Several of the men described him as the clone of the nasty Gunnery Sergeant Hartman from the movie *Full Metal Jacket*.

"Forget Sergeant Miller," Michael said. "Just keep at it. You've got what it takes, but you should have known it's not a walk in the park."

"Oh, I knew what I signed up for. Never mind. I'm just tired, I guess."

When they had both cleaned their plates, Michael said, "Let's split this fine dining scene."

Outside, Michael held a flattened hand up to his brow and looked at the sky. "Man, I knew it was hot in Texas, but this is a little extreme."

They walked toward the barracks, and Michael brought up a topic they had both been avoiding. "You ready for tomorrow?"

Joel replied, "I have to be, right?"

"You're my partner, so you'd better be."

"I'm all in. Don't worry. Do you have any idea what it's going to look like?"

"I've heard talk, but nobody has ever said. Supposedly it's an exercise that most trainees don't do until you're in the SERE training phase." He was referring to the most feared course of the process. SERE stood for Survival, Evasion, Rescue, and Escape. Special Warfare candidates didn't enter SERE training until near the end of the line, usually around nineteen or twenty weeks *after* Assessment and Selection.

"Why would they make us do it if we're not ready for it?" Joel asked.

"I think they want to see just how badly we'll fail right now. They want to know if we have any skills to problem solve without having all the tools yet. I don't think we're supposed to succeed, but just not totally blow it."

"Great. Sounds like a blast." Joel took a deep breath and beat his chest like a gorilla. "Bring it on, brother! I'm ready!"

"That's what I want to hear! Oh, I think I know what the exercise is called."

"What?"

"Saving the Bozo."

"*What?*"

"Really, that's what I heard."

"Who told you that?"

"Jenson."

"Eh, Jenson, he's a joker. I wouldn't believe anything he says."

"Just sayin'."

"Well, whoever the bozo is, it's not going to be me," Joel said.

They continued walking across the base.

"You're in this for life, right?" Joel asked.

"As in a career?" Michael shrugged. "That's what I'm thinking, sure. If I make it."

"You'll make it. I have no doubt."

"Eventually you age out of active duty, though. Then the real nightmare starts. You become Sergeant Miller!"

More laughter.

"Do you have a Plan B?" Joel asked.

"What do you mean?"

"I dunno … if you … for some reason if all this crashes in, or if you get hurt or something. What would you do?"

Michael stopped and faced the field where some men were playing touch football for recreation. "I once had my eye on football. I've still got a 4.3 forty in me."

"You'd be a hell of a tight end."

"But you know what? I kind of had it in my head that I'd go to law school if given the chance."

Joel looked at Michael sideways. "Michael Carey, Esquire. Attorney Michael Carey. Hey, it fits. I think."

Michael shrugged. "Like you said, it's a Plan B."

2

MTI Master Sergeant James T. Miller stood on the pavement next to two Air Force Jeeps. Drivers waited to transport the two men to the location of the training exercise.

"Carey!"

"Sir, yes, sir!"

"Hartbeck!"

"Sir, yes, sir!"

"Approach!"

Joel and Michael had reported for duty as instructed at six-thirty in the morning after a rushed breakfast. They'd been told to eat heartily, because, depending on the outcome of the exercise, it was possible they might not get lunch. If the exercise had not been completed by dinnertime, the activity would truly be deemed a bust.

Miller eyed them and nodded. "I will tell you now that you will fail this exercise. You do not have the mental and physical equipment to succeed. The purpose is to see how awful you really are. And I assure you, you will be awful. You will feel like idiots. However—maybe, and I mean *maybe*, you will show us that you possess a little critical thinking in those tiny brains of yours."

Joel swallowed. He was more nervous than he expected to be.

"This exercise is called Saving the Bozo. One of you will be the saver, and the other will be the bozo. The bozo is a prisoner, because that's what bozos always do—they get captured! He has been captured by the enemy and held in a secure site that is heavily guarded. The saver needs to figure out how to get past the guards, infiltrate the locale, and free the bozo. It's possible that the guards will call reinforcements and surround the place, so then the two of you, if you get that far in the exercise, will have to work together and successfully *break out* without getting shot to ribbons. The guards—and the saver—will be using paintball guns. If either of you is 'killed' or 'wounded' sufficiently to incapacitate you, the exercise is over. Now we will flip a coin to determine which one of you is the saver."

Miller pulled a quarter out of his pocket. He nodded at Joel. "If you win the toss, you're the saver. Call it." He flipped the coin into the air.

"Heads."

Miller caught the coin with one hand and slapped it onto the back of his other. He showed both men the results. "Tails. You're the big bozo, Hartbeck."

Joel cursed inwardly.

* * *

The two men were blindfolded, separated, and taken away in the Jeeps. After a bumpy forty-five minute ride, the blindfold came off and Michael blinked a few times to get used to the brightness. He stood facing a hilly, thick brush. No paths, no openings between the trees.

"Into the thick. That's the way. The clock starts now. Good luck, pal," one of the men said with a snicker. Michael turned to see him get into the Jeep. The driver waved, and they took off down a two-lane paved road away from the forest.

Michael faced the "thick" again.

Would the exercise be deemed a failure if I just thumbed a ride back to base?

The thought made him chuckle.

Might as well give this thing a try.

Michael was armed with a Tippmann Alpha Black paintball .68 caliber rifle that resembled an M16. It was a little on the heavy side at around eight pounds. There was no sight attached. He'd been told that his ammo consisted of only a hundred paintballs, which was a shame.

The Alpha Black could hold a thousand rounds. Michael would have to use the weapon sparingly and with accuracy. It had three settings—semi-automatic, which meant he could fire the paintballs quickly, but he had to squeeze the trigger for each round; fully-auto, which, with one trigger pull, the gun would fire twelve to fifteen rounds per second; and 3-shot burst, which unleashed three rounds with one trigger squeeze.

He was also supplied with an ASEK (Aircrew Survival Egress Knife), which could not be used as a weapon, but only as a tool for prying and other tasks.

That was it. No compass. No phone. No map. No water or food. No frills.

Michael moved forward, pushing his body into the mesquite, live oak, whitebrush, spiny hackberry, catclaw acacia, and other vegetation he couldn't identify. All he knew was that it was thorny, poked his clothing and exposed skin, and was unfathomably noisy to move through. He feared he was going to give himself away to the "guards" before he was even fifty yards from wherever Joel was being held.

The going was slow and tedious. Mosquitos and gnats quickly discovered his presence and swarmed around his face. He gave up swatting at them after a minute. It was pointless. At least these pests were merely annoying. Much worse would be the rattlesnakes and copperheads that supposedly occupied the area in big numbers.

After twenty minutes of this torture, Michael was beginning to wish he'd landed the job of the bozo.

After a half hour, Michael was certain that he was lost. Had he been traveling in a straight line? It was doubtful. It was more likely he'd been moving in circles. Looking up, he could see the full sky and the sun. The trees were not very high. This wasn't the Redwoods.

I'm an idiot!

He should have been noting the sun's position and using that to navigate.

From that point on, he was careful to keep moving in more or less one direction, although he had no idea if it was the *correct* direction.

After perhaps an hour, something made him stop moving. A sound. Up ahead somewhere. Unseen.

He listened as he attempted to temper his breathing.

Voices!

Two, maybe three men. Talking softly. He couldn't understand them. All he knew was that he heard the faint suggestion of human voices. Then there was a laugh, followed by a "Shh."

He was close. He had to be.

Michael looked around and saw that a nearby mesquite tree was unusually broad, tall, and covered with thick branches. The Black Alpha rifle had no strap, so he laid it on the ground at the foot of the tree. He then grabbed a branch and hoisted himself up, swung a leg over, and straddled the limb. Michael waited and listened. He no longer heard the voices, but he wanted to make sure no one had heard *him*. Finally, he stood on the branch, grabbed another, and climbed higher. One more time, and he was a good thirty feet above the ground. He could see over the brush for a hundred yards.

About forty yards in the distance was a clearing, and in the middle of it was a log cabin, a small, one-room variety that looked as if it might have been an old, abandoned hunting camp. It had to be his target, even though he couldn't see any guards. He'd have to get closer.

Michael carefully climbed down to the ground, picked up his rifle, and continued moving toward the clearing as quietly as possible.

Michael squatted behind a thick crop of whitebrush. The cabin was a mere 100-120 feet away. Two men, also Airmen in training, were in front of the one-room structure. One sat on a bench, smoking a cigarette. His Black Alpha lay on the bench beside him. The other man slowly paced; his own paintball gun strapped to his shoulder. Michael figured they had more than a hundred rounds in their weapons.

A dirt road lay horizontally between the whitebrush and the area in front of the cabin. The road likely wound through trees and heavy brush back to the highway, a way for the Airmen to go back and forth rather than walk through this desolate jungle of heat, bugs, and prickly vegetation.

Michael studied the structure. There was a front door and a window with dark curtains inside. He could see a little of the right side of the cabin, and there was nothing there—no windows or doors. He had no idea if there were a back door or other windows. The roof revealed a metal vent the size of a standard tire, only rectangular.

Could he pick off the two guards from where he was hiding? The range of the Black Alpha was about a hundred feet. It would be a gamble to attempt shooting at this distance. He might come up slightly short, and then the guards would be after him. Michael didn't relish running through the thorny thick. He needed to either get closer without being seen—which didn't seem possible—or *get them to come to him.*

Michael carefully moved back from the whitebrush and stood behind a mesquite. To his left was a better outcropping of trees that would provide more cover. He slowly crept over to it using what little stealth techniques he already knew from basic. At one point he stepped on a brittle fallen branch and it snapped loudly. Michael froze and held his breath. Several seconds passed and he didn't hear the guards speaking or moving. Maybe they hadn't noticed it.

He finally made it to the mesquite "nest," as he liked to think of it. Michael then held the rifle up and pointed it in the direction of the cabin, which he couldn't see now. The foliage of the mesquite was good camouflage for him and the rifle barrel. This might work.

He made a subtle coughing sound.

Silence.

Did they hear him?

He started to fake another light cough, but then he heard a voice. Then a "Shh" and a whisper. Michael was too far away to understand what they were saying, but they were communicating quietly. They knew he was there.

Surely at least one of them would investigate. Their self-assured cockiness would hopefully lead them closer.

Michael waited what seemed like an eternity, and then, sure enough, he saw the foliage moving ahead of him.

Hold … hold…

There! The guard's head and shoulders appeared just through a cluster of leaves, perhaps eighty to ninety feet away.

Michael held his finger on the trigger but didn't squeeze. He wanted the guy get closer.

The well-trained guard moved expertly, gun ready, scanning the thick from left to right. Then he took another step and repeated. Michael waited another three minutes until the man was seventy to seventy-five feet away.

Michael squeezed the trigger. The marker hit the guard square in the chest.

The man shouted a curse word and then, "I'm hit!" He remained standing, though, examining the splotch of paint on his uniform.

"You're dead," Michael spoke. "You have to lie down, damn it!"

The guard peered in the direction of the voice. "I can't see you."

"Get down."

"I'm not lying down here."

Michael set the gun for a 3-shot burst and squeezed the trigger, aiming at the man's upper torso right below his throat. *Pftap-pftap-pftap!* Now the guard was covered in paint across his torso, and some had splashed onto his face. Michael had made sure the shots would be painful and messy.

"Aw, man!" the guard cried. "Why'd you have to do that?"

"Get your ass down and play by the rules, or I'll unload this damn gun on you!"

"Okay, okay..." The man got on the ground, but he didn't lie on it, he just sat.

If the guy didn't give away Michael's hiding place, this could work. The conventional training would have had Michael move to another position, but he decided to stay put behind the mesquite and wait.

It was likely ten minutes later when the brush moved near the "dead" guard. The second man emerged and spoke to his fallen comrade.

Michael aimed just as the man on the ground pointed in the direction of the mesquite cropping. *Pftap-pftap-pftap!*

The 3-shot burst splattered the second man, who, like his colleague, began throwing F-bombs, thoroughly pissed that the new trainee had led him into a line of fire.

Michael moved into view and walked to the men. He addressed the guy who had pointed. "You know the rules, sir. Now stay dead while I go get the bozo." Michael eyed a set of keys on the second man's belt. "Key to the front door of the cabin?" he asked.

The guard made a disgruntled face and nodded. Michael unhooked the ring. "Thanks. Both of you look really good in yellow, by the way." Then he noticed three smoke grenades also secured to the belts of both guards. "Oh, could I have those, too? You don't need them, do you? After all, you're dead. Did I mention that you're dead?"

"Take them, asshole."

He did. "Thanks for your service."

He moved forward and made his way to the clearing and the cabin. There was no one else in sight. First, he did a reconnaissance around the cabin to check for potential well-placed traps, and he determined there was no back door or window. The only access inside was the front door or front window. Michael went to the door, checked for trip wires, and then used the key on the ring and opened the door.

Joel was tied to a chair in the middle of the room, blindfolded.

"Hey, bozo, I'm here to rescue you," Michael said.

Joel's head jerked. "Michael?" Then he burst out laughing. "You're the *maestro*, dude!"

"I told you I'd make it."

"Get me out of this!"

Michael untied Joel and removed the blindfold. Joel's eyes landed on the Tippmann and he asked, "I don't suppose you have an extra one of those, do you?"

Michael slapped his forehead. "I should have taken one from the dead guards! Damn, how could I be so stupid? I left them with their guns!"

Joel shook his head. "You knucklehead."

"I do have six smoke grenades, though."

"Well, don't stand here, come on!"

But before they could move to the open door, they heard the sound of vehicles pulling up on the road outside. Markers began pelting the front of the cabin and zipping through the open door. Michael kicked the door shut and quickly locked it from the inside.

Joel went to the window and peered out the side of the curtain. Paintball splotches covered the glass, but he counted three Jeeps and several men in uniform.

"There're five, six... no, seven real serious-looking dudes out there, Michael."

"Think I can take 'em?"

"Absolutely not." After a beat, Joel looked at Michael and asked, "Any suggestions on how to get out of this?"

"In the words of our pal Miller, 'There's always one more move.'" Michael crossed to a wall and gazed at the ventilation grill in the top corner. "I think that vent goes to the roof. I noticed the fixture outside."

"What, are you expecting a chopper to come pick us up off the roof?"

"No, but maybe I could pick off the guards from up there and put those grenades to good use. Come on, let's move the chair over so I can stand on it."

"It's bolted to the floor."

"Then give me a boost."

Using some awkward gymnastics, Joel hoisted Michael up against the wall. Michael removed the ASEK knife from his belt and pried off the grate.

Wincing, Michael said, "I think it's too small to get inside. Damn it." Joel helped him down. "There's no way my broad shoulders can get through that opening."

Joel stared at it. "I could fit. I'm a tall string bean with muscles. Look at me; don't you think so?"

Michael eyed the opening and Joel's size. "It's worth a try."

Joel smiled. "And I just thought of a plan."

The ventilation duct was absolutely a tight fit, but Joel was able to worm his way through it. The first part was the most difficult, as the duct went upward from the opening for three feet and then immediately curved to a horizontal position above the ceiling. From there it was a short few feet to the exterior fixture on the roof. Luckily, the width of the duct remained constant.

Joel made it to just below the fixture and examined the mesh grill. He didn't have a screwdriver, but Michael had given him the knife. He carefully cut away the wire mesh, allowing him to thrust his head and shoulders up into it. Once again, he performed the wormy slithering movements that inched him upward until his head and shoulders emerged from the vent on the roof. He could see the Jeeps and the men down below, but they weren't paying attention to him. Michael was busy taunting them by shouting insults through the door about them and the two "dead," but magically resurrected, guards he had hustled. The men kept up a barrage of high velocity paint at the front of the house with their Tippmann equipment.

Now completely free and standing on the roof, Joel unhooked the M15 smoke grenades Michael had also gifted him. He deftly pulled the rings and tossed three down between the cabin and the guards. They went off with a bang, and a massive grey cloud instantly enveloped the area. Then he threw the other three grenades. The men below coughed and shouted, and two of them began firing blindly at the roof. Joel lay flat as the markers flew past him over his head and back.

It was Michael's cue. He opened the door quietly. Nothing but smoke filled the opening. He squatted as low to the ground as possible and began auto-firing the Alpha Black into the smoke, slowly moving from left to right and back. *Pftap-pftap-pftap…*

The men hollered and screamed something about beating the Bozo's ass. They continued to fire at the door and front of the house. Markers struck Michael on the upper left arm and left knee. He was a wounded man, but he kept firing because he was still in play.

Nearly a minute later, a voice shouted, "We're dead! It's over!"

Was it a trick? Were they allowed to trick? Michael's experience with the other two guards in the brush indicated that they might cheat.

Nevertheless, he stood and stepped outside into the white cloud. Waving his arms around, he moved forward until he saw in the smoke the silhouettes of figures squatting on the ground.

"If you move, I'm shooting you again," Michael said. He went close enough to see the man's features.

"All right, I'm dead, ass clown!" the guard said. "But you look like you're crippled. I don't think you'd be walking out here like that."

"Joel?" Michael called.

"I'm up here!"

"Can you get down?"

"I can sort of see you down there. I assume the ground is there, too, but I can't see it."

"Well, get down here if you can."

Joel decided to jump. After all, he was planning to be a PJ. The height wasn't dangerous. The trick was touching down lightly on his feet, dropping, and rolling.

Unfortunately, he misjudged the distance to the ground and he landed too hard on his right foot. The pain shot through his lower leg as he crumpled on the rocky surface and writhed in agony.

"Joel?" Michael went over to him, waving smoke away.

Through gritted teeth and between grunts of torment, Joel said, "I think I broke my ankle!"

*   *   *

Joel was discharged from Wilford Hall Medical Center at Lackland Air Force Base. He wore a cast on his foot and ankle that came up to mid-calf. His self-diagnosis had indeed been correct. He had suffered a broken ankle, and it wasn't minor. In fact, Joel underwent a surgery called ORIF—open reduction internal fixation—in which the surgeon had to line up the ends of the broken bones and install a metal plate and a few screws. Joel had spent a night in the hospital post-surgery, but he was now anxious to get out of there.

As was prearranged, Michael was waiting beside an MP and a Jeep as Joel was pushed in a wheelchair out of the hospital. The nurse handed Joel crutches, he thanked her, and then the patient winced as he stood and positioned the crutches in his armpits. He took a few tentative steps and then strode forward with more confidence toward his friend.

"Hey, bozo," Michael said. "How do you feel?"

"I hope you're not going to call me that forever."

Michael laughed. "Sorry." He indicated the cast. "You going to be okay?"

"Yeah. I'm more humiliated than hurt. That was a dumb thing I did, jumping off a roof to a surface I couldn't even see. Think I can get worker's compensation?"

"I don't think it works that way in the Air Force."

They both climbed aboard the Jeep, and the driver silently took them to the barracks. Once inside, Joel sat on his bunk, then laid back and sighed. "Man, that was more tiring than I expected."

"You'll get used to it," Michael said. "And remember, you just had surgery yesterday, buddy, so don't rush it."

"Yeah. What did you find out from Sergeant Miller?"

Michael shrugged. "We flunked the exercise, of course. We scored some points in the beginning because I made it into the cabin, but then I got 'wounded' so badly that I shouldn't have been able to walk. Then your stunt put the nail in the coffin. So we both messed up. Miller did say we did better than most. So there's that."

Joel nodded. "Listen. I talked to the recruitment counselor this morning. I'm dropping out of the program."

"What? Come on, why would you do that?"

"Because I broke my damn ankle!"

"But that will heal! What the hell? In three or four months you should be fine."

"Not really. The doc said it will take up to twelve weeks just for the bones to heal, but then comes physical therapy and babying the thing for what could be six months. Maybe even a year. So we discussed my options, because I do want to stay in the Air Force. Becoming a PJ is out. I have to find another career path."

"So where do you go with that?"

"I don't know for sure, but I'm thinking I might go into EOD."

"Explosive Ordnance Disposal? That pretty much makes you certifiably nuts! You won't just break your ankle; you'll blow off your whole leg!"

That made Joel laugh. "Or other more precious body parts! I haven't decided for sure, but the training isn't what it is to be a PJ. It takes about ten months to be an EOD technician. After the healing is well on its way, I can start with the classroom stuff and save the physical training for later. It might work out."

"Didn't you once tell me you were good with math in school?"

Joel smiled. "I did, and I was. You told me that if you weren't going to be an airman, that you'd probably go into law. I once thought I'd be an engineer, maybe an electrical engineer. I'm pretty good with machines. I could always go into mechanics and do that for the Air Force, but then I doubt I'd see any action."

"Maybe not, but the Air Force needs mechanics. It's just as important as any job in the Air Force."

"Yeah, but being an EOD technician—the guy that disables roadside bombs and such—that's important, too. I'm leaning in that direction."

Michael thought it made sense. "Well, I hope that works out for you, then."

"That said, I'm shipping off the base tomorrow to recover. I sort of have to start all over once I'm healed. I'm going back to Kentucky for a while. My old hometown is a place where I can dig in and heal. Maybe a cabin in the woods. I hire a pretty maid, drink whiskey, smoke cheap cigars, and watch old western reruns. What could go wrong with that?"

"You don't have any other family?"

"Distant cousins, maybe, but I wouldn't even know their names. I've always been pretty much a loner."

Michael cocked his head. "Me too. I guess that's why we get along."

"Michael, you're going to fly through training. I can see it. You're going to be a PJ. And you'll be going to Afghanistan or Iraq. You'll be over there a lot sooner than I will. But maybe we'll run into each other again."

"It's possible, Joel. The Air Force is a tiny world."

Joel held out a hand.

Michael slapped his palm on Joel's and the two men held a firm grip. "Good luck, brother."

"And to you, too, Michael. I hope to see you again soon."

They both knew, however, that this was unlikely.

3

Balad Air Base, Iraq

"Listen up," EOD Superintendent Mathers said to the team. "An infantry patrol has indicated insurgent activity in Baqubah, just thirty-nine klicks southeast of Balad Air Base. You know the area."

Baqubah was a sizable hamlet of nearly a half-million people. A major supplier of the fruit in Iraq, it was known for its immense orange groves. Sadly, the place had become the latest ground zero in the fight for Iraq, and many inhabitants had fled or were in hiding from the al-Qaeda in Iraq (AQI) fighters there. In 2006, AQI had declared Baqubah the "capital" of its Islamic caliphate and thousands of hardened AQI fighters migrated from within Iraq and Afghanistan to expel the "infidels" from the area with increased viciousness, using children, mentally disabled, and wheelchair-confined elderly Iraqi as mules for their suicide bombs that indiscriminately murdered US soldiers and innocent Iraqis alike. Now, in October 2007, the situation was worse.

"The patrol's Duke V3 jammed radio signals along the main drag, Baquba Street, heading east-west in front of the government building, a distance of about four blocks," Mathers continued. "Aerial Recon confirmed significant emplacement activities as well. The place is strung up like a Christmas tree, gentlemen. They're probably hoping to hit US forces known to stop in the area for the lamb kebab that the vendor 'Hassim Harry' serves from his cart near a playground at the east end of the road."

"That's awesome kebab," Joel Hartbeck interjected. "Worth the trip."

Mathers eyed Joel and said, "Since you know it, Hartbeck, you're on the team to check out the street. The mission is to locate and take out any IEDs in the area."

"Great," Joel said.

Mathers continued the briefing, laid out the rules of the mission, and chose team leader Derek Bolt, Kenny Charles, and Franklin Jones to accompany Joel.

Joel, whose ankle had healed and only seemed to bother him whenever it rained (luckily, it never rained in Iraq!), was slowly but surely becoming an expert in chemical, biological, radiological, and nuclear materials, as well as explosive devices. He hadn't yet mastered control of the robots used to disarm certain incendiary devices that were too dangerous for disabling in close proximity. Joel was, however, solid at analyzing signal jamming data and detecting and disarming remote-detonated IEDs.

The city of Balad, where the air base was connected, was still recovering from a deadly suicide bomber attack in September, and there had been others in the past few months. The use of IEDs by the enemy had stepped up in both Iraq and Afghanistan.

The EOD units had been kept busy, and Joel was dropped right into the quagmire. He had already gained experience disabling two roadside bombs wearing the eighty-pound protective bomb suit. The worst part about it was not its ergonomically challenged assault on the spine and muscles, nor its cumbersome weight—it was the immense heat inside. One could easily dehydrate within a half hour of wearing the bomb suit in the searing Iraqi sun. They were operating in one of the hottest deserts on earth.

* * *

At 1200 hours, the EOD team drove a Humvee equipped with a Duke to Baqubah. They were supported by an infantry squad and, in case something went terribly wrong, medics. The convoy moved from west to east on the mostly deserted throughway of Baquba Street. Only handfuls of civilians were about; granted, it was the hottest time of the day. Heat shimmer rose from the roadway, blurring objects in the distance. Aside from the more modern buildings in the center of town, many of Baqubah's buildings were made of mud bricks, and Joel was already concerned that many homes in the area had been damaged from previous incendiary activity.

Kenny Charles pointed out the various shops and markets across from the government building. "Seems like we're in the correct spot."

"Right," said team leader Derek Bolt, who was driving. "Any noise from the Duke?"

Joel was watching the instruments, but no indicator lights were active. "Nothing yet."

An outdoor market stood under a tent just west of the playground, which was devoid of children. Three women wearing burkas were shopping for what little fruit was available. And there, on the corner, was the cart with "Hassim Harry" written on the side in English and Arabic. The letters in the word KEBAB were illustrated with crudely painted ovals of lamb meat.

"Anyone hungry?" Kenny asked.

"I'm stopping there if we don't find any IEDs," Joel said.

At that moment, though, the Duke beeped and an indicator light shone red.

Joel sighed. "Well, we knew it was going to happen. Who's wearing the suit?"

"You are," the three other men said simultaneously.

Joel sighed again. "I guess it *is* my turn. All right."

Bolt stopped the Humvee and reversed the vehicle until the Duke indicator went off. It was easier to don the bomb suit outside, standing up. Joel got out and spent the next ten minutes putting on what felt like a deep sea diver's outfit, massive helmet and all. Once he was suited, he awkwardly walked alongside the Humvee as it slowly returned to the spot where the Duke had lit up.

Joel examined the street corner for trash piles, roadkill, overturned dirt, or surfaces that appeared to be recently disturbed, as if something might be buried. The kebab cart was just a few feet away, but no one was inside the cooking area. No customers were lined up to buy food. In fact, Hassim Harry wasn't there. All of Joel's Spidey senses were going off.

Over his radio he announced what he saw, and then turned toward the market. One of the burka-clad women held a cell phone, and she was frantically punching numbers on it as if it didn't work.

Joel made the connection. "Woman at five o'clock has a phone!"

The infantrymen, who had trailed the Humvee at a safe distance and had piled out to provide cover for Joel while he suited up, shifted their rifles toward the woman. They shouted for her to drop the phone. She started to run but there was nowhere for her to go. The market tent was directly behind her, the infantry was to her left, and the EOD team was to her right. An interpreter with the infantry shouted commands in Arabic. Ultimately, she must have known there was no escape. She dropped to her knees and put her hands behind her head.

Joel walked around the kebab cart and then looked underneath.

An ugly EFP was mounted to the curb, behind the cart's wheels. The Duke had done its job and blocked the phone signal to detonate the threat. Now all that was left to do was to disarm the damned thing. If that weren't possible, they would have to evacuate the market and surrounding buildings, clear the area, and detonate the bomb themselves.

* * *

All in all, it had been a good day.

Joel was tired and achy from wearing the suit. It always sapped the strength out of a person. The shower felt great, though, and he looked forward to some hot food and ice cream at one of the DFAC dining facilities at Balad. Amenities were fairly nice at the base. For fast food connoisseurs, there was a Subway, Pizza Hut, Taco Bell, Burger King, and a Popeyes.

He went over to the DFAC alone, and once inside, he was curious about a large group of men he hadn't seen before. They were chowing down and taking up a lot of space. Then he remembered—more units had arrived that day. Balad Air Base was in many ways a small town with a lot going on. Air Force units sometimes stopped at the base en route elsewhere.

Joel stood in line with his tray, waiting for his turn to be served. One guy he did know, a PJ with the 64th Expeditionary Rescue Squadron, spoke to a broad shouldered man beside him. "Balad isn't bad. You'll like it here."

"It's got to be better than Bagram, but it feels weird leaving the 83rd."

"You're needed with us, pal. We appreciate you making the transfer."

Joel thought there was something about the way the new guy moved that was familiar. Before he could say anything, though, the new air-man turned to him and asked, "What do think about the food here?"

Joel's jaw dropped.

The airman's eyes widened. "Joel?"

"Michael? Michael Carey? No way!"

* * *

The two friends had not believed their good fortune of running into each other again so far from Lackland Air Force Base in Texas. Even though they were assigned to different units housed in separate quarters at Balad, over the next four weeks they had attempted to get together during down-time to share meals and catch up. Michael had undergone the intense and lengthy training to become a PJ and had marked his achievement by acquiring two tattoos. One was a jade green "A+" on his chest, signifying his blood type. The other was a picture of green feet applied to one of his butt cheeks!

"You did *what*?" Joel had asked.

Michael laughed and explained. "It's the 'Jolly Green Feet,' a symbol for PJs. Back in the Vietnam days, PJs rode in Sikorsky HH-3E helicop-ters, and they were known to leave marks resembling green feet on rice fields and green paddies."

Michael revealed that he had been with the 83rd Expeditionary Rescue Squadron based at Bagram Airfield in Afghanistan until some reshuffling had occurred. Some PJs were needed in Iraq, so Michael had been transferred to the 64th.

"Well," Joel said, "we are glad to have you here. I'm thinking your commanding officers figured they needed *me* to keep an eye on you so you don't screw up!"

And yet, as determined as they were to see each other at the base, the two men were rarely able to do so. Different units, different missions.

Then, a month later, Joel and the EOD team were assigned to investigate the bridge in Kirkuk, and Joel experienced firsthand what an EFP could do to a human.

But unlike many soldiers who fell victim to the insidious devices, Joel miraculously survived.

4

Plainsburg, Kentucky

The first half of 2008 had not been pleasant for Joel Hartbeck.

Following the incident at the bridge, Joel was evacuated to the field hospital at Balad Air Base, where preliminary triage was performed. He had received multiple fragment wounds on the upper left torso, arm, neck, and the bottom and side of his face. The exposed skin—the neck and face—suffered second-degree burns. The concussive force of the blast knocked him out, but he had been able to regain some alertness on the way to the hospital. But in regaining consciousness, Joel was acutely aware of the pain. It felt as if his entire body had been bludgeoned by sledgehammers. The concussion alone was bad enough to cause vision problems, extreme disorientation, and a vise-like headache that took a month to dissipate.

At some point in the first couple of days after the incident, Joel learned that the infantryman who had reached for the backpack was killed in the blast, and three more men behind him had also been seriously injured. The doctors said that Joel was "lucky," but the rumor mill was already filtering in—Hartbeck had failed to find an EFP and was at fault.

Joel was flown to Landstuhl Regional Medical Center in Germany for further treatment. An assessment was made regarding the severity of his burns. Skin grafting was not absolutely necessary, but it was an option to lessen unsightly scarring. Joel made the decision to go ahead and do it. But it was a decision he quickly came to regret as they debrided the burnt meat from his body to prepare it to receive the grafts of flesh harvested from undamaged areas of his body. Autografting was performed and Joel spent another week in the hospital. He was then moved to a veterans care center. It was there that he learned he had received a medical discharge from the Air Force. While it was true he had received injuries while on duty, it wasn't an honorable discharge. It wasn't a dishonorable one, either, nor a general discharge or "other than honorable" discharge. It was a "you screwed up and got hurt" discharge. They may have well tacked on "and got others killed" to the label. It meant he would have to apply for disability aid through the veterans benefits system, a notoriously slow bureaucratic process that was usually less than fair.

He was saddened by this news. His disillusion was further compounded when he realized that others with the same injuries might have received a Purple Heart. Joel didn't.

Returning to the United States was not the celebrated homecoming it should have been. He went to the place he called home, which was nowhere.

Plainsburg was a home-rule class city—where local laws could be passed as long as they didn't conflict with state laws—in southeast Kentucky. Population: less than 15,000. Joel had been born and raised there, and it was where he had gone through two foster homes after his parents had been killed in a traffic accident.

Every hometown carries with it memories ranging from magic to tragic. One of Joel's big nights at a bar was something in-between. He had been celebrating his twenty-first birthday when his night progressed from his fourth tequila shot to the back seat of a female Air Force recruiter's Toyota. After a weekend fling, she had talked him into enlisting. He never saw her again after that.

Nothing had changed in Plainsburg since he had left for basic military training in 2006. He always believed that this was both the positive and negative sides to small Kentucky towns. He also recognized that Plainsburg had raised him to be the person that he was, and most days he was good with that.

Now he was back in town, and he needed a place to live and something to drive. He found a used white 2005 Ford Explorer SUV with 45,000 miles on it for a price he could afford. It would do. For lodging, Joel at first took up residence in a cheap, abandoned hunting cabin that was listed on Craigslist. It was located in the hills of the eastern woodlands. He quickly grew tired of the lack of amenities.

After cabin life, he rented an apartment in Plainsburg and spent the months of February through June in a funk. Mostly he was depressed about how he looked. The plastic surgery had covered the more grotesque appearance of the left side of his face, but he would never consider himself "normal" again. Overall, he simply felt tired and spent. All the time.

So he ate pizzas and drank beer. He gained weight but didn't much care.

By June he had found that his medical claims were moving through the system at the speed of a sloth. One of the biggest mistakes he ever made, he'd found, was that he hadn't taken out supplemental insurance beyond what the Air Force had provided. The healthcare system in America was in the toilet. One non-VA clinic he'd gone to in Plainsburg told him that his wounds were a "preexisting condition" and that they didn't take veterans insurance. Other times his claims were not "preauthorized." Or they needed "additional information" that he didn't have. The worst was that the skin grafting he'd received had been deemed "elective surgery," and ended up not being covered. After three months of phone calls and threats to contact his virtually useless congressman, partial payments were made because of his "medical discharge status."

It made all those "Thanks for your service" comments he routinely received from strangers who stared at his scarred face even more difficult to hear. Even worse were the times he had to listen to all the war pimps that made appearances on CNN or Fox News to unload bullshit about how they supported the men and women in uniform who sacrificed so much.

In fact, most of the news on television compounded the situation. The stock market was a roller coaster, and talking heads were predicting doomsday. Catchphrases like "mortgage crisis," "credit crisis," "bank collapse," "government bailout," "interest rates," "consumer debt," and "too big to fail" were bandied about as if the average viewer actually knew what they meant. Folks were saying that the wars in Iraq and Afghanistan were taking their tolls on the American economy, and there was going to be hell to pay.

I'm already paying it, Joel thought.

If only he weren't so tired all the time. A doctor in Bowling Green told him it was called CFS—chronic fatigue syndrome. And guess what? Many of the medical clinics refused to accept CFS as a real diagnosis without more "evidence" of the condition. Simply stating that the symptoms were present apparently wasn't enough.

And what about chronic nightmares? Joel wondered. *Is that a thing? CNS? Chronic* Nightmare *Syndrome?* He relived the terror on the bridge in his dreams, waking up with a scream, his skin clammy, and his wounds aching. The head pounding always returned the following day after these nightmares. He'd feel miserable for twenty-four hours, and then it would pass. But, lo and behold, after three or four days went by, the whole joyride would occur again. It was driving him mad.

Damn it, Joel, what are you going to do about it? he asked himself. *Order a pizza and grab a beer or twelve. That's what.*

* * *

Ten long years passed and most of it was hell for Joel.

The memories were always with him. The nightmares persisted, the headaches came and went, and the areas itched where he had received new skin. There was a term being thrown around in the media—PTSD, or post traumatic stress disorder. It meant that the inflicted person would experience flashbacks, feelings, disturbing thoughts, and dreams related to the traumatic incident. It seemed that he could never escape the war. In order to help him fall asleep at night, Joel tried to depend on a white noise machine. But he could never put it on the "babbling brook" setting. The gurgling sound reminded him too much of the sound from the Khasa River that had been so prominent when he was above it on that bridge.

Trickle ... trickle...

In 2011, he finally found someone who could relieve the pain. Dr. Bock prescribed something called OxyContin, warning Joel that he should take it only as prescribed. Once every twelve hours. He had started with the lowest dosage of ten milligrams.

At first Oxy made him feel *great.*

In fact, Joel felt so energized and confident on the drug that he went to a singles bar and met a slightly older woman named Tracy. In 2012 they were married. Unfortunately, the OxyContin grabbed Joel by the soul, and he needed the drug more often and at higher doses. When Dr. Bock stopped prescribing the medicine, Joel went to black market dealers. The *need* for Oxy dominated every waking moment of his wretched existence.

Like many users, Joel had become addicted, and his marriage—and his life—fell to pieces.

It was only after he had truly hit rock bottom that things began to change.

* * *

"How do you feel today, Joel?"

It was a question he hadn't been sure how to answer until recently. Joel had begun seeing the VA psychologist, Zelda Watson, at the beginning of 2018. He had found her in the town of Middlesboro, a bit of a drive from Plainsburg, after he had explored veterans centers in neighboring towns and some cities as far away as Louisville. Too many of the counselors Joel had encountered were too bureaucratic for his taste. From the moment he saw his first shrink, Joel was sure that the entire psychology profession was overrun by a clown car cabal of oddballs who were quick to ask scripted questions and incapable of providing any meaningful answers. Finally, though, he came across Ms. Watson, an older woman to whom Joel was surprisingly able to relate. She was kind, empathetic, and seemed to understand everything he'd been through. They were even on a first-name basis. She was there to save his life.

"I'm so much better, Zelda," he said. "This time the rehab took. I think I'm a new man."

Zelda wrote on her notepad. "That's fantastic, Joel, but I must warn you. Don't get too cocky. Don't think you're 'cured.' You have to keep in mind that you will always be an addict. One slipup and you'll be back to where you started."

"I know that. Believe me. Sorry for the slipups you've had to pull me through already."

"That's my job, but I'm not sure you need me to do that any longer. Joel, let's do something new today. My experience has shown me that very often it helps if you review your journey verbally again and again. It gives you a sense of where you were, and where you are now. Why don't you tell me your story? Start at the point when you knew you were addicted to the drug and relate to me everything that has happened up to now."

"Really? As you know, that will take a while."

"You'll be surprised. Just hit the important things. Let's try and remember the milestones, and don't worry about whether we have talked about it before. Just humor me and try this."

Joel sat back in the chair in the woman's office and said, "Okay. Well, let's see. You know about the marriage to Tracy. That failed big time. She had a good divorce lawyer, and she took me for everything I had. I was practically homeless. I got into trouble with the law several times for vagrancy. I was arrested for assault in the boarding house where I was living. That was … gee, in 2013. But the charges were dropped when the police figured out that the guy who pressed charges was indeed a habitual thief. Stolen property from other residents of the boarding house was found in his room. But I still had to find another place to live, so I rented a mobile home in a trailer park. The first three years there are a blur. I was … out of my mind."

"Besides the addiction, what were the other events that caused you the most suffering?" she asked.

"The divorce. I was devastated by it. Just made me want to stay high all the time. So all my days were spent trying to score Oxy from shady dealers."

"And how did you pay for it?"

"Oh, I went through a bunch of odd jobs. Manual labor, mostly, and I barely had the strength to do it. I got fired a lot."

"And what turned you around?"

Joel chuckled. "A rabbi. I'm not Jewish, and I'm not overly religious at all. But I was in a bad place in my head one day. I think it was late 2016. I was sitting on the sidewalk in downtown Plainsburg with a cup in hand and a side of a pasteboard box where I'd scribbled the words 'Wounded Veteran, Please Help.' I was astonished how many people just walked past as if I were invisible. Can't say I blamed them. But one day this rabbi came by, plopped some money and a card into my cup, and looked me in the eye. 'Trust yourself' was all he said, and then he walked on. I looked at the card, and it was a phone number for a rehab place in the country in southern Kentucky. Remote location. I've told you about it. Normally I would have tossed the card, but something … *something* about that rabbi made me hesitate. I checked out the place. I liked it, and I enrolled. The thing is, it was a charity organization, and I didn't have to pay at first. It was a pay-as-you-can kind of place."

"And you did well there."

"I did. So I stayed. And I went through the wringer with withdrawal. I ran away the first time and fell off the wagon. But I came back. And it happened again. But the third time … well, they say, 'third time's the charm,' and it was. I've been clean for six months. I still crave the Oxy, but it's not the *need* anymore. Now it's just a … temptation. But it's a temptation to which I can say, 'No thanks.'"

"And you're working now?"

"I have a crummy job, but at least it's a job."

"You're still hauling trash?"

"Yes. That's my job. It sucks, but…" He shrugged.

Zelda read off an address from his chart. "You still live there? The trailer park?"

"Yes. And I have a P.O. box for mail."

"So, Joel, you see? You're in a much better place than you were five years ago. Listen to your story. Remind yourself about where you were and where you are today. Which brings me to the question that is so overused: How do you feel about all that?"

"Good. But..."

"But?"

"I'm angry, Zelda. Now that I'm sober and I've returned to reality, I'm really pissed off at the state of the world, the government, the Air Force, and people in general. The politics in this country has gone looney and it's dividing us more than I've ever seen. It seems like everyone is becoming more stupid. I keep thinking: is this what I sacrificed everything for? Was it worth it? It all just makes me ... angry. All the time."

"Joel, be angry, be very angry, if that helps, but not all the time. Go back to the basics. Relationships, service of some kind. Hobbies. Don't make all this more complicated than it really is. Maybe begin this week with something as simple as exercise."

Joel laughed and squeezed the handlebars of flesh at his sides. "You're right about that."

She glanced at the clock on her desk. "I'm afraid the time is up for today, Joel. I can honestly say that you are one of my most interesting patients, but I don't think you need me every two weeks now. How about you come see me again in a month?"

"Sure."

Later, at home in the Forest River Wildwood mobile home in the trailer park at the edge of Plainsburg, Joel retrieved a beer out of the fridge and sat at his little dining table. Although, as a recovering addict, it was best that he didn't drink alcohol, Joel had found that beer did nothing to him if he kept it to one or two. A beer was refreshing.

Beer calmed him down when he was angry.

And what he'd told Zelda was the truth. He was angry.

On a whim, Joel dug out the folder he kept in a metal strongbox that contained legal documents—his birth certificate, social security card, and all the paperwork pertaining to his time in the Air Force. There was also material from his classroom training sessions to be an EOD tech. These included diagrams and detailed information on how various types of IEDs, including EFPs, are made. Joel got these out and studied them.

Back then, he had known this stuff by heart. It made Joel feel good to refresh his memory about his prior technical expertise.

Later, sometime during the night, another flashback nightmare struck. He was back on that bridge, just before the EFP exploded, and he knew it was coming.

Trickle ... trickle...

Unfortunately, he had no mouth with which to warn everyone. He tried to scream and cry, but his chin was nothing but loose flaps of smooth, grafted skin.

He awoke in a panic. Once again, he was in a cold sweat and his heart was pumping like a jackhammer. After a few anxious seconds, Joel realized where he was and what had happened.

It's what I get for revisiting EFPs.

And this made him angry again.

Wide awake now, he opened the case that contained a Glock 19 that he had purchased back when he'd had money, a house, and before Tracy was in his life. He couldn't recall the last time he'd fired it. Maybe it was time to take out some of his aggression at a gun range. He felt an immediate need to get back into shape with his weapon. Zelda had suggested that he find a hobby to occupy his time. Shooting at a gun range could be just the ticket.

Besides, it never hurt to be prepared ... just in case.

* * *

In October 2021, the *need* was now a distant memory.

Joel finished his workout at the Fitnexx Gym, ignored his fellow obsessed fitness junkies who were staring at his skin scarring, and moved to the locker room. Few people went to the gym during the pandemic. Joel could exercise surrounded in peace and quiet, and since he'd already had the virus, he wasn't concerned about being in the facility. He left the building feeling energetic and pumped.

The white 2017 Ford Explorer was similar to the one he'd had before marrying Tracy, except it was updated with many new bells and whistles.

He'd bought it a year ago, used with 38,000 miles on it. He was now able to finance the payments since he had a steady job at Ace Hardware.

As he drove to the apartment building where he now lived, Joel spotted an Air Force recruitment billboard. He took his right hand from the wheel and gave a middle finger salute to the display as he passed it, and then laughed.

Although it had been years since he'd seen Zelda, he knew that she would be impressed with him now. He was much more together, although he was well aware that he carried a grudge and tended to be regularly pissed at everyone and everything. The best therapy for that was to keep to himself, stay a loner, and not socialize with the intention of making new friends.

He'd gained weight in the last ten years, and he hoped that the workouts at the gym would replace the pizza-induced lard with muscle. Squeezing out sweat, to him, was a continuation of the process that got rid of the old toxins in his body. For years he'd never thought he was healthy, but now that was a word he was proud to use. Contracting COVID a year earlier had kicked his butt. He'd caught the virus early on in the pandemic, and he'd felt like crap for three weeks. But he got over it without any serious issues, and he had no lingering effects.

Most importantly, he'd kicked the OxyContin for good.

Joel sipped a Budweiser as he flipped between CNN and Fox News on his new television. He was often amused by the clear distinction in worldviews they presented. Joel felt as if he were above it all now, not swayed by either.

His one bedroom apartment was frighteningly similar to the one he'd had during the time "Before Tracy." It was funny how he tended to demarcate his life. There was "Before the Bomb" and "After the Bomb." Then there was "Before Tracy" and "After Tracy." Now he was in the "After Rehab" chapter. So far, "After Rehab" was working out okay.

On CNN, a news report came on about a law firm in Florida, Bergman-Deketomis, that went after some kind of military contractor outfit and a bunch of hotels in a case of global human trafficking. Joel became engrossed in the story, as it also involved a strange, rich Howard Hughes–like recluse in Las Vegas who had held a girl captive.

The main lawyer in the case, a guy named Nick "Deke" Deketomis, was a guest talking head. Apparently he had been successful in bringing down the white collar, Wall Street network that financed a huge part of the trafficking.

"I couldn't have done it without my team. They truly are the best team in the business," Deketomis said. "I am especially grateful to my associate, Michael Carey, who was instrumental in busting through the Las Vegas component of the case."

The camera picked up the associate in question, and Joel nearly dropped his beer can.

"Holy mother of God, it's Michael!" he said aloud.

The anchor asked, "Mr. Carey, I understand you put to good use the training you had in the Air Force to accomplish what you did in Las Vegas."

"That's correct," Michael said with a slightly embarrassed laugh. "I was a pararescueman in the Air Force. Turns out I had to do a low altitude parachute maneuver from a Cessna onto a fifty-story hotel to help a client that was being held captive there. Not exactly an everyday event in the practice of law. But it was all good."

Joel burst out laughing. "Michael, my man! You insane son of a bitch! Good for you! You did it! You really *did* become a lawyer! A frickin' pararescue son-of-a-gun action hero lawyer!"

He held up his beer and toasted the image on the television. "Cheers, brother!"

5

Joel secured his Walker Quad 360 ear muffs, adjusted his protective shooting glasses, picked up the Glock that was already loaded with a full magazine, and aimed at the range target depicting silhouettes of "bad guys." He positioned himself in a classic Weaver stance, breathed steadily, and fired.

Multiple bullseyes. Only one or two rounds were a little off, but the grouping was still tight. All were kill shots.

Satisfied, Joel checked the gun's chamber before resting the weapon on the bench before him. He then flicked the switch for the retriever mechanism to pull the target closer to him so that he could examine his handiwork.

"That's fine shooting," a voice said.

Joel turned to see the guy in the next lane over. The man had been watching at a respectful distance.

"Thanks," Joel replied.

The fellow was dressed in a businessman's white shirt with the sleeves rolled up. He looked as if he'd come to the range from the office, except that he wore at his waist a holster stuffed with what Joel recognized as a Smith & Wesson Shield 9mm. The man was small in stature, wiry, and had a high, tinny voice that was almost comical. Joel figured he made up for being the "ninety-pound weakling" growing up by learning to shoot at the range.

The man held out his hand. "I'm Willis Lee."

Joel shook it. "Joel Hartbeck."

"Nice to meet you, Joel. You're a veteran, aren't you?"

"Air Force."

"Marines for me."

Joel blinked. *Really? Marines?* He tried not to show his surprise, but Willis chuckled and said, "I know, I know, I don't look like a marine. I'm a miniature version, but I assure you I was. I got in because of my knowledge of computers. I was a tech guy. Data network specialist." He grinned, revealing remarkably ugly teeth.

"Did you serve overseas?" Joel asked.

"Iraq. From 2008 to 2011. Four lovely tours. I got off on it, man."

Joel nodded. "I was in Iraq, too. A little earlier, and for not as long. 2007. I was EOD." He gestured to the left side of his face. "Even brought back a few souvenirs, so I got an early discharge."

"Wow, EOD tech! I really admire you guys. Did you see that movie? *The Hurt Locker?*"

Joel winced inwardly. It had been a painful, traumatic film for him. "Yeah, I saw it."

"I thought it was awesome. Hey, when you're done, do you want to go have a beer? My favorite watering hole is just a couple of miles away. Do you know Beggar's Ravine?"

"I've seen it, but I haven't been in there."

"Lot of ex-military guys go there. It's our kind of place. Want to go?"

There was something about Willis Lee's enthusiasm that creeped him out, but Joel didn't have many friends. It was likely that *he* creeped out other people, too, so he replied, "Sure, why not?"

* * *

The more the two men talked over beers, the more Joel loosened up and started to like Willis Lee. He was a hyperactive and talkative little guy, but to Joel he seemed to be sincere and passionate about the new connection between two veterans.

"Oh, I'm big on hunting and fishing," Willis said. "That's why living in southern Kentucky is fantastic. The woods and hills around here are great for that."

Joel agreed. "When I was a kid before my parents died, we'd go up to a cabin we owned. It was about sixty miles from Plainsburg. It was always kind of an adventure for me, even though there was no running water and we had to use an outhouse. Hey, sometimes I look on Craigslist and find some abandoned cabin to go crash in to escape the world."

"That whole one with nature thing. I get it. You got family around?"

Joel shook his head. "I was an only child and then an orphan. There are some cousins who live far away now, and we're not in touch."

Lee nodded and then drew a solemn face. "I had a brother. He was killed in Afghanistan. He was a marine, too."

"I'm sorry to hear that."

"Thanks. Hey, did you say you work in a hardware store?"

"No, I said I *worked* in a hardware store. I got fired a month ago. Some jerk came in and wanted a refund for a tool that he broke himself, and I wouldn't do it. He started cursing and pointing fingers, and I told him where he could stick the tool. The man complained on social media, exaggerated the entire incident, and the store got a bunch of one-star reviews as a result. So I got the blame and was let go."

"That sucks, man. So does that mean you're looking for work?"

"I guess it does."

"I might know of something for you, if you're interested."

"Sure, what is it?"

Lee said, "Today's my day off, but I'm working for this bank. They set up an anti-money laundering unit in town. Have you heard about it?"

"No."

"Bank Antriol. It's a big New York bank. Anyway, the DOJ came down on them a couple of years ago for allowing money transactions between US government sanctioned entities overseas."

"Sanctioned entities?"

"Groups or individuals who have been put on the government's shit list for allegedly supporting terrorism and drug cartels. Banks aren't supposed to do business with any of the people and companies on the sanctioned list. As part of the settlement with the DOJ, the bank agreed to set up this AML unit—the anti-money laundering unit—and audit thousands and thousands of transactions over the past few years. They're hiring big numbers of people to do the work. Are you good at computers? Good at math?"

"I'd say I'm proficient with computers, and I'd say I'm damned good at math. I was going to be an engineer but I joined the Air Force instead."

"You'd probably be perfect, then! They're hiring, like, bunches of young people. With your age and experience, you'd probably sail right through the entry-level positions and get promoted to something higher pretty quick. And the pay is outstanding."

"Really? What does it pay?"

"I started at twenty-five bucks an hour. Now I'm making forty."

"Holy crap, Willis. Sign me up. What do I have to do?"

Willis dug into a pocket and pulled out his phone. He fiddled with it and showed him the address and phone number. "Take this down. Call and make an appointment with Freddie Barton. He's the manager of the unit. Tell him I sent you. I'm telling you, I'll bet he'll hire you without a second thought." He then looked at the time on his phone. "Aw, geez, I think I have to go." He plopped some cash onto the table. "It was really nice meeting you, Joel. Maybe I'll see you soon at the range again, or maybe at the AML unit!"

"That's a good possibility, Willis. Good meeting you, too."

The men shook hands, and Willis left the bar. Joel still had some beer left so he stayed in the booth.

It was just a few minutes later that a group of five men came into Beggar's Ravine. All of them appeared to be in their twenties. Two had long hair and beards, and the other three had shaved heads and goatees. They were dressed in military fatigues, were covered in tattoos, and they all carried long guns of various types. Open carry was legal in Kentucky except in businesses that prohibited it.

The men appeared to be already on their way to falling-down drunk. They were laughing loudly, shouting at each other, and carrying on as if they were the only patrons in the place.

Joel knew who they were. He'd seen members of their little organization around town. They were similar to the various fringe, far-right wing, paramilitary, white supremacist outfits that had sprung up and been in the media for the past several years. Now, in September 2022, it seemed they were everywhere. These were members of the Mohawk Warriors, or MWs. They took their name from the 1773 Boston Tea Party protesters who had called themselves the Sons of Liberty and had disguised themselves as Mohawk Native Americans during that fateful protest. Of course, these guys weren't dressed like Native Americans. The tattoos they sported were symbols of hate that had either been around for decades or were new to the scene. Swastikas, along with Iron Crosses and the SS insignia of the Nazi Gestapo seemed to be popular with this particular bunch of drunks. Some had tattoos of numbers that no doubt had some goofy secret meaning to all the losers who had just walked into the bar. There were a few about which Joel could guess. The number "4/19" was on the arms of each of the five men. Joel knew that April 19 was the date of both the Branch Davidian siege in Texas in 1993, and of the Oklahoma City Federal Building bombing in 1995. Obviously, it was an anti-government statement.

Joel had seen the MWs marching through Plainsburg with their guns and signs that attacked Democrats, Jews, people of color, and ANTIFA. He had a sudden thought that perhaps there was a thin line between these guys and himself. After all, Joel was willing to admit that he had anti-government thoughts, too. He was aware, though, that these derived from feeling that the government had failed him. The cretins in the bar were simply motivated by hate.

Other patrons in the establishment quickly paid their tabs, got up, and left. Joel still had a third of a mug to finish, so he wasn't about to move. Still, he couldn't help himself. He said aloud, mostly to himself, but intentionally with enough volume for the entire room to hear.

"What a freak show. If they want to shoot those long rifles, join the damn military."

All five of the MWs abruptly went quiet and turned toward him. Two of them—one of the skinheads and one with long hair—took a couple of steps forward from where they were standing. They stared at Joel as if he stank of skunk.

The skinhead with the goatee wore a military jacket that was missing its sleeves, baring his muscular arms. On his upper arm was the tattoo of a skull. Joel knew that the symbol was a "death head." It allegedly signified that the bearer had committed a homicide, usually of a Jew or a minority. A patch on the front of his jacket proclaimed: CHOKE THE WOKE. The man's eyes blazed with fury, and his pale white skin was flushed.

The other man's long blonde hair was tied in a ponytail. He had a beard and mustache, and he wore a ring pierced into his right eyebrow. He, too, had bare arms that displayed tattoos, notably of spider webs on his elbows. Joel wasn't positive, but he thought that meant the man had spent time in prison.

Joel took a sip of beer and ignored them.

The two kept staring. Their companions eventually gave up, turned back to the bar, and started laughing. Joel heard several unsavory words used to describe him.

Finally, after nearly a minute, Joel gazed back at the two men who hadn't moved and barked, "You got something to say?"

Skinhead immediately started forward, but Joel smoothly laid his Glock 19 on the table in front of him, his hand resting over the grip and his index finger outstretched over the trigger guard.

Blonde Guy grabbed Skinhead's arm and stopped him. "Not here," he whispered. Skinhead backed down, but he shot arrows of rage at Joel with his eyes.

The other three had also regained interest in the drama going on between their comrades and the loner in the booth. After a few moments of tension, Blonde Guy reached into his jacket pocket. Joel's hand twitched over the Glock, but all Blonde Guy brought out was a bunch of 8 ½ x 11 sheets of paper rolled up and secured with a rubber band. He pulled off the band, peeled off one of the sheets, and dropped it on the table in front of Joel. It was an announcement for a "Take Back Our Country" rally in Plainsburg Park coming up on the calendar.

"You've got balls, mister," Blonde Guy said. "Why don't you join us? We could use someone like you."

One of the three other guys hollered, "Come on, Rusty, Chad. Leave Scarface alone. We got you some shots of tequila."

The Blonde Guy was apparently Rusty. The skinhead was Chad. Of the two, Joel sensed that Chad was easily the more dangerous of the two. "Psychopath" was written all over him.

Joel didn't acknowledge Rusty's invitation. He simply took the mug of beer in hand and downed the rest of its contents. He then threw some money on the table, stood, holstered his handgun, and walked out of the joint. He left the flyer on the table.

6

E xactly two weeks after meeting Willis Lee at the gun range, Joel was hired by Bank Antriol to work in its pop-up anti-money laundering unit.

The place was situated in an empty storefront in a strip mall. Joel couldn't remember what the old business had been, but for the past several years the location was used as a temporary seasonal Halloween shop. It was large enough to have been a department store along the lines of a TJ Maxx or Stein Mart.

Joel had been interviewed by Freddie Barton, the manager of the site. Freddie was a man in his forties who wore a suit and Clark Kent glasses. He struck Joel as someone who was likely a strict, quota-enforcing bureaucrat with no sense of humor.

Freddie was impressed that Joel had experience in the Middle East, as this would be an asset in the work. Joel's math skills and experience in working in teams with clear chains of command were also considered a plus. In short, though, Joel figured he was hired because the AML unit needed bodies. At any rate, he would start at an entry-level position at twenty-five bucks an hour. If Joel exhibited strong proficiency after a couple of weeks or more, then this past experience would play into rapid promotion and more money.

"Why is the unit in Plainsburg, Kentucky?" Joel had asked.

Freddie had shrugged. "It's as good a place as any. The space was available at a good price, I guess. We're a global bank. We can work from anywhere. It's the new normal."

Joel thought it was probably because they could get cheap labor, and this was confirmed when, during the "nickel tour," Joel was surprised to see so many high-school-age employees and temp workers who didn't appear to have much life experience or office familiarity. The unit was laid out with rows of inexpensive cubicles and workstations. Stairs at the back of the space led up to a balcony where management, behind makeshift walls and glass windows, oversaw the factory-like atmosphere.

"Exactly what will I be doing?" Joel asked.

"Ah," Freddie said. "You'll go through a day of training, but it's really easy. Bank Antriol is headquartered in the Netherlands, but we have a main branch in New York City. My immediate supervisors are Blake Dullea and Karl Maher, executive vice presidents of the branch there, and they were personally in charge of the creation of this unit. This is uniquely their program. Very sharp guys. They come down here for a visit fairly often, so you'll get to meet them soon."

"I look forward to that."

"Anyway, after 9/11 the Department of Justice leaned hard on banks to do its job tracking bad guys, requiring us to institute a whole bunch of internal procedures for flagging suspicious customers. You've heard about the $10k rule?"

"The what?"

"If a person deposits more than $10k in cash at a bank, it gets reported. That rule."

"Oh, yeah. I've heard that somewhere before."

"It's really like that. The US got caught so flat-footed by 9/11 that its knee-jerk reaction was to clamp down on everyone's civil rights. Patriot Act and all, you know. Illegal cell phone tracking, domestic spying, you name it. Well, that included banks, too. Now we have to jump through a bunch of hoops here in the States so Uncle Sam can sleep better at night thinking that we will be able to help prevent some nut job from buying a five-dollar box cutter and boarding a plane again."

"How's that even possible?" Joel asked.

"Sanctions. The government sanctions people they deem 'bad guys' and then it falls on banks like us to help freeze them out of their money and stop them from using it for whatever bad shit they've supposedly done or plan to do."

"Okay. So what's that have to do with what we're doing here?"

"A few years back, it was Bank Antriol's turn to be some buffoonish overpaid and underworked government regulator's punching bag. As usual, someone at the Treasury Department was trying to make it look like they actually worked for a living. Then the no-count DOJ had to pile on and look like they're actually winning whatever war they've decided to wage that day—the war on drugs, the war on terror—hell, if you ask me, it's just more of the woke's new war on capitalism. A routine audit detected a minor technical glitch in the systems Antriol had set up to flag suspicious banking activity. Treasury and the DOJ jumped on their soapboxes claiming we had violated banking laws and failed to file what are called Suspicious Activity Reports, or SARs. It's really a bunch of BS. Anyway, we paid a fine and agreed to a re-review of transactions. We report the results to Wall Street watchdogs so they can say they're doing their part fighting terrorists and whatnot."

"Willis Lee told me a little about that."

"Right. Willis has rapidly moved up the ladder here to a management position overseeing the Asian branch. Anyway, the DOJ has this list of sanctioned companies and individuals who have been suspected of supporting terrorism, drug trafficking, invading other countries ... all that kind of stuff."

"And here I am."

"Yep, welcome to the party," Freddie said with a smile. "Here, we do the re-review of decades-long backlog of transaction data. The bank has a customer account monitoring program—called CAMP—that stores the bank's transactions, including wire transfers. On top of that, the bank has an alert monitoring system, or AMS, that monitors CAMP. If the AMS comes across a transaction that involves a sanctioned entity, it sends out an alert of suspicious activity. It will be your job to examine the alert and deliver a report about it."

Joel nodded. "I get that. I assume there are various degrees of suspicious activity?"

"You catch on quick! Yes, there are three ways an alert can be handled. The best outcome for the bank is for you to clear it. That's what the bank really wants. What it boils down to is that we're in the customer service business. Our customers are billion dollar entities that keep the world's economy moving. They expect us to provide the best service, which means to facilitate their financial transactions with as little delay and interference as possible. We encourage everyone here to find every opportunity to clear any alerts. The more alerts that are cleared, the more satisfied our customers are and the more money the bank makes, and that will factor into your promotions and increases in salary. To close an alert, you'll personally write a brief narrative that reviews all the facts and information about the transaction in question and show how there is no need for the alert that is being reported. That wipes the alert clean. Of course, in rare circumstances, clearing an alert is not always possible. A second option for dealing with an alert is that it is escalated to an SAR. Those are rare occurrences that would go to me personally, and after reviewing it, I forward it to Mr. Dullea and Mr. Maher in New York, and to the Treasury Department. The third way an alert is handled is to simply place it 'on watch.' This means the alert is not suspicious enough to be escalated to an SAR, but there is enough so that an investigation should be done comparing it to any other suspicious activity in the past or in the future. All in all, it ain't that complicated for a smart guy like you."

Joel thought he could handle all of that. Freddie offered him the job, and Joel accepted.

Now, a week into the work in the Asian branch, which included the Middle East, he was a bit overwhelmed by how much data there was. The bank had literally thousands of transactions. It was no wonder that the AML unit had hired around two hundred bodies to work there, packed into cubicles like sardines.

From day one, Joel would meet up with Willis Lee for their lunch break. Willis was now his immediate supervisor. On the eighth day of Joel's employment, Willis said, "I think Freddie likes your work. You're far surpassing all those kids out there with your output. You're going to advance quickly."

"I appreciate you letting me know that. I'm happy to have the job."

"You'll be a valued member of the team."

Joel had noticed something about Willis, who had had a hand in Joel's training. Willis seemed to be able to calculate complicated equations in his head. His brain was like a massive storehouse of information that he had no problem accessing. When Joel mentioned this to Willis, the man replied with modesty, "I'm what doctors call a savant when it comes to memory. I am blessed and cursed with a brain that stores way too much information. That's why I was good as an ORSA analyst in the Marines. Operations research/systems analysis. I guess I was born this way. I don't think anything of it, but, yeah, I can remember stuff. I'm told there are very few of my types walking around. Not sure whether that's good or bad."

All Joel could say in reply was, "Wow." He had previously thought of Willis as a bit of an odd duck, but a likeable one. Now he regarded the guy with a certain amount of awe.

* * *

A month into Joel's employment at Bank Antriol's AML unit, he was promoted with a good raise to overseeing the review of transactions involving West Asia. This encompassed Middle East countries including Israel, Turkey, Saudi Arabia, Yemen, the UAE, Lebanon, Syria, Iran, Afghanistan, and, yes, Iraq. Willis Lee had been promoted and now worked in the management office with Freddie Barton. Joel was still friendly with Willis, and on days off they spent time at the gun range together, and, afterwards, drinking beer at Beggar's Ravine. He and Willis talked little about the work itself. Their topics of conversation mostly consisted of the various women working at the unit.

One such lady that Joel had noticed was Janet Blanco, an attractive brunette who was supervisor of the Latin America branch. Her cubicle was just across the aisle from Joel's. They had spoken occasionally at first, and that had led to meeting up for lunch during the break. Joel knew he shouldn't even dream about a possible relationship with Janet … well, he could *dream* about it, but he wasn't going to act on it. Not unless she showed some kind of sign that she might be interested. So far, though, it was all platonic.

One day Janet asked him, "Have you kept track of the percentage of SARs you submit versus the ones you clear?"

"I'm clearing more," he replied. "I haven't thought about the percentage. Maybe ninety-five percent are cleared. Why?"

"It's the same with me. I suppose with Middle East transactions, the sanctioned people are suspected of funding terrorists, right?"

"Uh huh."

"With my area, it's more about drug cartels. I can't believe the bank was doing business with them, but they were."

"Why would the bank knowingly do this?"

Janet rubbed her fingers and thumb together. "Come on, why do you think? Cash-ola!"

He smiled. "Yeah, I figured that much. But I have to say, there's something odd that—"

Freddie Barton walked into the break room, and they went quiet. He said hello and then stood at the vending machine. Janet shook her head at Joel and said no more with the boss there. They continued to eat their sandwiches as Freddie painstakingly pondered which candy bar to buy. Once he finally made his purchase he turned to them. "Ah, look at you two branch heads showing genuine camaraderie. I like that, I think. Hey, I'm about to make an announcement over the intercom. Mr. Dullea and Mr. Maher just arrived in town and will be addressing the unit at three o'clock. They'll want to meet with you both after that."

"Oh, cool," Joel said. "Thanks. I look forward to that."

When Freddie left the room, Janet whispered, "Have you met Dullea and Maher before?"

"No. They haven't been here since I started."

She simply nodded and rolled her eyes a little.

"What?"

"Nothing. I'll let you make an assessment on your own."

"What were you about to say earlier?"

"Never mind. I'll tell you later, but not here."

* * *

Blake Dullea was a man in his forties who wore a fancy suit with a brand name that Joel guessed was likely Italian. Dullea might have stepped out of an ad for the bank. Joel thought he looked more like a male model than a bank executive. Still, he projected an aura of confidence and slick charm. He spoke with a pronounced New York accent, but he seemed to work at covering up the harsh edge with an Ivy League polish. The women in the unit were definitely paying attention to him. Joel sensed that Dullea could very well have his pick if the guy wanted a conquest.

Karl Maher was also dressed in a sharp suit. Again, Joel didn't know anything about Fifth Avenue or Madison Avenue men's wear, but whatever it was, it screamed *expensive*. Maher, too, was a good-looking man, a little younger than Dullea, maybe late thirties. Joel guessed that he had Middle Eastern or Mediterranean attributes because of a swarthier skin color, dark eyes, and black hair. When he spoke, his English was unmistakably "American," although there was no regional inflection that Joel could pinpoint.

"Karl and I have to congratulate all of you on the tremendous work you're doing," Dullea said with gusto. "The number of alerts cleared in the past month surpassed September, so give yourselves a round of applause!"

Everyone did so.

Dullea and Maher stood on the balcony outside the management office to address all the employees in the unit. Most people were standing outside their cubicles to get a better view.

When the applause died down, Dullea continued. "That said, it *is* important to flag suspicious transactions; that is, those made to or on behalf of DOJ-sanctioned organizations and individuals known to support terrorism or drug trafficking. That's why you're here. But at the same time, it's just as important to clear as many transactions as possible. Bank Antriol is depending on you to clear these alerts quickly and in mass quantities. That's why we've come here today to announce a new incentive program. Karl's going to tell you about it."

Karl took the microphone and said, "Thank you, Blake. Good afternoon, everyone. We at Bank Antriol are happy to announce that beginning this month, the thirty employees who clear the most alerts will receive a fifteen percent raise in salary. If you are in the top thirty next month, you will *again* get the raise, and so on, as long as you're employed at the unit. Furthermore, the person who clears the most alerts between now and December 31 of this year will receive an all-expenses paid trip for you and your immediate family for three days at Walt Disney World in Orlando, Florida!"

The employees applauded and oohed and aahed with glee.

Blake took the microphone back. "And ... depending on how all that works out, that little perk may continue in 2023. Maybe the next paid vacation will take you to Las Vegas! Or bring you to New York City to see some Broadway shows!"

More applause and delight.

Joel rubbed his chin. Both men sounded like barkers at a second-rate carnival. It was clearly a blatant attempt to get the not-so-smart employees to cut corners and clear alerts. Maybe that was okay. Perhaps there was no harm done by that. The problem he was having was that he had already connected the dots on how money flowing through the New York branch could end up in the wrong pockets. The process of scanning the data and writing reports had made it clear to him. If he were honest with himself, it wouldn't take detailed analysis to understand how easy it was to make a transaction appear legitimate and produce a limitless cache of weapons for drug cartels in Central and South America. In his new position, Joel had gained deeper access into the bank's transaction data, including more insight into customer details. While he had been clearing alerts at a rapid rate, he had also placed many of them on "watch" and issued several SARs. He had noticed that Freddie was never happy when SARs were forwarded to him. It was as if he didn't want to deal with them, or that they somehow made him look bad in the eyes of his New York superiors. Wouldn't Dullea and Maher have been pleased to get the SARs as proof that the AML unit was doing the job it was created to do? The more he thought about it, all those dots were becoming heavier to carry around.

He remembered Janet rubbing her fingers and thumb together.

Of course! It's all about the money to be made. It's how the world turns.

It reinforced the beliefs he'd been nurturing over the past several years that all of government and big business were corrupt.

And now the question he had to answer for himself was whether he had become part of that corruption.

7

It was in mid-January 2023 that Joel came upon a group of transactions that the AMS flagged as suspicious. Several small companies located in Saudi Arabia and Lebanon—Dhalm Tools Enterprises, Chtoura Oasis Ltd., and others—had been using the bank to advise and negotiate letters of credit to purchase equipment from SeedDotz, an American tool company. SeedDotz owned and operated manufacturing facilities in Europe and Asia, and it specialized in designing and building machine tools for industrial manufacturers. Dhalm Tools Enterprises and Chtoura Oasis Ltd. were at various times either on the sanctioned list, or closely related to other entities that were, and they had been flagged for being possible fronts for Hezbollah. The United States designated Hezbollah a terrorist organization back in 1997 due to its systematic targeting and killing of Americans overseas.

As Joel traced the transactions through the bank's systems and reviewed the letters of credit, bills of lading, and other information about the funds and transfers of goods, he learned that the Middle East companies had used the bank to purchase industrial grade pneumatic presses and "assorted tooling."

Joel double-checked the dates of the transactions. They spanned years, even after some of the entities had been blacklisted. Digging further, Joel found that the pneumatic presses arrived at ports in the Middle East unusually far from the Lebanese customers by which they had been allegedly purchased. Once off-loaded at the ports in the Arabic Gulf, the bills of lading were signed over to individuals who had misspelled the names of the companies, and in some instances even the spelling of their own names changed across the documents. Despite these discrepancies, the bank treated the transactions as complete and released payment for the goods. The bank's fees were then swiftly assessed, and at much higher rates than normal. Joel scoured the data, but no record existed to show that the presses arrived where they were supposed to go, and even more documents purported to show the presses being loaded onto trucks for which no proof of final delivery at the factory, or to the named customer identified on the original transaction record, existed.

To close the loop, Joel punched one of the final destination addresses provided in several of the shipping documents into Google Earth. A 3D globe in the program spun and zoomed to a pin dropped in downtown Beirut. Joel wheeled the mouse, zooming closer to the pin, and suddenly the names of landmarks, streets, and places of interests materialized on the map. The program switched to street view, and quickly Joel was given a visual perspective, as if he were standing directly in the middle of a narrow street in Beirut at midday. The sun was shining, but the tall balconied buildings squeezed the road, casting a shadow over most of it. The street was paved with black flagstone that glistened with moisture from a recent rain. Parked cars lined both sides facing opposite directions, making it wide enough for just one vehicle. A person on a scooter, frozen in time, the face blurred by Google's amazing technology, passed closely to the car-mounted camera that had collected the 360-degree photograph. Foot traffic and shopkeepers, similarly obscured, crowded the curb and were suspended mid-motion like statues. Joel clicked and dragged his mouse across the screen, spinning the street view photo to scan the storefronts and coming to a rest on the pin. What he saw made him triple-check the address in Google Earth's search bar. Once he was sure he hadn't fat-fingered the coordinates, he almost laughed out loud. He was staring at the façade of a Starbucks.

The fact that this had gone on for years at the bank and hadn't yet been reported, along with the bank's premium fees for these transactions, sealed in Joel's mind that this wasn't a result of a technical glitch in Antriol's systems. This was a red flag on top of a red flag.

He needed a breather.

Joel sat in the break room eating a protein bar and running what he had learned about SeedDotz through his mind. As he stared at a motivational poster espousing "Teamwork!" by depicting four people assembling large puzzle-piece shaped blocks into a square, a young woman walked in and began filling a large tumbler from the water cooler. As the tumbler filled, the sound of the water splashing into it seeped into Joel's thoughts.

Trickle ... trickle...

Instantly he was back in Iraq standing on the bridge with the babbling brook flowing below. And then it clicked.

Joel stood and walked briskly to his desk. Punching his login credentials into CAMP, he knew what he would find before it materialized on his screen. And then, there it was. The insurance inventory of the goods shipped with the presses included precision rollers, mandrels, and dyes. Tools used to shape thick metal sheeting into solid concave plates, and in turn, the tools could press the conical plates tightly into variable diameter tubing—the exact same kind of tools and materials his EOD training had taught him that were used to form high-grade copper sheets into cylindrical cones. Joel, of course, knew from firsthand experience that those were critical components of EFPs.

It was time for Joel to finally start asking the tough questions that everyone at that hole in the wall facility should have been asking. *Does the bank* really *want to stop these transactions? Are they covering them up? Is this place nothing but a sham set up to appease the dysfunctional DOJ?*

He rubbed his eyes and laughed to himself. He couldn't ignore the obvious. It was possible that a United States bank the size of Antriol was more than likely deliberately committing a whole host of crimes. Still, maybe it was a mistake. Perhaps it was an oversight. Maybe his imagination was running wild.

Joel decided to talk to Janet Blanco about it to get her take.

* * *

It was their third date, although Joel didn't like to call their liaisons as such. The first time was meeting for a Thanksgiving dinner at a local restaurant that was open on the holiday. Janet's mother lived in Monticello, and she would normally have spent the holiday with her. But her mom came down with COVID, so Janet was staying away. Being single and alone, Janet had otherwise nowhere else to go, and neither did Joel. It had been a pleasant, enjoyable luncheon together.

Joel asked her to go out for pizza one evening after work during the second week of December. She happily accepted the invitation, and again it was a good experience. They talked mostly about work. Like Joel, Janet was beginning to feel uncomfortable about how the AML unit was run. The emphasis on clearing alerts at the detriment to due diligence was becoming more of a distraction for both of them.

He had presented her with a holiday card prior to the unit's break—a closing for four days—and he was happy to see her reaction.

Now, at Grill Happy, Plainsburg's finest barbecue restaurant, Janet boldly stated, "I was wondering if I'd said something wrong last time. We haven't been out together in a month."

Joel winced. "I'm so sorry, Janet. Believe me, it's not you. I was … I'll admit it … I was afraid of rejection. My past … it's not pretty. I'm gun-shy when it comes to women. I didn't want to overstep too soon and find myself embarrassed and disappointed."

She placed a hand over his and said, "It's all right. I don't know if we're 'seeing each other' or not, and it's best not to put a label on it. Let's just take it one day at a time. That's perfectly fine with me. You can relax."

He smiled at that. "All right. Thanks."

The beef brisket, ribs, beans, and potato salad tasted particularly good to Joel after Janet's encouraging words. In between napkin wipes, she spoke again. "You said you wanted to talk to me about something at work."

"Right. I was wondering if you've encountered something like what I have." He told her about the group of transactions he had been investigating and what he'd found. "I hope I'm wrong, but it strikes me that the bank knows full well these transactions are illegal, and yet they're continuing to take place."

She nodded. "To answer your question—yes. I have had to flag several transactions that should have triggered wide open alerts. I have found recent money transfers to companies and individuals in South and Central America—mainly Colombia—that have been sanctioned. I'm convinced they're associated with drug cartels and their paramilitary protectors. I've reported them to Freddie, and he said he would put them in the pipeline to New York."

"But is New York doing anything about them?"

"That I don't know."

"Should I just do what I'm supposed to do and report these things to Freddie?"

"What else can you do?"

"Maybe I should talk to Willis. I could draw a diagram that connects all the dots, and it will be easier to comprehend."

"I guess that wouldn't hurt. But ... you know ... we could report this stuff to the FBI. Or something."

Joel made a face. "Yikes. I'm not sure I want to go that far. Besides, Freddie sends these things to New York anyway, right? I don't really want to lose this job just yet."

"Yeah, I know what you mean. Still ... it's something to think about."

The restaurant had a couple of flat screen televisions above the bar, and Joel couldn't help but notice a headline on one that read: MWs GANG MEMBER ARRESTED AND RELEASED. News footage displayed a house with yellow DO NOT CROSS tape in front, and several of Plainsburg's finest milling around police vehicles at the curb. Janet started to say something, but Joel gently held up a finger. "Hold on, I want to hear this."

"...was arrested on suspicion of distributing cocaine and methamphetamine, but he was later released," the anchor voiceover was saying. "Chief of Police Burt Wainwright confirmed that a lack of evidence was the reason for Blueson's release."

A mug shot flashed on the screen of one of the MW members who had accompanied "Rusty" and "Chad" at Beggar's Ravine the night they had harassed Joel. The name "Ronald 'Blue' Blueson" captioned it. This was followed by B-roll from the "Take Back Our Country" rally in Plainsburg Park, where the MWs were seen marching with their

AR-15s, the usual right-wing propaganda signs, 4/19 and Nazi insignia, and other offensive imagery.

"I hate those guys," Janet said. "They're knuckle-dragging racists and big-time drug dealers."

"I saw the man they arrested at Beggar's Ravine one night. Two of his pals got in my face a little bit, but I walked away."

"Good for you. I've heard they've got ties with the Colombian drug cartels."

"How do you know that?"

"Word gets around in the Latino community."

"I wouldn't be surprised if it's true. Funny how they're white supremacists, and yet they have no problem working for non-whites when a lot of cash-ola is involved."

"Bingo," she said with a chuckle.

They gladly changed the subject of conversation, proceeded to ignore the TV screens, and talked about more pleasant topics. Eventually they got into revealing bits and pieces of their former lives. He told her about his childhood as an orphan and the horror of foster homes. She revealed that her mother in Monticello was in the dementia wing of an assisted living home. They talked of family, love affairs, failed marriages, and dreams of the future. The trust—and intimacy—definitely became more palpable as the evening went on.

When they realized that they had stayed at their table nearly an hour after finishing dinner, they finally got up to leave.

Joel drove her home. Janet lived in a small ranch house in a working class area of town. She had told Joel that she had purchased the home because it was affordable, not for the real estate. Besides, the small melting pot of diverse ethnicities in her neighborhood were more in tune with her own, and she felt safe and happy there.

He was about to say goodbye and that he'd see her at work, but she surprised him by asking, "Would … would you like to come in for a drink and some TV?"

His heart skipped a beat before he managed to nod affirmatively.

* * *

Joel sat in his cubicle trying to concentrate on the AMS data for the day. It was difficult to focus because all he could think about was Janet. For a week and half, they had "taken it to the next level," as she had put it. Joel had been under the impression that he would never be with another woman since the Tracy debacle. Both he and Janet thought it would be wise not to let on at work that they were truly now "seeing each other."

Funny how life throws good and bad curve balls at you. This was definitely a good one.

A tap on his shoulder jolted him out of his reverie. Joel turned to see Willis standing behind him.

"Hey, Willis. What's up?"

"Sorry to disturb your work. I just wanted to tell you not to worry about those transactions you told me about. I discussed them with Freddie and he agrees with you. He's going to report them to New York and will also send along that diagram you made that illustrates the connections. He said to tell you, 'good work.'"

"Oh, that's great. Thanks for telling me, Willis."

"You ready to go to the range again soon?"

"I am. What are you doing after work?"

"Going to the gun range with you!"

"Ten-four, buddy."

After Willis went back upstairs, Janet stood and went over to Joel's cubicle carrying some printouts. She sometimes did this simply to say hello or flirt a little under the pretense of asking a question about the paperwork.

"What did he say?" she asked.

He told her.

"I did the same thing," Janet said. "Yesterday I found transactions that were so blatantly illegal that I marched upstairs to show Freddie myself. He said he would 'take it under advisement.'"

Joel spread his hands open. "Nothing else to do, right?"

"Yeah. Well, maybe. Do you actually think Freddie follows through?"

He shrugged in reply. "He's supposed to."

"I don't trust Freddie," Janet confided with a whisper.

Joel blinked. He rubbed his chin and considered that. "I trust Willis, though. It's out of our hands, isn't it?"

"Maybe." She raised her eyebrows. "But maybe not."

* * *

A few days later, Joel decided to dig into the AML systems and check on the final status of some of the SARs he had sent up the line to Freddie and ultimately to New York. Technically, he wasn't required or even supposed to do this, but with his promotion and new responsibilities, he had better access into deeper levels of the machine. He looked up the transaction for which he had used Google Earth, and he was shocked to find that it had come back cleared. The entities involved in the transactions had been placed on the "green light" list; in other words, upper management in New York had allegedly investigated the players and deemed them to be safe.

But did the DOJ agree with those assessments? Did they even know?

Joel continued the deep dive into the transactions in question. The American tool company, SeedDotz, and its manufacturing colleagues in Europe that he had identified earlier were continuing to use the bank's money transfer system to export raw materials that were components of a variety of products, but even a surface investigation would show that these materials could be used to make specific copper-alloy capable of allowing EFPs to pierce thick American military armor. This information might be gobbledygook to a layman, but Joel had been an EOD technician. He had studied EFPs extensively—the materials that went into building them and how they were constructed. To him, it was obvious what was going on with these companies and the transactions they initiated for transferring funds. Even without this technical knowledge, the bank's handling of the transactions and business with sanctioned entities in and of itself was illegal and blatantly reportable.

Luckily, in Joel's capacity as a supervisor in the West Asian branch of the unit, he could look up the original digital paperwork behind these recent transactions. It took some doing, but he eventually found them. As suspected, the recipients of the money transfers were again dodgy, near-anonymous entities in the Middle East. They were well-developed, perfect fronts for terrorists in the business of building bombs.

Joel's jaw dropped when he saw the names of the bank executives who had signed off on these deals.

Blake Dullea and Karl Maher.

8

Joel watched as Willis Lee fired his Smith & Wesson at the "bad guy" target in the lane. Over the period of time that the two men had been shooting together, Joel had given Willis a few tips that improved his aim. "The Marines taught me how to shoot," Willis had said, "but I was never great. I do okay."

When Willis finished, they packed up, secured their weapons, and made the obligatory trek to Beggar's Ravine for a beer. Once they were in a booth, Willis noticed that Joel was edgy and apparently uneasy about something. When Joel looked at his watch, Willis asked, "Is anything wrong? You have to be somewhere?"

Joel smiled sheepishly and replied, "I, uh, have a dinner date."

"Oh? Some pretty young thing?"

"You could say that."

"Are her initials J. B.?"

Joel blinked.

Willis laughed. "Don't look so surprised. I know what's going on. Well, I at least suspected it. Don't worry, man. Good for you. Janet's a knockout."

"We were trying to keep it quiet," Joel said.

"Hey, there's no law on the books that says employees at the unit can't date each other. Maybe if you were in the New York office it might be a little different with all that woke insanity up there, but here ... don't sweat it."

"Please don't tell Freddie."

"I won't. Freddie and I aren't friends like you and me. Freddie's a corporate shill. I do what he tells me to do, and that's it."

Joel nodded. "Okay, Willis. Thanks."

"No problem, buddy. Is there anything else bugging you?"

Joel paused a moment and then said, "Willis, I'm concerned about something at work."

"What is it?"

"It's some of the transactions I'm dealing with."

"More of those fishy SARs?"

"The same ones, really." He told Willis what he'd discovered and why he was so disturbed. "I'm kind of an expert in IEDs, and I can read this information a bit differently than someone else. I really think there's a problem."

Willis laughed. "Man, you're overthinking it. This is way over our pay grades. We work for the bank in New York. It's their problem. Not mine, and definitely not yours. My advice is to just do what your job description says and let those rich bastards up there handle it. If they're doing something wrong, it's their asses, not ours. Relax. You don't want to cause yourself any unnecessary trouble. Freddie will just as soon let you go as easily as he hired you."

"I know. I like the job, too."

"Then don't say a word to Freddie."

"I won't."

* * *

Joel knocked on Janet's door and waited until she opened it. She gave him a hug and a kiss, and then they both went to the dining room. A glass of red wine and an open bottle was already on the table.

"Are we celebrating something?" he asked.

"You want some? I'll get you a glass." She moved to the kitchen and retrieved another goblet for him. After she poured wine into it, she sat and took a swig from her own. "I needed a drink after work," she said with a slight smile, "and this is my third."

Joel could see that something was off. He sat and asked, "What's going on, Janet?"

She proceeded to tell him how the more she looked into the Colombian transactions, the more she was convinced that drug cartels were involved. "I finally realized I needed to do something about it. The bank is covering it up. I'm sure of it. They're just going through the motions so that the useless DOJ can do what they've been doing forever with this bank, which is to ignore the obvious. They are a joke when it comes to controlling white-collar crime. This is just another example."

She handed him a large envelope full of papers.

"What's this?" he asked.

"Copies of everything I've uncovered. Complete with my notes connecting the dots. I don't want to be the only person with this material."

"What am I supposed to do with it?"

She was quiet a moment. "Just hold on to it. Keep it safe."

"You're not thinking of confronting Freddie with this, are you?"

Janet blinked but didn't say anything.

"I was talking to Willis earlier," Joel said, "and he was pretty clear about how Freddie could really fly off the handle if we make any waves. You could get fired. You need to be careful."

"If he fires me, he fires me. And if that happens, Joel, I could go to the FBI."

* * *

The evening consisted of love, followed by restless sleep for the both of them. Janet had then risen early, dressed, and departed for work. She surprised him by saying she had a meeting with Freddie, but she didn't seem to want to tell him why. Joel took his time to shower, have some breakfast, and depart for the unit. He took care to make sure the lights in her house were off and the door was securely locked, and then he drove to the strip mall. He normally arrived a little early anyway.

Janet's car was not in the parking lot.

On a whim, Joel hid her envelope full of papers under the seat of his car. He then went inside, stopped by his own cubicle to drop off his coat, and then he moved directly to Janet's cubicle. It was empty. None of her personal items, such as the photo of her mother that usually sat near the computer, were present.

Joel looked up at the balcony. The lights were on in Freddie's office. Joel walked briskly to the stairs and made his way to the door, which was open. Freddie was at his computer.

He knocked and said, "Good morning, Freddie."

The manager looked up at him. "Morning. What can I do for you?"

"Janet Blanco had asked me about some protocols on RFIs, and I promised to show her some examples of mine. I went by her cubicle and it's all cleared out. Have you heard from Janet?"

Freddie swiveled in his chair and faced him. "Janet is no longer with us, Joel."

"What?"

"I can't discuss employee records with you. All I'll say is her work performance wasn't meeting the standards that we require. We'll be looking to promote someone to her position from her branch as soon as possible. Anything else I can help you with?"

"Uh, no. Thanks. Sorry to hear that."

Freddie shrugged as if it were no big deal. "People come and go through here all the time. It's a revolving door. The work isn't particularly stimulating, you know? I'm sure she'll land on her feet somewhere else."

Joel left the office and returned to his cubicle. He got his cell phone out of his pocket and phoned her, but he reached voicemail. He then sent her a text message: CALL ME.

He knew damn well that Janet was one of the best employees at the unit. The bastard had fired her for making waves.

9

When Joel took his lunch break, he noticed that Janet had left a voice message on his phone. The AML unit rules were such that employees' cell phones needed to be silenced during work hours, so he hadn't heard the call. He took it outside to the parking lot and phoned her back.

"Joel!" she said. "I was fired."

"I know. Freddie told me. Did he say why?"

"Some bullshit about not doing my job properly. But it was really for reporting those suspicious transactions and questioning Freddie's clearance of them. I did it, Joel. I pointed out the connections to the drug cartels, and he said that I was imagining things. He told me they can't have someone in the unit who 'makes stuff up.' Those were the exact words he said."

"Geez, I'm so sorry."

"They made me sign an NDA in order to receive a severance. And the severance was only two weeks' worth of pay. Pretty meager. Now, I wish I hadn't signed it, but at the time I was too shaken to think straight. There's definitely something criminal going on with the bank and this AML unit. Joel, I'm going to the FBI. I'm going to report them."

"Janet, be careful. Remember, you just signed an NDA. You could get in legal trouble."

"There are whistleblower laws, Joel! I think I can be protected. I told them that, too."

"Wait," he said. "You told Freddie you might go to the FBI?"

"Yes. Then they made me sign the NDA. I still think I can be a whistleblower."

Joel rubbed his head. He was beginning to get a headache again for the first time in a long while. "Janet, you might need a lawyer. I don't think you can just do this on your own and be protected."

"I'm going to spend the afternoon researching it. But don't be surprised if I put in a call to the FBI before you get off work today."

"Listen … wait until I come over, okay? I'll shoot right over to your place as soon as I get off."

"Oh, damn," she said. "I forgot to tell you I have to go to Monticello today and see my mom. It's her birthday, and I promised to go have dinner with her. Since I don't have to go into work tomorrow, I'm going to spend the night."

"I could go with you. I'll stay in a motel and drive back early."

"No, I need to leave before you get off."

"I'll skip out on work the rest of the day."

"Joel, I think I need to go alone. I'm sorry; it's nothing to do with you. I'll call you tomorrow when I get home, okay?"

"All right, Janet. I'm sorry this happened. Do me a favor—call me tonight from Monticello, will you do that?"

"Sure. Of course. And keep those papers I gave you safe!"

"Okay, I will. Drive careful."

He hung up and went back inside the unit to eat his lunch. The headache was getting worse, so he popped a couple of ibuprofen tablets. When he finally returned to his cubicle and sat in front of the computer, Joel's thoughts lingered on a notion about which he had been in denial.

Am I now part of the banking cesspool, contributing to the support of terrorism?

* * *

Janet Blanco stepped out of the kitchen door into her garage, where she kept her 2017 Toyota Camry. She pushed the button to open the big garage door to the driveway, flooding the place with sunlight. The brisk cold wind blew inside, and she shivered. The weather reports warned that snow was on the way. She hoped that she could get to Monticello before the storm hit. Luckily, it wasn't a great distance.

She opened the car's back door on the driver's side and threw her overnight bag onto the seat. She now just needed to go grab her purse, a bottle of water for the road, and her phone.

Back in the house, she paused in front of her laptop computer. Perhaps she should bring it along as well. After speaking with Joel at lunchtime, she had gone online and researched reporting tips to the government. The FBI had a site where one could do that. Janet investigated it and found several options of departments that she could contact. One was the United States Drug Enforcement Administration. She figured that might be the best place, considering her concerns regarding the bank's transactions with drug cartels. The Department of Justice also had a website upon which she could report a crime related to drugs, but she was wary of the DOJ. They were supposed to be monitoring the re-review of the transactions, and they had already messed up handling the bank.

Instead of doing anything immediately, she chose to heed Joel's advice and wait. However, if she took the laptop with her to her mother's place, perhaps she could send reports to both entities that evening after she'd had more time to examine the websites' instructions.

Janet started to shut down the computer when the voice came from behind her.

"Your door was open."

* * *

When Joel arrived at work the following morning, he was depressed. The snowstorm overnight hadn't helped, and the roads had not yet been cleared. Driving was hazardous, and there were a lot of idiots skidding and sliding everywhere.

Of bigger concern was that he hadn't heard from Janet the night before, and he had called twice to leave messages. He had also texted, and she didn't reply. Was it over between them? Was it something he'd said? Had he blown it?

He entered the building and went to his cubicle. A note affixed to his computer keyboard read: SEE ME. FREDDIE. Sighing heavily, Joel removed his coat and draped it on his chair. This was all he needed.

Upstairs, Joel knocked on the door, and Freddie answered, "Come in." Once in the office, the boss ordered him to close the door and sit down.

To Joel's surprise, Blake Dullea and Karl Maher were sitting at the table. Freddie joined them, and Joel felt as if he were under interrogation at the police station. It was him against three bad cops and no good ones.

"Joel," Freddie said, "we've decided to move you to the filing division."

It was well understood that this was where they put newbies or employees who couldn't handle more complex tasks. After SARs had been cleared, the info went to filing, where digital transactions were logged into a database to be sent to the bank's storage unit in Antioch, Tennessee. There it would remain under lock and key until the end of time. It was the dead end job of the AML unit.

Do they know about Janet and me? he wondered. *I haven't rocked the boat, at least not officially. Unless...*

"Um, why is that?" Joel asked.

Maher answered, "We feel it's best that you no longer have access to the raw data anymore."

Dullea shot his partner a glance, as if that were something Maher shouldn't have said. He jumped in. "Don't get us wrong, Mr. Hartbeck. You are a valued employee. You've done great work. We don't want to lose you. We think with your organizational skills, you'll be better suited to managing that massive log of data that needs to be sorted and filed. Your pay will stay the same, don't worry about that."

Joel felt his anger building. The bitterness he had carried inside ever since the incident in Iraq abruptly resurfaced. He felt the anger in his chest and gut, and all he wanted to do was lash out.

Control it, Joel ... be cool...

"With all due respect," he managed to say, "my expertise in the Middle East was something that has been an asset in my branch. I've been able to recognize and act on seriously suspicious transactions. I thought that's what our purpose is, right?"

"You are correct," Freddie said. "And we appreciate what you've done so far."

"Why don't you fire me like you did Janet?"

Freddie narrowed his eyes. "Joel, if you no longer want to work here, you know where the door is."

"You want me to resign, is that it? That's what you are really hoping I'll do."

"Mr. Hartbeck—" Dullea began.

Joel stood. "Fine. I resign. Get someone else to cover up your big bank crimes. But you and all you Wall Street punks better dig in when people start to understand that you were killing American soldiers."

There, he thought. *I said it.*

"Joel!" Freddie barked. "That kind of talk is uncalled for."

Maher opened a manila folder and slid forth a sheet of paper. "If you want to leave, that's fine, but you'll have to sign this first."

"What is that?"

Maher attempted to sound as pleasant as possible. "Bank Antriol is willing to offer you a severance payout, even if it's your choice to leave your employment. You'll need to sign this NDA, though."

"What, it says I can't talk about what's been going on here?"

"Right."

"What do you mean, I have to sign it *first*? What if I don't sign it?"

"Then you don't get the severance payout."

"You said, if I want to leave, fine, but I have to sign that first. Are you saying that I can't just resign and walk out the door? What if I don't want your pissant severance payout? Fact is, I'll leave under my terms, not yours, and that should scare the hell out of all of you because I don't think you are going to like my terms."

"Come on, Joel," Freddie said. "We've been good to you here."

Joel's headache made him want to pound the table with a fist, but he refrained. Instead he moved toward the door. "Gentlemen, have a good day. Be careful driving in the snow. It's a treacherous world out there."

He slammed the office door shut and bounded down the stairs. As Joel passed the break room, he saw Willis Lee getting coffee. The man caught Joel's eye and started to say something, but Joel was on a mission—to get the hell out of there without another word. And he did.

* * *

Joel imagined that the "bad guy" target in the lane was Freddie Barton. He aimed the Glock, breathed, and squeezed the trigger. The gun recoiled six times, perforating the bullseye exactly where he had intended.

Next up—Blake Dullea and Karl Maher. All he had to do was change the target on the retriever mechanism.

He hadn't slept well the previous night. Joel was angry about what had happened at the AML unit, and he was frustrated with Janet not returning his call. Hopefully, she'd be back home later in the day, and he could go over and find out what was wrong. He had gone back over their conversations, and he was damned if he could figure out if he'd said something out of line. How had he upset her? He had no clue.

"Joel?"

He turned to see Willis standing at a safe distance.

"I thought I'd find you here when you didn't answer your phone. I went by your place, too," the man said.

Joel reached into his pocket and pulled out his mobile. Sure enough, there were two missed calls from Willis.

"Sorry," Joel said. He removed the earmuffs. "I guess I didn't hear it since I was here." Then he cocked his head. "Why aren't you at work?"

"I called in sick," Willis answered. "I heard about what happened and wanted to make sure you're all right."

"I'm fine. I'm glad to get out of there. Willis, I think something is going on with Bank Antriol. They fired Janet because she was making waves. They threatened to fire me because *I* was making waves. Janet is going to report what she found out to the FBI. They thought she might do that. There has to be a connection."

"No, man," Willis said. "I don't think that's true. That's conspiracy theory stuff."

Joel rolled his eyes. "I don't know, Willis. If you ask me—"

"Joel!" Willis looked around and lowered his voice. "Listen to me. I've been looking for you because I need to tell you something."

"What?"

"It's Janet."

Joel holstered his gun. "What about Janet?"

"She's ... she's dead."

The words slammed Joel in the chest with the force of a roadside explosion. He felt dizziness and his vision blurred ... and he was back in Iraq. He heard the screams of his fellow airmen followed by the terrible ringing in his ears.

Trickle ... trickle...

"Joel?"

He shook his head and rubbed his eyes, and then he was back in the gun range. Joel's voice cracked as he responded. "What ... what did you say?"

"She was found in her home this morning. Joel, she was murdered."

"What?"

"A neighbor woman had seen that her garage was open. Her car was there, and the rear door was open. The neighbor thought that was odd, so she went over to tell Janet that she'd left the garage and car door open. Apparently, the kitchen door was ajar. Janet was on the floor in the house. She'd been shot."

Joel squeezed his eyes closed. He slumped against the wall and slowly dropped to the floor.

10

He went straight to Janet's house and found that it was marked off with police tape. Two patrol cars sat out front and a handful of uniformed beat cops were just beginning to shut down the crime scene. The forensics work had already been performed, the body had been removed, and the lead detectives were gone.

"What happened? What happened?" Joel cried as he ran to the first policeman he saw.

"Whoa, sir, slow down. This is a crime scene."

"I just found out! She's my ... she's my girlfriend!"

"Oh? I think the chief will want to talk to you, then."

The officer asked for Joel's name and address, and then he called it in. He listened, and then addressed Joel, "Can you come with me to the station, sir?"

Police chief Burt Wainwright and Detective Ken Bostick interviewed Joel for an hour. Joel kept his opinions to himself, but he felt that neither man knew what he was doing. Wainwright was a typically overweight redneck who seemed to think that Janet's home was in a "bad neighborhood," as he described it, and that this was a factor in the case. Bostick did most of the talking, though, and he asked the expected questions about Joel's relationship with Janet, how long they'd been seeing each other, and, most importantly, where Joel was yesterday between the hours of noon and six. Bostick had another officer check Joel's alibi that he was at work. For a few moments Joel knuckle-clutched the arms of his chair as he waited for the verdict, but the alibi came back confirmed.

Joel explained that Janet had planned to drive to Monticello to see her mother and spend the night. The overnight bag in the back seat of her car backed up Joel's assertion.

Wainwright said, "This was obviously a robbery gone wrong. We've seen a lot of crime in that part of town. The perp was probably on the street and saw her in the garage. He accosted her, took her inside, and did the deed. We'll be investigating the crime further, but I'm betting it was some illegal immigrant with a drug problem. Quite a few of them have shown up in that area lately."

Joel thought the man was insane. "What did he steal?"

"I beg your pardon?"

"You said it was a robbery. What was missing from her house?"

Bostick answered. "We didn't find a computer. Did she own one?"

"Yes, a laptop."

"It wasn't in the house or in the car. Oddly, her purse was there on the kitchen counter. He didn't take that."

That was no robbery.

"We'll of course be running ballistics tests on the bullets. Do you own a gun, Mr. Hartbeck?" Wainwright asked.

Joel told them about his Glock.

"Nine millimeter?" Wainwright asked.

"Yes."

He nodded. "Well, when ballistics comes back we may want to do a comparison with your weapon, just to rule you out. I can't reveal what we know, but I don't think she was shot with nine millimeter rounds."

Joel also showed them the many texts he had sent to Janet on his phone, saying how concerned he was that she hadn't answered him. His service record and his employment with Bank Antriol went a long way toward convincing the officers that he likely had nothing to do with the murder. They cut him loose with the stipulation that he remain available should they have further questions.

When Joel got into his Ford Explorer, he finally allowed himself to break down and cry.

* * *

Snow was falling thickly when Joel parked in his space in front of the apartment building. He got out of the car, avoided the ice on the sidewalk, and hurried up the stairs to his door.

To his horror, he found that it was ajar.

Once again, he felt a seizure of anxiety in his chest. He knew very well what he was about to see when he pushed the door all the way open.

His apartment had been ransacked, and his strongbox had been busted open. Private papers were scattered everywhere. The furniture had been overturned. The kitchen cabinets had been emptied and all of his dishes were in fragments on the floor. His television screen was cracked like a cobweb. The laptop he had left on the dining room table was gone.

He immediately called 911 and then began taking stock of what else might be missing. Thankfully, personal records such as his military discharge papers, his passport, and Social Security card were still there—they had just been dumped on the floor.

What had they been looking for? Janet's documents?

Luckily, those were safe.

When the police showed up, they performed a cursory search of the premises and determined that Joel's apartment door lock was likely jimmied with a screwdriver or other tool. "Sorry, sir, there's nothing much we can do," the officer said. "Burglaries are a dime a dozen." They filled out a report and gave Joel a copy for insurance purposes. Unfortunately, he didn't have renters insurance. The TV, laptop, dishes, and other items were a big fat loss. But TVs and laptops were nowhere on his list of important things at that moment. The edges of that extreme, violent anger he worked so hard to control were breaking through again.

* * *

Joel sat in a booth at Beggar's Ravine, nursing a beer and drowning in his sorrows. Things had been going so well for him, and now everything had gone to hell. *Again.* Why was he destined to get the shit end of the stick? It was a never-ending spinning cycle of one step forward, two steps backward. And then he remembered the real victim. What was he doing feeling sorry for himself, when that wonderful, beautiful person with a kind soul was stone cold *dead?* Shot in the back by some unknown intruder.

Janet ... I'm so sorry ... I'm so sorry...

Was it really the work of a burglar? First there was Janet's murder and then the ransacking of his apartment. Were they connected?

All roads unquestionably were leading back to the bastards in New York.

Joel stared at the glass of beer in front of him. The plan had been to get very drunk. For some absurd reason, though, the lack of a healthy head of foam on the beer suddenly gave him a burst of clarity. It was as if the "foam" had been cleared away to reveal what was underneath.

He was in danger.

What am I doing? I'm a sitting duck. I'm obviously a target. There could be eyes on me at this very moment. I need to get the hell out of here. Now.

Joel threw money on the table, left, and walked outside to his car. He almost slipped on the slush, but he caught himself and cursed aloud. And then the sight of his SUV halted him in his tracks.

He'd been right. He *was* being watched.

Red paint. Written in broad strokes across the windshield: "4/19."

* * *

Joel quickly gathered his important documents, packed a bag full of clothes, took his phone charger, and piled it all into the back of the SUV. He locked the door to his apartment, muttered a "goodbye," and drove away into the snowstorm. He didn't know where he was going, but he knew he needed some space between himself and Plainsburg.

There was a target on his back, and he was feeling those same unmistakable sensations he had always felt when he was approaching an IED that needed to be disarmed.

He needed gas, so he pulled into a Shell station. While he filled his tank, Joel's attention focused on the pump's tiny video screen that displayed advertisements and the news. He immediately recognized the

Florida lawyer, Nick Deketomis. Joel's jaw dropped as his old friend, Michael Carey, appeared with him.

And they were talking about the possibility of representing Gold Star families and disabled veterans by going after banks that were supporting terrorism!

Joel got back in his car and opened one of the envelopes he'd retrieved from his files at home. It was something he'd scribbled on a piece of paper not too long ago after seeing a news item on television. It was only a name and a location, but it would be easy to get the phone number from the firm's website.

MICHAEL CAREY. BERGMAN-DEKETOMIS LAWYERS. FLORIDA.

It was time to make a phone call to a *real* friend ... a brother in arms.

PART TWO

11

Spanish Trace, Florida

Nick "Deke" Deketomis called the meeting to order.

Most of the veteran trial team of the Bergman-Deketomis firm were all present in the Spanish Trace office—Deke and Michael Carey, both of whom had returned from the conference in Chicago a few days earlier; Carol Morris, the head of Safety and Security and Investigative Services; Jake Rutledge, investigator; Gina Romano, associate attorney; Diana Fernandez, the office administrator; and Sarah Mercer, the firm's chief trial paralegal.

"Good morning, everyone," Deke began. "I hope you've had a chance to read the summary of the 'Let's Do Something About It' conference that Michael and I attended over the weekend. As you know, I've become interested in cases concerning Gold Star families and wounded veterans, and the illegal funding of terrorism by US banks. Michael and I heard and saw evidence at the conference that points to Wall Street corruption that is extreme, even by the standards that we are used to seeing. Even though the DOJ has placed several banks on notice for conducting money transfers for potential terrorist organizations and drug cartels, we all know that the DOJ is often little more than a paper tiger—understaffed, overworked, and rarely the solution to big problems. So, the question here today is whether or not this firm should saddle up and go after these banks for all the suffering they have caused so many military families. And it's not just military families. Border law enforcement doing battle with drug cartels are the latest victims being murdered with the help of half a dozen New York banks. Setting aside the moral obligation to do it, know that it would be a few years of courtroom combat. But imagine that combat on steroids, with an army of two thousand dollar an hour corporate defense firm freaks breaking all the rules we usually see, but on a much, much bigger scale. It goes without saying that we have all seen these silk-stocking corporate lawyer types push the limit of ugly. But my prediction is that this limit may edge closer to lawyer criminality because there is so much at stake for their banker clients. Before I open the topic up for discussion—" Deke nodded at Michael, "—tell the crew what you've learned from your pal in Kentucky."

Michael opened a manila folder that contained his notes. "Okay. An old friend from the Air Force, Joel Hartbeck, recently contacted me." He proceeded to give everyone a brief history of how he had met Joel at the Special Warfare Assessment and Selection Course at Lackland, and their subsequent reacquaintance in 2007 in Iraq. "The last time I saw him was before that bomb went off at the edge of the bridge that he was working. I was in a helicopter when it happened, but I saw the explosion from above. I knew he had been wounded, he survived, was discharged, and went back to Kentucky, where he was from. We lost touch after that, until this past weekend when he contacted the office trying to reach me. When we finally connected, Joel was frazzled, which is unusual for people who are used to disarming massive bombs. He told me he believes his life is in danger and that he's in hiding. We talked three different times at length, and he told me a remarkable story."

He then outlined the substance of his phone calls with Joel: Bank Antriol, the AML unit, the SARs and suspicious transactions, the murder of Janet Blanco, and Joel's leaving his employment. There was mostly silence in a room full of people who were used to hearing incredibly outrageous setups for cases. Michael had their attention. "Based on Joel's information, if it's true, there's enough there to seriously go after Bank Antriol, for starters."

Carol, a slim, fit woman in her mid-fifties with brown hair and eyes, spoke up. "You said that Joel sounded 'frazzled.' Is Joel … okay? I mean, in his mind? From what you've said, it sounds like he's had a difficult time since his discharge from the Air Force."

Michael shrugged. "I can't answer that. Joel was a good guy and a hell of a special operator when I knew him, but that was sixteen, seventeen years ago. I think we'd have to find him and talk to him in person to know for sure."

"Thanks, Michael," Deke said. "So the question is the same that we always ask at the start of a potentially huge case. Should the firm begin to take a serious look at this, knowing it's going to involve a commitment by everyone in this room?"

Gina raised her hand and Deke acknowledged her. "We would need an official affidavit from Michael's friend," she said. "What he said over the phone won't cut it."

Michael answered, "Joel said he would provide a notarized affidavit. I would want to go to Kentucky, though, and get a full recorded statement from him. Video and the works."

"In that case," Gina continued, "*if it's true*, I think there are plenty of reasons to 'saddle up,' as you put it, Deke, and do some preliminary work."

Carol jumped in. "Prior to filing a lawsuit, much of the critical material we would need to look at with both the New York banks and the overseas banks is going to be really well hidden. We'll need some funds to get us going. I'm thinking twenty grand to start an investigation."

Sarah Mercer, a woman of Lebanese descent in her mid-thirties and the head of the twenty-five-member paralegal team at the firm, piped in. "I'm saying what must be obvious to everyone in this room, I'm sure, but if those companies overseas are really funding terrorists and drug cartels, then we'd be indirectly going after some seriously deadly people who are capable of most anything. I'm assuming our primary target would be Bank Antriol, but we'd also be pissing off some dangerous people in the Middle East. This is turning it up a notch from beating the hell out of the pharmaceutical bad guys or tobacco manufacturers. Death and murder are side effects of their greed-driven love of money, but terrorists murder out of deep-seeded hatred."

"That's a good point," Jake said.

Diana raised her hand.

"Yes, Diana?" Deke asked.

"I just want to say I have a cousin who served in Afghanistan. He's missing a leg. It was a roadside bomb that took it off. I, for one, can sympathize with those Gold Star families who want justice. And the wounded and disabled veterans in this country don't always get a fair shake. If we can get jury awards against Bank Antriol for these brave men and their families, I'm all for it. But I'm just the office administrator." She smiled.

"Your opinion is just as valuable as anyone's," Deke said. "It's why I often have you here in our strategy meetings. You're an important part of the team."

"Hear, hear," Gina said.

"Anyone else have anything to say?" Deke asked. "Michael?"

Michael nodded. "I think it's worth pursuing Joel, getting an affidavit and a video recorded statement, and see what we've got to work with. If his testimony is the smoking gun I think it is and we can back it up at all with a scintilla of evidence, then we should be all in."

"I agree," Deke said. "Michael, tell Accounting to set aside about fifty thousand dollars as a preliminary budget. I have no doubt we are conservatively looking at a ten million cost to this little adventure. Everyone, give it your best in this early evaluation. We need to be right about everything before we spend that kind of money."

"Got it," Michael said.

"Okay. Michael, you need to make your way to Kentucky. What's the town where your friend is hiding out?"

"Plainsburg. It's a small town in the southeast part of the state. Close to the Tennessee border."

"Jake?"

"Yes, Deke?" the investigator asked.

"Why don't you go with Michael? While Michael's tracking down Joel Hartbeck and getting an affidavit, why don't you look into the murder of that woman ... what was her name?"

"Janet Blanco," Michael answered.

"If there is any evidence at all that someone associated with the bank is responsible for her death, then that's something else we can work with."

"Got it," Jake said. A black-haired man in his early thirties with a linebacker build and an incongruous but handsome baby face, he gave Deke a thumbs up.

"Gina, why don't you see what you can dig up about Bank Antriol? I want to know all the details about what brought about that first DOJ action against them. I'm betting there are plenty of dirty little secrets we can uncover there."

"Will do," Gina answered.

"And Carol, Sarah... Why don't you take a deep dive into the terrorist organizations and the companies cited by Mr. Hartbeck? Who are these people that the bank is doing business with? I want to know all the details about how dangerous these dirtbags really are."

12

Plainsburg, Kentucky

The flight to Knoxville, Tennessee, was uneventful, despite the threats of winter storms. Michael and Jake rented separate cars, since they each had different missions. They caravanned north over the border to Kentucky and reached Plainsburg in three hours. Travel time would have been faster had it not been for the icy roads and a traffic pileup due to an accident. They both checked into different rooms at a Holiday Inn Express and then set about their separate agendas. Michael told Jake to keep in touch; otherwise they'd meet back at the hotel at night.

Joel had instructed Michael to call him and leave a message when he arrived. Michael did so, and an hour later his phone rang with an unknown caller ID.

"Hello?"

"Is this PJ Michael Carey, the parachuting super lawyer?"

Michael laughed. "It is I. How are you, Joel? And what's this number?"

"A burner phone. Can't be too safe."

"Are you keeping warm? Coming from Florida, I'm freezing my butt off."

"I'm as warm as this hidey-hole hangout can be."

"Where can we get together? You want to come to my hotel?"

Joel suggested a diner on the outskirts of Plainsburg. They hung up, Michael grabbed his coat and laptop, and off he went in his rented Nissan Altima.

* * *

Diner-24, with its "We Never Close!" marquee, was a 1950s dive on the edge of town more accommodating to truck drivers and early rising farmers. Michael felt as rural as he could get, and he realized how absurdly overdressed he was when he walked in. Only a handful of booths were occupied and there were a couple of solos sitting at the counter. They were all white male senior citizens in cowboy hats, baseball caps, overalls, and workmen jumpsuits. Michael supposed some of them *weren't* senior citizens, but they were losing the battle where it came to aging well.

He spotted Joel Hartbeck sitting in a booth with his back to the wall as far away from the other patrons as possible. He wore a camouflage-patterned Kentucky Wildcats baseball cap and a red and black plaid wool shirt. His hair was slightly longer than shoulder length, tied in a ponytail. He was sporting three- or four-day stubble.

The man stood and spread his arms. Michael and Joel gave each other bear hugs and slapped each other on the backs. Michael observed that Joel had gained way too much weight since Iraq.

"Michael, you are looking *good*!" Joel said as they sat down. "But hear it from me, you don't need to wear your lawyer clothes in this town. People will think you're either an evangelist come to save their souls, or an undertaker come for their bodies."

Michael laughed. "Okay, I get it. As soon as I walked in here, I knew I stood out like a turd in a punchbowl."

Joel asked where he was staying, and Michael told him.

"What about you? Where are you living?"

Joel lowered his voice and spoke in a measured tone. "Take it down a notch, Michael. We can talk here, but I don't want anyone to be able to even guess as to what we're talking about. Know what I mean?"

"Sure."

"So, I had a nice apartment in town, but when it got ransacked, I moved out. I packed up in the middle of the night, made sure no one was watching the building from the street, dropped a note in the manager's mail slot, and left in my car. There is no way that it's safe for me to stay there. Now I'm at the Mountain Man, a fleabag motel not far from here. The best thing I can say about it is that it's cheap and remote. But let's order and catch up before we talk business, okay?"

"Sure thing, Joel."

The men ordered food from the waitress who appeared to be north of eighty years old, and then they talked about their years since Iraq. Michael went first on Joel's insistence, so he delivered the short version of his life story since the war—his Air Force accident and injuries, the marriage to Mona, a woman he'd met and whose life he'd saved while on duty in Iraq, and the newborn daughter who had arrived in their household a year ago.

"Congratulations, Michael! How fantastic is that! I'm happy for you."

Michael felt guilty explaining his almost perfect life to the old friend who was barely connected to anything that looked remotely similar. "Thanks. She's a dreamboat, too. I think you said on the phone you're divorced?"

"Yeah. That was a few years ago. And it was a mistake. The marriage, that is, not the divorce. Nothing interesting in that department until Janet. Geez, Janet..." He shook his head and bit his lip. It was evident that he was trembling.

"I'm sorry, Joel. Our investigator, Jake Rutledge, is here with me, and he's looking into the crime. But please ... we talked a little about what all that's happened to you after your discharge, but please get me up to date with your life and everything that's been going on that you couldn't say over the phone."

Joel proceeded to fill in a lot of the details about his difficult years, including a confession of becoming an Oxy addict and the hellish recovery. Then he moved to the job at the AML unit. While he was telling his story, Michael noticed that Joel's eyes continually darted around the diner. He was visibly nervous and extremely jumpy. Michael wondered if perhaps Joel was *still* on OxyContin. Along with the nervous jitters that were so evident when Joel spoke of the bank managers, his speaking voice turned from normal to more of an angry snarl. He then went off on a rant about banks, terrorists, the government, the VA, and how the "little people" keep getting screwed. To Michael, some of his diatribe was pretty fringe stuff, but he could see that his old friend definitely had plenty to justifiably be upset about.

"And the police here make the Three Stooges look like nuclear scientists," Joel said. "They've done *nothing* about Janet's murder. There's no news at all from the local media, much less beyond Plainsburg. If they're investigating, they're keeping it close to the chest."

"Jake will find out something," Michael said. "You watch."

"Michael, I'm sure the bank is behind it. Those people are covering up a bunch of shit. *Serious* shit. They don't want it getting out. Janet found some buried bodies, and they took her out. I know the same facts she discovered and more. That's why I'm hiding out like a damned terrified school kid, like *I'm* the one who broke the law. Hell, I'm even embarrassed to admit that, after all the tough talk I unloaded on them when I quit and stormed out of their building."

"I get it. Anybody in their right mind would panic over the story you just shared with me. Why don't you just leave town?"

Joel shrugged. "Nowhere to go. No one to go to and no way to pay for getting there."

They continued to discuss the transaction data Joel had found, and the handling of the SARs that implicated two of the bank's executive vice presidents. Michael started to make notes on a notepad he always carried in his jacket pocket, but Joel held up a hand. "Again, please don't do that while we're sitting right here. I have it all on paper here in my backpack." He indicated it, sitting on the seat beside him. "A complete affidavit."

"You've already written one?"

"Yes, sir. It's as detailed as I could get it. I typed it on a computer at the library and printed it out."

"Can I see it?"

Joel pulled a stiff mailing envelope out of his backpack and handed it over. Michael removed the twenty-seven-page document and began to skim it.

"I looked online to see how affidavits are written," Joel said. "I hope I did it justice. I can make changes if you think I need them."

"Joel, this is great," Michael said. "I'm very impressed. There's terrific detail here. I'm convinced you have always been the smarter of the two of us. I'll read it in detail when I have some privacy."

The food arrived with a coffee pot for manual refills. The two men put work aside to eat and continue catching up. They reminisced a little about their time in Air Force training and had a few laughs. Joel loosened up a bit, but Michael recognized that the kind of stress Joel was feeling was going to take much more than a meal and conversation with an old friend to cure.

After the waitress removed the plates, they spent the next twenty minutes just talking about the details that Joel had included in the affidavit, and Michael made notes in the margins. When they were done, Joel said, "These fixes are no problem. I can make these corrections at the library in the morning, get a new one printed, and give it to you tomorrow afternoon? Is that okay?"

"Joel, there is one more step we need to make with this affidavit. It needs to be notarized by a neutral notary in case anything happens to you. Technically, it would be difficult for us to actually use it in a court proceeding, although there is a way ... but just as importantly, it creates credibility with my law partners who I'm asking to take a huge risk in going after one of the largest banks in the world."

"I have no problem with that if it has to be done."

"And you have the documentation referenced in these pages?"

Michael detected that a shadow passed over Joel's eyes. The man answered, "I have those papers safely hidden."

"Perfect. Then we can have it done at a bank or wherever you feel comfortable."

Joel began to take pictures with his phone of every page of the affidavit. As he was doing so, he said, "I'm going to let you keep this original affidavit. I'm taking pictures of your notes on every page. Yours is the only copy out there other than the one on my well-hidden flash drive. It is very well possible that my life depends on the dates and details reconstructed in those pages, since it might be my only bargaining chip if I get cornered. Take good care of it, brother."

"You bet." When Joel was finished, Michael put the notated document away and said, "Oh, just for our records, I need to take a photo of you on my phone. Okay?"

Joel shrugged. Michael pulled out his mobile and took a picture of the man across the table. He then said, "You can call me if you have any questions. Should we meet here tomorrow at, what, noon? One?"

"Make it one. And by the way, the phone number you have for me? You can leave messages on it, and I'll get them. But that phone isn't moving around. I don't want anyone tracking me. I use a burner phone to make calls and check my voicemail box, but you can't leave messages on it." Joel held it up. "And I change burners every few days. So the number I called you from won't be good in a couple days. Tomorrow it should be fine."

"Joel, we were pretty much up shit's creek in that training rescue mission so many years ago. Trapped in that prisoner shack. Surrounded by a dozen guards who wanted nothing more than to beat our asses. It was you who really saved our bacon by throwing all those smoke grenades at exactly the right time in exactly the right place. Well, I'm going to need *that Joel* by my side right now. Can you do that?"

Joel poured himself a refill of coffee from the pitcher on the table, and for a beat he stared into his cup as he stirred it. Then he looked at Michael.

"Just hand me the grenades again, brother."

13

Spanish Trace, Florida

On the same day that Michael and Jake traveled to Kentucky, Gina Romano arranged to meet with Deke to present what she had learned so far about Bank Antriol. Gina may have been the youngest associate at Bergman-Deketomis, but she had a reputation for being a powerhouse when it came to social justice. Deke liked to say that Gina didn't just upset the apple cart—she liked to blow it up.

She carried her preliminary research in hand and sat at the round table Deke always used for one-on-one discussions.

"You've already got material for me?" he asked. "How long has it been? Twenty-four hours?"

"It's just a start, Deke," Gina said, "but it's probably stuff you need to know from the get-go."

"Okay, let's hear it." He shut the door and sat across from her.

She cleared her throat and began. "So, the headline here is that Bank Antriol is one of the 'big' banks in this country and in Europe, and it's considered to be one of those institutions that is 'too big to fail.' That means, according to the government, it's also too big to shut down. One of the talking points the DOJ always hides behind in their failure to actually do their job with all the big banks is that they are afraid to shut them down or even make them suffer at all because of all the financial turmoil it might cause. For the most part that is absolute nonsense. What's really at work here is the age old story of 'money talks.' These big banks have mastered the art of spreading billions of dollars around to the right senators, congressmen, and presidential hopefuls to where they are virtually bulletproof. You might remember, not one banker went to prison when they burned down our entire economy with their endless mortgage scams. Thousands of Americans lost everything because of that blatant fraud, but not one of those bottom feeders went to prison."

"Has there been any changes to the politics of all that since that fraud tsunami?" Deke asked.

"Not at all. The DOJ and the political protection they had then is the same protection they have with these money laundering cases today. It's a tight arrangement these big banks have with the US government. Victimize American consumers. Steal as much as you need, and if you get caught, pay a big fine, and live to steal another day. And you will really love this ... pass the cost of that fine on to taxpayers as a deduction on your tax payments!"

"Give me the good news now," Deke responded sarcastically, but with obvious disgust.

"There really is nothing great to report, aside from a tiny victory for the good guys now and then. There are small examples of the DOJ's cases against other banks in past decades, but very few. The case against the HSBC banker-organized crime syndicate was a somewhat significant case."

"I know about that one."

"Then you know that since the Treasury Department and the DOJ won't allow the free market to work by allowing these skank big banks to shut down and fail, the so-called 'penalties' imposed on the banks end up being pathetically minor. The fines can give the impression of being very large, but in relation to what one of these banks makes in profits, that monetary fine might be a month or two worth of transaction fees the bank charges its customers. It's barely a slap on the wrist."

Deke shook his head. "Crime really does pay in America if you're dressed up in Wall Street criminal garb. The CEOs and presidents and vice presidents take home massive salaries and bonuses, the banks pull in obscene profits, and meanwhile all the dispensable types—our men in uniform—get blown to hell by roadside bombs. It gives me that gag reflex."

Gina nodded and moved on. "Bank Antriol was founded in Utrecht in The Netherlands, in 1947. It benefitted from war reparations, and there were two or three older banks that were folded into its creation. Within twenty years, it was one of the major banks in Holland, and it started expanding globally. There are branches in London, Tokyo, Tel Aviv, Zurich, Moscow, and the United States. Some US cities have smaller branches. The New York branch is the largest and most influential of them all. You could say that even though the bank's headquarters is in The Netherlands, its worldwide business operates out of New York."

"Okay."

"The bank's New York president is Nigel Beech, sixty-two years old, a New Englander, and he reports to the CEO in The Netherlands, but he pretty much has complete autonomy in running the branch. Mr. Beech has a board of directors, of course, five executive vice presidents, a few lower level VPs, and so on. The organizational structure is just like any big bank. Mr. Beech lives in a huge mansion in Woodsburgh, Long Island."

"Of course."

"Anyway, four years ago, Bank Antriol was flagged by the DOJ for failing to file Suspicious Activity Reports—SARs—over a period of nine years. These involved customers making wire transfers of large amounts of money, and the players involved were on the DOJ's list of sanctioned individuals and companies that were suspected of supporting terrorism. And, as it usually happens, the DOJ prosecutors and the bank's attorneys spent a few weeks in conference rooms and worked out a settlement. The bank agreed to pay a fine of $1.7 billion dollars. They also agreed to set up an anti-money laundering unit to re-examine all the transactions going back ten years. That's the outfit in Plainsburg, Kentucky. It's in an old department store space in a strip mall. The bank hires high school kids, college-age people, and just about anyone who has minimal computer skills. Michael's friend, Joel Hartbeck, was working there. His claim is that the bank is purposefully ignoring new SARs and quickly clearing them, and they're doing everything they can to clear the old ones flagged during the re-review so they can carry on 'business as usual.' In other words, the DOJ is allowing the bank to self-police itself, and the bank isn't doing a very good job of it."

"As if that's a surprise," Deke muttered. "There is no question that the DOJ could do plenty to put a stop to that criminal conduct and still not shut down the bank. Throwing a few of the white-collar critters at the top into a federal prison comes to mind."

"Of course, I'm going to keep digging," Gina said.

"Gina, in just one day, that's good work. If these facts keep developing the way I think they will, we are soon going to be plastering this story all over the front page of the *Wall Street Journal* and leave the banks and the DOJ twisting in the wind."

14

Plainsburg, Kentucky

Jake had been a West Virginia lawyer with less than two years of experience. He had helped Deke build out a national opioid case against the drug manufacturers and distributors of OxyContin that had resulted in a multibillion-dollar national settlement. When fifty court-protected and incriminating documents ended up in the hands of the *Wall Street Journal*, the young lawyer admitted that he alone was the source of that leak. He had made the decision to violate a federal judge's gag order that was clearly protecting the corporate drug pushers. It resulted in his disbarment, but experts who later analyzed the chain of events concluded that his action had prevented the deaths of thousands of people. Deke was more impressed than angry with Jake's tough decision and offered him a job as an investigator in his Florida-based law firm. Jake had simply made a wrong decision for the right reason.

Deke liked Jake because the investigator was wise beyond his years and could morph into different guises and personas. He was a rugged, tough individual who could appear to be a Southern redneck, a California beach bum, or an Appalachian mountain man; but put a suit on him and he might be a hotshot attorney from Boston. Jake had an ability to speak without a discernable accent, so he was useful as a chameleon. While he hadn't served in the military, he was well-versed in firearms and street brawling because he had been raised around it.

He was also good at solving puzzles, which made him an ideal sleuth for Bergman-Deketomis. It also helped that Jake and Michael worked well together, as they were roughly the same age.

Being from West Virginia, Jake still knew some folks in law enforcement there. In fact, one of his best friends was still a city cop in Logan, which wasn't very far from the Kentucky border. The first thing Jake did was to pick up his phone and call Lester Hawkins.

"Hawkins."

"Lester, it's Jake Rutledge."

"No, it isn't."

"Yes, it is!"

"Jake, you rascal, how are you? Is this really you?"

"It's me, and I'm in Kentucky at the moment."

The two old friends caught up for a minute or two, and then Jake brought the conversation to the matter at hand. "Lester, do you know anyone in law enforcement in Plainsburg, Kentucky?" He explained why he wanted to know.

Lester laughed. "I don't believe this."

"What?"

"My ex is an officer in a town not far from there. When we split up two years ago, she accepted a job out of state just to get away from me. I suppose I can ask her if she knows anyone in Plainsburg."

"I hope that wouldn't be too awkward for you."

"Nah. Julia and I still talk all the time. I think deep down she misses me. Let me give her a call. Can I reach you at this number?"

"Yes, sir. Thank you, Lester."

Jake remained in the hotel room and continued perusing the internet on his laptop for more information about the Blanco case. He had the ability to log into various law enforcement sites thanks to a hack that an IT buddy had done for him. Jake had a fake identity with the FBI and the National Crime Information Center (NCIC) data bases, but so far they were devoid of any material on the case.

Lester returned the call in thirty minutes. "Jake, you're in luck. Julia knows an officer in Plainsburg! Her name is Sheila Denning, and—no surprise—she's the only woman on the force. They have her doing traffic control. Julia reached out to her, and Sheila says she'll meet with you. It sounded to me like Sheila isn't real happy working there."

"That's fantastic, Lester, thank you!"

Jake immediately called Sheila and got her voicemail. "Officer Denning, my name is Jake Rutledge, investigator for the Bergman-Deketomis law firm. I understand that Julia Hawkins reached out to you a little while ago. I'd really like to meet with you, if possible, as soon as we can." He left his number and waited.

Sheila called him back five minutes later, saying that she was currently on duty but would be off at six. She gave him the address of a bar where she would meet him, but it was out of town where they wouldn't be seen by anyone local.

* * *

The Kentucky Spoon was located thirty minutes out of Plainsburg. Western music blared on the jukebox and the place was a third full of mountain folk types that Jake had been mostly raised around. A no smoking ban was apparently *not* in effect, as the joint was thick with haze from cigarette smoke.

Jake was savvy enough to know that jeans, work boots, and a flannel shirt would help him blend right in. He made a straight line to the bar, ordered a beer, and then turned to survey the surroundings that made him feel right at home. A lone woman sitting in a booth nodded at him. Jake took his beer and joined her. Sheila was a freckle-faced, ginger-haired woman in her thirties who gave off the impression she could wrestle an alligator and probably win.

"You must be Jake."

"I am. Nice to meet you, Officer Denning."

"Please, call me Sheila. I'm not on duty."

"This is quite a place."

She laughed. "Rustic, huh? I was born not far from here. My daddy used to own this place until he died, and it got sold. Greg, the bartender, knows me, though. None of the locals who frequent the Kentucky Spoon remember me now. I've changed a bit since my debutante wild girl days. And none of the MWs like to come here."

Jake frowned. "The MWs?"

"The Mohawk Warriors. You don't know about them?"

"No, I don't, but there's a lot I don't know and that's why I need your help."

"Well, let's not waste any time, then. I'll start at the heart of the matter." She began naming off a short list of some similar right-wing paramilitary groups that were better known in the media. "You've heard of *them*, I bet."

"Yeah."

"The MWs are just like them. It's a smaller group and local to Plainsburg. They don't come here because they used to get into fights here. Greg took out a restraining order against any member wearing MW regalia. They tried to jump Greg in the parking lot one night, but Greg unleashed his sawed-off shotgun, fired off a few warning blasts, and they scattered like a bunch of scorched jackals. They haven't bothered him again. Needless to say, *I* would have unleashed hell on those sons of bitches, myself!"

"Are they relevant to the Janet Blanco case?"

Sheila took a swig of her beer, swallowed, and then looked at Jake. "Yes. Janet Blanco's murder holds few clues about the perps. Police Chief Burt Wainwright is leading the investigation along with his deputy and one other officer who they *call* a homicide detective, but truthfully, he couldn't find his pecker in a well-lit room. So far, I've been kept out of the loop. They keep me out of most everything except finding lost dogs and handing out parking tickets. I was hired because the mayor insisted that the chief put some women in the department. Wainwright hired *one*, and I got the token job of making fresh coffee and sitting around the office like a damn oddball gewgaw."

"That sucks."

"Tell me about it. But I hear things, and I can sneak a look at files and such. There's one big item that has been withheld from the media about the case, and it's your lucky day—I'm going to tell you what it is."

"Okay."

"The killer left a 'calling card' at the scene. Someone had used red paint to write something on the wall in the kitchen where her body was found. You know, 'Helter Skelter' style, the way those Manson freaks did."

"What was written?"

"The numbers four and nineteen, with a slash between them. Like a date. April 19."

Jake rubbed his chin. "That's a gang symbol. April 19, the day of the Columbine massacre?"

"Nope. That was April 20. Also, Hitler's birthday. The day before, April 19, was both the Oklahoma City Federal Building explosion as well as the Branch Davidian disaster with the FBI down in Waco, Texas. And guess who around here likes to flash that symbol around, along with Nazi swastikas and other far-right symbols of hate?"

"The MWs?"

"Give the man a cigar!"

"Why are they called the Mohawk Warriors?"

Sheila proceeded to give Jake the rundown on the group. How they took their name from the disguises the Sons of Liberty used at the Boston Tea Party, and how they held marches and protests in town. "Several of the members are known felons and former convicts," she said. "Others are just deluded wannabes, extreme right wingers who have drunk the Kool-Aid."

"Why would they have a motive to kill Janet Blanco?" Jake asked.

"That's the million-dollar question. There doesn't seem to be any connection. We've looked at her background and social media and everything—she seemed to be squeaky clean. She didn't flash any kind of liberal or 'woke' messaging in her life, so I can't imagine what she did to piss off the MWs. But here's the thing..."

"What?"

"None of the MWs have been questioned."

"*What*? Why not?"

"Chief Wainwright believes it's a false flag left by the perpetrator. That whoever did it was trying to throw off law enforcement and make it look like the MWs were involved."

"That doesn't make any sense," Jake said. "With no motive, it's your only lead. Any investigator worth wearing a badge would at the very least question some of them. How does your chief know for sure that it's a false flag?"

Sheila wiggled her eyebrows. "The chief's son, Rusty Wainwright, is the leader of the MWs."

15

Spanish Trace, Florida

Deke liked to refer to his head of Security and Investigative Services, Carol Morris, as "Southern steel magnolia." A little older than Deke, Carol was a dynamo in the office and out in the field. She had grown up in the South, the daughter of an army staff sergeant. Some of her father's hardness must have rubbed off on Carol, because she easily intimidated anyone with her "in your face" presence that she could control like a light switch. Deke himself wouldn't want to be on her bad side. She did have an impulsive nature, and Carol had been known to lose her temper. That said, she could be polite and charming when that same switch flipped.

Carol had worked for years in law enforcement, and she was especially good at speaking to and comforting female victims or interrogating women suspects. Heaven help male suspects if they faced Carol Morris across the table from them! She could be "good cop" and "bad cop" at the same time.

She had many connections in the world of law and order. Carol had go-to sources in the DOJ, the Treasury Department, the FBI, the CIA, the DEA, and in police departments around the country. Given Deke's task that she look into the terrorist organizations that Bank Antriol was doing business with, she knew who to contact.

Tyra Schilling worked in the Treasury Department. Like Carol, Tyra was a no-nonsense career woman who took the job seriously and suffered no fools. She was often at odds with her superiors, which, in Carol's book, meant she was trustworthy. Carol gave Tyra a call.

"Carol Morris, are you still alive and kicking up dust?" the woman answered, recognizing the caller ID.

"I'm as mean and ornery as ever," Carol answered with a laugh. "How are you, Tyra?"

"Working my butt off. The Treasury never sleeps. What can I do for you?"

"Tyra, aren't you part of a team that compiles the list of sanctioned individuals and companies that banks aren't supposed to do business with?"

"Uh huh. You mean the Specially Designated Nationals and Blocked Persons List. The SDN. You'll find my fingerprints all over that thing. Why do you want to know?"

Carol launched into the story. "My law firm is doing preliminary investigations into possibly taking on a civil action against a bank that we believe is still doing business with players on the SDN list. I was wondering if you might know something about the bank and any of these places."

"Maybe. Who are we talking about?"

"Bank Antriol."

Tyra laughed. "Oh, Lord. Funny you should mention them. I am well aware of Bank Antriol's case with the DOJ. We have them under a consent order now, with auditors in place monitoring their SAR compliance and look-back review. The DOJ got after the bank for allowing money transfers between wealthy individuals in Europe and the Middle East to fund companies identified as fronts for fundraising entities linked to Iran and other entities suspected of supporting terrorism. We were never able to tie the bank directly to a terror group though. You know what reverse money laundering is?"

"Theoretically."

"Well, you know that money laundering is when criminals turn dirty into clean money. It's like when drug cartels make a million dollars in cash for selling drugs, and then they find ways to filter that money through various channels so that it comes out looking like the money was made through legitimate means. We just handled a case where a small-time jeweler in New York was money laundering for some heroin distributors. Let's say they made $10,000 from selling drugs. The jeweler would take a cheap diamond worth, say, $150. He would then throw that diamond into New York Harbor. However, he'd then create a receipt of purchase for selling the diamond to a nonexistent customer for $10,000. Ta-da. That dirty ten grand is now clean ten grand."

"Yeah, I understand money laundering."

"Well, reverse money laundering is the opposite. It turns clean money into dirty money that is used by the bad guys for illegal purposes. It's a lot more difficult to flag and trace. In a case like this, say you have some alleged upstanding citizen who deposits legitimate money into a bank or investment firm. Those funds are then moved to make fictitious investments, or into shell companies, or offshore tax havens, or whatever. Then the bad guys withdraw those funds from the financial system, and they use it for illegal means. Here's an example. Someone buys a bunch of kitchen equipment for ten grand. But it's a 'gift' for some relative in the Middle East. When the recipient receives the kitchen equipment, it turns out to be guns, or grenades, or material to make bombs. Somewhere along the way, the company that was supplying the kitchen equipment did a switcheroo through a series of in-between companies—shadow companies—and the original clean money came out dirty."

Carol said, "That's kind of what's going on here. We have a source who has told us that Bank Antriol is still doing business with sanctioned companies. Have you heard of SeedDotz Manufacturing? They're American but have facilities in Europe."

Carol heard Tyra typing on her computer. "Yeah, I'm pulling their information now. US-based machine tool company with subsidiaries in Europe and Asia. Specializing in supplying industrial metal manufacturers with custom tools. Their website doesn't tell you much. It's almost as if they deliberately make their business vague so no one will bother them."

"Exactly. We think they're just one of the groups involved. What can you tell me about the bank?"

Tyra answered, "The president of the New York branch is a guy named Nigel Beech. He's actually been very cooperative with the DOJ. From what I understand, he seems like he's decent. For a rich bastard, anyway. I'm pretty sure he's under a lot of pressure from the board of directors and other officers to put up more resistance to the DOJ."

"Have you heard of Blake Dullea or Karl Maher? They're executive VPs."

"No. They're not on my radar. But I tell you what. We have files on *all* the bank's officers. Complete bios and profiles. And we have all the case files of the settlement agreement with the DOJ."

"Oh, my. Who do I have to buy dinner for to get copies of that stuff?"

"Me? Next time you're in DC?"

"Done!"

"Do me a favor, Carol. I'll send the files to you, but don't tell anyone where they came from, okay?"

"I'm not a dummy, Tyra."

"I know that. And also … keep me informed? We're very interested in Bank Antriol. If your case actually goes forward, perhaps we can help each other out."

"You got it. Thanks, Tyra."

"As soon as I round up everything, I'll send you a secure zip file." She confirmed Carol's email address, and the two women hung up.

Carol thought, *Not bad for an hour's work!*

16

Plainsburg, Kentucky

Michael and Jake touched base the next morning at the hotel's breakfast buffet. They shared what they had learned so far, and Michael mentioned that he was just killing time until his one o'clock rendezvous with Joel back at Diner-24. Jake said he was going to try talking to the chief of police that afternoon, so he had the morning free, too. They hopped into Jake's rental, and the two men spent the next two hours riding around Plainsburg to get a feel of the town. The temperature was a brisk thirty-eight degrees. Remnants of the recent snowstorm had been plowed to the sides of the roads and were turning a grey-white from the daily grime. They went through the "downtown" area, the section where Janet Blanco lived, and noted the schools and strip malls and industrial complexes. The working class vibe was strong, but so was the poverty and elements of a struggling community living in the past.

"What a sad, ugly town," Jake remarked. "Everything's dull and blah."

"It *is* winter, dude," Michael countered.

They found the strip mall where Bank Antriol's AML unit was housed. Jake parked the car in the lot, and they sat for a moment watching the place. The doors to the unit were made of glass, but it was difficult to see what was beyond them.

"Shall we innocently take a look inside?" Jake asked.

"Why not?"

They got out of the car and strolled to the front door. Michael opened it, and they both stepped into a prefab-built foyer with a window much like a doctor's office reception area. A few empty chairs lined the wall. A closed door read "Employees Only," presumably leading to the warehouse-like space where everyone worked. A young woman who might have been a senior in high school sat on the other side of the window. She gave them a big smile. "Good morning, gentlemen!"

"Good morning," Michael said.

"Are you here for interviews?" she asked.

"Interviews?"

"Are you here for a job?"

"Oh, no, we thought this was..." Michael looked at Jake. They hadn't really thought this through. "Did this used to be a TJ Maxx?" he asked her.

"I don't know," the woman said. "Maybe. I know they used to sell Halloween stuff here sometimes, but we've been here for a couple years now."

"And what's your name?"

She recited it as if she were reading from a cue card. "I'm Bambi Barnett, and this is the Bank Antriol remote data center."

"This is a bank?" Jake asked.

"It's an important division of the bank," the woman answered.

"So you're hiring? You mentioned job interviews."

"Oh, yes, we're hiring. If you're looking for jobs, I'm sure they'll grant you an interview. Would you like to fill out an application?"

Michael asked, "Could we take a couple with us?"

"Sure." She handed them through the open window two sheets of paper that had been right at her fingertips on her desk. "Just fill those out and bring them back when you're ready."

"Thank you, Bambi." Michael gestured to Jake with his head, *Let's get out of here.*

Back in the car, Jake drove slowly back to the hotel while Michael looked at the forms.

"They sure don't require much from applicants," he said. "Here's a list of office skills it asks if you're competent in—computer use, Excel,

Word, alphabetizing, data entry … It doesn't even ask for former employer information. I think these guys will take anybody!"

"Well, Michael," Jake said, "if this lawyer thing doesn't work out for you…"

"I'm always looking for challenges. Let's go get a cup of coffee. I'm freezing."

* * *

The two men walked into Diner-24 ten minutes early, grabbed a booth, and ordered more coffee. It was the only thing that seemed to warm him up. Living in Florida year round had spoiled him with his real love for the warm beach life.

One o'clock came … and no Joel.

At ten after, Michael started to become concerned. "I'm pretty sure this is not a good sign," he said. He checked his phone to make sure he hadn't missed any messages. At twenty after, he phoned Joel's burner. He got the electronic beeping and the auto voice proclaiming that it wasn't a working number. He then dialed the older cell phone number and got the familiar voicemail.

"Joel, it's Michael. I'm at the diner. Just wondering where you are. Give me a call." He left his own number again and disconnected.

At 1:45 p.m., Michael gave up, Jake paid the bill, and they made their exit. Sitting in his car, he tried to remember the name of the motel where Joel was staying. Something about mountains. Mountain View? Mountain Lake? Mountain … *Man!*

He looked it up on his phone and found the Mountain Man Motel on a state highway between Plainsburg and the Tennessee border. It took thirty minutes to get there, and they found a dilapidated structure that reminded him of the Bates Motel in *Psycho*. A total of two pickup trucks were parked at the twelve-unit facility. Michael and Jake got out of his rental and went to the door marked "Office."

An extremely thin woman who appeared to be in her seventies was watching a game show on a portable black-and-white analog television with rabbit ears. The woman looked at them with surprise, as if she never had customers. "Are you here about the water bill?"

"No, ma'am, I'm looking for one of your guests," Michael said. "Do you have a Joel Hartbeck registered here?"

The woman frowned. "That name's not familiar." She stood from her comfy chair that was missing much of its upholstery and moved to the counter where the registration book sat. She opened it to the most recent page. Only two lines had names on them. "No Joel—what did you say?"

"Hartbeck."

"Nope. Not here."

Michael decided to be bold. He reached for the book and turned it around toward him. "May I?"

She didn't protest.

The two names were "Ronny G." and "James Miller."

Master Sergeant James Miller.

Michael had to smile. Joel had never liked that guy.

"This is him," Michael pointed. "Can you tell me what room he's in?"

The woman looked at the register. "That's not the name you said."

"It's who I'm looking for." He flashed his business card. "I'm an attorney, and this is my associate." He nodded at Jake, who grinned at her. "I have confidential business with Mr., uhm, Miller. I have something he really needs to take a look at."

"He's in number eleven. Don't think he's there, though. His car ain't out front."

"I'll take a look. Thank you, ma'am."

They walked out of the office and down the walkway past the numbered doors until they came to the correct one.

"Joel? You in there?" Michael knocked on the door, and the thing creaked open. Jake then noticed that the knob and lock were broken.

A chill went up Michael's back.

He pushed the door open all the way and stepped inside.

The bed was unmade, and it appeared as if the occupant had checked out. No bags or clothing or anything. The place was empty.

Except for the numbers "4/19" smeared in red paint on the wall over the bed's headboard.

17

Spanish Trace, Florida

Two days later, Deke held another meeting in the conference room at the firm. Michael and Jake were back from Kentucky, and Gina, Carol, Sarah, and Diana were also present.

"Let's review what we know," Deke said. "Michael, why don't you start?"

Michael cleared his throat and began. "I'm sorry to say that Joel Hartbeck is MIA right now. We don't have any leads about where he might be. I have a real uneasy feeling about it. I've left messages on his voicemail, but he hasn't returned them. I tried calling the burner phone number he gave me, but it's out of order or no longer active. His motel room had been vandalized with the 4/19 symbol, which is something that is prominently used by a hate group in that area called the Mohawk Warriors, or MWs. Joel mentions in his affidavit that his car was vandalized with that same symbol sometime last week before he reached out to me. According to my conversation with Joel, he has a feeling that there might be a connection between this hate group and the bank, but he had no real specifics to offer except the fact that the '4/19' we are starting to see sure isn't random. Jake has something to say about this, too."

Deke said, "I read your report of the trip, Michael. What did the police say when they came to the motel to investigate Joel's room?"

"It was the county sheriff's department that came out. The motel is out of the Plainsburg city limits, so their police wouldn't have been involved. A couple of deputies showed up, saw the room, and spent ten minutes sniffing around. According to them, they found no evidence of foul play. They took our names and numbers, and I gave them Joel's real name—he'd been using a pseudonym at the motel—and that was it. They're relegating it to random vandalism and the probability that Joel was simply skipping out without paying the room bill. In other words, they're blaming it on Joel. And to be fair, he does have a little bit of criminal incident history. Minor stuff. In his years since Iraq, Joel was arrested for assault, he was cited for vagrancy more than once, and other minor offenses. I'm afraid Joel is known by law enforcement in Plainsburg and the county as being a troublemaker of sorts."

Carol asked, "But you got an affidavit, right?"

"Sort of." Michael distributed copies to everyone. "It's the draft he and I worked on and I marked up. He was going to correct it, print it out, and sign it in front of a notary on the day he went missing. So this is all we've got right now. That said, pertinent details and names and dates are all there. Joel was heavily detailed in the chain of events. Dates, document descriptions that prove criminal conduct, and Joel's first-hand observations are all there. It's something we can use to supplement our investigation, but obviously not something we can offer in court without Joel's direct testimony to its truthfulness."

"Signed, notarized, or not, it sounds like a powerful document," Deke added.

"Yeah, not exactly a perfect situation for the case, but it sure gives us a lot to work with, Deke. I'm particularly interested in the boss at the AML unit in Plainsburg. Freddie Barton. Then there are the two executive vice presidents of the bank who are based in New York. Blake Dullea and Karl Maher. Joel's friend, Willis Lee, might know a few things. From Joel's narrative, it sounds as if Mr. Lee might be a potential ally. I attempted to contact Mr. Lee using the number for him that Joel provided in the affidavit, but the man never returned my call while I was in town. Maybe he still will. That's all I have for now."

Deke nodded. "Thanks. Jake, what else do you have?"

Jake related his tale of meeting with Officer Sheila Denning and what she told him about Janet Blanco's murder. "She believes that this far-right group is definitely involved in the murder. Given that Mr. Hartbeck also had some experiences with the MWs, it leads me to believe that something is all jacked up in that town. I went to speak with the chief of police there, Burt Wainwright, but he refused to see me. The police in that area are obviously not very friendly to out-of-state lawyers and investigators coming in and asking questions. It is mighty suspicious that, according to Mr. Hartbeck's affidavit, Ms. Blanco had informed the AML unit boss, Freddie Barton, that she was going to the FBI with what she knew—and then she was fired and after that she was murdered. The police are writing it off as merely a robbery gone wrong in a bad part of town, but as Officer Denning pointed out to me, the leader of the MWs is Chief Wainwright's son."

"These facts are getting creepier by the minute," Gina said.

"Exactly. Anyway, Officer Denning has promised to keep me apprised of any news. That's it."

Deke replied, "Thank you, Jake. Good work. Carol?"

Carol passed around copies of her report. "My contact at the Treasury Department, Tyra Schilling, is very interested in our case, should we decide to pursue it. She sent me detailed profiles of Bank Antriol's key figures and all the files regarding the settlement agreement with the DOJ. I'm turning all this information over to Gina and Sarah, who are handling all the documents related to the bank. In short, these two VPs that Mr. Hartbeck talks about in his affidavit, Blake Dullea and Karl Maher, are of interest. Mr. Dullea is a native New Yorker. Mr. Maher, however, is an Egyptian American whose birth name is Karim Maher. Maher is an Egyptian surname, and Karl has an extensive family in Egypt. Does this mean Maher has sympathies for extremism? We don't know, but there's a web of connections here that needs to be untangled."

"I'll be doing more research into these characters," Gina said.

Carol continued. "As far as the settlement files go, it's what we already knew. It was a slap on the wrist. It was the DOJ at its very worst. Read it and weep."

Deke said, "Thanks, Carol, the tears are already rolling down my cheeks. Gina, what do you have for us?"

Gina sat up straight and spoke. "Well, I think I might have the answer as to why the DOJ gave only a slap on the wrist to Bank Antriol. Take a look at these summaries of annual reports of subsidiaries that are in the bank's global network and what those entities do." She handed sheets of paper around. "The bank has a major role in processing petrodollar transactions for crude oil. A *substantial* part of the bank's business is trading in crude oil. In short, hindering the bank at all might have a negative impact on crude oil supply. Also look at page fifteen of the report and you will see that at least five major weapons manufacturers are leveraged to the max with Antriol and a half dozen other international banks. If you will notice on page twenty, both the oil industry and those folks on the weapons industry list gave mega money to both political parties in the run-up to the last presidential election. I'm pretty sure the White House is not dying to kick over all the rotted logs surrounding the relationships of its major donors. In fact, if you look at the dates of the settlement agreement, you might recognize that it was an election year. As you say all the time, Deke, 'There are no coincidences where politics are involved.'"

"Unbelievable," Jake said. "Facts might be stranger than fiction."

"It's all connected, isn't it?" Carol asked. "The bank helps the Middle East. Whether or not it's intentional that they're helping terrorists at the same time is irrelevant. Then, the DOJ helps the bank in order to protect the administration. The bank pays lip service to the DOJ to fulfill the settlement agreement, and the DOJ says, 'Thank you very much; it's all fine and dandy now. We'll just look the other way. Carry on.' There are no lines separating good guys and bad guys in this story."

Deke slapped his hands on the table. "Right. Great work, everyone." He then held up the day's issue of the *New York Times*. "Not sure if you saw this. There's a piece on the front page that caught my interest. EFPs are still going off in Afghanistan. The US is now out of the country, which is a good thing, but the vacuum we left with our debacle of a departure means the Taliban is going full speed to fill it and is not putting up with any local resistance. A suspected group of anti-Taliban freedom fighters were all killed by roadside bombs yesterday, and a bus of school children, all little girls, was shredded by what is reported here as a 'copper-plated shape charge bomb.' The terrorism is still happening, which means so is the funding to these bad actors. I'm sure Bank Antriol isn't the only US bank that's doing it, but it's the one we've got a shot at targeting. If we can bring down one of them for their clever little reverse money laundering, it will at least be a good start. I have visions of dominos falling, people. The terrorists are still out there, our financial system is making that possible, and we happen to be in the center of all that. What could possibly go wrong?"

18

The press conference was held at one of the major chain hotels near the Bergman-Deketomis office.

Deke and guest Bernie Serling, who had flown in for the event, were the principals doing the talking. Bernie also managed to bring in two wounded veterans to speak firsthand about their experiences in the Middle East. One was Scotty Weiss, the vice president of Gold Star Plus. The second was Darren Whitsell, a marine who had lost both legs, his right arm, his eyesight, and much of his upper body's outer layer of skin to an EFP. His presence, in a wheelchair, made a powerful statement.

The three major networks, plus CNN, NPR, PBS, and MSNBC, sent camera crews to the event.

Deke and the team had prepped Bernie earlier, saying they were already talking to forensic experts who could trace laundered money and illicit trade finance transactions through and from the bank to the terrorist groups, and then from the terrorist groups to the region and even the village where a bomb was detonated. The bombs had "fingerprints" that a material expert could analyze and then trace backwards from the bomb to the washed money that paid for them. Deke was careful to mention that the team would need an airtight case that unquestionably illustrated that the bank was knowingly covering up illegal transactions going to entities on the DOJ's sanctioned list. Bernie had already been compiling a list of victims and families who indicated that they would join in a lawsuit.

At the appointed time, Deke launched into it. From the get-go, it was clear to anyone tuning in or present that this was a man that the cameras loved. Deke was used to being on television, and he was comfortable and confident being in the public eye. His voice, good looks, and forceful demeanor commanded attention. He had a charisma that was worthy of Hollywood motion pictures. While he instinctively knew this and used it to his advantage, Deke still managed to convey an intangible sense of modesty and humility that was palpable. These character traits made him all the more likable.

"Good afternoon, everyone. We are here today to announce the filing of a lawsuit against Bank Antriol, a Dutch bank with a prime branch in New York City. It's a lawsuit on behalf of an astounding number of Gold Star families and injured veterans who have knowingly been maimed and murdered by a cabal of money changers who have made a fabulous living on Wall Street but never experienced the terror of war on a street in Iraq or Afghanistan. The purpose of the lawsuit is to fully expose the bank's willing support of groups that are killing Americans— and others—overseas. My law firm has already obtained evidence that the bank is *intentionally covering up* illegal money transactions between individuals or groups that support or fund terrorism. The Department of Justice has already had to punish Bank Antriol for doing business with entities on the Specially Designated Nationals and Blocked Persons List. However, that list did not stop Bank Antriol from helping those folks in the murder and maiming of US soldiers. The bank told the US government that they would stop assisting terrorists. In fact, they told the government that they would set up a program to monitor all new transactions that had any possibility of funding terrorism. We are here today because they have been lying to all of us. They have, in fact, phonied up documents and bank transactions that clearly show that it is business as usual between Antriol and terrorists killing American soldiers. I'm going to turn the microphone over to my colleague, Bernie Serling, the attorney for Gold Star Plus, a not-for-profit organization that helps Gold Star families and wounded veterans try to put their lives back together after their battle experiences in the Middle East. Bernie?"

Bernie took the podium and proceeded to take the attendees on a brief, but harrowing, journey of what was at stake. He explained what IEDs and EFPs were, and how they had been used against Americans during the Iraq and Afghanistan wars, and how they were still in operation today. He rolled graphic footage of EFPs in action—some of the same material Deke and Michael had seen at the conference in Chicago—as well as newer, animated creations that illustrated how EFPs work and the damage they could cause to a human being.

To emphasize that last point, Bernie introduced Scotty Weiss, who told the crowd about his experience in Kandahar, Afghanistan, when a roadside bomb killed several of his fellow infantrymen in 2009. The same blast took off his own arm, blinded him in one eye, and burned his face badly. While he acknowledged the receipt of a Silver Star, and was thankful for that, he named the figure he was given as compensation by the US government—and the audience gasped. It was ridiculously low.

Scotty then introduced Darren Whitsell, who had an even more compelling story to tell. He had been in Iraq in 2005 when fourteen Marines were killed by a gigantic roadside bomb in the city of Haditha. Darren had escaped with his life, but he left behind three of his four appendages, both eyes, and much of his face. Indeed, the grafting on his features was not the sort of thing that was normally seen on network television. He had been awarded a Purple Heart. However, the compensation he and his family had received was, again, shockingly poor.

Both men received ovations from the crowd when they finished speaking.

Deke returned to the podium to wrap it up.

"So now you have heard only a few unpleasant truths. As facts are disclosed in our case against Bank Antriol, you will see that their greatest sin is their love of money. It is a sin that distorts their basic sense of decency. They ignore the fact that the very soldiers they put in harm's way were the soldiers who were fighting for Antriol's right to conduct their business in a free and vibrant democracy. Every year thousands of soldiers are injured and killed just doing their jobs. Then, when they are crippled for the rest of their lives, *taxpayers* step in to make sure those soldiers are paid disability to live a tolerable life. When Bank Antriol helps create those disabilities, they never are asked to pay a penny to help these soldiers. By the time this case is over, my goal is to make damn sure Antriol pays their fair share for the suffering they have caused. But the unfortunate truth is that nothing we accomplish in a courtroom will ever reverse the suffering that Bank Antriol's love of money has created for so many American families."

He paused to allow that to sink in.

"The law firm of Bergman-Deketomis will be filing the lawsuit shortly. Thank you very much."

By nightfall, the message from the press conference was all over traditional and social media. Reaction from the public was swift, positive, and supportive. It was only Wall Street pundits that night who mounted an all-out attack on Nicholas Deketomis.

Deke was fine with that.

19

New York, New York

Nigel Beech, the president of the New York branch of Bank Antriol, entered the conference room, sat at the head of the long table, and confronted the six attorneys already present. Four men and two women, all ranging in ages from forty-two to seventy-three.

The two top US lawyers for the bank, George Mendel and Oliver Wrecker, of the prestigious firm Mendel, Wrecker, and Platt, were the senior partners and policy makers when leading the bank's legal defenses … and offenses. Both men were billing machines and had built one of the country's most prestigious corporate defense firms by mastering the art of extracting billable time from remarkably wealthy, affluent corporations and white-collar upper management people who were usually willing to pay as many billable hours as needed to save themselves from potential criminal prosecution. Beech knew them to be ruthless in courtrooms and intimidating in most any other legal setting. Beyond that, he had little respect for the two lawyers who had moved on to their third and fourth trophy wives.

Beech, a tall, handsome man in his early sixties, would best be described as a moderate Republican with a genuinely deep religious center. While he tended to be reasonable and righteous, he could be firm and tenacious in getting things done. The rise in his career in banking was full of awards and achievements, and no one could argue with his stellar record of honesty and fair dealing. It was genuine.

He didn't like the announcement of the Bergman-Deketomis lawsuit one bit. He took it personally, as if somehow *he* had sinned in some way and caused it to happen. Of course, lawsuits against the bank were a dime a dozen. None of them ever amounted to much, thanks to the bank's high-priced legal team.

Still, there was something about this particular suit that made Beech uneasy. None of the words that had been spoken at the news conference described what he wanted for his bank.

"Good morning," Beech said, calling the meeting to order. "We've all heard about the pending lawsuit and that's the agenda today. I'll begin by saying I'm incredibly disturbed by it. It's not something I ever expected to see, considering that the bank already went through a painful and embarrassing bout with the Department of Justice in the not-too-distant past. So, my question to you is: *why is this happening?* It was my understanding that we were complying with the DOJ's terms in the settlement. That was a demand that I unequivocally made clear to every employee in this organization."

George Mendel spoke first, as was his prerogative. "Nigel, I can assure you that the bank *is* complying with the DOJ's terms of the settlement, and that this lawsuit is frivolous. Just another ambulance-chasing, hungry puppy trying to extort money from your bank. We will see to it that it is swiftly dismissed."

"Just like that?" Beech asked. "Snap your fingers and it's dismissed?"

Mendel glanced at his partners, who all gave him slight nods. "Yes, Nigel. Poof. Gone. I guarantee it."

"All right, fine. Since it's my job to play devil's advocate, what happens if it's not dismissed? This Deketomis fella does not strike me as just another run-of-the-mill lawyer. From the little bit I've been told, he certainly doesn't need more money, and he has an impressive history in the courtroom. That doesn't add up to an easy dismissal to me."

Oliver Wrecker answered this one. "Nigel, we have the law on our side. Besides, you may recall that we have an ace in the hole at the NYDFS."

The NYDFS—the New York Department of Financial Services—was responsible for issuing licenses and regulating banks operating in the state. This bureaucratic watchdog had the power to shut down financial institutions. It rarely happened, but any bank problems that landed on the desks of the NYDFS's staff could cause some hair-pulling angst. Losing a license to operate in New York posed an existential threat to a bank's business. Conversely, an ally in the local regulatory establishment could grease the way through any big obstacles.

"Remind me," Beech said.

"As nothing leaves this conference room and stays with us present, we can safely say that there's a recent appointee as the head of the NYDFS who was 'greatly assisted' by banks and insurance companies to the position. A man with—" Wrecker chuckled, "little experience. He's too green to be effective. This appointment was by design."

"What's his name?" Beech asked.

Wrecker looked confused and turned to one of his female associates.

"Dan Lawson," she said.

"Dan Lawson," Wrecker unnecessarily repeated to Beech.

"I heard her. So you're saying Mr. Lawson is on our side and will just willingly go along with whatever we want? That sounds a little far-fetched to me, to be perfectly honest."

"Nigel," Mendel said, "if it will make you feel better, bring in your men who are in charge of the anti-money laundering unit. That's what the lawsuit is targeting. Get them to supply you with documentation and the proof that they're complying with the DOJ. We will need something from them, anyway, to prepare the defenses and present at the hearing for dismissal."

Beech nodded. "You're right. I'll do that." He stood. "Thank you all. I'm sure you'll keep me apprised of developments." With that, he left the conference room with no further eye contact or pleasantries with the lawyers.

They may be the bank's attorneys of record, but that didn't mean he had to like them or even trust them.

* * *

Blake Dullea told the others, "Let Karl and me do the talking," and without waiting for a response, he, Karl Maher, and the three other executive vice presidents entered the inner sanctum. Nigel Beech was sitting behind his expansive mahogany desk that was an antique from the time of the Revolutionary War. The office itself was akin to a suite at the Four Seasons Hotel—the luxuriousness and artistic aesthetics were more conspicuous than any sense of a productive atmosphere for work. Blake and Karl knew, though, that the bank president managed to perform the latter quite effectively from his fiefdom.

"Sit down, please," Beech told his underlings without looking up from the paperwork on his desk. All five of the VPs did so in elegant, comfy chairs that were positioned ten feet away from the boss. Blake expected that the man would be somewhat dramatic, and so he was ready to play along.

After a few seconds of the silence that Blake knew was supposed to make them squirm a bit, Beech raised his head and addressed them. "Thank you for coming in. I know you're busy."

"No problem, sir," Blake answered.

Beech shot him a glance, probably to indicate that he didn't approve of Blake assuming the role of spokesperson for the group. It didn't bother Blake.

"You all have seen the memo about the lawsuit that has been filed, or is about to be filed, right?" Beech asked.

There were nods and murmurs of "Yes, sir."

Beech then looked directly at Blake and Karl. "Your anti-money laundering unit is under attack. Why?"

Blake cleared his throat. He had prepared his answers in advance. "Sir, I have no idea. The AML unit is operating beautifully. Its progress is, well, off the charts. The employees there are doing everything they can to comply with the mission statement, sir."

"And you have documented proof of this?"

"Of course, sir. The unit is clearing more transactions than ever. Karl and I set up a new incentive plan for the employees, and it's working like gangbusters. Paying for a couple of employees and their families to go to Disney World and increasing the salaries of a few of the higher producers are small prices to pay in the grand scheme of things. The number of clearances increase every month."

Blake then glanced at Karl, giving him his cue to speak.

"At the same time, sir," Karl added, "the territories of the bank that were flagged—West Asia, Latin America, East Africa—they are still doing a booming business, despite the sanctions the government has imposed. We are doubling our efforts to make sure that customers are still being serviced while also policing suspicious activity. We're naturally not going to let illegal transactions occur, but, as you know, not every transaction flagged as such is necessarily illegal. After proper investigation is made, we are almost *always* able to clear a transaction and mark the players as non-risks. All of these are then sent first to the accounting company we hired for auditing the process, and then to the Treasury Department for double checking. We're doing what we're supposed to, sir."

Blake piped in again. "Based on the results, sir, we believe our business in high-risk areas generates returns and strategic benefits that are still commensurate with the potential risks involved."

Beech studied them for a beat and then spoke. "Blake, Karl, you're the ones here who are in charge of that operation. I want to see a full report on the progress of your unit and its positive results on my desk *tomorrow*. It needs to be something our lawyers can present to get this lawsuit dismissed. Is that *clear?*"

"Yes, sir," Blake said. "We've already been working on that."

"I'm counting on you, gentlemen. I don't want another round of sanctions that make all of us look like dishonest charlatans who would ever have an ongoing relationship with murdering terrorists. If we say that we're abiding by the DOJ's rules, then by God we'd better be doing that. I had my misgivings about the AML unit, especially with it being all the way down in Kentucky, but I will have to trust you. If the numbers speak for themselves, and, as you claim, you're clearing more transactions than not, then I have to believe you. Can you promise me that you're not cutting any corners? Everything is on the up and up?"

"Of course, sir," Blake said.

"Absolutely," Karl echoed.

Beech stared at them for a full thirty seconds without speaking a word until Karl shifted uncomfortably in his seat.

"Very well. Tomorrow on my desk by noon, please. That's all."

The other three VPs looked at each other as if to ask, *Why the heck did we have to come in here for this?*

They all stood and began to leave the office.

"Blake? Karl?" Beech barked.

The two men halted and turned to him as the others went out the door.

"Yes, sir?" Blake asked.

"No games here. Your future in this industry depends on that. Am I clear enough?"

All they could do was nod, turn on their heels, and depart. Outside the door, Blake looked at Karl and rolled his eyes.

20

A month passed.

Bank Antriol's team of high-powered lawyers filed a motion in Federal court to dismiss the Bergman-Deketomis lawsuit within the allotted deadline to do so. A hearing date was set, and Deke, Michael, Carol, Sarah, and Bernie flew from Florida to New York to appear and argue against the dismissal. While technically only Deke and Bernie needed to be at the plaintiff's table, Deke thought that since Antriol had a battery of six attorneys, then he would show up with at least the five-member core of his trial team assigned to the Antriol case. Deke was never one to ignore the obvious truth that the success of every major case he had ever handled was more dependent on his remarkable team of legal professionals than his trial skill alone. He didn't count on intimidating anyone on the opposite side, but at least his team's presence would indicate that Bergman-Deketomis was all in with their effort to take down Antriol. The case had already captured the attention of serious journalists throughout the country merely by what was detailed in the filed complaint and the response to that complaint by the Antriol lawyers. The *Wall Street Journal, Forbes, Fortune, The Economist*, and *Harvard Business Review* were sure to be present outside the courtroom because of the dramatic impact the Antriol case potentially could have on the banking industry.

Deke was well aware of the reputation of Mendel, Wrecker, and Platt, but he had never met George Mendel or Oliver Wrecker. Perhaps the gentlemen knew who *he* was, though. Deke was never one to acknowledge that he had developed somewhat of a "well-recognized lawyer" status, but in this case it would be a plus. A key factor to a successful outcome required keeping the discussion about the case alive in news reports and journals of every conceivable kind beyond a forty-eight-hour news cycle. All the lawyers and staff at the Bergman-Deketomis law firm were well trained in exactly how to accomplish that, and they knew that what took place in the courtroom that week would impact that goal.

The team set up at the Roxy Hotel on lower Sixth Avenue, which was a mere ten-minute walk across White Street and down Centre Street to Foley Square and the huge, impressive Thurgood Marshall US Federal Courthouse in its Classical Revival glory. Deke had booked the one-bedroom suite at the Roxy for himself so that the team could meet in its comfortable living room area prior to the hearing, which was scheduled for 11:00 a.m. After a quick breakfast in the Roxy Bar, the foursome gathered in Deke's room for a final huddle and pep talk.

Carol started off the session. "Okay, everyone is well aware that we didn't draw the best judge for this case. Senior Federal Judge Carroll Patterson is a hardline conservative. He's a man who will predictably side with big business virtually all the time. To be exact, the count is … big business forty wins; regular Joes and government regulators five wins, just in the last seven years. Pretty much a nightmare for the little guy and anyone not connected to Wall Street or Madison Avenue."

"We can't control who we draw. We kind of have to deal with that reality," Michael said.

Sarah piped in. "Maybe not. Gina wanted us to call her when we got together this morning because she was still digging into any potential connections the judge or his family might have with the bank. If there is even a scintilla of evidence of a conflict of interest anywhere, we need to raise it, no matter how far along the case advances. No doubt he is going to act like a prick, and we need to do the same for the record." She dialed the number on her phone.

"Gina," Deke asked, "do you have anything we need to know about his highness the judge?"

"Weak, but I found this information late last night. So, it turns out that Judge Patterson is a member of the Fields. That's an exclusive country club in the Hamptons. Very chichi. Members include former presidents, congressmen, CEOs, and so on. Men only, of course. Even in this day and age."

"I get the picture," Carol said. "All white guys who are wannabe golfers."

"Right. Well, guess who else is a member of the Fields?"

"I'm afraid you're going to tell us," Deke said.

"Nigel Beech, president of Bank Antriol, and the current US attorney general."

"I can read between those lines," Bernie muttered.

"Yeah, it's not good."

"I don't think that alone gets us anywhere," Deke said. "It certainly isn't enough for a cause challenge to this judge. Even though we all know how those kinds of relationships impact cases. We would need something much stronger to get rid of this guy with a conflict argument."

"I agree," Michael added.

"Is that all you have right now, Gina?" Deke asked.

"I'm afraid so."

"Keep working it. I'm thinking this guy will do everything he can to deep-six this case."

"You know I will." With that, Sarah ended the call.

"Well, folks," Deke said, "we go in with what we've got and do the best we can. Ready to take a walk?"

* * *

Deke always hated to hear that 'worn-out Philistine giant versus the poor little shepherd boy' comparison in cases like this, but if he were honest with himself, today he felt a little like David with that one damn rock and sling.

Three attorneys from Bergman-Deketomis and the one from Gold Star Plus sat at the plaintiff's table with Sarah and Carol in position behind them. On the other side, the six attorneys from Mendel, Wrecker, and Platt were arranged at the table with an army of associates and paralegals sitting behind them. Anyone doing the cost calculations would accurately conclude that Antriol was spending close to $150,000 in legal fees for this one hearing.

Antriol's lead attorney, George Mendel, was the first to stand and speak with a "Good morning, your honor," and then some ridiculous ingratiating inside story comment about the judge's flower garden that no one in the courtroom except the judge and Mendel could have possibly understood. That didn't prevent the low-level hangers-on sitting around Mendel's table to fake a laugh at the judge's meaningless response.

"Your honor, the facts of this case turn on a simple interpretation of the existing law. We have provided the court with a fifty-page brief that establishes what that interpretation should be. In a nutshell, it is this. For the past thirty-three years, US law has provided anti-terrorism measures that, among other things, provide a provision for both criminal and civil liability in order to combat terrorism and those who provide material support to international terrorist activities that result in harm to US citizens. Recently, Congress amended the law with something titled JASTA—the Justice Against Sponsors of Terrorism Act. If you will turn to page four in our brief, we discuss the scope of that legislation." Mendel stood silently at the podium as the judge gave the impression of actually reading what he had been directed to.

"Mr. Mendel," the judge said, "let me assure you that both I and my three law clerks have thoroughly reviewed your brief ... so get to the point."

"Your honor, this JASTA legislation has nothing to do with the banking industry or my client. JASTA is written for the purpose of preventing foreign states and their terrorist-connected charity organizations from collecting donated money and then directing that money to be used for global terrorist activity. Mr. Deketomis is trying to place words and meaning into that JASTA law that simply do not exist. His interpretation is an absurd and frivolous attempt to use smoke and mirrors and bilk Bank Antriol out of billions of dollars. He knows that they are legally not even a permissible defendant in a case like this."

"Again, Mr. Mendel, I can read. That argument is clearly all through your brief, and I'm inclined to agree with most of the legal precedent you analyzed in it. Let me hear from you, Mr. Deketomis. Did I say that right? Deek-a-toe-mis?"

Deke approached the podium. "Yes, judge, you stated my name correctly. I'm certain you and your law clerks have reviewed my lengthy brief as closely as you reviewed Mr. Mendel's, so let me highlight a few important points.

"First of all, there are at least two other federal courts that completely agree with our interpretation of the JASTA law. They clearly point out that it makes no difference what the source or vehicle of support actually is. The law clearly states that providing, directly or indirectly, *any* support to certain terrorist groups like Hezbollah or al-Qaeda, including financial services, may give rise to civil liability. Congress expressly stated that the purpose of JASTA was to give victims of terrorism the broadest possible basis, within the bounds of our Constitution, to hold *any* person or entity, even banks, accountable for their conduct that results in reasonably foreseeable acts of terrorism. Simply put, it makes no difference if a terrorist receives support from a foreign country, a charity organization, a mom and pop corner drug store, or even by a global bank, the spirit of the law is the same. If our soldiers are being murdered by terrorist groups whose capability to commit violence was enhanced by the use of that support, be it money or material, then we have the right to make a JASTA claim for those soldiers. So, I agree with Mr. Mendel as to one thing, at least. It comes down to a simple reading and interpretation of law that totally supports our position. Also, Your honor—"

"Enough, Mr., um, Deek-a-toe-mis. If you are telling me it comes down to only interpretation, then let me save all of us a lot of time because I agree with the position Antriol has taken in this case. You are way overreaching in this claim, edging on being frivolous. If you want the law to say what you have stated in your brief and in open court, you best spend your time seeking legislation that makes your farfetched position much clearer. Mr. Mendel, please prepare an order for me to sign granting your motion to dismiss."

As the judge stood and made his exit from the courtroom, he took with him all the air Deke and his trial team had been breathing up to that point.

21

D an Lawson, the newly appointed head of the banking division of the New York Department of Financial Services, winced when he saw the email that his assistant had sent to him. If it had been a real piece of paper, he might have wadded it up and thrown it across the room.

The Bergman-Deketomis mass tort action against Bank Antriol had been dismissed in federal court.

Dan shook his head. *Well, it figures*, he thought.

The lawsuit had gotten his attention when it had been filed, for the name of Bank Antriol had crossed his desk in the past.

Dan rubbed his chin and thought about the implications. His department supervised and regulated the activities of New York State financial institutions, including regulating, licensing, and servicing the banks in the state. While he was aware that many thought of his staff as "policemen" of sorts, Dan liked to think they were there to help nurture the growth of the industry and encourage economic development.

Unless crimes were being committed.

Right on cue, Jean, his assistant, came into the office. "I guess you saw the email about Bank Antriol?" she asked.

"Yes, I did, thanks. I was going to talk to you about that."

Jean, a woman in her fifties, sat across from him. "You had asked me to keep an eye on that case."

"That's right. When I was at the Treasury Department, something involving Bank Antriol crossed my desk. They had negotiated a settlement agreement with the Justice Department to resolve some issues over suspicious wire transfers and a feeble customer due diligence process for overseas trades. It caught my eye because the settlement occurred pretty quickly into investigation, which either means it was a very weak case, or a very strong one. And the folks handling it for Justice seemed quite pleased with themselves over it. But allegations like that aren't just bandied about. It seemed to me that the bank had to be doing some pretty questionable things and in some very high risk parts of the world—all primary areas of money laundering concern. But all that was above my pay grade. *Then.*"

"Why do you think the Gold Star Plus lawsuit was dismissed?" Jean asked.

"I was afraid it would be. But even this is much rougher justice than I expected. Maybe they didn't invite the right people to their wedding," he wryly noted with a wink.

Jean smiled and nodded.

Dan appreciated that his wise assistant had been an ally from his first day on the job. She was aware that *he* was aware that the people who appointed him believed—and wanted—him to be predictably incompetent. The financial world was a dark cesspool of greed and avarice, and it wasn't beyond the powers-that-be to use influence to get who they wanted in key positions. They expected Dan Lawson to be their puppet, but he wasn't about to play that game. He had spent most of his young adult life trying to do the right thing, even knowing it was the kind of steadfast commitment that could often go badly for him personally.

"Bring in the team, Jean," he ordered. "I've read the Gold Star Plus lawsuit, and there's something there. We're going to launch our own investigation into Bank Antriol. And we're going to be very vocal about it, too."

She observed, "That could place the bank's license and ability to operate in the US in jeopardy, won't it?"

He nodded. "That's the idea. Get me that lawyer, Deketomis, on the phone. He and I need to talk."

* * *

Two months passed. Joel Hartbeck was still missing. The news cycle had dropped any mention of the Gold Star Plus lawsuit and moved on to the next shiny thing. Bank Antriol's Anti-Money Laundering unit was still functioning, and it was business as usual.

Deke and members of his team, however, had several productive virtual meetings with Dan Lawson in New York, and by the end of the second call they had decided to join forces. It was time to meet in person, so Deke and Carol flew to New York to talk strategy. They met in Dan's offices at One State Street in Manhattan, which was a twenty-five minute walk from the Roxy Hotel, Deke's preferred spot downtown. He and Carol didn't mind the walk—it was now May and the weather was beautiful.

Jean Moore welcomed the two Floridians and ushered them into a conference room where lunch from a nearby Chinese restaurant was brought in at Deke's request ("I've had Chinese food everywhere, but outside of mainland China, the best is in New York City!"). Dan joined them for the meal and began the meeting over cold sesame noodles, fried dumplings, and four different main dishes shared family style on flimsy paper plates.

"Let me bring you up to speed with what we've uncovered in the past week," Dan said. "We obtained all the transaction data that was initially provided to the DOJ in order to negotiate that sham settlement agreement. Even though what Antriol provided was a sampling of transaction data that it was able to cherry pick, we believe Bank Antriol is intentionally scrubbing SWIFT messaging data so that sanctioned customers can still process transactions undetected by regulators."

Carol interrupted him. "We know generally what the scrubbing of data means, but it might be helpful to give us your Scrubbing 101 tutorial."

Dan explained, "To get away with what we suspect the bank is doing, even with the DOJ now looking over their shoulders, they need to use a process we call 'wire stripping.' Basically, modern banking doesn't deal in paper fiat. It's all bits and bytes now. Electronic wire transfers rely on standardized messaging systems. SWIFT messages are based on a system developed by the Society for Worldwide Interbank Financial

Telecommunication. These messages are how the banks' computers talk to each other and know when and how much money to exchange and to which account it goes. The electronic data attached to wire transfers is behind-the-scenes information. A good analogy is email. Emails have what computer people call 'headers' and 'metadata,' and these things contain a bunch of coding gobbledygook that tells where an email came from and where it went to and the path it took. Forensic computer investigators can read this stuff like it's English."

"I know about metadata," Deke said.

"So, if someone clever can get hold of the transaction data at a specific point in the process, they can scrub it of any data that may cause the transaction to trip any of the alarms built into the messaging systems designed to flag seemingly suspicious transactions. Most commonly, these alarms look for designated customers, suspicious amounts and frequencies, and other known red flags based on the locations of the customers or banks handling the transaction. Certain types of goods or transactions can't involve customers in specific locations either; that is, any transactions coming from certain areas or for certain types of goods are immediately suspicious. Some banks are even blacklisted entirely. Simply put, banks are required to know exactly who their customers are, what business they conduct, how they conduct it, the purpose of the transactions, and who may be the ultimate beneficiaries of the transaction, with an even more watchful eye out for bad guys using their banks to do bad stuff."

"And so?" Deke asked.

"And so, banks have an affirmative duty to be the front line of defense to prevent terrorists from accessing the money and goods they need to operate. The chance of a glitch or clerical error in all of this is slim to none. To bypass all the laws, ignore all the standards, fool all the alarms, and to do all that while you're being audited, especially after already getting popped for it like Antriol did, takes a huge set of brass balls, and those are going to be attached to someone inside the bank." Dan, remembering Carol was there, sheepishly looked her way.

Deke noticed the glance and jumped in. "She's heard worse, trust me. So, they're doing it willfully and knowingly then, but how?"

"Back to wire stripping. Someone inside the bank has to first know that a transaction will trigger an alarm to know it needs to be stripped. They need to know what information the system is looking for so they can remove it, or alter it, to bypass the filtering tools the alarms use. Once stripped, the system can't tell if a customer or transaction should be flagged. Usually the person stripping the wire will omit just enough data, alter it ever so slightly with a typo, or perhaps the real recipient is replaced by a front company or series of intermediary entities. There are all kinds of things they can do."

"Got it. And let me guess, the bank doing this charges a premium for this special service?"

"Exactly!" Dan said as he broke a fortune cookie and popped the edible portions into his mouth without looking at whatever the slip of paper inside may have predicted for him. "We hired some computer and financial experts to examine the sampling given to the DOJ. Our guys think there's just enough there to show that the information on these messages normally used to identify sanctioned companies and individuals has indeed been stripped, and it's not a glitch. Unwanted data was stripped and replaced with false entries. *Or ... get this ...* the bank itself returned the payment message to the client who initiated the transfer with instructions to *them* to wire strip the message and resubmit it with different data. In other words, they were given specific instructions about the need to strip and exactly the best way to do the stripping by the very people who were supposed to prevent the suspicious activity that was surfacing through Bank Antriol. We believe that's what they've been doing after the AML unit in Kentucky sends an older SAR to the bank. The bank 'takes care of it' and sends it back to the AML unit *cleared.* Do you know about StoneWall?"

Deke frowned. "StoneWall?"

"That's another thing we've learned from the DOJ material. Bank Antriol uses a CPA company called StoneWall to help them with the clearing of problem transactions. They were supposed to be an independent auditor hired by the bank to ensure its compliance with the earlier settlement. The DOJ even blessed their involvement when it negotiated the settlement with the bank. StoneWall came in and audited the data sample submitted to the DOJ that was used to negotiate the settlement penalty. Our forensic analysts who looked at the same data think there is subtle evidence that other methods were being used to hide the true nature of the transactions, too, and yet StoneWall looks at everything before the bank reports its progress to the DOJ. How Antriol is pulling the wool over the eyes of StoneWall and the DOJ is going to be a tough nut to crack."

"Smart little freaks, aren't they?" Deke noted. "Our witness, Joel, never mentioned StoneWall."

"It was likely he didn't even know about them. They were part of the shell game."

After lunch was cleared away, Dan displayed printouts and other material that highlighted the issues he had discussed. The entire time, Carol would occasionally make a peculiar groaning noise to which the rest of the team had grown accustomed. She was someone who *despised* corporate wrongdoing after so many years of going toe-to-toe with the worst of the worst.

Deke eventually sat back in his chair and said, "What's most interesting about the way you have presented all of this to us is that it is almost trial ready."

Dan shrugged. "I never actually used my license to practice law, so maybe what you see is a frustrated trial lawyer coming out in me."

Deke rubbed his chin and looked at Carol, who raised her eyebrows. He then stated, "I'm going to be conservative here and say there is not an all-out smoking gun that would be enough to criminally prosecute the CEO of Antriol, but there certainly is enough to go after the individuals connected to these transactions. And the way I see it is that the public display of this kind of conduct would absolutely be enough to create a long line of angry shareholders. It would also more than likely force them to a negotiating table with the Gold Star families. Still, my take on it is that we need powerful direct evidence that the bank's top management *intentionally* set up work-arounds to clear SARs, and those transactions can be traced to terrorists in Iraq. You've seen Joel Hartbeck's unofficial affidavit?"

"Yes, your associate sent it to me and I read it. That's powerful stuff," Dan said.

"He's a star witness here, and unfortunately, we don't know where he is. He might be dead, for all we know." He nodded at Carol. "I think it's time to send Investigator Jake back to Kentucky to exhaust every effort to find Joel."

"I agree," Carol said. "I'll get that started."

Deke's cell phone rang, and he saw that it was Gina Romano calling from the Florida office. He answered, "Hi, Gina. What's up?" He listened for a minute, and then he abruptly sat up in his chair. "You're kidding! Really?" The one-sided conversation went on a little longer, and Deke began to make some notes on a pad of paper. "Uh huh. Oh, that's fantastic." He scribbled a little more, and then said, "That's wonderful news. Does Bernie know? Oh, good. Thank you for letting me know. I'm sitting here with Dan Lawson and Carol right now and we're going over some things. This news will be a boost for morale. Thanks!"

When he hung up, Carol asked, "What was that?"

"Well!" Deke said. "Dan, all along since the case was dismissed here in New York, many more Gold Star families and wounded veterans have joined this fight. The good news is that we have been looking for the next best place to make our stand, and we have been hoping to sign up this particular group of veterans based in Richmond, Virginia, so we could file another lawsuit there. Well, today they agreed to act as plaintiffs. That's in the Eastern District of Virginia."

"That certainly creates a new jurisdiction for a completely new lawsuit. A second shot!" Dan stated. "More importantly, it is a district where most of the judges run an aggressive rocket docket. They force all parties to trial with very few delays."

Deke added, "That's exactly what we've been counting on. Everything in that district moves fast. Based on the research we have done on all of their prior rulings I believe the federal judges there could very well be willing to hear our case. Dan, we can *refile* the lawsuit in Virginia! It means we can be in business again, and maybe this time we can find a judge with a soul and a conscience. I think Carol and I should head back to Florida tonight and get on it. The sooner we file, the better."

"From here on," Dan said, "let's be sure to share every bit of new evidence that surfaces in discovery. I would also very much appreciate you sharing with me all the recorded statements you take from your wounded clients and their families. It will help motivate me even more. I'm always embarrassed to admit that I never had to battle for my life in my two tours in the desert. I was always tucked away in a safe air-conditioned office reviewing data while so many of my friends were sacrificing their lives on the front lines."

"You got it, my friend. We're in this together now. And please consider that even though there are still no roadside bombs going off around you, be very aware that there will be plenty of ugly bullets fired in your direction as you try to get a little justice for these soldiers."

22

Plainsburg, Kentucky

Jake Rutledge dutifully returned to Kentucky to search for Joel Hartbeck. Michael had supplied Jake with everything he knew, including the various phone numbers and the photo of Joel that Michael had taken at the diner. Jake's first attempt was to again call the message phone. Joel's voicemail greeting played, a sign that the bill had been paid, or at least that the phone still worked. After the beep, Jake said, "Joel, this is Jake Rutledge of Bergman-Deketomis. I'm here in Plainsburg. Michael Carey and Deke Deketomis sent me to try and find you. If you get this message, please call me." He left his number and the date. Jake then attempted to call the burner number, but, as before, it was out of service.

The next step was to contact Willis Lee. Michael had left a message for the man when he and Jake were last in Plainsburg, but Willis had never returned the call. This time, however, when Jake called the number, someone answered.

"Hello?"

"Is this Willis Lee?" Jake asked.

"Who's calling?"

"Mr. Lee, my name is Jake Rutledge. My associate, Michael Carey, attempted to phone you a couple of months ago when we were in Plainsburg. I'm an investigator for a law firm in Florida. I'm wondering if you might be willing to meet with me on an informal basis—somewhere so I can ask you a little bit about Joel Hartbeck. I understand you know him?"

"Uh, yeah, I know him. I don't know where he is, though."

"That's partly what I want to talk to you about. Lunch, dinner, or drinks is on me. Would today or this evening be good for you?"

Willis hesitated, but he finally said, "Okay. Meet me at a place called Beggar's Ravine at, say, five thirty?"

Jake quickly looked it up on his phone and found directions. "That's fine, Mr. Lee, thank you. See you then."

* * *

Willis Lee was not what Jake had expected. The man's wiry, diminutive frame did not scream "marine," but it was apparent that he had more energy than a power plant. Jake noted that Willis seemed extremely nervous.

"Mr. Rutledge," he said, "I don't mind talking to you, but I have to be careful. I'm now in an upper management position where I work, and I can't be seen with you. We have a strict NDA in force and all that."

"I understand, Mr. Lee. Can I call you Willis?"

"Sure."

"Call me Jake. So, can you tell me about the last time you saw Joel?"

Willis rolled his eyes. "Man, the guy was about to blow a gasket. Between you and me, Joel is terribly unstable. His behavior was becoming more and more erratic and paranoid. He was starting to spout off bizarre conspiracy theories about the bank where we work—er, where *I* work. He was fired. Or he resigned. That's right, he walked out. They probably would have fired him, though, if he hadn't left first."

"And you haven't heard from him at all since that day he left?"

"Nope. And I'm concerned. He and I became buddies. We'd go shooting together at the range to blow off steam, you know what I mean?"

"What's the name of the range?" Jake asked.

Willis told him. "Don't waste your time going there, though. I asked the manager just yesterday if he'd seen Joel. He hadn't."

"Did Joel ever mention anything that might indicate where he would go?"

Willis made a face and rubbed his chin. "Nah, he didn't. He didn't have family around. I think he mentioned a cousin who lives far away. Someone he wasn't close to."

"We checked out the motel where he was last known to have been. Are you sure he never talked about any family residences, favorite hangouts, or, I don't know, do you think he might have just left town?"

"He could have. Actually, come to think of it, he did tell me he likes to look on Craigslist for old, abandoned hunting cabins up in the hills or in the woods. He said that sometimes he goes to those kinds of places for a day or two to be 'one with nature,' or something goofy like that." Willis then frowned and muttered to himself, "Shoot, I should have told..."

"I beg your pardon?"

"Oh, nothing. I was just thinking out loud. I should have told you that earlier. I normally have a great memory. I guess I just wasn't putting two and two together with regard to where Joel might be. That's all. Although I think a rented cabin is a long shot, if you ask me."

"Anything helps. You said he was talking conspiracy theories about your bank. Like what, exactly?"

"Not sure I should say. Oh, hell, I told him I'd help him. He was concerned that the bank is intentionally covering up money transfers that should be sanctioned. You know, transactions between bad actors, like terrorists or drug cartels."

"And what do *you* think?" Jake asked.

"Oh, the whole reason we're working for the bank is because it got busted by the DOJ. Our job is to find anything suspicious and report it. I think there was something going on, and now the bank paid a big fine and have to fix it and all, but if you ask me, all banks are kind of corrupt here and there, don't you think? Give a man millions of dollars, and he's going to do whatever he can to keep it. Bank Antriol is a big frickin' bank. All the top dogs who run it are rich as hell. But I don't think they're committing crimes in the way Joel was talking about."

"Willis, we're involved in a lawsuit against the bank for Gold Star families who have lost loved ones to terrorism, specifically roadside bombs over there in Iraq and Afghanistan. The men and women who survived those types of bombs and returned home without limbs are our clients. At this point we already have clear evidence that the bank is allowing money to go to the terrorists who build those bombs. By the time this is over, I'm predicting that it will turn into not only a massive civil suit, but also a significant criminal case. The truth is, as you know, Bank Antriol has already been busted for doing exactly what I just described to you. It might not be a bad idea for you to distance yourself as far as possible from that operation as soon as you get the opportunity. You could sure start that by giving us a little help."

"Look, Jake, I'd like to, but my job is important to me. Like I said, I'm in a management position now. If they found out…"

"When everything goes sideways, which it will, wouldn't you be better off being on the right side of all this? Don't get me wrong. We know about Janet's death, and it's clear that Joel is on the run because he fears for his life. You have every reason to keep your mouth shut and just sit on the sidelines here, but it is just a matter of time before that management position you have now becomes a liability for you rather than anything positive."

Willis looked away and drummed his fingers on the table. "I've kinda seen all this coming, even though I wish I hadn't. I like what I do."

The man stared at Jake without a word passing between them for a solid, uncomfortable minute. Jake knew to keep quiet and simply stared back.

"Okay, pal, here's the deal. I'm sure as hell not going to be a whistleblower, if that's what you're leading up to here," Willis said. "But I'll do anything I can do to help you find Joel. And if I find something that sounds like it fits into the case you're building, I'll share it with you if it's possible. Beyond that, Willis Lee is going to show up at work every day as if this conversation never took place. I'll worry about the possible fallout of all that when the time comes. Are we good with that?"

Jake knew it was the best he was going to get from the guy. "Okay, that's fine, Willis. We don't want you to do anything that makes you uncomfortable. Is it okay if I call you again? Or if my colleague Michael Carey calls you?"

"Sure, just don't make it a habit, if you know what I mean?"

* * *

Jake touched base with Michael down in Florida to give him a report. The rest of the veteran trial team was about to hop on a plane for Richmond, Virginia, to attend a new hearing regarding the Gold Star case. The refiling in district court there had been accomplished.

"Tomorrow I'm meeting with that police officer, Sheila Denning, again," Jake said. "Hopefully, she'll have some more info for me. So far, though, Joel hasn't left much in the way of bread crumbs."

"He's had specialized military training that taught him how to disappear," Michael said. "Well, keep at it, Jake. You're a great investigator. You'll turn up a rock or two and find something."

"Michael, I just had a thought. If Joel's laptop was stolen when his apartment was ransacked, how did he print out that affidavit he gave you?" There was silence at the other end of the call for a moment. "Michael?"

"Yeah, I'm here. You know, I'm pretty sure he said he did it at the library. You can go to a public library and use a computer for personal things and even print stuff out. That's what he did, I remember now. He said so."

Jake smiled. "You know, pal, that's actually *very* helpful."

* * *

The Plainsburg Public Library was open late on weekdays. It was a relatively small establishment that housed mostly current bestsellers. Its back collection was meager, and there was little in the way of audio-visual material. It appeared that the periodicals were the most used items, for several senior citizens sat in easy chairs scattered around the space with newspapers and magazines in hand.

The young woman at the Reader Services desk was plain in appearance, but she had that "sexy librarian" vibe that Jake couldn't resist.

"Can I help you, sir?" the woman asked. Her name tag read: "I'm KIM."

"Hi, Kim, I was wondering if you have computers that patrons can use?"

"Yes, sir, we do. Do you have a library card with us?"

"Um, no, I don't. I'm from out of town." He handed her a business card. "I'm an investigator with a law firm." He leaned closer to her and whispered, "I'm looking into a very serious *murder* in town, and my own laptop is on the blink. I was hoping maybe you'd make an exception for me in this case."

Her eyes widened at the mention of a murder, and she took his card. "Oh, my. Well, technically we're not supposed to do this…" She blinked, and there was a hint of a smile. "Well, this sounds exciting in a mysterious kind of way. Take a few minutes with the computer. I'll make an exception here but be quick. We'll be closing soon."

"Thank you, Kim. This is a huge help. Where are your computers?"

"There's only one. It's over there in that alcove." She handed him a slip of paper. "Here's the login information. Again, we'll be closing in an hour. I hope that's enough time for you. Sounds important." Kim added with a flirtatious smile, "I'd love to know you got your big break here in my library."

Only one computer. That was the best news Jake could have heard.

"One other thing I was wondering. Maybe you can help. There's a man in town who is a person of interest for us. He's not a suspect, mind you, but rather a witness. Someone who can help us." He leaned in and whispered again, "We think he's in hiding. From some real *bad guys*."

"Wow, this plot is thickening by the minute!" she whispered back.

"Do you recognize this man?" Jake asked. He pulled up Joel's photo that Michael had taken at Diner-24.

"Oh, yes, that's Mr. Miller! Nice man. He comes in here pretty often and uses the computer. Well, actually I haven't seen him in a while. Gosh, maybe not for a month or so. Is he okay?"

Jake smiled and nodded. "Can you tell me when Mr. Miller used the computer last?"

"We do keep records of users," she said. "Just a second." She typed on her keyboard and read the results on her screen. She gave him a date that was six weeks earlier. This confirmed for Jake that Joel had not been killed in the motel.

"Thank you, Kim." Feeling proud of himself, Jake went to the computer, which was also connected to a printer. It was several years old and wasn't running the most up-to-date software, but it would do. He logged in and immediately opened the Google Chrome browser. He went to Settings and opened the browser's history page.

Oh, thank God, he thought. *I'm in luck.*

All of the computer's browsing history was there, dating back months. No one had bothered to clear it at such a small and little-used library.

He scrolled down to the date in question and examined the various URLs that users had accessed.

Craigslist ... Craigslist...

Yes! There were indeed some Craigslist URLs around the date Kim mentioned. Some were innocuous searches for things like washing machines for sale, but after only a few minutes of scrolling, Jake found what he was looking for.

Hunting Cabins for Rent.

There were several URL links for cabins. Joel must have been perusing a bunch of them, but two of the links had been brought up several times. This indicated to Jake that Joel had looked at each of those more carefully, likely trying to decide which one he should go for.

Jake printed out both entries. They pictured dilapidated rustic log structures that he guessed were some miles away from Plainsburg, definitely remote, and in the woods and/or up in the Kentucky hills. There were no addresses, just general descriptions of where the cabins were located and the closest major roads. Owners' phone numbers were included.

Jake folded the sheets of paper and stuck them in his pocket. He logged out of the computer and went back to the Reader Services desk.

"Did you find what you needed?" Kim asked. "You know, if this mysterious mission you seem to be on turns into a great mystery novel, you'll owe me a signed copy." She removed her glasses and gave Joel another one of her remarkably sexy smiles.

"I'll do better than that. How about dinner and champagne if it makes it to the bestseller list?" Joel flirted back as he started to make his exit.

"I'll be pulling for that. Nice to meet you, Mr. Inspector. Glad I could help!"

As Jake left the Reader Services desk, he failed to notice the man sitting in a comfy chair with a newspaper hiding his face. Even if he had, Jake would certainly not have known that the man's baseball cap covered a shaved head and the many tattoos on his arms were concealed by the long-sleeved army jacket.

Feeling as if he had accomplished something, Jake went out the library door to his car. He didn't know that the man who'd been carefully following him all day had immediately stood from his chair in the library and gone over to the same computer.

Jake wasn't the only person who knew how to access browser history.

23

Richmond, Virginia

It was the New York motion to dismiss hearing being played out again, this time in Richmond, Virginia.

The veteran trial team, consisting of Deke, Michael, Carol, and Bernie, with Sarah providing invaluable assistance, gathered in Judge Eleanor Trackman's courtroom in Richmond. Dan Lawson had also flown down from New York to watch from the gallery. The team once again faced the powerhouse juggernaut of Bank Antriol's attorneys, led by George Mendel and Oliver Wrecker and the usual assortment of orcs in tow.

Standing in downtown Richmond, catty cornered from St. Paul's Episcopal Church, the United States District Court for the Eastern District of Virginia had an aesthetically pleasing façade with curved sides that, in some ways, reminded Deke of the ancient Colosseum in Rome. When he'd mentioned that to Michael, his associate had replied, "We're all gladiators in the courtroom, aren't we?"

From the get-go, Deke had a much better feeling about the proceedings. Judge Trackman listened to the arguments of both sides with intense concentration.

Then, when Deke had less than thirty minutes left to make his points, he said, "Judge, we believe the material we have already provided the court in our brief shows overwhelmingly that the defense's argument about JASTA having no application to banks is totally without merit. Three separate jurisdictions agree that it has a critically important application to cases like this. I won't spend any more time arguing that issue. Instead, I would like to spend my last bit of time showing you how all the other parts of this case fit together."

George Mendel rose to his feet. "Your Honor, anything beyond the simple question of whether or not JASTA applies here is quite irrelevant in this dismissal hearing!"

The judge's response was quick and edgy. "Mr. Mendel, I have already moved beyond that question in my mind, so, yes, I would like to know what to expect as this case moves forward."

Mendel was visibly shaken by the judge's response. It was clear that she had decided to deny the motion to dismiss. Anything else that his opposing counsel would be presenting was going to look like a slow motion truck collision for the defense team. He sat down without another word.

As Deke proceeded to take his time torturing Mendel with his words and presentation, the judge's brow creased several times, but especially when Deke ran through a PowerPoint-driven argument that showed an exceedingly simplified timeline. The judge could easily visualize how all the dots were connected. Deke used the presentation to display how the terrorist money was first received by the bank through specific deposits and then how that very money was the source of four specific roadside bombs that had left four of his clients permanently crippled or dead. The affidavits of forensics experts who had provided the detailed data for the PowerPoint were presented as well. To humanize the presentation, Deke used a video collage of Iraq and Afghanistan footage. It was as if EFPs had exploded in the courtroom itself. The sworn affidavits of Gold Star families and wounded veterans that Deke had selected were also extremely powerful. Finally, the preliminary evidence of the bank's wrongdoing was more than compelling.

Deke could feel the bloodsucking vampires at the other table shifting uncomfortably in their chairs. Even *they* knew that the fearful daylight was creeping upon them.

The judge called a brief recess when both sides were done, allowing time for the team to grab some lunch and cautiously congratulate each other on a fine presentation. "I think we did our best," Deke told them. "You heard the same thing I did from the judge already. I think we're okay, but this is an unpredictable business."

The recess, however, went longer than Judge Trackman had indicated. That was not a good sign.

"What do you think is keeping her?" Michael asked.

"Beats me," Deke said. "Have patience, my friend."

Michael was always amazed by Deke's ability to remain calm within a courtroom setting. If need be, his boss could be passionate and persuasive when he was "on stage," as it were, but behind the scenes he was always as cool as a Blues Brother.

Finally, the team was informed that they should return to the courtroom.

When both armies of attorneys were assembled, the judge entered the court.

"I have carefully gone over the materials presented by the plaintiffs and the defendants in this matter, and the reason for my delay in reconvening is that I wanted to read in detail the reasoning the DOJ gave for not criminally prosecuting the decision makers at Bank Antriol the first time they were caught engaging in their money laundering scheme. To say I am dismayed by the slap on the wrist the DOJ handed out is putting it mildly. To be frank, the FBI and all the entities of the DOJ involved with the handling of that settlement owe the American public an apology. It is an embarrassment."

Mendel rose to his feet. "Your honor, on behalf of my client, I need to state on the record that the prior conduct of the DOJ in that event has nothing at all to do with this case at hand, and—"

"Stop right there, counselor," the judge snapped. "Until we shine a light on what has been presented before me today, we can't be sure that the facts of this case don't directly tie into what transpired between the DOJ and Bank Antriol in that prior case. And let me be clear about something. I'll be looking at all possible connections. Mr. Deketomis, please prepare an order for my signature denying the motion to dismiss."

With that, the judge slammed her gavel and left the courtroom, visibly agitated.

Any experienced trial lawyer in the courtroom would clearly read the significance of the hammering the judge had just administered to both the DOJ and Bank Antriol's trial team. She was a skillful, and unusually clever, senior judge sending a clear message to the defense lawyers.

Negotiate and settle the claim before it gets any uglier than it already is.

* * *

Deke had a plan of action in place that he routinely used in cases where the defendants were starting off having to overcome the risks of a massive financial loss. The team referred to it as their "shock and awe" strategy. Based on what had just happened in the courtroom, he could visualize how well that strategy would play out in the Antriol case.

After congratulations were enthusiastically traded around the team, Deke called Gina back in Florida to set everything in motion. They had already drafted requests to send to Bank Antriol's lawyers. In terms of discovery, the veteran trial team wanted all of the bank's transaction data for the last fifteen years, as well as current data. The request would include all emails, all recorded notes that were created at staff meetings in every department of the bank, and two more type-written pages of disclosure requests drafted in a way that could possibly reveal bad conduct in events completely unrelated to the case at hand.

It was just the first minor shot across the defendant's bow.

Much of this information, which included the bank's SAR data meant to be audited at the AML unit in Plainsburg, was stored in the IronVault Document and Data Storage Center, located in Antioch, Tennessee. The IronVault facility was like a miniature Ft. Knox. The center's clients included not only high profile banks, but also government institutions and law enforcement agencies around the country. The security there was second to none, and it was heavily guarded. Since much of the data stored there was electronic, the center was filled with servers and data banks that were backed up by power generators in case of an electrical failure.

Drafts of subpoenas were already in place to get access to the data in the vault. Deke merely pulled the trigger for his highly efficient team in Florida to finalize and execute them, and they went out the same day as the hearing.

Deke and everyone on his team could already predict Mendel's only move—delay and obstruct the progress of discovery at every turn. Deke had seen the same scenario play out so many times that he had lost count. He welcomed the dishonesty and deceit that always seemed to flow from lawyers like Mendel, because he knew that the attorney would dig a deepening grave for his client at every unscrupulous turn. To lawyers like Mendel, there was no moral bottom when it came to generating billable hours, client be damned! There would be motions to quash subpoenas, failures to respond to interrogatories, and meritless objections to requests for admissions. One big defense focus would be creating motions to protect documents from any disclosure because of "confidential business strategies" and attempts to shield itself with "European privacy laws." When all that failed to succeed, the wholesale destruction of all smoking gun documents would begin.

24

Plainsburg, Kentucky

Jake could already smell the fried eggs and hash browns in the parking lot of the Kentucky Spoon diner, and his mouth immediately began to water. There was something about the cooking in this area of the country, including his home state of West Virginia, that he always regarded as special. Calories and an overabundance of fried fat were of no concern to him. It was comfort food, plain and simple.

He didn't spot Officer Sheila Denning when he walked in, so he grabbed an empty booth. He placed an order for coffee with the waitress and said that he was expecting a friend. Jake then looked at his phone and saw a message from Deke. The case was moving into discovery phase. Good news, but the missing part to fully building the case centered around Joel Hartbeck. Jake knew that a lot was resting on his shoulders to find Hartbeck, or at least figure out what the hell had happened to him.

Ten minutes passed before Sheila Denning came through the door. This time she was dressed in her uniform, and she carried an 8 x 12 envelope in her hand. She hustled toward the booth and sat across from him.

"Sorry I'm late."

"I just got here myself. Want some coffee?"

"Sure, but I'll get it to go. I don't have a lot of time, so I can't join you for breakfast. As you can see, I got called in for a shift today. Right now I'm out 'patrolling for parking tickets,' so I'd better not stay. The chief point blank asked me yesterday if I've been talking to any 'outsiders' about any of the department's business. I guess I need to be a little more careful."

"I don't want to get you in any trouble," Jake said. "If you'd rather meet somewhere less public..."

"No, no, we should be fine for a few minutes. You go ahead and order food."

The waitress came by again and was told about the coffee to go. She quickly fetched it, and Jake then ordered the breakfast special. When the waitress was out of earshot, Jake asked, "Anything new on the Janet Blanco murder?"

"I can't tell you much more. The chief and his doofus detective, Bostick, still insist that an illegal immigrant on drugs was the perp. And they're not doing much to *look* for that alleged illegal immigrant on drugs. As far as they're concerned, Janet's murder will be relegated to the cold case file. With prejudice."

"But I bet you have other ideas about the crime, right?"

"You bet I do," Sheila said. "Before I only suspected it, but now I'm convinced that she was killed by the MWs. I mean, come on, they left their creepy calling card of the four-nineteen date painted on the kitchen wall. Seriously, who else would do that? False flag, my ass. I still can't figure out *why* they would kill her, though, or why they would leave that stupid ass four-nineteen. Makes me think there *is* a link between this and your man who's missing—the same calling card was left in his hotel room! Unfortunately, my hands are tied in the case. Others in the department have made it very clear to me that *they're* in charge of the investigation, and I'm nothing more than a token charity case who should be thrilled to work with a flock of dodo birds."

Jake broke into one of his trademark loud laughs. "I understand. I guess, if you can, just keep your ear to the ground. You may pick up something."

"I plan on it." She handed over the envelope she had brought. "Here you go. I've made copies of everything we have on Joel Hartbeck. His arrest records going back twenty years, some tax returns that he had to submit for something at some point, some phone records ... but they're not very recent. Going back a few years, you'll see he was arrested for assault—a charge that was dropped—but he was picked up a few times for vagrancy and suspicion of distributing opioids. I think he was just a user, not a pusher. We know he was in rehab two or three times, but I guess it finally took, and I would suspect that he's clean now."

That news struck a nerve in Jake. He had experienced his own battles with that demon.

"Joel apparently also had some altercations with the MWs," Sheila said. "At a bar called Beggar's Ravine—"

"I know that place; I've been there."

"Right. Joel was a regular there for a while, according to the bartender. One night violence almost broke out between him and some MWs that came in drunk. You'll also see in the packet records a couple of 911 call logs that Joel made to the police regarding the MWs."

"What were the calls about?"

"Nothing, really. He just wanted to report them, as if we didn't know anything about them. 'Why are you allowing these right-wing Nazis to march in our streets? Why do you let them carry guns while they spew so much hate? There are children watching!' That kind of thing."

"Which, I imagine, your chief blew off as being rants of a deranged drug addict," Jake ventured.

"You got it."

Jake reached into his backpack and pulled out the sheets of paper he had printed at the library. "I might have a lead to find Joel. We know he liked to occasionally hide out in abandoned hunting cabins way out in the woods somewhere. I'm pretty sure he searched for and looked at these Craigslist ads on the dates indicated there at the top. Do you know where those places are?"

Sheila took them and studied the descriptions of the cabins. "They say to call the owner for directions. You don't want to do that?"

"I'd like to find them on my own. Joel might be squatting in one, trying to stay off the grid."

"Okay." She pointed at the pages one at a time. "From what it says, it sounds like this one is close to State Highway 1534. You'd have to explore the roads that splinter off of it on both sides, but 1534 isn't very long. Some of those roads might be paved, but likely not. The cabin is probably deep in the woods, up in the hills in the southeastern part of the state. Maybe close to an hour's drive from here. The other one … it says it's off of State Highway 190. Same thing—you'll have to find roads that shoot off from it. This one's a little closer, maybe a forty-five minute drive. It's still deep in lumberjack country. It could take you a day or two to go up and down 1534 or 190 to find those trails. It's going to take a lot of time and patience."

"I guess I've got some adventuring to do, then," Jake said, taking back the sheets.

"Just so you know," Sheila said, "the MWs like that area of the state, too. It's been said that their headquarters is deep in the woods. They take over those abandoned hunting cabins as well. They like to play soldier boy in those woods, practicing half-baked combat tactics and any number of things rednecks with low IQs might be interested in. There are likely *hundreds* of those old cabins scattered about. Some are still owned by people, and others are completely derelict and were left to rot a long time ago. Joel could very well have found one of those, too."

"Maybe I'll get lucky." Jake looked past Sheila's shoulder and muttered, "Shit. Your chief just walked in."

"Oh, Christ…" Sheila bowed her head, as if that would hide her; but of course, it didn't.

Chief Burt Wainwright strode over to their booth with his hands on the hips of his large frame. He spoke in a booming voice that everyone in the diner could hear.

"Officer Denning!"

"Yes, sir."

"What in the *hell* are you doing here? You are supposed to be out writing parking tickets!"

"I stopped in for some coffee to go, sir." She lifted her cup. "See?"

The man's face turned red. "You're sitting here talking to this Yankee investigator! Officer Denning, you need to get out of here *now* and stick to your job as a police officer. You are not to speak to this man or any other mutt investigators or lawyers who come sniffing around our business!"

Jake said, "Well, just to be clear, this Yankee mutt is from West Virginia and you can absolutely count on the fact that there will be more Yankee mutts on their way because … well, because we just love this part of the country."

The chief turned to Jake and growled, "Shut your goddamn face. You're not wanted in our town, so I suggest you get the hell out."

"Mr. Sheriff, you can count on the fact that that's probably not going to happen. As a matter of fact, as we speak, there are about half a dozen more mutt lawyers and mutt investigators that should be right here with me in your beautiful city within the hour."

Jake recognized that the sheriff believed this "mutt" was by himself. This could be a threat, but Jake also knew that the character standing before him would do what most cowards do—back down.

Wainwright's eyes looked as if they might pop out. "You. Are. Not. Welcome. *Here!*"

With awkward timing, the waitress brought Jake's food. "Um, breakfast special?"

"Right here, ma'am," Jake said. The woman set the plate on the table and, sensing trouble, quickly moved away. Jake picked up a fork and looked at Wainwright. "I'll just eat my breakfast and wait for the rest of my team. Join me. We can chat about your distinguished career in law enforcement."

There was a beat of silence, and then the chief lowered his upper body so that his face was close to Jake's. He whispered menacingly, "Stay here too long and you're gonna learn firsthand more than you want to know about me." The man then straightened and turned to Sheila. "Go on, Denning. Now!"

"Yes, sir." She slipped out of the booth and hurried toward the diner door.

Wainwright gave Jake one more grimace of disgust. Jake calmly thrust a bite of hash browns into his mouth and slowly chewed them, all the while keeping focus on the sorry excuse for a police chief. Finally, Wainwright followed his officer outside. Jake watched through the window as Sheila got in her patrol car and backed out before the chief could say anything else to her.

Jake hoped that she wouldn't be disciplined too badly, but he knew that Sheila Denning was a hell of a lot tougher than her rotund, redneck boss.

25

The following morning, Jake set off east in his rented Hyundai Elantra. The weather was perfect, and the scenery in that part of Kentucky was gorgeous. The forests were dense with yellow poplar, oak hickory, sugar maple, beech, and other varieties of trees that combined to create thick tracts of green and brown timberland. The terrain ascended into rolling hills that eventually morphed into the Appalachian Mountains. The pockets of civilization became more sporadic with little whistle-stop towns, coal mining communities, and rural agricultural dwellings.

Jake thought he would try State Highway 190 first. Perhaps he would get lucky. Besides, 190 went diagonally northeast from the bottom of the state alongside and through the Kentucky Ridge State Forest until it intersected with north-south US Route 25E, which, in turn, would take him down to an intersection with Highway 1534. Jake figured if he struck out on 190, he could then try 1534, which also went northeast, but on a more haphazard, twisty-turny course.

He started at the bottom of 190 and headed northeast, eyeing the sides of the two-lane highway as he went. Every once in a while, there was an unmarked road on the left or right side, and he took the time to turn and venture in that direction. If there were no cabins or if he came upon private property, he simply turned around and went back to 190. After an hour of driving, Jake realized that this could likely be a long and tedious process, just as Sheila had said.

He came across his first hunting cabin on a dirt road just past a tiny community called Chenoa. The place didn't appear to be in use and didn't match the library printouts. He stopped the car and got out to take a closer look. He saw no recent tire treads in the dirt at the side of the cabin where a vehicle might park. No one had been there in a long time. He moved on.

Next he found a cluster of cabins on a succession of paved roads off 190 near the area around Pine Mountain State Park, a resort that encompassed a hotel, a golf course, and a restaurant. Jake figured that these might be too close to civilization for Joel, but he had an excuse to stop there for lunch.

Jake eventually discovered the Craigslist Highway 190 cabin just east of Clear Creek Springs, a tiny hamlet at the center of several farms. It was up a paved road that wound around a sizable mountain. He had almost given up driving on the seemingly deserted path until a structure appeared. He recognized it from the Craigslist photo. After parking the Elantra, Jake got out and walked around the structure. There were signs of use, as trash bins outside appeared to be full. A sign out front indicated that the place was for rent, and the phone number matched the one on the Craigslist ad.

With careful consideration, Jake determined that this couldn't be where Joel had been hiding. It was too "commercial," if such a word could be said to describe such a no-frills abode without sewage facilities.

It was nearing four in the afternoon when Jake reached the intersection of 190 and Route 25E. Since Daylight Savings Time was in effect, he knew he had several more hours before darkness descended. Jake certainly didn't want to be traipsing down creepy unlit paths in the woods after dark, but he estimated that he had enough time to get down to Highway 1534 and explore it for three or four more hours before packing it in for the day.

As Sheila had guessed, Highway 1534 was extremely backwater, barely paved, and not quite wide enough for two vehicles side by side. Jake had to stop twice and pull over onto what constituted as a shoulder so that an oncoming pickup could pass.

Within two hours on 1534, he found more possibilities, but they were not viable candidates for Joel. Jake was becoming tired and hungry, so he allowed himself another hour before heading for the best route back to Plainsburg.

It was around six thirty in the evening when he hit pay dirt. He found the other Craigslist property on a dirt road off of 1534 in the middle of nowhere. Jake parked the Elantra in front of the old cabin and got out. This time there was no rental sign in front. The place looked empty, but he went to the door and knocked anyway. The door creaked open, unlocked and ajar. He stepped inside to find a discarded sleeping bag, an oil lamp, a fireplace with cinders in it, and a bit of trash. A bin held empty cans of beans and soup, and a few beer bottles. *Someone* had obviously been squatting here. Could it have been Joel? Jake wanted to believe it was so, but where was he now?

As he looked around, Jake picked up the sound of vehicles in the distance growing more pronounced. He peeked out the front door and at the dirt road leading off into the woods. Sure enough, a small caravan of pickup trucks and SUVs was headed his way.

Not good.

There was no way he could jump into the rented Elantra and high-tail it out of there, because that was the only road. It was probably best to hide somewhere and wait to see who was paying a visit to the cabin.

Jake ran out the back door. A footworn path led to an outhouse some thirty yards into the trees. Figuring that the visitors might need to use that facility, he darted into the brush on the side of the cabin. There, he hid behind a large tree, but he could still see the structure's front. Two pickup trucks and two SUVs pulled up to the cabin and stopped. All of the trucks were adorned with Confederate flag decals and an assortment of other insignia that screamed out a high level of hate.

"Who's heeeere?" one of the men sing-called when he got out of a pickup. "Anyone hooooome?"

"Here kitty, kitty, kitty!" another one called.

A guy with a shaved head examined the Elantra. "This is the rental car, all right. Where is he?"

They were all dressed in fatigues and were covered in tattoos that Jake knew signified every iteration of white supremacy. The men were also equipped with their obligatory props—long rifles, AR-15s, and the like. Several also had pistols both on their belts and in shoulder holsters.

Two went into the cabin, found no one there, and returned. As they approached the rest of the group, Jake could see bright 4/19 patches on the left shoulders of their road worn biker vests.

A lump formed in Jake's throat. The cabin was a hideout of the MWs.

"Check the outhouse," Shaved Head commanded. Two of them ran behind the cabin for a look-see.

In the meantime, Shaved Head opened the Elantra's door and peered inside. Jake hadn't bothered to lock it. Had he left anything inside? Likely only the Craigslist printouts. The material Sheila had given him was back at his hotel. Luckily, there was nothing in the car that would identify him, although it seemed as if they already knew who he was.

"Hey, Chad," called one of the outhouse searchers. "There's no one back here!"

Shaved Head's name was Chad. Good to know.

The rest of the MWs—eight in all—gathered in front of the cabin. Chad addressed them. "First we take care of his car. Then we spread out and look for him. He can't have gone far. He wouldn't leave his rental here." With that, Chad drew a handgun from a holster at his waist, stepped back, and pointed the weapon at the car. The others followed suit. Some aimed handguns, while others pointed their long rifles.

Chad counted them down. "One ... two ... three!"

The group unleashed a tremendous tsunami of firepower onto the Elantra, blowing out the tires, windows, and perforating the body with a hundred holes. The cacophony was so loud that Jake thought it could be heard miles away. Unfortunately, the likelihood of a single soul present within that range was slim.

The men laughed and hooted in an almost childlike way amidst the smoke and strong smell of cordite.

"Sure hope he took out the optional coverage!"

More guffaws.

"Okay," Chad said. "Spread out and find that smartass bastard."

Time to leave.

Jake took off running into the dark forest. He knew he wouldn't survive if they caught him. He was a tough guy, but not against eight of them.

He was immediately aware that this wouldn't be easy. It was rough going through the brush, and the tops of the trees blocked the waning sunlight. Not good at all.

He dug out his cell phone and turned on the flashlight. It helped illuminate the way in front of him. It would be a disaster if he tripped over something, fell into a hole, or sprained his ankle with a misstep.

Jake heard them calling for their prey behind him. They were confident. He kept running and dodging trees, but he invariably scraped his arms on sharp bark and brush. Something jagged ripped his jeans at the knee.

What am I doing? he thought. *I'm going to kill myself out here.*

The last thing he needed was to get lost in the woods after dark.

Jake stopped running and leaned against a tree to catch his breath. He could still hear the MWs in the distance calling to each other. Stalking him and making him run for his life seemed to be a game for the gang of sick pricks that were after him.

Running is no good. What can I do? I wish I'd brought my damned gun so I could fire a few random shots myself!

Jake scanned the area around him and ultimately gazed at the branches above. The foliage was thick up there. Would it serve as a hiding place?

He began to climb. Getting atop the first branch at the height of his head was no problem. The next one up was a little trickier, but he made it. One more branch, and he was able to nestle into the thick leaves. He positioned himself so that he could rest his legs over two branches and lean his back against the trunk. For support, he held onto two smaller stems at his sides. This would do, as long as the MWs didn't look up. Even so, it was now dark enough that his body might just blend in with the tree limbs.

Two minutes later, a couple of MWs came uncomfortably close.

"I can't see a damn thing! He ain't here."

"Where is he, then?"

"I'm going back. It's too dark!"

"Wuss."

They argued with each other, but eventually they did turn around and head back to the cabin. Jake waited a good thirty minutes before attempting to move because the MWs never got into their vehicles to leave. He would have heard the engines. The gang was probably going to crash in the cabin for the night.

When he felt that the forest was quiet enough, Jake slowly and silently descended to the ground. He pulled out his phone again.

Of COURSE there is no reception here!

At least he had plenty of battery power that would last a few hours. He turned on the flashlight again and began walking in a direction that he *thought* might lead him to the dirt road but far enough away from the cabin to avoid the MWs.

Another hour passed and he was still trudging through the forest. The sun had long disappeared, not that it had made much difference before. Now everything was totally lost in darkness. No moonlight or star shine filtered through the tops of the trees. All Jake had to guide him was the phone.

It was nearly eleven o'clock when the trees finally began to thin out. He came out of the woods onto a narrow paved road. He had somehow bypassed the dirt road that led to the cabin and was back on Highway 1534! Jake checked his cell phone coverage again and was disappointed to find that there was still no service. His sense of direction told him that to go right would likely take him toward the dirt road, the cabin, and the MWs. Going left would take him, eventually, to Route 25E, which had heavier traffic.

He was exhausted, but he set out toward the highway. Not a single automobile passed him, and only a half moon in the sky was his traveling companion.

26

Spanish Trace, Florida

Two weeks later, the veteran trial team remained busy with the continuation of recorded video statements of Gold Star families and injured veterans, as well as the back-and-forth process of filing motions and subpoenas to counteract the strong resistance of Bank Antriol's attorneys.

Jake Rutledge was back in Florida, too, after running for his life in the Kentucky forest. On the night that he had set out hiking along Highway 1534, he was lucky not to have encountered any more MWs. He had reached US Route 25E around one in the morning and then continued south toward Middlesboro, occasionally passing small, isolated homes or trailers. He had considered knocking on a door and asking for help, but he figured that might not be a good idea after midnight in that part of the country. Someone could have shot first and asked questions later.

Then, just as the battery on his cell phone was at 11 percent capacity, signal bars appeared at the top of the screen. He immediately phoned Michael, waking him up in Florida.

"Jake? What the ... are you okay?"

"Pretty wild few days, pal," Jake said. "Right now I don't have much juice left on my phone. I have to talk fast." He gave a brief rundown of what had occurred and that he was stranded without a car on a lonely, dark, two-lane road. Together, they figured out where on the map Jake was and how far he had to walk to reach an all-night gas station. After hanging up and trekking for another hour, Jake had made it to a combination truck stop-convenience store and hitched a ride to Plainsburg with an agreeable trucker.

An hour and a half later, Jake was back at his hotel. He would let Bergman-Deketomis worry about the claim for the rental car. Having escaped with his life, all he wanted to do was to get the hell out of Kentucky.

The debriefing back in Florida had been depressing. The mystery now was why the MWs appeared to have been involved in the AML unit's business, and why and how they had tracked Jake to the cabin. It meant that the MWs had trained their sights on the veteran trial team for whatever reason. Jake had been in their crosshairs that night. How they had known he was looking for cabins, though, was a big concern. Jake did believe that the structure he had found was recently a hideout for Joel Hartbeck.

Now, Michael Carey sat at his desk reviewing an index of documents that had been shared with Deke's team. The number of documents to be reviewed by the firm would be in the millions. Antriol's strategy would be to give the appearance of complying with all of Deke's discovery requests by providing gigabytes of unusable and mostly manufactured garbage designed to overwhelm the Deketomis team. At the end of the day, Michael knew that the gold mine of critically important discovery material would be found in two locations. The StoneWall files and the IronVault facility were where all the proverbial bodies were buried. Michael's strategy would be to allow Antriol to hang themselves by swearing to the court that every bit of relevant discovery information had been provided to the Deketomis team, when in fact it hadn't been. After Antriol's lawyers had inevitably perjured themselves in federal court, Michael would then issue a subpoena for all information from StoneWall and the IronVault. It was a checkmate move that would likely end with huge money sanctions against the opposition. More importantly, it would justifiably turn the judge against Antriol and their corrupt lawyers for the rest of their time in front of her.

There was a knock on his door. "Come in!" he called.

Diana appeared and said, "I have a FedEx envelope for you. It came from Tennessee."

"Tennessee?" He took the envelope and examined it. No name, just the address of a FedEx unit in Tazewell, a small town not far over the border from Kentucky. He pulled off the tab on the envelope and brought out … Joel's affidavit.

"What the…?" He quickly flipped through the pages. "Oh my *God*, Diana, this is Joel's complete, corrected affidavit. And it's *signed* and *notarized*." He held it up and showed it to her. "Joel's alive!"

"That's wonderful news!"

Michael jumped up and ran down the hall to Deke's office. He didn't bother knocking; he just burst in to find Deke on the phone. The boss gave him a perturbed look and held up a finger to indicate *one minute, please*. Michael thrust the document in Deke's face and pointed to the notary seal.

Deke's eyes widened, and he said into the phone, "Teri, I have to call you back!" He hung up and grabbed the affidavit. "Where did this come from?"

"From a FedEx shop in Tennessee. Joel's alive, Deke!"

"This is fantastic!" He thumbed through the several pages. "It looks to be in order. Was there a note or anything?"

Michael still held the envelope in his other hand. "I don't know…" He looked inside and, sure enough, there was a piece of FedEx stationery with handwritten scribbles on it. "It says, 'Michael, my brother—I will call you soon! Leave me a message and let me know you got this!' There's a new phone number here. I'd better give him a call. Where the hell has he been all this time?"

"I suppose he's going to tell you," Deke said.

Michael grinned. "Deke, I have been thinking about the strategy we should use in the depositions we set. Ordinarily I would never want to build a depo around an affidavit, but what I like most about this one from Joel, a former employee of the company, is that it becomes a perfect vehicle. I have no doubts about the details he laid out. I am convinced they are credible. Every Antriol witness we depose is going to perjure themselves and deny every part of that affidavit. When they do that, it should get really ugly when we show them documents from StoneWall and the IronVault that, I'm guessing, establish exactly what Joel has in his affidavit. At this point, the Antriol team doesn't seem to be aware of the fact that we even know about the IronVault. What do you think?"

"I think most of the time in this business, Michael, we plan and God ends up laughing at all those plans. But on any given day, with a few breaks, every now and then it comes together. That's all you need here. A few breaks and we are going to have more fun than a monkey in a banana tree. Nice work so far, Michael. It only gets better from here."

Michael knew it was always Deke's way to stay positive in front of his team. But even in the short time he had been lawyering, he knew that monkeys in banana trees were usually far from the reality of handling a case against players like Bank Antriol.

27

New York, New York

Dan Lawson was frustrated.

He and his staff were going through the transaction data that the NYDFS had received from Bank Antriol. The subpoenas from his institution had produced a truckload of material that was going to take weeks, if not months, to examine. The bank had dumped the transaction data in a way that made it feel like it had been loaded into a digital blender and puréed. Dan's team was trying to reorganize the data so that it could be chronologically mapped and examined for signs that certain customers or bank employees were using a method to circumvent the AML review process. About 99 percent of the time the data was so disjointed that it appeared benign; but occasionally, the team would find a transaction with customer information seemingly omitted or altered. One common thread found so far was that the signoffs on the AML team's review work was directed through the bank's upper management in New York. Interestingly, two names of bank personnel were appearing more frequently than most—executive vice presidents Blake Dullea and Karl Maher. The biographies supplied by the Bergman-Deketomis team indicated a possible red flag on Maher. He had family in Egypt and was half Egyptian, but that certainly didn't mean the guy was a terrorist. Like most wayward bankers, he was likely only in it for the money. What was striking, though, was that both Dullea and Maher were in charge of the AML unit that was supposed to be the watchdog.

Dan continued his work with the transaction data until the mail clerk came by the office to deliver the daily batch. "You have a package, Dan," the man said. He placed it along with the regular mail in Dan's inbox on his desk. Dan thanked him and picked up the parcel. It was the size of a ream of copy paper and just as heavy. He guessed that it was indeed full of paper. There was no return address, but it was clearly labeled to go directly to Dan and was marked PERSONAL.

He used a letter opener to slit the end, and, sure enough, the box contained a big stack of documents. An anonymous, typed note on plain paper on the top was signed, "A Friend."

Dan read the letter twice and then immediately called Deke.

* * *

Spanish Trace, Florida

The core veteran trial team gathered in the conference room at Deke's request—Michael, Carol, Gina, Jake, and Sarah—and they could see that the boss was excited about something.

"What's going on, Deke?" Michael asked. "You sent up a flare."

"I did, and you'll see," Deke answered. "I need to get our friend Dan Lawson back on the phone. He called me a few minutes ago with some news, and I want you guys to hear it from him." He dialed the NYDFS and placed the conference room phone on speaker when Dan answered.

Dan said, "Hi everyone. I just received an anonymous package with a cover letter. I'm going to read it to you. 'Dear Mr. Lawson. My name is not important but what I know certainly is. I have read about your investigation into Bank Antriol and the suspicions of reverse money laundering, as well as about the lawsuit that the firm in Florida is pursuing on behalf of Gold Star families and injured veterans. I have a brother who was severely maimed by a roadside bomb in Iraq in 2009. He is unfortunately in constant care and is mentally and physically incapacitated. I mention this so that you might understand my motivation here. I am a former employee of an accounting firm called StoneWall CPAs. They are auditors who were hired by Bank Antriol to examine the wire transfer data that you and the Florida firm are concerned about. When I was working for StoneWall, I became aware that Bank Antriol became a client several years earlier. I was in the division handling their material. Because I had a vested interest in the case because of my brother, I began compiling a file of documents that I found to be highly irregular. One of these is an internal memorandum from the president of StoneWall, Charles Torn. It is addressed to the auditing staff in charge of the Bank Antriol account. You will see that it outlines financial and promotion incentives to the auditors to clear as many of the transactions as possible. Furthermore, it instructs the auditors to *continue to ignore* what would normally constitute a red flag Suspicious Activity Report. The use of the word *continue* prompted me to search our archives and files that existed prior to my joining StoneWall, and I found the company's work with Antriol around the time that the bank agreed to a settlement with the Department of Justice. From what I found it became egregiously apparent that StoneWall was taking orders from the bank to whitewash the audit reports so that the DOJ would merely administer a slap on the wrist to the bank. StoneWall was paid handsomely. I herewith enclose copies of all the pertinent documents, including emails and in-house memos, that back up my assertion. I hope you will find it useful. Signed, a friend.'"

Michael let out a low whistle. Carol and Sarah simultaneously said, "Wow."

"Dan," Deke said, "this is indispensable ammunition for us. It sounds like StoneWall is doing exactly what Antriol tells them to do. I already have a deposition scheduled for Bank Antriol's president, as well as for his VPs. I think what we do first is fire out a few discovery requests that ask for the exact material that is contained in that new package you just got. They will deny any of it ever existed, and the first time we will disclose it is during the deposition of this Charles Torn character at StoneWall. We will also target the emails and communications between Antriol and StoneWall to see just how 'independent' the auditor is being with its work."

"I'll copy all of this material and FedEx it down to you today," Dan declared.

"I'll bet you a Chinese food lunch that it helped Antriol cherry-pick the data sample submitted to the DOJ that was used to negotiate the shamelessly low settlement penalty, and probably even approved the whole AML operation so that the DOJ agreed to it. I don't know how often you've received whistleblower material like you just described to us, but I can tell you it has only happened once with me in my thirty-plus years of lawyering. And here's the good news—it ended well."

* * *

New York, New York

Blake Dullea and Karl Maher were the last to arrive. When they were seated, Nigel Beech called to order the meeting with Bank Antriol's officers. The executive vice presidents, the chief financial officer, the chief audit officer, the head of human resources, and others were present.

Beech held up a document. "My summons to a deposition from the Deketomis law firm." He nodded at Dullea and Maher. "I understand you two received summonses, as well."

Dullea nodded. "Yes, sir."

"Anyone else?" Nearly everyone at the table raised hands. "Ah, I see. They've also targeted our accounting firm of StoneWall CPAs. Charles Torn, whom some of you know, has received a summons, as well as a few of his people. I'm in constant contact with our attorneys for their supposed expert guidance on these depositions. As you might expect, I'm at the point of doubting much of what they have to say these days. Nevertheless, you will soon be contacted by someone at Mendel, Wrecker, and Platt to discuss your options. If it turns out we have to do these depos, then, from what I've been told, our attorneys will bring in a team of media experts to coach us in how we should handle ourselves in the way we testify. Lead counsel George Mendel insists that this Florida law firm is on a fishing expedition. It's what 'discovery' is all about—fishing, meaningless fishing, according to him! We shall soon see."

"I'm not worried," Dullea interjected.

Beech shot his younger colleague an angry glance. "Well, that should make us all feel better, Mr. Dullea, the fact that you are not worried." Beech's level of sarcasm was palpable, and Blake didn't appreciate it. Next would come the lecture.

"What is it that you don't seem to grasp here, Mr. Dullea? The bank is in a legal vice. We're being squeezed on two sides. One side is Mr. celebrity lawyer Nick Deketomis and his law firm. The other side is Dan Lawson and the New York Department of Financial Services. It's clear that they're working together. These are serious people obviously undertaking what they believe is a serious case. The NYDFS has the power to pull the bank's license to operate. Does everyone in the room understand what that might mean?"

"It means we could lose our jobs," Karl Maher said.

"Karl, if these people succeed in prosecuting the bank and extracting a settlement, that's one thing, but if the case moves into criminal liability—which I understand is improbable but not *impossible*—then the *best case* scenario is that you will lose your job. Am I making myself clear enough for you? Who among you wants to go to jail? Perhaps some of you in this room know more than what you are sharing with me? I certainly hope that is not the case. Notwithstanding my suspicions and concerns, we have to be diligent and prepared."

"Yes, sir, we will be ready," Karl said with feigned enthusiasm.

Beech took a deep breath and paused to gather his thoughts. Finally, he said, "I, for one, plan to fully comply with the summons. Even if George Mendel can get me out of it, I personally want to be deposed. I have nothing to hide. Besides, and this may be news to some of you, I had planned to retire at the end of this year anyway. I would like to go out with a clear conscience. Some of you know I'm a man of faith and have strong moral convictions. I didn't rise in my career to this position without having these virtues. I plan to tell the truth; at least, what I know the truth to be. I suggest you all do the same."

Blake leaned forward. "Sir, with all due respect, I feel—" He looked around at his colleagues. "I think we *all* feel that you might be taking the wrong approach. This action against us is frivolous and without merit. In the conversations I've had with our attorneys, they stress again and again that we should be resisting as strongly as we can."

Karl spoke. "We are all honest here, sir. We have the utmost respect for the integrity of the bank. We all need to have a united front and fight these ridiculous charges together. There doesn't seem to be any reason to fall on our swords based on the material I've reviewed."

Beech responded, "I didn't imply that the bank doesn't have integrity. In fact, I want to nip these accusations in the bud by showing the opposition that we are not only complying, but that we are actually making changes in the way we do things." He looked at Blake and Karl. "The sore spot in all this is that AML unit in Kentucky. You two need to clean house. I want to see a new, improved plan of implementation of procedure at the AML unit by the end of the week. I'm going to have this same talk with Mr. Torn at StoneWall. I want to show Mr. Deketomis and Mr. Lawson that Bank Antriol was never guilty of anything we're being accused of, but also that we are putting new systems in place to go even further in complying with the settlement agreement with the DOJ. Am I making myself clear?"

All the VPs looked at Blake and Karl. It was obvious who was *supposed* to make the acknowledgment.

"Yes, sir," Blake finally answered.

28

Harwood, Maryland

Sandro Savoldelli enjoyed working nights.

As a truck driver who worked for a lumber company, he could manage his own hours with the only big requirement being that he deliver the wood on time to the various hardware stores around the country. Seeing that he was behind the wheel of a heavy Kenworth T800 five-axle logging rig with a Cummins X15 565 horsepower engine, driving at night was much less stressful than the opposite shift. As long as his destination, be it a warehouse owned by a mom and pop shop or a big box store like Loews or Home Depot, could accept deliveries at night, then Sandro much preferred performing the task between the hours of midnight and five in the morning.

At nearly two o'clock, he pulled off of Highway 214 north of Harwood, Maryland, and entered what appeared to be a two-lane country road. This was in the section of the state that was east of DC and west of the Chesapeake Bay. The closer one got to the bay, the more rural the landscape surprisingly became. Homes in that area had large spreads of land and it was dense with forest. And, at that time of night, not a soul was around. No other cars or trucks were on the road and in the way. He would arrive at the warehouse in Harwood in thirty minutes. The unloading would take a couple of hours. After that, he planned to go to the motel he had booked, set himself up with a bottle of wine that was in a bag in the truck cabin, and not worry about food until that afternoon.

The truck entered a three-way intersection of country roads. Sandro had to quickly think and remember to pull the wheel to the left at this fork to continue toward Harwood.

In that same second, he was hit with a thousand sledgehammers.

The truck had been suddenly launched airborne by a powerful blast from the center of a thunderclap. An intense heat and a blinding flash of yellow and orange light slashed through the cab and whooshed across his body, singing the hairs of his exposed skin, and slamming his head hard against the driver's side window ... and then there was blackness.

When he opened his eyes, he felt warm asphalt beneath him and he was lying close to something that was *very hot*. Confused and disoriented, he pushed himself off the ground and felt serious pain in his left leg. His neck and face seared with pain and he slapped at it instinctually to extinguish the flames his facial nerves told him were there. There were none, but his face and head felt tacky. The blurriness in his vision began to clear, his right eye able to open only partially because the lids stuck together each time he blinked.

As the night wind moved the smoke up and away, he could see that his truck was upside down in a field beside the road. It was engulfed in fire. Timber and burning truck tires littered the road and rolled, fortunately in a direction away from where Sandro had miraculously ended up outside the cab. He was immediately overwhelmed with the sense to move away from the growing inferno and began crab-crawling backwards away from the inferno.

What the hell happened?

He knew he hadn't hit anything. There hadn't been any other vehicles on the road. He remembered that much.

The shock of the incomprehensible trauma that had just occurred caused Sandro's strength to fail him. He stopped moving some twenty yards from the burning truck and dropped flat again. As his eyes fluttered closed and the cloak of unconsciousness buried him, he thought he saw the taillights of a truck in the distance moving away from the wreckage.

* * *

Sandro Savoldelli had been rushed to the nearest hospital, where the emergency room doctors diagnosed him with a life-threatening brain bleed and a left leg that had been mangled so badly that amputation would likely be inevitable.

The local police were bewildered. What at first appeared to be a terrible accident on a lonely road in the middle of the night became something far more sinister. As firefighters secured the scene and finally extinguished the flames, it was determined that a massive explosion had occurred, and it was powerful enough to launch an eighty-five thousand pound trucking rig fifty yards through the air and into a field.

The first theory on the scene was that the truck had surely been carrying C4 or nitroglycerine.

Once daylight cast a clearer picture on the scene, investigators ruled out any notion that the truck had been carrying explosives. Remnants of explosive materials and small fragments of electronics were found at the side of the intersection of the three country roads. A large tree had fallen, lifted from its root system. What remained of its trunk in the ground revealed evidence that told a story.

Because a United States senator lived some twenty miles from the intersection, the FBI was called in for an opinion. Arson and ordnance experts examined the remains of the device and the truck itself. After three days of forensics study, the FBI agents made a startling announcement.

The truck had been hit by a bomb planted on the side of the tree. The electronic fragments revealed that the bomb had been triggered by a cheap disposable cell phone. The timing of the blast, on an empty roadway at night, suggested that the perpetrators had to have been within eyesight of the scene.

The most obvious questions that needed answers began with whether or not it was a terrorist act. If so, why would it be in the middle of the night on a lonely country road where fatalities would have been at a ridiculous minimum? It wouldn't have been much of an attack. Had something gone wrong? Had the bombers installed the device with its intended use for a different day and time? Had they accidentally triggered it prematurely? And, given the remote location, for what purpose had the bomb been implemented? It became quickly clear that the truck, the payload, and its driver, Mr. Savoldelli, other than being in the wrong place at the wrong time, were not tied to anything that would warrant being targeted.

Most of the investigators were stumped.

FBI Special Agent Kirk Turkel, however, had a theory.

A veteran of the Iraq War, he recognized the components and techniques as the same used in IEDs in the Middle East. With no motive for the attack and its random location, he knew this bomb was likely a trial run.

29

New York, New York

Blake Dullea was first in line for a deposition conducted by the veteran trial team. Deke had wanted to get Nigel Beech in the hot seat first, but scheduling conflicts pushed the Antriol president's appearance out several days.

The team had arrived in New York the day prior to Dullea's depo and once again camped at the Hotel Roxy downtown. Michael had almost stayed behind in Florida. He had not yet heard from Joel, despite receiving the notarized affidavit and the note promising that his veteran colleague would soon get in touch. Michael had left several messages on the voicemail of the new phone number that Joel had provided, but so far there had been no response. He was becoming concerned about his old friend once again.

He joined Carol, Bernie, and Sarah in Deke's suite to talk strategy and make sure all of their ducks were in a row. The deposition was scheduled to take place the following morning at the law offices of Mendel, Wrecker, and Platt, which was located in the Wall Street area of lower Manhattan. Deke was counting on what usually occurred at depos of low to mid-level management witnesses—the lead counsel top dogs rarely appeared. Instead, they would typically send lower-level partners or associates with marching orders to "protect" the witness with a senseless barrage of meaningless objections and arguments.

"Well, I think we are as ready as we possibly can be, Deke," Sarah observed. "It is pretty much shock and awe time at Mendel, Wrecker, and Platt."

Deke smiled at that. This was because he never took the traditional kind of depositions where actual questions were asked. The "shock and awe" method immediately began with an attack centering around the hottest and ugliest documents that had been uncovered prior to the depo. Typically thirty to fifty of the most damning emails, memos, and text messages were displayed on an eight by eight foot video screen, one by one, for hours. Simultaneously, Deke would both humiliate and put the witness in an impossible position of explaining what was plastered across the screen. In all likelihood, the young corporate lawyer there had never seen these carefully chosen documents prior to the depo, and their efforts to defend the indefensible simply made what was happening in the videotaped questioning look even worse.

"Bernie, has our tech team completely set up?" Deke asked.

"Locked and loaded," the Gold Star Plus attorney answered with a grin.

Bernie was referring to four high-quality video cameras and a sophisticated computer stack that retrieved and displayed select documents on a screen in seconds on demand.

Carol held up the morning's *New York Times*. "Y'all see the news out of Maryland?"

They had all seen coverage of the bombing incident the previous morning on CNN, and now, forty-eight hours after the event, the major newspapers featured pieces that were lacking in detail. The *Times* hadn't bothered to place their article on the front page, but rather it had been relegated to a brief mention on page three. The headline was vague: ROADSIDE BOMB DESTROYS LUMBER TRUCK.

"We don't really know much about it, do we?" Michael asked. "The media doesn't either. What we do know is that a roadside bomb like the one described is way far from an everyday occurrence in the US. Terror comes in many forms on our shores, but rarely anything like what I saw every day in the Middle East."

Deke rubbed his chin. "I don't see anything here that leads me to believe that the bombing is in any way related to our case."

"I'm not ready to make that conclusion, either," Michael said.

"Me neither," Carol echoed. "However, you know I have my tentacles in a lot of places. Between us, Sarah and I have a dozen contacts at the FBI. We'll start making calls today and see what surfaces."

"If you can, find out what components were in the bomb," Michael suggested. "And where they might have come from. That will tell us a lot."

"The FBI plays it close to the vest, as you know," Carol said. "Sometimes it takes an excavator to weed just a tiny morsel of information out of them. But I'll do what I can."

Deke said, "We know if anyone can make a federal agent reveal trade secrets, it's you, Carol."

"Ve have vays to make zem talk!" she said with an exaggerated accent.

"Michael, what was the name of that manufacturing company that Joel Hartbeck talks about in his affidavit?" Deke asked.

"SeedDotz."

"How big are they?"

Michael went to his laptop to retrieve his notes. "Surprisingly not that big. They do have four subsidiaries overseas. One in Germany, one in Turkey, and one in China. Joel didn't mention this one, but there's also a SeedDotz affiliate in Saudi Arabia. It doesn't use the SeedDotz name, but it's owned by them."

"And they manufacture materials that could be used to make EFPs?"

"They export machine tools like pneumatic presses and lathes to companies they do business with—and some of them are on the DOJ-sanctioned list. They're the ones that use the tools and have the capability of manufacturing components that *could* be used for bombs. They could also be used for a number of other things, too." Michael shrugged.

"Could SeedDotz make bombs if they had someone there who knows how to do it?"

"Anyone with the know-how can get the materials needed, like copper plates and pipes, but they'd also need highly explosive material, too. I seriously doubt SeedDotz is making bombs, though."

"And where is the US headquarters of SeedDotz?"

Michael glanced at his notes. "Hmm. West Virginia. It's a bit of a leap I'm making here, but you know what? Geographically, that's awfully close to Maryland."

* * *

Long Island, New York

On the morning of Blake Dullea's deposition, Nigel Beech strode from his palatial Woodsburgh mansion and, nodding to the driver holding the door, settled into his chauffeured bespoke Rolls Royce Phantom Oribe to travel into the city.

Woodsburgh, a village in the town of Hempstead, Long Island, is generally considered one of the wealthiest of the twenty-two villages and thirty-eight hamlets that comprise Hempstead, which lies in Nassau County. The home where Nigel Beech and his wife lived stood on four acres of spectacularly landscaped grounds with lush gardens. The traditional Georgian house, built in 1912, contained eight large bedrooms, a gym, library, office space, a walk-in vault, and a ballroom.

If Beech had wanted, he could have easily taken the train to Manhattan from the nearby Woodmere Long Island Rail Road station. The bank also had a fleet of three helicopters from which he could choose. But Frederick, his English chauffeur, was always on hand to drive Beech to work every morning and bring him back home at the end of the day. Never mind that it took a bit longer with the usual traffic to drive from Woodsburgh to the Bank Antriol building on Wall Street than it did to ride the train to Penn Station, where a different driver would be waiting to deliver Beech to the bank.

The normal route to the city, via the Belt Parkway that ran to Kennedy Airport and around the southern bulb of Brooklyn, competed with the sometimes better-paced alternate course via the Long Island Expressway, which went up to Queens and then west to the FDR Drive for the leg south to the tip of the island. Frederick thought either way was horrendous during rush hour. On this particular morning, he checked the GPS and determined that traffic was lighter going via the Belt. The first part of the route, though, was the same. The Rolls would leave the Beech home, travel north through Woodsburgh, and get on Rockaway Boulevard.

Contrary to his driver's feelings about the commute, Beech didn't mind the ride and used the time in the Rolls to catch up on work, read the *Wall Street Journal* and *New York Times*, or make phone calls. It was his "alone time," and he relished it.

He was well aware that this was the morning of Blake Dullea's deposition. Beech had never liked Dullea or his shadow, Karl Maher. There was something way too smug and self-promoting about those two, and he should never have allowed them to be in charge of the AML unit in Kentucky that was causing all the trouble. It would be interesting to see what the lawyers from Florida came up with, and how Dullea would answer what would certainly be intense questioning.

The Rolls soon entered the stretch of Rockaway Boulevard that was four lanes with a concrete median down the middle. Trees and brush surrounded both sides of the road, giving the false impression that the city had disappeared and the boulevard was in the country. Traffic was uncharacteristically light. Frederick, a man of few words, concentrated on his driving; but he did announce to Beech that they would probably reach the office fifteen minutes earlier than usual.

As soon as Frederick had spoken those words, however, the Rolls Royce was slammed by a force so powerful that the automobile shattered into three sections and catapulted over the concrete median and into the oncoming lane. The massive twelve-cylinder engine block from the Rolls was turned into a seven-hundred-pound missile, slicing through the concrete barrier and sending engine parts and rock through windows and doors of the oncoming vehicles on the other side. Flame and debris showered the boulevard as black smoke rapidly swelled to the size of a building. Other vehicles on the road in front and behind the Rolls were also hit, and some were thrown a distance of thirty yards. Horns blared and people screamed and cried in anguish. Death and destruction had stomped on this little piece of civilization in an instant.

The first emergency crews that arrived on the scene were instantly overwhelmed by a tableau of carnage. It was as if a forty-yard flaming tornado had briefly touched down and gouged a scar across the roadway. The cries of the dying and maimed flittered through the smoke. As the seconds passed, the distant sounds of sirens floated above the scene, but to those there and still able to hear, the wails did not approach quickly enough.

After hours of cleanup, evacuation, and halted traffic both ways, it became clear that the bomb had instantly killed Frederick, whose identity was confirmed by the three remaining teeth that had managed to stay in the clump of flesh that had once been his head. Nigel Beech was found alive in the back third of the Rolls wreckage, gravely wounded. There were sixteen other fatalities that day, including four children.

The second roadside bomb had hit a bullseye.

30

New York, New York

As Nigel Beech's Rolls Royce left his home in Woodsburgh, a large conference room at the law offices of Mendel, Wrecker, and Platt had been transformed into what appeared to be a Hollywood studio set. Four cameras on tripods were set up—one focused on the witness, one directed at the plaintiff's questioning attorney, one aimed at the defense team, and one pointed at the TV screen upon which images would be shown.

Representing Blake Dullea of Bank Antriol were Lisbeth Hawkinson and Griffin Aaronson, two senior associate attorneys who sat with no less than two junior associates and four paralegals, plus a couple of law clerks. Each of them was charging Bank Antriol thousands of dollars in billable hours.

On the side of the plaintiffs were, of course, Deke Deketomis, plus Michael Carey, Carol Morris, Bernie Serling, and Sarah Mercer. Dan Lawson was present to observe. Deke had brought four law clerks from the office to run the cameras and recording equipment.

The stenographer sat directly beside the witness with headphones and a computer screen.

Blake Dullea was sworn in right on time. Deke began. "Would you please state your name for the record?"

"Blake Dullea."

With that out of the way, the shock and awe began.

"Mr. Dullea, I call your attention to the video screen. Is this your signature?"

The image was that of an elaborate signature made with a pen. It could be made out to read "Blake Dllll."

"That appears to be my signature," Blake answered.

The image changed to another signature. "Would you say that this is your signature as well?"

The second picture was almost identical. "Yes," Blake said.

"Finally, please identify the signature on this third document."

Another photo appeared with the same handwriting.

"They're all my signatures."

Lisbeth Hawkinson spoke. "Objection. Relevancy."

Deke continued as if the young lawyer was not even in the room. He read out several document numbers and instructed his tech specialist to display them on the screen. "Please pull back and show the entire documents upon which Mr. Dullea's signatures appear." The magic of technology beautifully displayed images of SARs that had been cleared. "Mr. Dullea, do you recognize these documents?"

"Uh, no, I don't think so."

"Are you saying someone else signed your name, Mr. Dullea? Because your signature is right there on the bottom of all of them. Am I right? Yes or no."

"They appear to be my signatures."

"And, Mr. Dullea, these are Suspicious Activity Reports that were generated at the very Bank Antriol facility that you are in charge of. Isn't that true?"

"Yes, they appear to come from the Antriol AML facility, sir, but I'm not the only one in charge."

"Yes, but you're the one I'm talking to right now," Deke responded with a snarky, subtle laugh. "And, Mr. Dullea, you can see right from the documents with your signature that they show transactions processed by Bank Antriol. Am I right?"

"They appear to. Yes."

"Objection!" Hawkinson shouted. "Mr. Deketomis, you need to change your tone in the way you are asking my witness questions. This is not your opportunity to harass Mr. Dullea with your flippant attitude."

Deke again continued as if he had not heard even a word spoken by the defense lawyer, who likely understood where he was going.

"Mr. Dullea, you knew when you signed those documents that the transactions were between your bank and entities that had been designated by the US government as having potential connections to terrorism, isn't that right, Mr. Dullea?"

"Well, sir, I don't have all those entities memorized, but it's possible."

"What are the dates shown on the documents? Can you see them, Mr. Dullea?"

"Yes, sir. They appear to be November 3, 2022, December 12, 2022, and January 14, 2023."

"Would you say those are fairly recent dates, Mr. Dullea?"

"I guess so."

"You guess so? They're just a few months ago, and that is long after your bank was flagged by the DOJ and directed not to clear transactions with entities suspected of terrorist activities. Is that right?"

"Yes, sir."

"And you knew the reason you were investigated and paid a fine is because some of the money that your bank transferred ended up in the hands of entities associated with terrorist groups in the Middle East?"

"Yes, er, well, that was one allegation, but it was never proven to be true. Look, we're a global bank. We do business in all parts of the world, and some of those places are not Disneyland, okay? The DOJ investigated us thoroughly and determined that there were a few transactions that could have involved materials and goods that could be used to build bombs or other weapons. But they could have legitimate purposes, too, and any use of those goods or money in a specific terrorist attack was never proven, either."

"Well, one thing we can agree with is that your signature is on these documents. Am I right? That means you cleared them just several months ago, is that correct?"

"Uh, I don't..." He looked at his defense lawyers with a wide-eyed face of terror. *Help me!* it said.

Hawkinson scrambled some papers on the table. "Uh, objection!"

"On what grounds?" Deke asked.

"Form." As soon as she said it, her colleague Aaronson leaned over to her and whispered frantically. He, too, began shuffling papers.

"Form? Really? *Form?*" Deke immediately went back to the witness. "Mr. Dullea, I ask you again. This requires only a yes or a no. Did you clear these SARs?"

"I suppose I did. But I can tell you that diligent—"

"Thank you. I now direct you to a new image—"

"Research was made to the legitimacy of those transactions, and—"

"Thank you, Mr. Dullea, we're moving on."

"Objection!" Hawkinson shouted. "You need to allow him to fully answer your question!"

Deke continued. "Mr. Dullea, the new image on the screen shows a signed and notarized affidavit that was provided to us by a former employee of Bank Antriol's anti-money laundering unit in Kentucky, Joel Hartbeck. I direct your attention to the lines highlighted on the screen. Could you please read them aloud? Just read it to us, Mr. Dullea."

Dullea did his best to sound unshaken, but his voice betrayed him as he read. "Uh, 'The SARs I had actively researched and pinpointed as blatantly illegal and were, in fact, criminal conduct, were cleared anyway by Blake Dullea.' I can explain that."

"Gee, that would be great," Deke said. "Take your best shot, Mr. Dullea."

"Joel Hartbeck was an unstable employee. He had a history of opioid addiction and was a man prone to conspiracy theories. His position at the unit was low level and unimportant. He was terminated from the AML unit. Everything he may have told you is a lie."

Deke made a show of scratching his head. "Really? Well, since you brought it up, I'm wondering why someone like you, an executive vice president of the bank and a member of the senior management team here in New York, would even be aware of a low level and unimportant employee's behavior down in Kentucky. Isn't that an HR issue down in Kentucky?"

Dullea cleared his throat. "Uhm, Karl Maher and I are in charge of the AML unit there. We created it together. It is our responsibility to know what goes on."

"Ah!" Deke exclaimed. "So you are saying that the buck stops with you and Mr. Maher, right? That whatever goes on at the AML unit in Kentucky is ultimately yours and Mr. Maher's responsibility?"

"I didn't say that."

"Objection!" Hawkinson yelled. "Stop putting words in his mouth!"

Deke gave her an icy look. "You've got to be kidding, Ms. Hawkinson." Deke went back to the witness without a second's lapse. "Mr. Dullea, let's look at the screen again." Deke gave the signal for his law clerk to change the image. "Do you recognize the first page of this document?"

"Uh, it appears to be the report that Karl and I did for the DOJ to show that we were in compliance with the settlement and non-prosecution agreement with Bank Antriol."

"And what does that report tell the reader? Give us a brief synopsis, please."

"Again … it was created to show the government that everything we're doing at the AML unit is aboveboard and complies with the settlement agreement the bank made with the DOJ."

"Does it really, Mr. Dullea?" Deke nodded at the tech assistant and called out a number. An image of dozens of transactions appeared on the screen. "Every one of these transactions was originally flagged as suspicious, but you never included them in your report to the government, did you? Isn't that correct, Mr. Dullea? Take a minute and look."

Dullea delayed as long as possible as he appeared to be studying the screen. "Yes, but we performed due diligence and—"

"And you or Mr. Maher cleared them. Every one of them. Thirty suspicious transaction reports and you and Maher personally cleared every one of them. You had the last word. Did I get that right, Mr. Dullea?"

"Yes, I suppose!"

"You suppose? Is that really your final answer? Because I want to display a document that shows you and Mr. Maher never failed, not one time in years, to—"

The door to the conference room opened and Oliver Wrecker entered. In a loud voice, he boomed, "Excuse me. Pardon my interruption! I need to speak to the defense counsel here. It's an emergency."

Deke, perturbed, threw up his hands and walked back to his team, all of whom had dropped their jaws at the uninvited outburst. Wrecker moved to Hawkinson and Aaronson and whispered intensely. Both Hawkinson and Aaronson's faces registered shock and surprise. The trio continued to consult in hushed tones for another minute.

"We're in the middle of a deposition here," Carol announced, unable to control herself.

Hawkinson finally stood and addressed the room. "I'm sorry to say that something terrible has happened. The bank president, Nigel Beech, has been severely injured in an explosion that occurred while he was commuting from Long Island on his way to the bank. His driver was killed. We've just learned that Mr. Beech has been placed in a medically induced coma at Mount Sinai South Nassau. Due to security concerns about the safety of Bank Antriol's employees, we need to end this deposition immediately."

With that, she motioned for Blake to stand and leave the room with her. Looking dazed and confused, he rose and quickly made his exit. The defense lawyers began gathering their materials.

"Are we going to reschedule?" Michael asked.

"Not right now," Aaronson said.

Deke told his law clerks. "Okay, pack it all up. Sorry, guys." He addressed the defense team. "We're sorry to hear about Mr. Beech, and we hope he'll be all right."

They ignored him and left the room.

Bernie muttered, "That's the best thing that happened to Dullea all morning, Deke."

"Well, this is terrible news," Deke said. "We would have done the same thing if it were one of ours. We'll need to regroup and find out what the hell is going on. To be continued, folks."

31

Spanish Trace, Florida

A day later, Deke and the team were back at the office in Florida. He called a meeting and once again sat with Michael, Carol, Gina, Jake, and Sarah in the conference room. After dialing up a Zoom call with Dan Lawson, whose face appeared on the big screen, Deke began the meeting.

"I just want to take stock of where we are," he said. "First, we need to make sense of what happened on Long Island to the very person who conceivably holds the road map of every important trail in this case. At the same time, I'm thinking that everything about Beech pushes me to believe that he is not the kingpin here even though he is president. Take a look at his history. He's a billionaire handing out millions to charities all over the planet. His choirboy credentials are almost overwhelming. It's not like he needs to be doing business with terrorists to make money for the bank that he is leaving in a year or two."

Dan answered, "I'm just as bewildered as you are, Deke. Your take on Beech is the same as mine. His bio reads like the antithesis of everything we now know about a typical Wall Streeter. Was Beech simply in the wrong place at the wrong time? Or was he specifically targeted? You know, he wasn't the only one who was injured. That scene on the road was a macabre massacre. It was a terrorist operation, to be sure."

"But what terrorists are we talking about?" Carol asked. "Middle East terrorists? Are the bombers al-Qaeda? Are they Taliban, Hezbollah?

Are they people not connected to the Middle East? No group or individual has claimed responsibility yet."

"Or are they domestic?" Jake asked. "Frankly, I'm leaning in that direction."

"*Or...*" Michael began with guarded, but dramatic, emphasis, "is it Joel?"

Deke flinched. "Joel Hartbeck?"

Michael raised his eyebrows. "It hurts me to say this, but he has kind of gone off the rails. When I last saw him, his mind seemed all stretched out. I mean, he gave us that great affidavit and everything, but he was also spouting off against the government and the VA, and most of all he sounded like he was considering a personal vendetta against Antriol. He had no doubt that Antriol murdered his girlfriend. Let's say Nigel Beech was indeed the target of this bombing. With the facts we have in front of us, who has expertise in roadside explosives? Who knows how to make them? Who do we know who has a grudge against Bank Antriol? It's probably harder for me than anyone on this call to come to terms with the possibility that our terrorist operation might be Joel, but it has to be put on the table."

Deke asked, "Jake, how do you read this?"

Jake held his hand in the air. "I'm a big believer in the duck principal. If it's quacking like a duck and it has feathers and flat feet like a duck, I'm usually going to call it a duck. And even though Joel didn't look like a feathery creature when Michael knew him fifteen years ago, I don't believe we're dealing with that same person today."

"We all change over time," Gina said. "And the history I reviewed tells me his life has been pretty upside down over the past decade."

Carol spoke up. "For what it's worth, I've been trying to reach my FBI contact for weeks, and he simply won't return my calls. They are as quiet as a mute church mouse about this bombing, and that weird one in Maryland, too. I have no idea if they know anything about Joel or whether he's a suspect, but I'll do my best to find out without tipping our hand at all."

"What's the name of the fed you are wanting to talk to?" Jake asked.

"Special Agent Rick Bushnell. He's based at Quantico."

"Well, keep at him," Deke said.

"For the record," Carol said, "I'm wondering about Joel, too. He does have the know-how and the means to do something like this. I mean, if he's not *dead*, then he's been living off the grid and avoiding talking to us. He surely knows that we're the only people on his side, but nevertheless he stays hidden from us. From a law enforcement standpoint, I'd be putting him on the top of the suspect list, for sure."

There was a knock on the door, and Deke called, "Come in."

Diana stuck her head in the door. "Sorry to interrupt but you need to turn on CNN right away. Something's happened."

Jake grabbed the remote that was on the table and pointed it at the television screen on the wall. CNN immediately came on.

Dan, looking at his phone, said, "For Chrissake, there's been another explosion."

"What the hell?" Michael muttered.

Sure enough, the anchor on CNN revealed that another roadside bomb had detonated on the outskirts of Philadelphia, this time killing several people and wounding dozens more. Live aerial footage revealed another scene of carnage on a busy road. Wrecked and burning cars and trucks, along with emergency vehicles, were everywhere.

"My God," Deke said. "What is *going on?*"

* * *

A week passed.

Deke's team plowed ahead and filed a subpoena requesting a specific list of more than a thousand items, including material that was in the anonymous package that Dan received. The list was partially a trap into which Deke believed Antriol would fall. He typically counted on a foreseeable level of dishonesty from lawyers like Mendel and was seldom disappointed.

Bank Antriol's data was kept in the IronVault storage facility in Tennessee, and it was the target for both sets of lawyers. Dan Lawson would file a similar set up subpoena a week after Deke filed his.

A one-two punch. Their plan was to give Mendel a lot of rope so that he would more than likely claim that the requested documents "did not exist."

While Deke and Dan were meeting daily and focusing on discovery strategy, the bombings were taking up large portions of the national news cycles. The attacks appeared to be random, even though they were all mostly clustered in the northeast near Washington, DC. Pundits speculated wildly in the media. Was it the act of one person or many? Who was it? What was their motive? Were al-Qaeda sleeper cells now awakened and at work once again in the United States? Who in the government has been asleep at the switch and allowed this to happen? Depending on the channel, the talking heads spun it away from their special interests and toward their political and ideological foes. The one constant question on everyone's mind was—were more attacks coming?

On the morning before a scheduled press conference with the director of the FBI, Carol finally heard back from her contact at the Bureau, Rick Bushnell.

"I'm sorry, Carol," he told her. "I haven't been avoiding you on purpose. As you can imagine, it's been chaos here. We've had to put just about everything else on the back burners and focus on these damned bombings."

"I totally understand," she replied. "But I need to pick your brain while I have you."

"I have a few minutes. As long as you don't ask me to give away any classified information. I'm not forgetting about all the help you gave me in Miami. I'm still grateful, but I am limited in what I can say about the bombings, if that's what you want to talk about."

Bushnell was referencing a time when Carol was still in law enforcement and had agreed to provide testimony at a federal trial of drug smugglers that the FBI agent had nabbed. She had been involved in the case on a local level in Miami, having worked undercover and placing herself in serious harm's way.

And I hope that's not all you're forgetting, she thought sardonically to herself.

"What I need to talk to you about concerns a case we're working on." She gave him the elevator pitch on the Bank Antriol lawsuit and the connection to terrorism. "So, there may be absolutely no connection at all with what you're investigating, but if there is, I may be able to help you in a big way. I can keep it really simple. Is it more likely than not that critical tools and materials for these bombs are being manufactured on this side of the Atlantic?"

Bushnell was quiet for a moment.

"Rick, are you still there?"

"Yeah, I'm here," he said. "I'm trying to decide what I can tell you. Seriously, there isn't much. The agent in charge of the case is Kirk Turkel. He's an expert in crimes involving explosives and arson. He works with the Terrorist Explosive Device Analytical Center."

"TEDAC."

"Right. Everything has been turned over to TEDAC, and they're analyzing all the evidence that they've uncovered."

"What kind of evidence?"

"Actually, the director is doing a press conference today. You should watch it. He's going to lay out a lot of pertinent evidence they have in the hopes that someone will step forward and help identify these creeps."

"So this is not a single person operation?"

"Carol, watch the press conference."

"We know about the press conference. So it's someone domestic doing it, isn't it?"

"Yes, we believe so. It's true, the bombs are similar to those used in Iraq and elsewhere, but these have come from within the US."

"Can you tell me anything else?"

"Watch the press conference, Carol. Seriously, anything I could tell you will be revealed there. Sorry I don't have more."

"All right, then, could I get in contact with Kirk Turkel?"

"Carol, I'm sure you know the standard format of FBI email addresses," Bushnell said. "I'll bet you could figure out how to reach him that way without putting myself at risk."

"All right. You always did make me *work* for what I want!"

"You've always been a hard worker, Carol. Oh, I thought of something else. You mentioned Plainsburg, Kentucky. I know a field agent in that area. Well, Louisville, anyway, but she sort of covers the whole state. I don't know if she might be of use to you—"

"Yes, she could. What's her name?"

"Felicia Paul."

"Let me guess. I have to figure out her email address, too."

"Listen, I really have to run."

"Okay, Rick. Thanks. I think."

"You're welcome. And needless to say…"

"Don't let Turkel know you talked to me."

"Hey, she's not only a hard worker, but she's smart, too!"

"Don't be patronizing, Rick."

"You know I love you, Carol. Take care." With that, he disconnected the call.

She couldn't help but grin. The guy really *did* love her once, a long time ago.

* * *

That afternoon, the team gathered in the conference room to watch the press conference on television. The director of the FBI was already standing at a podium, supported by a quartet of slick-dressed men and women behind him. None of them were introduced, but Carol pointed out the man wearing glasses to the right of the director.

"See the Clark Kent-looking guy? That's Kirk Turkel," she said. "I looked him up after I spoke to Rick today."

The director spoke in measured tones. "The FBI is taking these attacks on American soil very seriously. We are busy analyzing the debris from all the bombing locations, and we will soon determine where the materials used to make these devices came from. We are studying certain closed camera security footage that has been uncovered from one of the sites. The incident in Philadelphia has revealed that a lone figure dressed in black placed the explosive at the side of the road at night when traffic was practically nonexistent. He apparently traveled to the site in a black or brown unmarked box truck. In the next day or two, we will be releasing a sketch of a person of interest."

"Rick didn't tell me that!" Carol muttered.

"That said," the director continued, "our agents are working around the clock to stop this violence. I urge citizens to dial 911 and report any suspicious activity that you might see on highways and roads. The more vigilant we are, the sooner we will catch these monsters and bring them to justice. Thank you."

As the news anchors wrapped up, Jake said, "Well, that was mostly typical bureaucratic noninformation, but to give him credit, his delivery was good."

Michael added, "All he really said was, 'we don't know a damned thing but we're working on it.' But I'm interested to see the sketch of the person of interest."

"Maybe I can get some more information from Turkel," Carol said. "I've already emailed him. I've also emailed an FBI agent in Kentucky who might be of assistance."

Sarah, looking at her phone, said, "Hey, guys, I'm seeing on social media that something's happened in Baltimore." She continued to scroll and read posts.

"What do you mean?" Deke asked.

She groaned and shut her eyes. "Oh, for God's sake, it looks like another explosion!"

"No!" Michael spat.

"What? Is it a roadside bomb?" Deke asked.

"Looks like it," Sarah said. "They're saying there are more casualties and wounded. A lot of damage. Happening right here on American soil. For the love of..."

Right on cue, CNN went to a breaking news report, confirming what Sarah had just seen on her phone.

32

Spanish Trace, Florida

Michael had lost count of the number of voice messages he had left on Joel's newest phone. It was Jake who suggested that he contact the FedEx facility in Tazewell, Tennessee, from where the notarized affidavit and note had been sent. Reaching out to the notary, whose contact information was in the stamp/seal, might be of use, too.

He phoned the FedEx office. When the clerk answered in a thick Tennessee accent, Michael said, "Good morning. My name is Michael Carey, and I'm calling from Spanish Trace, Florida."

"Yes, sir?"

"Not long ago I received a FedEx envelope addressed to me here at the law offices of Bergman-Deketomis, where I am an associate attorney." He read off the tracking number and the date of the shipment. "I was wondering if you have any information on the sender that you can give me?"

"Let me look on the computer; hold on a second," the man said. Michael heard a bunch of typing in the background. After a moment, the man came back on the line. "Was the sender not indicated on your envelope?"

"No. Just your address."

"Huh. I must not have noticed that. Anyone shipping is supposed to put their info on the envelope, too. Hold on."

More typing. Michael was beginning to think this might be a dead end.

"There is some information here," the clerk said, "but I can't give this to you over the phone."

"Sir, I really wish you could make an exception here. The case I'm working on involves protecting the safety of a lot of people."

"Can't help you. If you'd like to come in with some identification of who you are and all that … Sorry, we have procedures and rules here."

It was looking more and more as if Michael would need to return to the area. He thanked the man and hung up. His next call was to Jane Parent, the notary public, who apparently worked at a bank in Tazewell.

"Ms. Parent, I'm calling about a document you notarized on…" Michael consulted the date of the seal and stamp and read it out to her. "A man named Joel Hartbeck brought in an affidavit to sign, and you apparently notarized it."

"I remember that. Lord, that man smelled as if he'd been living in a skunk nest. Sorry, I hope he's not a friend of yours."

Michael let that one go. "I'm trying to locate Mr. Hartbeck. Did he leave any kind of contact information with you?"

"Isn't his address and phone on the affidavit?"

"Yes, but the address was his old apartment in Plainsburg. He's moved since then."

"Oh, well, no, I can't help you with that."

"Did you happen to read the affidavit?" he asked.

"No, I never read those things. I'm not required to. I just watch a person sign it and date it, and I give it the stamp and seal. I charge a small fee, of course."

There was nothing much more she could tell him. Michael ended the call. At least he had confirmed that the affidavit was legitimately notarized. He then looked over his notes and came across Willis Lee's phone number. They hadn't spoken since their meeting at Beggar's Ravine in Plainsburg, when the man had promised to "help" him search for Joel and pass on any new information about the AML unit. Of course, Michael had not heard a word from him. Michael decided to try him again, and surprisingly, the man answered.

"Willis Lee."

"Mr. Lee, it's Michael Carey calling from Spanish Trace, Florida."

"Oh. Mr. Carey. How are you?"

"Fine, and you?"

"Okay."

"Is this a good time to talk?"

"Actually, no. I'm at work, and we're not supposed to take personal calls here. My boss is out of the office for a minute, so I can talk just a second. What's up?"

Michael said, "The last time we talked at that bar, you said you'd keep an eye out for anything regarding Joel Hartbeck's whereabouts, or anything pertaining to our case against Bank Antriol."

"Yeah, and I also told you I couldn't really tell you anything about the bank because I value my job too much! And as for Joel, hell, I don't know where he is."

"Do you think he's alive?"

"Damn straight, he's alive! He's the one setting off all those bombs!"

Michael blinked. "Wow, that's a pretty strong accusation, isn't it, Mr. Lee?"

"Sure, it's got to be him. He was an EOD guy in Iraq. He knows all about those things. He was acting like a certified crazy man those last few days I saw him. He was ranting about the government and the military and his job. He was a powder keg!"

"So you're telling me Joel has become a domestic terrorist?"

"Yep. I have no doubt."

"Have you reported your suspicions about Joel to the police?"

"No, it's just my instincts, man. I know a psycho when I see one, and Joel is a psycho. I gotta go."

"Wait, Willis, just another second. If I return to Plainsburg, can you meet with me again? I'm going to convince my boss to let me come back and do another sweep. I have to find Joel."

Willis, suddenly less harried to get off the phone, tittered quietly and paused for a moment. "Sure, Mr. Carey. Come on back. We can meet up again. I can't promise we'll find Joel, but who knows."

"Thanks, Willis. I'll be there in the next day or two. I'll call you."

"You do that. Bye."

Jake called from down the hall. "Michael! You have to come see this!"

Michael went and joined Jake, who stood with Deke in front of the TV screen in the conference room. CNN had Breaking News on again.

The anchor was speaking, "...has released this sketch of a person of interest in the recent bombings. He is wanted for questioning. If anyone has any information on this man's whereabouts, please call the FBI hotline shown here, or your local law enforcement. The FBI warns that you should not attempt to approach the man, as he may be armed and dangerous."

The crudely drawn, almost generic sketch of the face could have been any long-haired, bearded man with dark glasses.

Michael, however, recognized him. "Crap. That sure looks like Joel the last time I saw him."

* * *

The following day was Sunday, but the law offices of Bergman-Deketomis rarely shut its doors when the team was in the middle of an important case.

Jake had become obsessed with the MWs. His experience in the woods had given him some insight into the group's potential for random violence. He shut himself away in his office with a computer to study any available footage of the right-wing group to see if he could start identifying some of those characters who had seemed more than willing to kill him that night.

At the same time, Gina concentrated on filling out a biography of Willis Lee.

Deke had given the green light for Michael and Carol to return to Plainsburg, Kentucky. Michael's task was, again, to find Joel. "Turn up every rock and fallen tree if you have to!" Deke had admonished him.

Carol had contacted FBI Special Agent Felicia Paul in Louisville, who, at first, was wary of talking to the law firm's head of investigations. Rick Bushnell hadn't exactly prohibited Carol from telling Felicia that he was who had passed on her name, so Carol dropped his.

"Oh, Rick..." Felicia said with a laugh. "I refer to him as Agent Casanova."

Hmm, you, too? Carol thought. She avoided the temptation to ask Felicia what she meant and instead moved on and presented the brief rundown of her own background in law enforcement and a bit about the Antriol case.

"I served in Afghanistan," Felicia said. "I had friends who got blown up over there. Sure, we can talk. You say you're coming back to Plainsburg?"

"Yes. We plan to stay until we solve some of the mysteries surrounding the case."

"Well, I can't really talk now, but I'm driving downstate on Monday morning. It's a case of my own involving drug trafficking. Call me on my cell, and I'll tell you as much as I'm permitted to say. Maybe if I have time during the week, we can meet up. I might be near Plainsburg."

"Will do. And thank you."

Now, Michael and Carol waited at the gate for their flight from Pensacola to Knoxville. The pair sat quietly looking at their phones, checking email and news sites, when their attention was pulled away by the overhead TV screen displaying CNN.

"Breaking news," the anchor said. "There's been another bombing, this time in Antioch, Tennessee. A single business appears to be the target this time."

Aerial footage displayed a gigantic cloud of dark smoke billowing over a large fortress-like facility. Emergency vehicles, their colored lights flashing, surrounded the area.

"The IronVault Document and Data Storage Center, located on the edge of Antioch, was struck by multiple detonations this morning. A spokesperson for the business stated, 'This is a tragedy, but thankfully it occurred on a Sunday. A skeleton crew was inside, and 98 percent of the employees were not in the building. Sadly, the bodies of eight individuals who were working this morning have not been found in the wreckage.' I believe we now have a statement from local law enforcement."

The image cut to the Antioch police chief, who was outside of the burning building. "It's a mess in there. Management of the center is with me now, and they tell me that the areas of the building that have been damaged were large electronic data storage spaces and not offices or common areas where weekend employees would have been routinely stationed. We're hopeful that we will be able to account for any of those still missing. Unfortunately, security camera data for the facility was being stored in the same areas that were destroyed. Anything near or in the path of the explosions was melted by the intense heat of them."

At that instance, Deke called on Michael's phone.

"This is Michael."

"Are you and Carol seeing this?"

"Yeah. We're still processing it. I can't believe it. It's terrible."

"Terrible? It's a disaster! I feel for the loss of lives, but you know what this means for our case, don't you? All of Bank Antriol's data that we subpoenaed is likely *gone.*"

"Yeah. That's probably true."

"Michael, it means you *have* to find Joel Hartbeck. Otherwise, our case has literally gone up in smoke!"

"Hey, Deke," Michael said, "I want to remind you of something."

"What's that?"

"Joel didn't know about the IronVault or StoneWall. He couldn't have been responsible for this."

Deke inhaled deeply. "You have a point. Find him, Michael."

On cue, the airline staff announced that boarding for the flight to Knoxville had begun.

33

Spanish Trace, Florida

On Monday morning, the media had exploded with some startling revelations, sensational speculations, truths, and outright propaganda.

Deke arrived at the office to find Jake, Gina, and Sarah watching the news in the conference room. Later in the day, he was due to board a flight to Virginia for a court appearance on Tuesday. Only Bernie and Gina would accompany him. Sarah would remain behind to act as point person for both out-of-state parties.

"What's going on now?" Deke asked, weary of the setbacks that were hampering the case.

"There's been some kind of leak from the FBI about the bombings," Jake answered. "Take a look."

The TV screen was flashing the overused graphics indicating that yet again CNN was "breaking news." An author of several bestselling nonfiction books on politics and the war on terror was on CNN and speaking with the anchor, "...but we must remember this was an anonymous source. Maybe it's true, maybe it's not. I tend to think it's true, though." Below the talking heads, a rapid scrolling chyron moved across the screen in all caps, theoretically asking viewers, "THE NEXT 9/11?"

Deke's eyes returned to the talking heads above. "Thank you for your insights," the anchor said, completely ignoring the speculative non-answer of their guest "expert." It did not prevent the CNN anchor from breathlessly reporting, "Once again, for those of you just tuning in, we have learned that the FBI TEDAC laboratory—that's the Terrorist Explosive Device Analytical Center—has determined that the same design, that is, the use of military-grade PE4 explosives and high-grade copper warheads, just like those used against US troops in the Middle East, called explosively formed penetrators, EFPs, have also been used in the recent bombings here in the United States. Hezbollah-linked terrorists may very well be operating right here at home, waging an extensive new war on America."

Jake said, "Reports with this same slant are on almost every channel." He pointed the remote at the TV screen and switched to MSNBC. One of the network's popular frenzied pundits was raging. "Hezbollah or al-Qaeda is on the home front, people!"

Jake flipped through three other corporate media channels before he turned his attention to social media reporting. He typically relied on the internet when TV news transitioned from actual reporting to sensationalism.

A well-respected journalist appeared on *The Young Turks*, one of his go-to sites. "When politicians ignore the threat of domestic terrorists here in our own country, this is what happens. To be clear, we don't know for certain if an al-Qaeda or Hezbollah sleeper cell has been activated in the United States, and the FBI leaker didn't indicate as such. It's important to note that *anyone* can build these types of roadside bombs with the right materials and the technical know-how, and frankly one can get the how-to instructions on the internet! The raw materials can be found in this country. So, we don't want this to create hysteria about foreign attacks on our soil. Personally, I have doubts that whoever is behind the bombings are foreign enemies of the United States."

"It's a Monday morning," Gina observed while Jake continued his internet searches. "All these breaking news stories will cease at the top of the hour, and I imagine each station will resume its regularly scheduled programming."

The image of the FBI sketch of the "person of interest" flashed on the screen.

"Hold it there," Deke said. "I want to hear this."

"So who is this person?" a new anchor asked. "Is this the face of a radical Islamic terrorist? Does he *look* like someone we think of as a member of al-Qaeda? I don't think so. This guy looks like a street person we now see too often these days at every busy intersection in our big cities. And, besides, this sketch doesn't tell us much, does it? Sunglasses, facial hair, long hair … this could be anyone. Remember the Unabomber sketch? It was not even close to reality!"

A guest talking head barged in, "Other than the sketch, the FBI hasn't provided much detail. This person could be Middle Eastern or Scandinavian for all we know. To me, with all that hair, if he is motivated by radical jihadist ideology, then he's not even gone through the final shaving of his facial hair in preparation for martyrdom by suicide like most Taliban or ISIS terrorists would be expected to do. So if this is indeed a Salafi jihadist, this may mean he's not done with his attacks. I think we're in a heap of trouble here."

"My lord, turn it off," Deke said. "You see what's happening, don't you? Politics and media ratings are already driving this story. Hell, they'll have us bombing Iran before the day is out."

"I bet your take is the same as mine," Gina said. "The fact that one of the bombs targeted the president of Bank Antriol and another one targeted the storage unit where Antriol kept all the data that we desperately need is like a red flare to me. I'm thinking the other bombings apart from these two are a distraction from what's really going on here."

"I wonder if the FBI has considered that," Sarah said.

"I don't know," Deke answered. "Still, let's not forget that these are the same federal agencies that missed all the signs that allowed 9/11 to take place." He held out his arms. "Hey, what do I know? But right now, I'm squarely in line with what Gina is thinking. I'm always going to favor facts over coincidences. Two out of five bombings have connections to our case. Those are facts that we are going to operate with. Michael and Carol are in Kentucky now. Let's hope they're successful in throwing some light on the darkness that's still dogging our case. If our theories are correct, we all need to be diligent."

"In other words," Jake added, "we're entering dangerous territory."

PART THREE

34

Plainsburg, Kentucky—Monday

After they had met on the hotel's ground floor for the complimentary breakfast, Michael and Carol independently felt the same sense of foreboding and uncertainty that their colleagues in Florida were experiencing. They both knew that their actions in the coming days could determine the fate of the Antriol case as well as that of the missing Joel Hartbeck, and perhaps their own well-being. They split up their tasks and agreed to move about in their separate rental cars.

Carol took the job of driving to the FedEx facility over the border in Tennessee. Michael wanted to get hold of Willis Lee. "We'll touch base tonight back here," he told her.

Carol took off and called FBI agent Felicia Paul from the road.

"Where are you?" Felicia asked.

"I'm on my way to Tazewell, Tennessee, to talk to a FedEx employee," Carol replied. "How about you?"

"I'm driving down from Louisville to the Federal Correction Institution at Manchester for that drug case with the DEA. I'll be interviewing an inmate there who's one of those right-wing 'Look, I'm a gun totin' bad ass' fella who likes Confederate flags and swastikas."

Carol perked up. "Hey, he wouldn't be a member of a group called the MWs, would he?"

"The Mohawk Warriors? Yeah, they've become the gang of choice in this part of the country."

"Well, there's a good chance they're involved in the bank case we talked about."

"How so?"

"We're working on those details right now." She told Felicia about Janet Blanco's murder and how the MWs could be implicated in that, even though the Plainsburg police had swept that idea under the rug. Then she related the story of Jake being hunted like a big-game animal through the forest.

"You know who the self-appointed leader of the MWs is?" Felicia asked.

"Yes. He's the police chief's son."

"Makes you wonder, don't it?"

"Oh, we're confident that the cops in Plainsburg are corrupt," Carol said. "But there's one officer, Sheila Denning, who our firm's investigator befriended. She has helped us fill in a few blanks in our case, but they've pretty much chained her to desk duty. So what do the MWs got to do with your drug case?"

Carol sensed that the FBI agent was considering what she could reveal. "Well, we have good reason to believe that these dirtbags are the distribution network for a South American drug cartel built on cocaine and meth. Listen, Carol, I could maybe meet you in Plainsburg tomorrow, and we can compare some notes. How'd that be?"

"That sounds good. Let me ask you one thing, though."

"Shoot."

"These bombings that are going on. The FBI released a sketch of a person of interest. Do you know if there's a name possibly attached to that face that your posse is keeping close to the chest?"

"Why, is there someone you have in mind?"

Carol would normally keep this information to herself, but she had a good feeling about Felicia. "We have an important witness who was an EOD specialist in Iraq. He has disappeared and that's the main reason my colleague and I are here—we need to find him. He might be in danger. He's already supplied us with an affidavit that implicates Bank Antriol in a huge way."

"And?"

"Well, our witness, um, he kind of looks like that sketch."

"What's his name, Carol?"

"Joel Hartbeck."

Felicia was quiet for a moment. "Well, I can neither confirm nor deny that the individual you named is wanted for questioning. Sorry."

"Hmm. I understand. Okay. Well, I look forward to meeting up tomorrow."

"Call me in the morning."

Carol ended the call just as she crossed the border into Tennessee.

* * *

Michael pulled into the strip mall parking lot where the AML unit was located. As there weren't many other businesses other than a Subway sandwich shop, a Goodwill store, and a State Farm agent's office, the nearly two hundred automobiles parked there likely belonged to employees of the unit. Michael had driven there on a whim, figuring that Willis Lee would likely be unable to speak to him in person. Nevertheless, he dialed Willis and waited for him to answer. As he expected, the call went to voicemail.

"Hi, this is Willis. Leave a message."

"Willis, this is Michael Carey. It's 10:30 a.m. on Monday, and at this moment I'm sitting in my car in the parking lot of the AML unit. I need to talk to you. If you can come out for a couple of minutes, that would be great. I'll wait for a half hour. You have my number."

Michael got out of the car and leaned against it. The sun shone brightly in a cloudless sky, but the hint of autumn was in the air. The woodlands, mountains, and higher elevation of the community provided Plainsburg with a cooler climate in the waning weeks of summer than most spots in the region.

Five minutes passed. He figured he'd wait another ten and then go inside the place and insist to Bambi—if she were still working there—that he needed to talk to Willis.

After eight minutes of waiting, Michael's phone rang.

"Michael Carey."

"This is Willis. Are you still outside?"

"Yes."

"Well, I can't come out. We're in the middle of stuff here. This is my job, man."

"We need to talk. When's good for you?"

"Never. I told you before I can't really talk to you."

"On the phone you had said we could meet up again. I need to find Joel."

"And I said I couldn't promise anything."

"Willis, you know, we can subpoena you for a deposition. I don't want to play that card, but it's a fact."

Willis sounded flustered. "You're wasting your time looking for Joel."

"Do you know any more about him?"

"No! If you ask me, he's fled to Mexico. You know the FBI is looking for him, don't you? Did you see that sketch of him that's been blasted all over the news?"

"You think that's Joel?"

"Don't you? It looks just like him! Hey, hold on a minute, will you? I'm putting you on hold a second."

Michael heard a click and then silence. He waited at least a full two minutes before Willis came back on the line.

"Sorry, Michael, it was my boss. I'm not supposed to talk on the phone at work. Look ... can you meet me at my house this evening? We can talk there. Around eight o'clock?"

"Sure. What's the address?"

Willis told him. "Okay. I'll see you tonight, then."

They hung up.

Now Michael wondered what the heck he was going to do for the rest of the day.

* * *

Tazewell, Tennessee—Monday

Carol arrived at the Tazewell FedEx facility just after lunch. She went inside and found a tall, thin young man who appeared to be barely out of high school working the counter. The fluorescence of the shop lights accentuated the losing battle his acne-pocked face had been waging with his adolescent hormones.

"Can I help you, ma'am?" he asked, struggling with eye contact.

"You sure can," Carol said. "On Saturday you got a call from my colleague in Spanish Trace, Florida, asking about a FedEx package he received that was shipped from this facility. He was asking about the sender's contact information."

"That rings a bell."

"You told my colleague, Michael Carey, that he needed to come in here in person before you would release that information."

"Uh, I think I said that. That's the policy."

Carol slapped her business card on the counter. "I'm the head of safety and security and investigative services for the Bergman-Deketomis law firm in Florida. We are investigating a serious criminal case. Michael Carey, the *attorney* you spoke to on the phone, sent me to retrieve the information he asked for." She gave him her signature unflinching stare. "I've come a long way, do you understand?" Without looking away, she handed him a photocopy of the shipping label from Joel's envelope. "There's the tracking number and everything else you need to look it up."

Her no-nonsense demeanor and intimidating presence made the young man pay attention. "Yes, ma'am, right away!" He began to type on the work station. "Uh, okay, here we go. I have it. He gave his name as, uh, 'J. Miller.' There's an address in Pikeville, Kentucky. I'll read it off to you and the phone number he gave us, too."

Carol wrote them both down. She checked them against a list of Joel's former phone numbers and addresses that Michael had given her. The number provided was an old one, no longer active. The address, however, was a PO Box at a PO Box Ltd. store in Pikeville. That was new.

"Thanks," she said. "That is very helpful. Hey, do you remember what, um, Mr. Miller looked like?"

"Yeah, I do. He looked like a hermit who lived in the mountains! He kind of stank like one, too. He had long hair, a beard and mustache, and he was wearing sunglasses."

"How was he dressed?"

"I noticed he was carrying."

"A gun? What kind?"

"Pistol. In a holster on his belt. I don't know what kind of gun it was, but it looked like a serious piece. Frankly, I didn't like the looks of the guy. He creeped me out a little. He had on camo pants, I think, but maybe they were just dirty. And a flannel shirt, like a lumberjack, and his jacket was army surplus."

Carol made the switch to be charming. "Say, you'd make a fine witness on the stand! You have a good memory."

The young man grinned and blushed. "Aw, thanks, ma'am." But then he looked horrified. "Wait … am I gonna have to be a witness?"

She shook her head. "Nah, it's not likely. Let's just keep our conversation between us. Thanks for your help. FedEx needs more folks like you." With that, she left the bewildered young man wondering if he had just done something right or wrong.

Outside, Carol called Michael from the car. "Hey, cowboy, what are you doing?"

Michael laughed. "I'm riding the range, what do you think I'm doing? Where are you?"

"I'm sitting outside the FedEx place in Tazewell. I got the information we wanted. The phone number Joel left with them is an old one. But the address is one of those PO boxes you rent from a place called PO Box Ltd. It's located in Pikeville, Kentucky."

"Hmm, that's almost a three-hour drive from Plainsburg."

"It's about the same distance from here. I'm not sure I can get there in time before they close for the day at five. Weird that they close so early. Must be small-town hours. The PO boxes are apparently accessible 24/7, though."

"What, you want to break in to Joel's PO box?"

She laughed. "Not unless I have to! I've done it before. Not exactly a secure system they have in place."

"Why don't we go to Pikeville in the morning together?" Michael suggested.

"That's a good idea. I can get back to Plainsburg in time for dinner. I have a date with that FBI agent, Felicia Paul, tomorrow. Let me call her back and leave a message and see what's up with her. What do you have going on?"

"Right now I'm stopping by all of Joel's known addresses in town and checking them out. I just left the apartment building where he once lived with the woman he married and then divorced. I talked to the manager, and she hasn't seen Joel for years. I've got three more addresses to hit, including that old motel that Jake and I were at before. Deke wants me to turn over every stone, and that's what I'm doing. Tonight, though, I'm supposed to meet up with Willis Lee after he gets off work."

"Sounds positive. You want me to come along?"

"Probably not. Willis seems to be so nervous about talking to me that it might shut him up completely if I show up with someone he doesn't know. Best I deal with him alone."

"Okay, I won't take it personally."

"Let's just meet back at the hotel tonight. We can drive to Pikeville tomorrow after you hear from your FBI agent."

Carol hung up and then called Felicia. She got the agent's voice-mail and left her a message to ask about meeting up late Tuesday afternoon. She then pulled out of the lot and headed back over the border to Kentucky.

35

Spanish Trace, Florida—Monday

Jake stared at his computer screen as he played various YouTube videos that were shot by civilians during protest marches where the MWs had taken part. He had found a few, as well as a couple of big ones that featured only the MWs, such as when they paraded in Plainsburg for the "Take Back Our Country" rally that took place in October of 2022.

The investigator was frustrated because so far he had not recognized any of the MW members from that night in the woods. Of course, he had not really gotten a good look at them at the time. The only one he had focused on was the skinhead they called Chad. Unfortunately, Chad had not shown up in any of the videos.

He and Sarah had worked together to find any information that existed about the MW members. They knew that Rusty Wainwright, the son of the Plainsburg police chief, was the leader of the group. He seemed to be the only one who was the "face" of the MWs in the media. He was savvy enough to cover up his tats and wear a suit and tie, making himself appear professional, and he fluently spoke the coded dog-whistle vernacular of white supremacy. He had been quoted in several news articles and was interviewed many times. Video footage of him was readily available on YouTube.

Jake was about to give up for the day when, at the very end of one of Wainwright's interviews, the camera swung to the right to reveal several

MWs standing behind their leader. There, in the center of the group, was the familiar shiny bald head.

Chad.

Jake smiled and said, "Well, hello! Let's put you into facial recognition software, my hateful friend!"

* * *

Plainsburg, Kentucky—Monday

Michael sat in his hotel room waiting for Carol since they were planning to go to dinner prior to his appointment at Willis Lee's house. The phone rang and the caller ID indicated that it was her.

"You're not going to believe this," she said.

"What?"

"I got a flat tire, and I'm thirty miles away from Plainsburg."

"I'll come get you. Where are you, exactly?"

"No need. I already called the rental company and they've sent someone out, but I doubt I'll be back in time for dinner."

"Seriously, I can get there before roadside assistance does."

Carol sighed. "Don't worry about it, Michael. I'll be fine. Go to your meeting with Willis and let me know how it went in the morning at breakfast before we head out. I've actually got a splitting headache and should crash early tonight."

"Well, text me and let me know you made it back to the hotel, okay?"

"Sure."

"Talk to you later. Good luck with the road service."

They hung up and Michael set out to have a bite to eat. He knew Carol was more than capable of handling herself.

* * *

The sun was still shining but rapidly descending. Michael arrived in Willis Lee's neighborhood at 7:45 p.m., knowing it would be dark soon.

The street was on the outskirts of Plainsburg, almost beyond the city limits. It was a rural area with more trees and roads than homes, and the houses were few and far between. Some of them appeared to be foreclosed or in disrepair. He passed a few lots where only slabs of concrete and cinder blocks remained from where mobile homes once perched, as if this were a long forgotten farming community that had died a slow death. Willis's brick ranch-style structure, certainly built in the 1950s, was at the end of a long dirt road. Unlike the others in the area, it had been kept in relatively good condition and it sported a nice lawn, on which Willis had posted a message for the uninvited—NO TRESPASSING. VIOLATORS WILL BE SHOT, SURVIVORS WILL BE SHOT AGAIN.

Michael parked along the creosote-soaked railroad ties that curbed the driveway, got out, and went to the front door. He looked around and couldn't see the nearest neighbor. Willis Lee liked his isolation.

Michael rang the doorbell, and after no answer, he knocked loudly.

Willis had not come home yet. After all, Michael was early, so he decided to go back and wait in the car. He phoned Carol from there and got her voicemail. "Hey, it's me," Michael said. "I'm at Willis's house out in the boondocks, waiting for him to come home. Just checking to see if you made it back. Talk to you later." He hung up, and three minutes later a text arrived from Carol stating that she was back at the hotel. He sent back a smiley face emoji.

Willis had still not shown up at ten past eight. Michael decided to get out of the car again and take a look around the house. Since dusk had taken over the landscape and the house was secluded, Michael felt bold enough to take a walk around the home. There was no fence, so Michael didn't see the harm.

The back of the house was nothing much to look at. A Weber grill, a picnic table, and benches occupied a cement patio that was full of cracks that had caught several cigarette butts and bottle caps. A sliding glass door led inside to the kitchen/dining room space. Michael looked in and didn't see anything out of the ordinary.

He looked at his watch. It was 8:15 p.m. Checking his phone again, he saw that there was a new text message from Willis. *I'm running late. Be there by eight thirty. Wait for me on back porch.*

Michael grumbled to himself and sat at the picnic table. He sat there for another minute feeling foolish, but then he had an idea. He got up and, on a whim, tried the glass door. It slid open!

He stepped inside. His first thought as he eyed the kitchen and dining area was that Willis Lee was a bit of a slob. The sink was full of dirty dishes, and there were empty beer bottles and ashtrays full of cigarette butts everywhere. A half empty bottle of Kentucky bourbon was on the counter, along with a stack of unopened mail. The house reeked of stale tobacco and booze. Either Willis had lots of friends who came over to party, or he was on his way to becoming a serious alcoholic.

"Hello?" he called, just to be safe.

Nothing.

Michael figured he would surely hear Willis's car pull up into the front drive in time for him to slip back outside to the patio, so he went further into the space and checked out the living room and foyer by the front door. A hallway led to a couple of bedrooms and the bathroom. He was tempted to explore Willis's personal spaces, but something drew him back to the kitchen instead. There, he noticed a door in an alcove. Curiosity got the better of him, so he opened it. A wooden staircase led down to a cellar, where the water heater and furnace could be seen off to the side. Michael saw a light switch to his right, so he flicked it on, revealing that the cellar was much larger than he'd originally thought. He took a few steps farther down and saw that behind the staircase was a complete man cave complete with a sofa, coffee table, several comfy chairs, and a big flat-screen television. And more empty beer cans and ashtrays full of butts. Michael went all the way down and stepped into the space.

Covering the back wall was a huge Confederate flag. Michael thought it might be in fact an original relic from the Civil War.

Really? I missed this about our boy Willis?

The sight was such a surprise that at first Michael didn't notice the *other* emblems that told Willis's story such as a smaller Nazi swastika flag, Iron Crosses, and a space where Willis and possibly others had used markers and paint to scribble crude gang symbols and numbers like 4/19, graffiti style.

Before he could catch his breath, Michael heard car doors slam in the distance above. More than one.

He leaped for the stairs and ran up to the ground floor, hitting the light switch as he passed. Michael slammed the cellar door behind him and hurried toward the sliding glass door.

Three men dressed in fatigues stood on the patio. One of them was a skinhead, possibly the same man Jake had described as being the ringleader of the gang that chased him through the woods.

They each had a gun pointed at Michael.

"Get your sorry-ass hands behind your head and get on your knees," the skinhead ordered. "Now."

36

Deke, Bernie, and Gina sat in the Hilton Richmond Downtown's dining area over breakfast discussing the day's plans. Having arrived the previous evening, they were due in Judge Trackman's court in a couple of hours. Bank Antriol's lawyers had filed an emergency motion to completely stay the case, and Judge Trackman had agreed to hear the motion.

"It's a last-ditch, desperate attempt by Mendel and company," Deke said as he sipped his hot coffee.

"Is there any chance they can sway the judge?" Bernie asked.

"Bernie, in this business, anything can happen," Deke answered. "I expect a large dose of sympathy argument about Nigel fighting to stay alive."

"Oh, look," Gina said, nodding toward the door. "It's Dan."

Dan Lawson had flown in from New York for the hearing. "Greetings, folks," he said as he joined them at the table.

"I was just going over what we can expect this morning," Deke said to Dan.

"Just what *is* their best argument for a stay?" Gina asked.

Deke answered, "Oh, they're citing concerns over the safety and security of the bank's employees and facilities. In addition to that, they're voicing concerns about the bank's ability to comply with discovery obligations since the transaction data at the IronVault facility was destroyed. They will also argue that Nigel, as the CEO of Antriol, is not able to help in the bank's defense right now because of his injuries."

"It *is* concerning that the IronVault was bombed," Dan said. "And their president, too."

"The media is saying the bombings are random," Bernie observed, "but Antriol has some connection to at least two of the attacks, right? And from at least one angle, the bank seems to benefit from all this, at least when it comes to evidence needed in the lawsuit. I mean, look, the most senior witness and the transaction data have now been all but destroyed."

"Bernie, we've alleged, and I believe it's true, that this bank is willing to do business with the epitome of evil simply to make a profit," Deke said. "So if you're thinking that Antriol may be willing to cause more death and destruction to protect itself, then I don't think what you're suspecting takes too much of a leap. It's probably only a matter of time before law enforcement and the media make the connection between the bombings and our case."

The group sat in silence as they collectively digested Deke's words. He took another sip of coffee.

Dan shook his head. "Deke, I'm constantly amazed by how calm you can be in situations like this."

Deke winked at him. "I've just got a well-developed game face. Frankly, even I'm concerned."

* * *

Judge Trackman kept her eyes on George Mendel as he delivered a passionate, ten-minute soliloquy that expanded on exactly what Deke speculated at breakfast. There should be an immediate and total stay of the case because of the safety and security of the bank's employees. Mendel pointed to the IronVault bombing as an attempt by "foreign terrorists" to damage American interests by attacking such a "prestigious" bank as Antriol's New York branch. "Even aside from threats of terror, there is a war on against Wall Street by liberal politicians and attorneys who blame everything wrong in this country on bankers and Wall Street executives.

Mr. Deketomis is doing that very thing in this case, your honor. 'Big bad bankers killing American soldiers,' that's what he is trying to sell during a time when our CEO is at death's door and our banking facilities are being blown up. Banks are not terrorists, but rather they are victims of them, too. With all due respect, your honor, if we are going to adequately protect the Antriol business and its employees from the circus frenzy that Mr. Deketomis is trying to create, then we need an immediate stay for at least as long as it takes for Antriol to recover from the horrible events it has just recently experienced."

The judge gave the attorney a slight nod, and then turned to Deke. He couldn't tell if she had bought his nonsense. Unlike the previous hearing, Trackman was playing with her best poker face now, too.

"Your honor," Deke began, "if there ever was a case where delay would cause irreparable harm and, in fact, potential further death and injury to human life, it is this one. Mr. Mendel speaks about the possibility of harm to Antriol employees. He lays out his projections and guesswork about how Antriol employees are possibly in harm's way. Well, my clients are concerned that there is no need for guesswork. Evidence in this case tells us that people will continue to die every month because this 'big bad bank,' as Mr. Mendel correctly puts it, really did wash money for the ugliest cretins on the globe, and as a result we cannot stop or delay the inevitable murder that will continue as we sit back and wait while a stay on the case is in place. The DOJ was unable to force this bank to show decency and play by the rules, and we believe the only way to stop this killing machine that Antriol is a part of is to expose their criminal-quality conduct in a trial as soon as possible."

Deke paused a moment. All eyes were on him, including those of Mendel and Wrecker. "Judge, I also need to focus on something that has not been discussed in this case so far. Mr. Mendel brought up the recent terrorist bombings. These disastrous, terrible incidents have killed or injured dozens of people. No one has claimed responsibility, and on their face they do seem to be random. For some reason, the media and law enforcement have not made this connection, but two out of the five bombings have a direct bearing on this case. We believe that it is not only possible, but in fact probable, that someone is targeting not Bank

Antriol, per se, but rather this very lawsuit. We have evidence, your honor, that indicates some entity is engaged in conduct that will ultimately show a connection with at least two bombings and this lawsuit. Also, your honor—"

"Judge!" Mendel stood and shouted. "This is preposterous! Is Mr. Deketomis really suggesting that Bank Antriol is anything other than a victim of these horrible acts? At a minimum, counsel seems to be implying that we've gained an advantage from these tragedies, and if he is suggesting that we are involved in this somehow, that the bank tried to kill its own CEO with a bomb . . . if that is where he's going, then we're listening to the ranting of a crazy man!"

"Your honor," Deke calmly replied, "I have done no such thing. Of course, if the shoe fits..."

"Gentlemen! Control yourselves. Mr. Mendel, sit down. Mr. Deketomis, would you care to elaborate on what you have said?"

"Your honor, I never said Bank Antriol was behind the bombings. We could have the transcript read back for Mr. Mendel if he wants, but I merely suggested that whoever or whatever entity is behind these bombings is possibly trying to shut down this lawsuit. And, your honor, I would never stand here in court and suggest that if we did not have developing evidence pointing us in that direction."

"Very well, Mr. Deketomis, but be sure that I will expect more than your mere representations as we proceed. Do you have anything else?"

Deke took a breath and wrapped it up. "Your honor, it would be a miscarriage of justice for this case not to move forward. Too many lives are at stake. Delaying this case only gives rise to the opportunity for more witnesses and evidence to be lost. If the bank's lawyers are worried that the employees are in danger, and that these employees have done no wrong, then it is illogical to prolong the risk to them by staying the case. While it is unfortunate that we cannot get our hands on the data that was stored at the IronVault, we believe we are in possession of enough evidence to prove the bank's liability in this lawsuit. We are ready to proceed, your honor. Thank you."

Deke sat, and Judge Trackman made a note to herself at the bench. She then addressed the court. "Gentlemen, I have heard the arguments of both sides, and I will take everything under advisement. I want to reconvene in two days—that's Thursday—and I will announce my decision then. Court is adjourned."

She banged the gavel, stood, and left the courtroom.

Mendel looked both genuinely confused and perturbed as he leaned over and whispered to his colleagues.

Deke turned to Gina. "Two days?"

Gina checked her phone. "A bailiff I know here just texted me. The judge's mother is quite ill and may be dying. She has to rush off to another state."

"Got it. Have you heard from Carol or Michael?"

"I got a text from Carol. She has a full day planned. She and Michael are driving to Pikeville for some reason. She asks if we've heard from Michael this morning."

"Tell her I haven't," Deke answered as he gathered his materials.

* * *

New York, New York—Tuesday

Karl Maher knocked on Blake Dullea's office door.

"Yeah?"

"It's me."

"Come in."

Karl entered the spacious executive vice president's office on the tenth floor that was identical to his own. He shut the heavy solid wood door behind him.

"Have a seat," Blake said.

Karl did so and the two men stared at each other.

"What are we going to do?" Karl asked.

"It's already in motion," Blake answered.

"This doesn't make you nervous?"

Blake shrugged. "Why should it?"

"The lawsuit could still go forward. The hearing went well, according to Mendel's paralegal, but the judge is unpredictable. She's allowing two days to come to a decision."

"That's why we've taken out extra insurance."

"That's a pretty radical type of insurance, don't you think?" Karl noted.

"Too late to worry about that now. Just get back to work and play it cool. They can't touch us. Everything is bulletproof right now. We haven't done anything. Right?"

Karl looked at his colleague. "You believe that?"

"Don't you? It is just the business of banking. Sometimes we miss things." Dullea leaned forward and whispered with emphasis, "We have an exit strategy. You said you had it all arranged."

"I do, but—"

"But what?"

"Our man on the ground in Kentucky is working with lowlifes I consider to be loose cannons. We needed to buy time to tie up the loose ends, and he's providing it, but things are getting out of hand. We may need to execute the exit strategy sooner than we expected."

Dullea sat back and shrugged. "So what? I'm not worried. Look, Karl, the chaos they're creating will slow things down and give a layer of plausible deniability to the bank."

Karl waited a moment, and then he nodded. He stood and said, "I'll talk to you later. Keep me apprised of any ... developments."

"You know I will."

After Karl had gone, Blake took a handkerchief from his $5,000 Armani suit jacket and wiped the hint of perspiration from his brow.

37

Michael wasn't answering his phone.

At first Carol wasn't too concerned. There had been plenty of times when Deketomis team members were "out in the field," as it were, and temporarily failed to connect for some reason. However, she and Michael had agreed to drive to Pikeville together.

She called and left another message. "Hey, Michael, give me a call. If I don't hear from you by nine, I'm going to head to Pikeville alone." Carol also texted him the same info. Next, she went outside to the hotel parking lot, but she couldn't recall what kind of car he had rented, only that it was white. She dialed Diana down in Florida.

"Hey, Carol, how are things up there?"

"Okay. Listen, I can't find Michael. Do you have the details of what car he rented?"

"Hold on." Diana brought up the travel arrangements she had made. "It's a 2022 Hyundai Elantra. I just texted you the license plate number."

"That's right, I remember now. A white one. Thanks."

"I heard you had a little roadside trouble."

"Damn flat tire. Slowed me down some, but Hertz came through. Everything's good, now. Hey, if you happen to hear from Michael, have him call me."

"Will do. Should we … be concerned?"

"Not yet. It's early. I'm sure he's fine. I'll let you know when we connect."

Carol hung up and looked around the parking lot for a white Elantra, but she didn't find one. She knew that Michael had gone to see Willis Lee the evening before, so maybe he was out chasing a lead.

She wasn't going to worry about it … yet.

* * *

When Carol saw the sign that indicated Pikeville was ten miles ahead, she remembered to phone the FBI agent. She did so, and the woman answered after the first ring.

"Felicia Paul."

"Hi, Felicia, it's Carol Morris. You had said to call you this morning to see if we might be able to meet up in Plainsburg later today."

"Hmm, maybe, but I'm some distance away right now. I'm in a town called Pikeville, and that's about a three-hour drive from Plainsburg."

"Wait. You're in Pikeville?"

"Yes."

"So am I! Well, in ten minutes I will be."

"Really? What are you doing in Pikeville?"

"Checking out a lead. There's a PO Box Ltd. Store I have to visit and see if I can get into our witness's PO box there."

"I know that store; I think it's the only one in town. Hey, what are you doing for lunch? There's a Bob Evans Restaurant right across the street. Let's grab a bite, and I'll join you at PO Box Ltd."

"That sounds great, Felicia. I'll GPS it and see you there in … thirty minutes?"

"Copy that!"

As Carol drove into Pikeville, she noted that its small-town feel was homey and quiet. Even though its population was smaller than Plainsburg's, the vibe she sensed was infinitely more pleasant. Were the people happier? Carol thought that could be the answer, for she found the general atmosphere in Plainsburg to be curiously edgy.

It wasn't long before she found the restaurant, so she pulled into the lot and got out. Felicia Paul was already waiting in a booth. The woman waved at Carol, assuming that she was the face behind the voice. They greeted each other, shook hands, and then Carol sat across from Felicia. She noted that the redheaded woman was likely around ten years younger than herself, with the build of an athlete. Carol immediately discerned that they were two peas from the same pod.

Over food, they spent a half hour discussing their backgrounds and current jobs. "Why did you leave law enforcement?" Felicia eventually asked.

"The law firm made me an offer I couldn't refuse. I like the people there, and Nick Deketomis is a fantastic boss. He's also on the right side of most of the issues I care about. The pay is good, and I'm not beholden to the bureaucracy of an agency."

"I hear you. I may follow your path someday, but not just yet."

"At this point in my investigation, I really believe I can give you bits of information that might help you with your drug case, and I'm willing to do that, Felicia. But the information I have might be meaningless without filling it in with parts of what you know."

"Yes, that has crossed my mind, but I have limitations you don't have. Why don't you shoot a few questions my way? I'll see what I can do."

"So, can you tell me anything about these drug cartels and the case you're working? How did your interview with the MW go?"

"He wouldn't give up his pals. We know that there's a drug distribution center in south Kentucky. It might be here, it might be in Plainsburg, it might be … anywhere." Felicia drummed her fingers on the table. "The MWs are involved. We have evidence that connects them to a cartel in Colombia. Somehow the drugs are getting moved into this country from the border, and it could be by a means as simple as a private plane or a moving van. I have to say that your case interests me because we've been trying to figure out how the money side of the equation works. It's getting washed somewhere. As you know, we have had plenty of experience dealing with Bank Antriol and their terrorist activity, but we haven't paid as much attention to the cartel connection until now."

Carol nodded. "Like I told you, there was a murder in Plainsburg that could be connected. Janet Blanco worked for Antriol at the anti-money laundering unit there. According to our missing witness, she was in charge of the Latin America branch and had flagged a bunch of transactions between the bank and sanctioned entities in Central and South America and Mexico that the DOJ had identified as drug cartels. Most of our emphasis has been on the terrorist side of it, but it is becoming clearer that Ms. Blanco was focused on the cartel side. I personally have little doubt that she was murdered because of what she uncovered at work. The best way I can help you is to keep looking for who is responsible. The cartel? The bank? Or some random killer? One thing is for sure—the local police chief will never answer that question."

When lunch was finished, the two women paid up and left the restaurant. "Follow me to PO Box Ltd.," Felicia said. "Maybe I can assist you in getting what you want. I can at least help you get past go; then it's up to you. As you no doubt remember, the rights you have as a private citizen to dig around are a lot broader than what I have as law enforcement. You know the drill."

They drove their cars a block to the store and parked again. Inside, Carol found a worker who seemed even more gullible than the Tazewell FedEx employee. This would be easy.

Carol pulled out the piece of paper with the PO box number on it. "Hi, I'm investigator Carol Morris with the Bergman-Deketomis law firm in Spanish Trace, Florida."

"And I'm Special Agent Felicia Paul of the FBI," her new friend said, flashing her badge.

The worker's eyebrows rose. "Um, what can I do for you?"

Carol pointed to the PO box number on the paper. "What can you tell us about the owner of this box?"

"Uh, I can't … there are privacy laws that I…"

"Sir, we are conducting a sensitive investigation involving murder, drug smuggling, and terrorism," Carol said. "Now, we could go and waste time getting a warrant from a judge, or my law firm could *subpoena* you, or you could just help us out and maybe save some lives." She pulled out the FBI sketch of the person of interest. "Maybe you've seen this sketch on the news?"

"Uh, no."

"Does he look familiar to you?"

"Uh, sorta. Yeah, I think so."

Carol asked, "Is he the one who owns the PO box?"

The man nodded.

"When's the last time you saw him?"

"I don't know. A while. A few weeks, maybe."

"Could you please look up the box number and tell us what information you have on the box?" Carol asked.

Realizing he was in over his head and pay grade, and clearly confused about who was in charge between the two intimidating women, the employee went to his computer and typed. "The box belongs to James Miller." He read out the residence address and phone number. The phone number was another old one that was no longer in service, but the address was new. In fact, it was in Pikeville.

Carol immediately plugged the address into the GPS on her phone. She looked at Felicia. "It's a Dairy Queen."

"Hmpf. Sir, can you please open the box for us?" Carol asked, taking things a step further while Felicia stood by without saying another word.

Again, the young man weighed his options. "I don't think my boss would like that."

"You'd be doing a service to your country, sir. Or, like I said, we can come back with a warrant and you'd have to open it anyway. Or, then there's the subpoena from my law firm for you, personally."

"Oh, fine." He opened a drawer and grabbed a set of master keys. "Follow me," he said, and he led them through a door and to an alcove of PO boxes. The man opened the correct one and stood to the side.

"Could I have some privacy, please?" Carol asked.

The man rolled his eyes and walked back to the counter. "Let me know when you're done."

Felicia said, "Carol, I'm not going to be able to look through the box, so I'm going to start making my way to other appointments. I sure have enjoyed our time together. You have my phone number. Give me a call when you leave this place. I'll be anxious to hear from you."

"You'll be first on my call list. Stay safe, my friend."

As Felicia made her exit, Carol's attention was squarely on the task at hand. Carol pulled everything out of the tightly packed box and took it over to a counter in the store. She began her review of the items: a sealed, bulky bubble-pad envelope and a legal size envelope an inch thick with contents.

Carol tore open the padded envelope first. It contained four cell phones. A quick examination determined that three of them were burners. The fourth was a Samsung Galaxy S21. She turned it on, but it asked for a PIN. She consulted her notes listing Joel's phone numbers and found the one that Michael would call to leave messages. She dialed it … and the Samsung rang silently. It was the phone Joel received messages on. It could not be traced, but still allowed him to receive messages that he could check at intervals. The PO box area was open 24/7.

She turned off the phone and then opened the other envelope. She found Joel's passport, his discharge papers, his birth certificate, and other personal items that he must have regarded as important documents. Carol used her phone to snap pictures of all the items she found and then put them back in exactly the order she had found them.

As she worked her way through the stack of items, Carol came across an envelope with red letters scrawled on the front. It was marked "Antriol." It contained what looked like the mother lode of information Joel had itemized in his affidavit. Along with actual copies of bank transaction memos, she saw a document with red stars drawn down the sides. Someone, presumably Joel, had scribbled in pen, "Janet Blanco's transactions that she gave to me." The statement was signed JOEL HARTBECK and dated.

Contained in the Blanco document was a list of what appeared to be Central or South American companies. Next to the listings, in a different hand, was written, CARTEL FRONTS! It was potentially a document that would move to center stage in Felicia's cartel investigation. Attached to it was a collection of bills of lading itemizing various descriptions of furniture and furniture parts such as bed frames, mattresses, and table tops. Joel had circled KENTUCKY CLUB TRUCKING COMPANY, with an address on State Highway 92. Remarkably close to Plainsburg.

Rather than continuing to take pictures and placing these items back in the box, Carol decided that it was too risky to leave this material at the facility. She recognized the risk that posed for the criminal drug case because of chain of custody and evidentiary pitfalls that might later arise, but the documents were simply too important to risk losing. She was a firm believer in the 'bird in the hand' theory on collecting evidence.

Carol wrote on one of the envelopes: *Joel, I'm Carol Morris. I work with Michael Carey. We need to speak to you! I have taken the bank documents that were in the envelope and I will keep them safe. PS: I will leave you messages on your phone. – Carol.*

She put everything else back into the PO box and locked it. Carol returned to the counter and gave the man his keys. "Thank you for your service," Carol said. "We're going to leave five-star reviews for you on Yelp and Google."

The employee swallowed. "Uh, thanks?"

Outside, Carol made her first call. "Felicia, you had a good day today. I'm predicting that soon you are going to receive a package from an anonymous source that is going to make you one very happy FBI agent. No need for me to say more. It will all be self-explanatory when the package arrives."

"Crystal clear, my friend," Felicia replied. "I'll be standing by. Sorry I had to cut this interesting day short, but I thought it was best to let someone without a badge do the looking. It sounds like you might have gotten a break, and I'm happy for you."

"That's putting it mildly. It's been a pleasure, Felicia. Be careful out there. I'll be in touch."

Back in her car, Carol checked her messages. Still no word from Michael.

As it was midday, now she was concerned.

38

Somewhere in Kentucky—Tuesday

...tomorrow or the next day ... until the judge ... how it is, you got me?
...never find ... afterwards, then Chad can get his...
"...for the camera ... and, oh, look, is he waking up?"
"The punk is waking up.
He'll wish he hadn't.
Ha ha ha ha ha ha...

The voices were like ocean waves, the tide flowing in and out of his ears and brain. Several voices. Men. Laughing.

Michael opened his eyes to a blur. Sunlight. No ... yes, sunlight coming from somewhere...

Pain.

He was suddenly more aware of the aches in his shoulders, head, and stomach than of the lack of functioning core senses.

"You awake, asshole?"

Michael's eyes finally focused. The man standing before him was likely in his late twenties or early thirties. He had a beard, mustache, and long blonde hair that was tied in a ponytail. He wore an army vest and no shirt underneath, revealing a bare sternum and a ribbed stomach. A ring pierced his right eyebrow. His bare arms displayed tattoos, notably of spider webs on his elbows. A Nazi "iron eagle" adorned his chest, although the bird's wings were covered by the vest.

Two other MWs stood behind the blonde man.

It all came roaring back to him.

He'd been at Willis Lee's house. The MWs were on the patio, pointing guns. They had rushed in and there hadn't been a thing Michael could have done. With that much firepower aimed at him, the only option was to surrender.

The skinhead had punched him hard in the stomach. It caused Michael to bend over in agony, and one of the others slammed Michael's right shoulder with the butt of a rifle. He went down to the floor, and then the skinhead punted him with a steel-toed boot to the head. The trauma of that blow stunned Michael to near paralysis. He remembered being picked up and hustled outside and into an automobile. A van? Truck?

And then one of them plunged a hypodermic needle into his neck. Within seconds there was blackness ... and here he was.

Michael didn't know how long he'd been drugged and out of it, but it was obviously the following day. He tried to move, but his hands were duct taped to an armchair and his calves were adhered to its front legs. The chair seemed to be bolted to the floor.

Michael's eyes darted around his surroundings. He was inside a room where the walls were made of logs. A door about fifteen feet behind the blonde guy was open. Michael could barely see the ground outside. There was a window on the wall to the right, but it was covered by black drapes. The sunshine was coming through the door, and two burning oil lamps sitting on a table beneath the window also provided illumination. Michael noted a fireplace dominating the left wall. Five army cots occupied various spots on the floor.

"Nice place, isn't it?" the blonde guy said.

Michael's voice croaked. "Where am I?"

"You're in the middle of a bad scene that won't get any better. That's where you are, son."

The other two men laughed.

Michael studied the man in front of him. Based on Joel's affidavit, he guessed the blonde's identity.

"Rusty Wainwright," Michael said.

"Wow, look at Mikey showing off his big brain!" Rusty announced to more laughter. "Yeah, I'm Rusty. How'd you know?"

Michael just shook his head. He coughed a little.

"Oh, my," Rusty said, "you're probably thirsty. I'll bet you need to use the outhouse and maybe get some food in your stomach, am I right?"

The thought of water and food was overpowering. At the mention of the outhouse, Michael knew that Rusty spoke the truth about that as well.

"Okay, here's the thing," Rusty said. "We're going to let you up. You'll be marched outside so you don't shit yourself here. And so you know, my pals here would just as soon slit your throat as look at you, so no bullshit hero stuff or I'll put a knife in you myself. If everything goes well outside, you get something to eat and drink. It's two o'clock in the afternoon, so I'm pretty sure that's a big gift."

Where ... am ... I? Michael asked with more intensity.

"Fine, since you're dying to know ... you're tucked away in a cabin way out in the woods. The kind of place that's not on a map." Rusty reached out and touched Michael on the side of the head. Michael winced at the tenderness near his temple. "You're damn lucky they pulled Chad off you. Chad's a little hard to control. You cross him and it's an instant nightmare raining all around. Be cool and you might make it out of here."

All Michael could do was nod.

"First I need to do this." He held up a cell phone. "Look at me, Mr. Dick Tracy."

Michael was staring at Rusty until he realized the guy was taking photos of him trussed up in the chair. Michael turned his head and closed his eyes.

Rusty examined his handiwork on the phone and nodded. "Got a few good ones before he looked away. Okay." He turned to his cohorts. "Cut that tape off and let's get him up."

* * *

They allowed him to eat a plate of cold beans and drink rust-colored water from a tin can at a picnic table outside. One guy with an AR-15 stood a short distance away watching Michael's every move. Rusty sat on the other side of the table. Michael had counted a total of four men. Once he was free from his bonds and outdoors, Michael could see that the place was likely an old hunting cabin, the kind that Jake had been tracking. It appeared to be a century old. There was no electricity, hence the lamps inside. He had noticed that they'd filled his cup with water from a pump at the side of the house. That meant there was no running water, either. A dirt road led away from the place through thick trees. In fact, woodlands surrounded the property. He was really deep in it somewhere.

"See how easy this is? Be cool and all goes well," Rusty said.

Michael nodded.

"Good. We want our special guests to be happy. We want to keep those five-star reviews coming!" The others laughed at their leader's wit.

"So what's this all about?" Michael asked.

Rusty grinned. "He *can* speak in complete sentences!"

"You have me here for a reason. What's going on?" Michael snapped.

"All right, no harm in telling you, even if you do make it out of here alive. Your boss is in Richmond, Virginia. He's at a hearing that really matters to some friends of ours. We're gonna know two days from now how that hearing goes for you. If your Mr. Bossman wins, you lose. If he loses, your chances get a lot better. All you are right now, pal, is insurance that Mr. Big Lawyer drops a lawsuit against our good friends no matter which way that judge decides."

"He'll never drop the case."

"Then you won't live to see Friday if he doesn't. You done with your lunch? Tasty, huh? All right, we're going back inside. We're gonna ziptie your wrists, but if you're a good boy we'll let you lie down. It's just like it is up in Rikers … if you behave, you get privileges. If you don't, then hell rains down. Don't worry, we'll always be here to make sure you don't get too comfortable. And one more thing … I need the PIN to get into your cell phone, and it's probably not worth it to you for us to have to beat it out of you, so just give it up. Don't worry, I won't look at your personal stuff. I just need to send a text message … from you. Okay, off you go." He looked at the guy with the long rifle. "Smitty, take him inside."

39

It was late afternoon when Carol dialed her go-to right hand.

"Sarah Mercer."

"Sarah, it's me."

"Hey, Carol. What's up?"

"Listen, Michael is missing. I don't know where he is. He's been gone since last night. I didn't think much of it this morning, but I haven't heard from him in twenty-four hours. So I'm concerned now."

"Got it! I'm calling Deke and conferencing you in. Hold on."

Carol waited a few seconds and then she heard Deke's comforting voice. "Hello, Carol? What's happened?"

Carol repeated what she'd said to Sarah.

Deke said, "Sarah ... Is Jake there?"

She answered, "He stepped out to grab something for us to eat. We've been working all day on reviewing documents. He'll be back soon."

"Well, tell Jake I said he should get on a plane and get up to Kentucky to help Carol."

"I don't know if that's necessary, Deke," Carol said. "I'm going to report Michael missing to the police. What was the name of the officer that Jake befriended?"

"Sheila Denning," Sarah answered.

"I'll call her. I don't think anyone else in that PD will care much. I have his rental car information, so I hope that at the very least they'll keep an eye out for it." She then told them how Michael had gone to an appointment with Willis Lee at the man's house the previous evening. He hadn't been seen since.

"Do you know where Lee lives?" Deke asked.

"I don't. Michael didn't say. Sarah, can you find out?"

Sarah said, "Let me look; give me a second."

"I do have the guy's phone number, and I know where the AML unit is," Carol said. "Oh, let me tell you what I've found." She then proceeded to relate the story of Joel's PO box in Pikeville. "We need to look into this Kentucky Club Trucking Company right away. It might be important."

Sarah got back on the line. "Carol, I'm not getting any results for Willis Lee. He's completely unlisted. You'll have to get into the state's DMV data, and Jake has the ability to hack into there. It won't take him long."

"I can't wait for Jake," Carol said. "I bet Sheila Denning will help me. If not … get Jake to call me right away." She then asked, "Deke, how did the hearing go?"

Deke told her what happened in the courtroom. "We're just going to remain here in Richmond until Thursday. No point in flying back to Florida and then turning around to return the next day."

"Hopefully, the judge will do the right thing."

"Carol, if you don't have any good news by tonight, I still want Jake to fly up and give you a hand."

"Thanks. I'm outta here now."

Carol hung up and found the number she had for Officer Sheila Denning in her laptop. She dialed it and was relieved that the woman picked up right away.

"Officer Denning, this is Carol Morris. I work with Jake Rutledge at the Bergman-Deketomis law firm in Florida."

"Jake? Oh, right. Hello."

"Jake spoke highly of you, and I wanted to reach out. I'm in Plainsburg, and one of our lawyers is missing."

"Wait, what?"

"Are you able to talk right now?"

"Yeah, I'm in my patrol car."

Carol gave Sheila a quick synopsis of what had happened.

"Okay. How can I help?"

"I need the address for Willis Lee. Can't find it with Google, and I'm hoping you can get into the DMV…"

"Hold on, let me plug that in…" Carol waited a few seconds. "Here it is. Willis Bradford Lee." She read off the street address. "That's on the edge of town. Are you heading there now?"

"I am."

"I'll meet you there in thirty minutes."

"Sounds good. Thanks." Carol then texted Sarah to tell her and Jake that she had Willis Lee's address.

* * *

Spanish Trace, Florida—Tuesday

Jake got off the phone with Deke and immediately asked Diana to get him a flight to Knoxville on Wednesday morning. The thought of his friend's disappearance was a little overpowering, but he knew that Michael was a survivor with a unique skill set. Jake then checked with Sarah on her progress, and she told him that two of the firm's law clerks were helping to complete the Bank Antriol employees' profiles. She promised to report to both him and Carol when she had something. He figured that Willis Lee had to be involved, it simply made sense.

Jake went back to the firm's unique face recognition software that had been running for a few hours. It was far from a government quality program, but it seldom failed to at least provide tangible leads. A little luck was always required. The program had completed its search and come up with nine possibilities for identifying "Chad." Two entries in the results were similar-looking people in Oregon and Minnesota. Those were unlikely candidates. The other seven results, however, were photos of the same man throughout the years. One was even a mug shot.

Dean Chadwick Quigg.

"Bingo," Jake said aloud. "Now let's find out where you live."

He spent the next hour using every database he could hack and access, but he had no luck finding an address for Chad. The man wasn't listed in Kentucky's DMV roster. Jake tried Tennessee, West Virginia, Virginia, Indiana, Ohio, and Missouri, and still no luck. No driver's license—at least not a legitimate one—and no address.

Chad Quigg was a ghost. One of the scary, violent kinds.

* * *

Plainsburg, Kentucky—Tuesday

Carol found Willis Lee's home where the GPS had told her it would be. A Plainsburg Police patrol car pulled up not a minute later. There were no other cars in sight.

The two women got out of their respective vehicles and stood back from the house. They shook hands, introduced themselves to each other, and then turned their attention to the dwelling.

Sheila rested her hand over her sidepiece. "Seems pretty quiet," she said. "I don't think anyone's here."

"Michael's car isn't here either," Carol responded. "So he must have had his meeting and left. I'm going to call Willis's number."

"And I'll go ring the doorbell and take a look around."

Carol dialed the number and got voicemail. When the beep sounded, she stated her name and affiliation with Michael. "Mr. Lee, please call me back. Michael is missing, and you may have been the last person to see him." She left her number and hung up.

Sheila returned after making a trip around the house. "I rang the doorbell, went around to the back, and knocked on the glass door. Nobody's home."

"Crap. I'm going to the AML unit. Maybe Willis is at work."

"Do you have info on Michael's car? I can put out an APB."

"Yes." She gave Sheila the make, model, and license plate number.

"Let's fill out the missing person form here and now," Sheila said. Carol sat with her in the patrol car and recited all the details about Michael that she could recall. Too much of the form had to be left blank.

"I'll take care of it—this is enough for now," Sheila said. The radio on the dashboard squelched. "Hold on a sec, I have to get this."

While Sheila talked to her superiors at the station, Carol got out and looked up the AML unit's address, got in her own car, and backed away from the house. Sheila stuck her head out of her open car door and called out, "I have to go to headquarters! I'll put out that APB and file the missing person report. Call me later!"

Carol gave her a thumbs-up and a wave. Then she drove away.

* * *

A half hour later, Carol pulled into the strip mall parking lot where Bank Antriol's splinter office was located. It was just after five o'clock, and many cars were already departing. Carol got out and ran into the building.

A young blonde receptionist stood behind the doctor's office-style window, gathering her purse and pushing in her chair. "Oh, hi," she said to Carol. "We're just now closing. Is there something I can help you with real quick?"

"I'm looking for Willis Lee. I need to speak to him. It's an emergency."

"Oh, dear. Willis didn't come in today."

"He didn't?"

"No. He's off. I think he's on vacation."

"Do you know how to reach him?"

"Um, I can't give out that—"

Carol turned around and went out the door.

She was angry, worried, and ready to do some damage to somebody somewhere.

* * *

Richmond, Virginia—Tuesday

Deke was aware that his public and professional persona was that of a fighter who normally exhibited a cool, calm demeanor. The only times that image took a radical turn was during cross examinations in a courtroom.

Now, however, alone in the Hilton hotel room after nightfall, Deke was proverbially "sweating it out." He had been on the phone constantly with his wife, Teri, with Sarah and Jake in Florida, and with Carol in Kentucky. He was glad to have Bernie, Gina, and Dan in Richmond with him, but after a while the four-way angst session in the hotel bar became tedious.

He heard his phone buzz on the table in the living room area of the suite, indicating the receipt of an email or text message. Would it be good news? Deke picked up the device and saw that a text message had come in from *Michael*! His heart leapt with sudden excitement, and he quickly opened the message.

To his horror, Deke saw a distressing photo. His friend and colleague was bound to a chair with duct tape. The man's face was battered, and he looked like he'd been drugged. There was a visible lump covered in dry blood on the side of his head.

The message read: *Regardless of judge decision, please drop the Antriol case or I won't be coming home. They want you to tell judge you do not have enough evidence to go forward. Do not contact police or FBI or other authorities or my friends here are threatening to burn me alive. The threat is real. Michael.*

40

Spanish Trace, Florida—Tuesday

Everyone was on edge. They were all on a conference call late Tuesday night to weigh their options after Deke had forwarded Michael's photo to them. Everyone was of two minds. On the one hand, they could call the FBI and report the kidnapping, and Carol could inform the Plainsburg police. But on the other hand, the warning was explicitly clear. As with all kidnappings, the threat to the victim was ever present should anyone contact the authorities.

However, Carol suggested that they do reach out to the allies they had gained in recent weeks. Jake agreed that she should call Officer Sheila Denning to report the crime and see if anything could be done without alerting Chief Wainwright and his minions. Carol would also reach out to FBI agent Felicia Paul.

Deke had also broached a moral quandary to the group: "Guys, this is a serious question. Do any of you think Michael is in danger of being hurt *prior* to Thursday?"

"That photo you got shows that he's already been hurt," Carol observed.

"I know. That could have occurred when he was abducted. I mean, do you think these guys, whoever they are—"

"The MWs," Jake said. "That's who they are. They're the only ones who could be doing this."

Deke said, "Fine, I can accept that. The MWs have Michael. The question is, do you think they will keep him relatively safe and unharmed until the drop-dead decision has to be made on the lawsuit going forward? Because if we *do* contact the authorities now, I think it will place Michael in even more danger."

"In other words, you're asking if we can we stall until Thursday?" Carol asked.

"Right. That's my question. I don't want to place Michael at any more risk than he already faces. Do we really have until Thursday morning, because if not I'll make the call right now. What I'm missing here is how do these nutjobs believe that the announcement of a dismissal changes anything? It's not like we go away forever. Someone else will file the same facts on another day. Dan Lawson isn't going away, either."

"To answer the first part of that question," Jake ventured, "yes, I do believe we have until Thursday, but the next part of that question is more complicated. With a dismissal, regardless of the repercussions, someone buys more time. It makes no difference if the MWs are arrested and prosecuted. It makes no difference if the case is resurrected. Months will pass and whoever needs to make a run for it has bought more time. This looks more like an escape plan by the *real* bad planners than it does a practical solution for Antriol. My thought, Deke, is that whoever is behind this is just looking for a period of absolute confusion and chaos that is going to develop after the fat lady sings here."

"I would agree, Jake," Deke said. "That's the only logic I see. Otherwise a dismissal, even with prejudice, has no long-term positive impact for Antriol. Carol, what's on your mind about where we are?"

Carol answered. "The best part of this is that they want Michael alive and well as a hostage to their demands. We have all of Wednesday to make some progress."

"I hate to do this, but I want a vote. Do we officially contact the authorities before Thursday?" Deke asked with a tremor in his voice. "Yes or no."

Everyone ultimately said, "No." Carol added, "Except for doing what we said about surreptitiously telling our allies in Kentucky about it. Keep it on the sly."

* * *

Wednesday

Sarah, assisted by a handful of law clerks and interns, had been working for hours after very little sleep. They scoured the internet and worked the phone, scrambling to fill in many of the blanks in Gina's compendium of Bank Antriol personnel. Jake had given her the material he had scraped up on the MWs, so that he could catch an early flight to Knoxville. There, he would once again rent a car and drive over the border to Plainsburg.

Sarah spent a lot of her time concentrating on Willis Lee. While at the beginning of the case it appeared as if Mr. Lee was an ally of Joel Hartbeck, the Antriol employee's erratic responses to members of the Deketomis team seemed to indicate otherwise. The man's disappearance after Michael's visit on Monday evening was also a huge red flag. There had been some discussion among the team whether or not Willis had been abducted with Michael. Both Jake and Carol thought that was improbable and that it was more likely that Willis Lee was involved with the kidnappers. "Michael was lured to Willis's house, and I'll bet that's where they grabbed him," Carol had opined. It made sense.

Sarah already knew that he hailed from Brooklyn and was in the Marines from 2008 to 2011. He was forty-one years old. Willis had no social media presence, no LinkedIn account, and, oddly, two different Social Security numbers associated with what online history he had. She had only just discovered this discrepancy, and it was either a mistake or something engineered.

She thought about the man's age and something didn't seem right. When Willis joined the Marines, he would have been twenty-six or so. Wasn't that a little old to be joining the Marines? It wasn't inconceivable, but it was … unusual.

Sarah went to the Defense Finance and Accounting Service website. It held a database of military personnel. A user needed only a Social Security number to search the records. The Bergman-Deketomis firm already had a registered account on the site, so it was no problem. Otherwise she would have had to go to the Freedom of Information Act site and send a request—but that took days or weeks for a response. There were other online databases, but the DFAS site was the quickest and most efficient.

Sarah plugged in Willis's name and the first SSN she had for him into the search, adding the years in service, and pressed enter.

No results.

She tried the second Social Security number.

Again, no results.

Sarah had been diligent in checking Willis Lee's criminal record in the state of Kentucky, but she hadn't checked any other states. Since the guy was from Brooklyn, she went to the New York database and entered the details.

Her jaw dropped. How could they have not known this earlier?

Willis Lee had been convicted of sexual assault in 2008 and had served seven out of a ten-year sentence at Rikers Island.

He had spent years dressed up in prison stripes rather than marine green.

* * *

Plainsburg, Kentucky—Wednesday

"You've got to be shittin' me," Carol said when Sarah relayed the news on the phone. "Does everyone else know?"

"I'm calling Deke and the team in Richmond next," Sarah said. "I thought you should be the first to know, since you're in the belly of the beast up there."

"Thanks, Sarah, you're the best. I was just about to call Officer Denning. I wonder if the police here in Plainsburg know about him? Good work; let me know if you find more gold."

"You know," Sarah said, "something just clicked for me. I overlooked it before. I need to follow up on something else. Gotta run."

"Bye!"

Carol hung up and immediately dialed Sheila.

"Hey, Carol. How's it going? Any luck on finding your colleague?"

"Well. Have I got a story for you. Can you talk?"

"I'm in the patrol car again. Story of my life."

"Okay, here goes." Carol then told her about the message Deke received.

"Oh, my God. No wonder the APB hasn't brought us any results. I think I'd better tell the chief about this."

"No, don't, Sheila. We have until Thursday morning to pursue leads. Jake is on his way here, and together we'll do everything we can to find him. Besides, we believe that the MWs have Michael."

"Son of a bitch. Those animals," Sheila said. "If that's true, then you're right. Telling the chief won't do you any good."

"Yep, his son is their top dog. Do you have information on where the MWs hang out? Where do you think they'd be keeping Michael?"

"They have several places. Out in the woods, up in the mountains, somewhere that'd be hard to find," Sheila said. "They like those old hunting cabins that have been around for a hundred years or more."

"That's what I figured. What does Rusty Wainwright do for a living, anyway?"

"I'm sure he sells drugs! But as for what he tells the IRS, frankly, I have no idea. I know Rusty, but we do not talk to each other one bit. When he got out of prison and came back to Kentucky, he tried to hit on me a couple of times. I told him that if ever came within ten feet of me, I'd kick him in the balls."

"Wait," Carol said. "Rusty Wainwright was in prison?"

"He was. Up in New York. He was part of an armed robbery in one of those places near New York City. Westchester? New Rochelle? I can't remember. A suburb that people commute into the city from."

"How long was he in prison?"

"Five years, I think. I believe his sentence was eight, and he got out for good behavior or some nonsense. Oh, and get this. Rusty was suspected of killing an inmate while he was in the joint. A black man. It couldn't be proven. No one ratted him out. Rusty, of course, was part of the Aryan Brotherhood gang, so his racism and bigotry was on full display there. He bragged about the murder after he got out. He's not wired right."

"I guess that explains the spider web tattoos on his arms. What years was he incarcerated?"

"I want to say 2010 to 2015, something like that."

"And where did you say he was imprisoned?"

"Oh. Rikers."

Carol inhaled audibly. "Sheila. You know Willis Lee? Well, guess what." She told the officer what Sarah had just uncovered.

"Carol, is that your connection?"

"You tell me."

"Well, Willis isn't known to associate with the MWs. I mean, he's never been seen parading with them or hanging out in bars with them. At least, not that I know of."

"It makes you wonder, though," Carol said. "They definitely have the same political leanings from what you told me. And they could easily have met in prison."

"Yep. Not a stretch at all."

* * *

Spanish Trace, Florida—Wednesday

The day crept into afternoon. Sarah continued her research into the bank's personnel. Two of the key figures, Blake Dullea and Karl Maher, had extensive online histories. There had been questions about Maher's Egyptian ties. While he had been born in America, his online presence on social media indicated that he frequently went to Egypt to visit family. Sarah enlisted Doug, one of the younger law clerks who knew his way around social media better than anyone at the firm, to explore Maher's Facebook and Instagram connections to see what they might reveal. After a couple of hours, Doug presented his findings to Sarah.

"So, Karl Maher has several uncles and cousins in Egypt," he told her. "Like Karl, they have fairly impressive positions at financial institutions and in national politics. He comes from a very connected family. Interestingly, though, I found one photo on his cousin Ahmet's site. The privacy preferences, I think, must have accidentally been set to public. It's a picture of two cousins and an uncle at a meeting of what appears to be the Muslim Brotherhood."

"No surprise there," Sarah said. She knew that the organization for decades espoused teachings and ideas that helped establish groups like Hamas, Islamic Jihad, al-Qaeda, and other radical Sunni groups. "Do you think those relatives are involved in terrorist activities?"

"Hard to say," Doug responded. "Not sure what all you know about the group. After the ouster of former president Hosni Mubarak in the Arab Spring protests of 2011, the organization won a bunch of seats in Egypt's parliament and promoted Mohamed Morsi as their presidential candidate, and the guy actually won."

"Yeah, but that didn't last long."

"No, he was ousted by the military in July 2013, and the new Egyptian government banned the Brotherhood, jailed or exiled its members, and the group went deep underground. According to what I've read, most all of them have virtually disappeared or seem to be hiding in plain sight. The government doesn't seem to be much interested in hunting them down and the US hasn't designated the group as a terrorist organization. Seemingly for political reasons. They reserve that type of pressure for those other hyper-violent offshoots. Does this mean Maher has sympathies for extremism or Sunni terrorists, or is he just very well connected in the Middle East?"

"Those are good questions, and I will report those findings to the team. Thank you, Doug."

When Doug left her office, Sarah continued going down the path she had remembered to take while talking to Carol on the phone. She had plenty of information on Blake Dullea's professional life, but she didn't know much about his younger years. Through LinkedIn she had learned that he had gone to the prestigious Brooklyn Technical High

School, one that boasted high academic standards, especially in mathematics. The same online information indicated that he was in the class of 1999.

Sarah then used Google to see if there were any copies of the school's yearbooks online, and sure enough, she found the 1999 edition. She spent time looking through it and found Dullea's senior photo and other mentions. He had been a member of several academic clubs and was on the varsity basketball team.

And then she found the lucky penny while looking at the basketball team's group photo. There, standing near Blake Dullea and wearing the same school jersey and shorts, was Willis Lee. He stuck out like a tadpole out of water because of his small build. There was no mistake that it was him. Weak chin, awkwardly large head, and rat-like eyes. It was him.

"When you turn over rocks, there's no telling what you'll find," she said to herself.

Sarah then went back to the senior photos, but Willis wasn't there. She then checked the pictures of juniors, and she found him. Willis Lee was a year younger than Blake Dullea ... *but they had known each other since high school!*

41

Somewhere in Kentucky—Wednesday

The MWs allowed Michael to eat breakfast and lunch with them at the picnic table outside the cabin. They seemed to grudgingly respect that he had been in the Air Force and had been a special operator in Iraq. Michael had made it a point to "behave" in the hopes that they would relax more around him and thus become careless. He also wanted as much time as possible without the zip ties. They secured him when he was inside the cabin because they couldn't always keep someone in there watching him. At least they zip tied his wrists in *front* rather than behind his back. That made a huge difference in his comfort level. He was allowed to sleep on a cot, but his hands were still bound and a long leash attached to one ankle was fastened to the bolted chair.

Where the hell is Joel? Michael continued to wonder. The fact that the MWs had brazenly abducted him and were obviously more than comfortable with violence made him suspect that Joel, too, had found himself in the MWs' grasp and was now buried somewhere in the hills nearby. Michael's gut instincts were usually never wrong, and it was becoming increasingly clear to him that Joel was never the "terrorist" behind the bombings. He was likely a victim of these animals. When his thoughts would drift in this direction, Michael worked hard to force them to the back of his mind by refocusing on reading the men and his immediate surroundings for any information that may help keep him alive.

He noticed that different MWs would come and go during the day. They rode in on motorcycles, or in SUVs, pickup trucks, and vans. There was also a lot of whispering and side conversations going on around him. Michael could sense that some kind of plan was coming to fruition. Rusty hadn't been there on Wednesday morning when Michael woke up. He overheard mentions of "Chad" and "home" and a "shipment coming in." Also talk about "Virginia" and "hostage."

He knew that Deke had been sent the photo that Rusty had taken. It was humiliating to be seen trussed up and helpless by his colleagues. Michael knew that they were working on trying to find him. He was of the opinion that they *should* get the FBI involved. Michael wasn't afraid. Whether the MWs were capable of killing him wasn't the question, but rather when, how, and which one would do it. He had seen firsthand what Chad was like. Michael knew that he could be pit bull dangerous. Rusty may have believed that he was the leader of the gang, but Michael had seen power struggles occur within criminal packs all the time. Chad was no doubt biding his time and planning for a regime change that would be brutal in the end.

Michael figured he could sit there and project a whole list of possible bad endings or do what he was trained to do. That 'one more thing,' that 'one more move' that he was prepared to focus on his entire career as a PJ. In his prior life, he had been the last hope of rescue for people in their Lord's Prayer moments. Now it might be up to Michael to rescue himself.

* * *

Richmond, Virginia—Wednesday

Deke, Gina, and Bernie were killing time inside Richmond's Museum of Fine Arts late Wednesday afternoon. Deke felt helpless regarding Michael's situation in Kentucky, and he knew that his usual cool and calm veneer was exhibiting cracks. He'd been on the phone with Teri at home three times already since the morning, simply because her soothing voice really *did* quiet his nerves.

Dan Lawson had gone back to New York and was planning to return early Thursday for the judge's decision. Now it was just the three of them, as they meandered through the Modern and Contemporary Art section of the sizable collection. They were staring at Andy Warhol's striking black and white "Triple Elvis" when a phone call came in. Deke answered it quietly. He then moved away from the others to a corner of the room so that he wouldn't disturb other patrons. He spoke for a couple of minutes and then returned to his team.

"Well!" he whispered. "An interesting development."

"What's going on?" Bernie asked.

"That was the courthouse. I've been informed that Judge Trackman will not be returning to court until *Friday*. Her mother passed away last night, so the judge is staying where she is today and tomorrow in order to make funeral arrangements, but she will return on Friday for one day to handle some outstanding dockets, and then she'll take the next week off. It gives us another full day to find Michael. I'm stepping outside to call Carol and Jake."

* * *

Plainsburg, Kentucky—Wednesday

Jake was back in Plainsburg, and he had met Carol at the hotel. They hit the ground on fire and discussed everything they knew about the MWs. They were certain that Michael had been abducted by them and that they were somehow connected to some part of Bank Antriol. The situation had been made clearer by Sarah's news that Willis Lee was at least one linking piece. Blake Dullea and Willis had known each other for years, and Willis and Rusty Wainwright had possibly met in prison.

"Those greedy bastards in New York are using a right-wing domestic terrorist outfit to create as much madness as possible centering around our lawsuit! Bedlam is what somebody wants!" Jake snarled.

Carol responded to that with, "Jake, I don't know if this is a crazy idea or what, but what if the MWs are behind the bombings? Does that make any kind of sense to you? Think about it. Two of the five bombings will have a direct impact on our case. The fact that Deke believes we still have enough evidence to salvage a case suggests that the MWs took Michael as a backup plan just in case."

"But then all that really means is can we connect someone at Bank Antriol to the bombings? No way they're being run by a law firm; no way they're being run by a man like Nigel Beech. What we need most is to put a face to who's calling these shots, and it sure as hell isn't that little worm Willis. That narrows the field to at least two possibilities in my mind that I'm liking," Jake said.

Carol showed him Joel's printouts from his PO box. She pointed to the shipping address on the bill of lading. "This Kentucky Club Trucking Company. We need to go check it out."

"Let's do it."

"Are you armed?"

"Yes. Armed and licensed in this state."

"I wish I were," Carol grumbled.

They drove in Jake's rental, a black Chevrolet Tahoe. Carol navigated, and her GPS indicated that the trucking company was out of town to the east, just as Sheila had said.

"I tried to find more information on this company yesterday," Carol told him. "There's no website. No Google or Yelp reviews. There is no registration for them at the Federal Motor Carrier Safety Administration. I was beginning to think they didn't really exist, but then on a Reddit search I found some mentions. I'll bet they carry phony registration documents in case they're stopped on a highway. The company is small, and they're in business only with a retail store in a strip mall in Plainsburg. The shop sells exotic furniture, stuff from other countries, especially Mexico, Central America, South America … All the truckers do is move furniture from Florida and Texas to Kentucky. There are sister stores in Miami and Corpus Christi. The outfit trucks them from those places to their headquarters here, which is a warehouse. That's where we're going. Some of the furniture then goes to the shop in Plainsburg, and some of it is sold to other retailers," Carol said. "Oh, and Kentucky Club Trucking Company and the retail store are family owned. Been in Plainsburg for decades."

When they finally reached the facility, they were struck by how isolated it was. The company was off Highway 92 and down a well-worn dirt road that wound through a thick wooded area. The building was surprisingly small, about the size of a bowling alley. It sat behind a high chain link fence with barbed wire at the top. A sign on the gate across the entrance read: PRIVATE PROPERTY—NO TRESPASSING.

"That's it?" Carol asked. "Just 'Private Property'? No name of the company or phone number? What, no 'Beware of Dog' or no 'Violators Will Be Shot'?"

The place was eerily quiet.

"Joel thinks it means something," Jake said. "He wouldn't have circled it on that printout if he didn't."

Carol got out of the car and looked around outside the fence. "There's not even a call button. Is this place a real business?" She called out, "Is anyone here?"

Nothing.

Jake asked, "What did you say the name of the furniture store is?"

"Oh, I don't think I did." She got back in the car. "Quigg's. A couple or three generations have run it."

Jake manipulated his phone as he looked them up. He was impressed with the photos. "They sell nice stuff, it looks like," he said. "Wait."

"What?"

"Quigg's." He looked at Carol. "Could it be? One of the MWs, the one known as 'Chad,' his real name is Dean Chadwick *Quigg.*"

"Cha-ching! I think we should go see that store."

Jake backed up the car, turned around, and headed back to Plainsburg.

Carol asked, "Would you agree that suspicions of Joel being the terrorist bomber are misguided?"

"I would. I think we're on the same side in all this."

"Should we fill him in on everything?"

"If he's alive and listening to his messages, yes."

Carol made the call. "Joel, it's Carol Morris again. I don't know if you're getting my messages, but you should know that Michael Carey has been abducted by the MWs and is being held hostage. They're trying to influence Deke to drop the lawsuit against Bank Antriol. They've extended the deadline until Friday morning because the hearing was postponed until then. We don't have much faith that the MWs will keep their word and release him, no matter what we do." She then proceeded to tell Joel what they had learned so far about the MWs and the various personnel. "We need you to come out of hiding now. It's now or never. I've already left several phone numbers for you—mine, Deke's, Jake's, and Sarah's. We're all on your side. If you're receiving this, give us some help, please. Thanks."

42

Quigg's was located in one of the oldest and busiest strip malls in Plainsburg. Unlike where the Antriol AML-unit was operated, there were many storefronts and eateries in this block-long shopping center. It once might have been what locals would have called "downtown." Vintage buildings surrounded the area, and the strip mall had perhaps been built fifty years ago on top of an even older shopping center.

"When I found out his real name, I did some digging," Jake said as they got out of the car. "I couldn't find an address for the guy, but further deep diving into police records produced some info. He served eight years in the Federal Correction Institution in Manchester, here in Kentucky, for aggravated battery. He was sentenced to fifteen. I don't know how he got out so soon, because the woman he assaulted was raped and almost died."

"If he's related to these Quiggs, then they must have powerful friends." Carol then cocked her head and added, "My FBI contact, Felicia Paul … she was interviewing an MW at Federal Correction Institution on Monday. It was about drug smuggling. Cartel stuff. *South and Central American* cartels. So she has something we need, and I have something she needs. We are de facto friends."

"Carol, I think we're onto something," Jake said as he got out of the car. She followed.

"When I did jigsaw puzzles as a kid," she replied, "I always found that the closer you get to finishing them, the easier it is to find the next piece that fits. It's been raining puzzle pieces the past couple of days. So much it makes my head spin."

They went into the store, which was about half the size of a Staples or OfficeMax. It was stocked with a multitude of furnishings but seemed to heavily favor the southwestern-style furniture that Jake had seen on the website.

A tall, silver-haired man in a suit greeted them. "Good afternoon, welcome to Quigg's."

Carol smiled at him. "Hi. We're just going to look around."

"Be my guest. If you have any questions, please let me know." He gave a little bow and went back to his desk at the front of the store. He appeared to be the only person there.

Jake and Carol wandered through, actually admiring the fine crafts-manship and artistry that went into making the pieces. The cabinets and dressers were especially attractive, and they all exhibited the ethnic flavor of lands south of the border. One "selling point" of the cabinets and dressers was that they came equipped with hidden compartments "for those valuable keepsakes."

"You know," Jake whispered, "furniture can be a good hiding place for smuggled drugs."

"I've already made that leap," Carol answered. "Secret compart-ments, huge hollow table legs, bulky cushions. Whaddaya know."

They continued to browse and ultimately came to a wall near the front where many photos and city council awards were hung. The pic-tures portrayed the store and its employees throughout the years, back to the founder, Aaron Quigg and his wife.

"Look," Carol pointed at three photos from different decades that pictured young men and a truck. In the one from the sixties, the men looked fresh out of high school or college. In the middle one from per-haps the eighties, the team of employees had tripled in size as had the number of trucks, and most of the workers were now Hispanic. A few of the original faces were still there and some had longer hair. They were a little rougher around the edges than the boys in the first photo. Then, in the more recent third picture, likely taken in the early 2000s, the dynamics of the group had changed again. A few of the faces from the earlier photos were recognizable, but the majority of the men were white and looked like huge, roided-out thugs that were on a prison work release program.

Jake subtly pointed to figures in the third picture. "They're MWs. I was watching videos on YouTube of their marches and hate protests. This guy ... and this one ... and him ... I recognize. Oh, and look ... there he is." He pointed to another tall one. He had blonde hair and eyes that bore a hole through the camera lens. "That's Chad. Before he shaved his head."

"Then he *is* part of this family," Carol said.

"I see you're admiring our Wall of History," the proprietor said, standing up again and walking to them. Jake recognized the man in one of the family photos.

"Are you part of the Quigg family?" Jake asked.

"I am indeed. I'm Glenn Quigg. My grandfather founded the store." He shook hands with Jake and Carol.

"It's fascinating," Carol said.

"Are you from out of town?" he asked.

"Yes," she said. She indicated Jake. "My brother and I are passing through on our way to DC. I heard about your store from some friends who bought a beautiful coffee table I admired. So I roped Jake here into making a stop."

"Oh? What are your friends' names?"

Carol made them up on the spot. "The Andersons. Joe and Jill?"

Glenn Quigg wrinkled his brow. "I don't remember those names. But I'm not always here, either."

"How many Quiggs are in your family?" Jake asked.

"Of those still involved with the store, just me and my brother Lewis. My other brother Buster was working with us, but he died in a car accident about twenty years ago."

"Sorry to hear that," Jake said. He pointed at the pictures of the truckers. "These are your employees, too?"

"Uh, yes," Glenn said. "They're the shipping and warehousing team we work with that handles pickup and delivery of our furniture from the importers down in Florida mainly."

Carol asked, "Are any of them Quiggs?"

They both felt Glenn Quigg stiffen slightly. He said, "Um, yes, my nephew is in the most recent picture. He runs that trucking business. Buster was his father. Sadly, his mother is in a nursing home now. I think the grief of losing her husband sped up the decline."

"That's terrible," Jake said. "We've been through something similar with our parents. It's a lot to handle. How's your nephew dealing with it?"

The man shrugged a little and said, "He manages. He took over his parents' house and the shipping business with his … friends." He turned away a little and started to walk back to the desk. "Let me know if I can help you with anything else."

It was obvious that Glenn Quigg didn't want to talk about his nephew.

* * *

Carol tried calling Felicia Paul but got the agent's voicemail. Instead of leaving a detailed message, she simply said, "Felicia, give me a call when you can. I've learned some interesting facts even beyond what I found out at the PO Box Ltd. store. These new facts are probably related to that thing you're working on."

A bit stunned at what they'd uncovered in just a few hours, the duo sat in the strip mall parking lot. "We need to find the Buster Quigg home and see what's there," Jake said.

"I know how to do that," Carol said. She made another call.

"Denning."

"Sheila, it's Carol Morris. I'm here with Jake Rutledge. Can you talk? Can I put you on speaker?"

"Yes and yes. I'm at the HQ, but I'm pretty much alone," Sheila said. "Hi, Jake."

"Hello, Sheila."

"You're minding the fort?" Carol asked. "Where is everyone?"

"Out and about. I don't know where Chief Wainwright is. He does his own thing. This is a small-town police station. I've been put on desk duty for insubordination."

"You just can't stay out of trouble, girl. I can relate," Carol said. "What did you do? Or what does he *think* you did?"

"He found out I met you at Willis Lee's house. He didn't say how he found out, but I'm betting that Willis has a hidden home security camera. He must have told Rusty, and then Rusty told his father."

"Geez, you could be right."

"Yeah. Hey, I'm sorry I haven't been able to do anything about your colleague. Any luck on your end?"

"We have moved from pretty sure to almost positive that the MWs have him," Jake said. "Listen, do you know where the Buster Quigg residence is?"

"Uh, yeah. It's over there in the Struck Gold Estates."

"The what?"

Sheila laughed. "That's what locals call it. It's where the wealthy people in Plainsburg live. All the Quiggs live there. Why are you interested in them?"

"Sheila, Chad Quigg is one of the MWs," Jake said.

"Who?"

"Dean Chadwick Quigg."

"Oh, Dean Quigg. Dean's in prison. Who are you talking about?"

"The MW that's a skinhead. He's been out of prison for years, Sheila. He goes by Chad now," Carol said.

Sheila seemed genuinely surprised. "That can't be right. A while back, even Chief Wainwright told me that Dean was still in jail. So did Rusty!"

"Then they're lying," Jake said. "They're protecting him."

"Holy mackerel, I knew Dean twenty years ago and he had hair and was thin as a rail. This guy, Chad, is Hulk-level buff and creepy and *not* the Dean Quigg I used to know! Jesus, some police officer I am."

"Don't take it out on yourself, Sheila," Carol said. "He was gone for many years. Prison can change people right down to how they look, speak, and carry themselves. It's part of their survival mechanism in a place where your pals are all likely to kill you. Regardless of all the tats and body piercings, people like Chad have occasionally been known to hide in plain sight for years. But, just so you know, we suspect him of being a possible kingpin drug smuggler right here in your home town."

"*What?*"

Carol and Jake both told their stories and brought Sheila up to date. "But the first order of business is to find Michael," Carol said. "We want to take a look at the Buster Quigg home and see if Chad might be there."

"That Chad guy is way dangerous," Sheila said. "God, how could I have been so stupid? Chad is Dean Quigg. I never would have guessed it. They say *this* Chad is a murderer, that he's killed people. He was convicted of rape and an exceptionally brutal battery."

"We'll worry about the danger," Jake said. "Just give us the address, please."

"Sure." She gave it to them and then said, "You know you can't take the law into your own hands?"

"We're investigators, Sheila," Carol said. "We're not the police."

Jake added, "We're just gathering information. If we really need the police, then, of course, we'll call someone—but not your chief."

Sheila said she understood and then quickly had to get off. Her boss had just returned to the station.

* * *

"Struck Gold Estates" was really called Plainsburg Hills, and there were indeed some very nice homes scattered over a landscape of green, rolling hills and parks.

"When Michael and I did our driving tour of Plainsburg, we sort of skipped over the rich folks' domain," Jake said. "We didn't think it was relevant to why we were in Plainsburg. It represents old money in the town, and the Antriol AML unit is a recent pop-up business from another state that hired employees from the local pool of applicants. If only we'd known."

Jake drove over a hill to reveal a stately example of the Antebellum architectural style that dominated Southern estates in the mid-1800s. It was fifty yards below and looked a bit more rundown than the other homes nearby. The grass was not freshly mowed and had weeds scattered about, and the flower beds had been left to rot.

"Stop," Carol said, and he did, leaving the motor running at the top of the hill. "That's it," Carol said. "That's where Chad lives."

"Wow, I bet the local homeowners association is all jazzed up about this dump," Jake said.

"There's activity down there."

They saw two vehicles in the large driveway in front of a garage at the side of the house. One was a medium-sized white box truck. The other was a UPS truck. Two men were talking in the driveway, and one of them was bald.

"That's Chad," Jake said. "I'd know him anywhere after that night in the woods."

The other man wore a UPS uniform. The two men appeared to be examining the rear of the UPS truck. The driver pointed at something, and Chad nodded his head.

"I guess Chad got a delivery," Jake said. "Or he's shipping something that got picked up."

Then something peculiar occurred. The two men shook hands and then embraced, as if they were best friends or brothers.

Jake almost laughed. "Looks like Chad has a bromance going on."

The man in the UPS uniform got into his truck, backed it out, and drove toward Jake and Carol on the hill. The driver didn't seem to notice them as the truck went by.

They kept watching the house as Chad shut the door at the back of the white truck—which may have been empty—and then went inside the house. The automatic garage door closed.

"Now what?" Jake asked.

Carol looked at her watch. "I'd like to see what's inside that house. Could be that all the evidence we need is in there."

"We'll have to wait until Mr. Chad leaves."

"I'll bet he leaves soon."

"Why do you think that?"

"Because he's a bigshot in the MWs. The MWs have Michael. Chad will want to be involved in whatever goes down. He's not going to stay at home. He was here for a reason that I'm guessing has to do with what UPS delivered or took away."

"Carol," Jake said, "if we follow Chad when he leaves, he might lead us to Michael."

She gave him a thumbs up, so they waited. Thirty minutes went by. That turned into an hour. The sun sank and soon it was dusk. Just as Carol was about to say they were nuts for pretending to be staked-out cops, the garage door opened. Chad walked out, got into the white box truck, and started it up. The garage door came down, and the truck backed out of the drive.

"Here we go," Jake said.

The truck lumbered up the hill and passed them on the way out of Struck Gold Estates. Jake pulled away from the curb, made a U-turn, and followed their prey. It wasn't difficult to trail the truck. It moved slowly through town and soon reached the outskirts heading southeast. Jake kept the rental car three vehicles behind the truck, but he knew the pursuit would become more difficult once they exited city limits and traffic thinned out.

Then the truck crossed railroad tracks, barely making it across before the crossing warning bell clanged, the red lights flashed, and the gate came down. Traffic halted, and a freight train roared in front of them.

"Damn!" Carol spat.

Jake drummed his fingers on the steering wheel as the train cars passed by. Much too slowly for comfort. A minute elapsed. Then two.

"Oh, for God's sake!" Carol growled.

Four minutes. It was a long, shambling train.

"I'm going to scream," Carol said.

Finally, the caboose was in sight. It came and went. The gate raised and the warning bell stopped its racket. The cars ahead of the rental moved across the tracks and Jake gunned the car, pulled around them, sped forward, and followed the road.

The white box truck was nowhere in sight.

"It's got to be up ahead," Jake muttered.

He pushed the car beyond the speed limit and kept going. Darkness had enveloped their surroundings, and suddenly they were alone. No other vehicles anywhere. The rental's headlights cast a ghostly glow over the curving, twisting highway. They passed dozens of possible turnoffs onto country roads, but he kept going.

There was no sign of the truck.

They drove for another twenty minutes before Carol sighed and said, "Jake, turn around. We lost him."

"He must have turned on one of those roads back there." He cursed aloud.

"Come on, let's head back to town and get some food. I'm starving. Then, we'll go back to his house. Now I'm *really* determined to get inside that place!"

43

The sun had set. The woods were dark and full of sinister sounds of the night. In a weird way, the forest around Michael and all it had to offer was comforting. There, he knew he could survive. The biggest menace was right in front of him.

One of the MWs seared burgers on a small Weber grill that was outside by the picnic table. Rusty Wainwright was back, along with several other members of the gang. They had lit a fire in a barrel to provide light. The zip ties were removed, and Michael was allowed to sit with them at the table to eat. They even gave him a bottle of beer from a portable ice chest. The burger was surprisingly good. Michael ate slowly, using the time to listen. They asked about his time in Iraq, and he indulged them with a few high-intensity PJ stories while he ate.

Michael counted six vehicles parked at the side of the dirt road. Some of the MWs had come from "the other cabin" and others had appeared from town. Apparently they had several "safe houses," as they called them. It was as if they were playing soldiers at a homegrown military installation. The more he listened, the more disgusted Michael became. He knew better, but these buffoons had not once stood next to a real combat soldier as he gasped for his last breath after a real enemy in a real war had blown a hole through his chest. Maybe it was because Michael had seen so much of that. Maybe it was because these pretenders disrespected those brave soldiers with their half-assed militia charade. Whatever it was, he finally couldn't help himself.

"How often do you cats come out here and play make-believe soldiers?" he asked aloud. "You want to know what real combat feels like, go fight in a damned war."

The conversation came to a dead stop. They all turned to Michael, too stunned to say a word. The entire scene went from a relaxed meal to a full-blown shit show in less than a minute.

Rusty stood and walked around the table to Michael. "We feed you, we treat you like a guest, and you spout off like that?" He nodded at two of his cohorts, who then roughly grabbed Michael by the shoulders and hauled him off the bench.

"Hold him," Rusty ordered. The two men grasped Michael firmly. Rusty pulled back a fist and then let Michael have it in the mouth. Hard. The blow ruptured Michael's lower lip and blood spurted over his chin and shirt.

Rusty was ready to deliver another punch when the sound of a truck arriving interrupted the festivities. The two men threw Michael to the ground as headlights flooded the scene. Michael thought about bolting, but the punch had dazed him, and he figured he wouldn't get very far before they caught him. Best to stay on the ground.

It was a white box truck, and three men got out of it. The driver wore a UPS uniform, and Michael didn't know him. One was the skinhead named Chad, the thug who had beat him at Willis's house. The other one was Willis Lee himself. Michael was at first surprised to see him, but it made perfect sense that Willis was associated with the MWs. He had never been an ally—not to the team, and certainly not to Joel.

Willis came up to Michael and looked down at him. "Michael! How are ya? I gotta say, you don't look so good. Have you been misbehaving, Mr. Lawyer?" Everyone around him laughed. "Sorry I didn't make our meeting on Monday. But as you know, I sent proxies."

It was all too clear now. Willis Lee was a spy for Bank Antriol.

Michael rolled over and sat up on the ground. He wiped his face with the back of his hand, spit blood on the ground, and watched the men. Willis went over to Rusty, who said, "Willis, I'm happy you came out to see us."

"Dude, I would have been here sooner but I was busy at the bank. I have to keep up appearances," Willis replied. "Don't worry, I got all your accounting right here." He pointed to his temple.

"Well, our suppliers are getting a little itchy for their money."

"Don't worry. I'll get that taken care of."

Now Michael understood Willis's position with the MWs. The savant with the brain that remembered "everything" was their accountant. All the details of their illegal business—likely with drug smuggling and who knew what else—was done in Willis Lee's head. And the money was probably washed with transactions in the Bank Antriol system! The question for Michael, though, was—did executives at the bank sanction it? Were the MWs indirectly "employees" of Bank Antriol?

Chad moved to Michael. "So it's the celebrity hostage!" he said as he squatted so that his face was at the same level as Michael's. "You get another night of accommodations with us, shithead. The decision on the hearing won't be until Friday. You better hope your slimy shark lawyer boss drops the lawsuit, or we'll skin you alive and you'll be my bear rug. I'll call it a 'lawyer rug.' And everyone who visits me will walk all over you!"

Michael spit bloody phlegm in the man's face.

That caused Chad to yell like a banshee. He leapt on top of Michael, held him around the throat, and unleashed a barrage of punches to his face and head. Michael defended himself by kneeing his opponent hard in the crotch. Unfortunately, Chad moved just enough so that it wasn't a direct hit. Michael was much stronger than Chad, so he was able to push the man off of him. And then they were both on their feet.

Now it was man-to-man. The other MWs cheered on Chad, hollering for him to "punish the punk." The two men circled each other, fists held in front, but Michael quickly proved that the brawl would be a mismatch. His professional experience instinctively kicked in, and the cheers from the rabid crowd went silent as 'the punk' perfectly placed a lightning-quick boot kick to the target right below Chad's throat.

A dazed and visibly panicked Chad clutched his neck, made a choking sound, and struggled to stay on his feet.

Michael didn't stop. He moved forward, immediately turned sideways, and kicked upward at Chad's face. The maneuver was so fast that no one was sure it was another direct hit until Chad recoiled and fell backward to the ground.

Before Michael could advance on the man, Rusty called out for them to stop. Michael ignored him and kicked his opponent on the ground, but one of the others stepped up quickly and slammed a rifle butt to the back of Michael's head. Their captive collapsed in a heap. Three more of the once-cheering spectators piled on top of Michael's unconscious body, delivering furious blows that Michael wouldn't feel until he awoke.

* * *

His senses slowly returned. The cool night air on his skin. The smell of hot food. He heard voices in the distance, floating in a haze. Michael felt cold dirt beneath him. And the pain. A lot of pain.

He was lying on the ground not far from the picnic table where they'd left him after the beating. An attempt to move confirmed that his wrists were zip tied behind his back.

The MWs were eating at the table. Chitchat. Something about the color blue. Michael wasn't sure who was talking. Maybe Chad? He heard only snippets.

"Blue ... babysitting our surprise ... when he gets your call to leave the truck ... a car parked nearby that he can just ... escape route ... he knows to always keep his cap low on his head so it's harder ... security cameras. Don't worry about Blue."

Michael concentrated on shaking away the fog so that he could listen and understand what they were saying. None of it made much sense, but he willed himself to remember the bits and pieces he was able to comprehend. He lay still, kept his eyes shut, and listened.

On cue, though, Willis asked, "Should we be talking ... him there? Can he hear us?"

"I whooped his ass," Chad answered, "he's out. Forget him."

Rusty added, "It don't matter. He won't be telling…"

That clinched it. Michael had a clear enough head to know they weren't going to let him go, not matter what Deke did. Escape was 'that one more thing' he had to do.

"…have … thirty-six hours," Willis said. "…could go the Florida lawyer's way…"

Chad snarled loudly, "It doesn't matter what the judge says. It's bombs away … That's the plan."

"The *plan* is that Blue is driving the truck … Richmond … tomorrow." Rusty shot a look over at Michael and went, "Shh." Everyone hushed. Michael felt their eyes on him. He kept his own closed.

"I'm telling you, he's still out!" Chad said.

"Smitty, check him out," Rusty ordered one of the armed guards. Smitty went over to Michael, squatted beside him, and watched the man breathe slowly and steadily.

"He's dead to the world," Smitty said, and he returned to his position. The MWs continued to speak softly. Michael still heard only fragments, but some phrases came through.

Rusty's voice: "So, Blue … set up before dawn Friday … We show up around six thirty … park … coffee shop … one-way street … corner is perfect … fast getaway … great vantage point to watch the front … Chad … make the call … Goodbye Florida trial team…"

Michael put it together. They were talking about a bomb. The "call" was the cell phone triggering device. The MWs were planning to set off another EFP in Richmond, Virginia, possibly near the courthouse, and the targets were all his friends.

The men started whispering, and he couldn't make out what they were saying. Then there was laughter. Michael barely opened his eyes to a squint so that he could see them.

Without warning, Chad stood and strode quickly to Michael. The MW brutally grabbed Michael's hair and pulled up his head. There was a slap across his face, followed by, "Are you listening to us, asshole? Huh? Are you *playin' possum?*"

Michael did his best to feign rolling his eyes. He emitted a pained groan.

"It's going to be a pleasure to watch you burn," Chad growled. "We're going to put a stake in the ground and tie you to it. And I'm going to light the match. Rusty, I think this feller's faking it."

Rusty gave a command to Michael's regular guards. "Take him back inside and keep him tied. I think the lawyer's been a bad boy."

The men roughly pulled Michael off the ground and marched him back to the cabin.

44

It was after midnight when Carol and Jake left their hotel to drive back to Struck Gold Estates. They were surprised by how the town of Plainsburg completely shut down at night.

"There is *nobody* out at this hour," Carol observed as Jake drove for some time through the empty, quiet streets … until they passed a bar where cars and pickups were parked in front and neon lights blazed within.

"Rest of the town might be empty, Carol," Jake noted, "but there are plenty of people out drinking. I bet we can go to my favorite watering hole, Beggar's Ravine, and we'll find a whole bunch of folks."

"I bet we could spot plenty of our MW friends there, too," Carol said. "I'd like to try and avoid them, thank you very much."

They eventually reached the rolling hills of the estates. Jake once again stopped at the top of the hill so they could observe the Quigg home.

"What'd I tell you?" Carol observed. "Looks like he's gone."

"It does appear dark and sleepy," Jake said. "How many floors do you think that mansion has?"

"Two, and a basement, and probably an attic. No doubt five or six bedrooms. Does Chad live there by himself?"

"It appears he's taken it over from his parents. Back at the hotel, I looked up the house records online. It's still in his mother's name. She lives in a nursing home now. The house is also paid off. No mortgage."

"Lucky for Chad. Drive down slowly; let's take a look."

He did, and they glided past the place. Jake then pulled over to the curb about a hundred feet down the street. "What do you think?" He shut off the car. They quietly exited and stood on the street. Carol looked around to make sure no lights were on in any neighboring houses. The closest one was at least thirty yards away.

"This place is like a ghost town with all the ghosts sleeping," Carol whispered. "Come on, let's go." She led the way as they approached the front of the home. Jake kept an eye out for security cameras, but he didn't see any.

"You think anyone's hanging out in there?" he asked.

"Let's find out," Carol said. She rang the doorbell.

"Jesus, Carol ... really?"

They ran to the side of the house and waited at the edge. No one answered the door.

"The last time I rang someone's doorbell and ran was when I was about eight years old," Jake said.

"Hush." She left him at the side of the house, hurried to the front door and banged on it, rang the bell several times, knocked loudly again, and then rushed back to Jake.

Nothing happened.

"What the hell, Carol—stop with the noise!" Jake said. "No one's home."

She motioned him further around the side to the garage, where the mechanical door was down and secure. Carol kept moving around the structure to the backyard, where the landscaping had been neglected for a few months. The moon shone over a gazebo, a large patio with outdoor furniture, and several big trees. The ground sloped down to a small pond.

"This would be a beautiful home if anyone had taken care of it," Carol mused. She then turned, approached a window, and peered inside. "I see a dining room. Big table and chairs. Once upon a time, the Quigg family must have had a little class."

"Help me out here ... what are we trying to accomplish, Carol?" Jake asked.

"We're trying to find a way in."

"Oh, of course. Breaking and entering. Why didn't I think of that? Maybe leave here in handcuffs."

She eyed him. "And you've done a lot more of that kind of thing than I have, Jake, and you know it. Don't turn choirboy on me now."

He shrugged. "As long as we don't get caught."

Carol tried to open the window, but it was locked. "Let's try the back door." She moved to the patio and a sliding glass door. It was locked, too. Carol turned to Jake and said, "Okay, do your thing. Pull 'em out. I know you've got 'em. No more sanctimonious BS. We have to take a look. It's now or never."

"All right, all right, just chill a minute." He pulled out of his pocket a ring of lock picks. There were ten of them—thin metal rods of various thickness. "This should be a breeze—it's a standard lock. Can you give me some light with your phone?" Carol turned on her mobile's flashlight and cast the beam over the lock. Jake tried a pick, found it to be too large, and then went for another. He inserted it into the lock and manipulated it until there was a soft click. He removed the lock pick and opened the sliding door. "Voila."

They went in, shut the door, and Carol cast her light over the room. They were surprised that the place was so well kept. Jake got out his own phone and turned on its light as well. They were in a room that might be called a den. Modern furniture, a television, and an upright piano against a wall. A hallway led toward the center and front of the house. The kitchen was to the left. Beyond that was the dining room they'd seen earlier.

The kitchen appeared to be in use. There were dishes on a drain board by the sink, but nothing dirty. Carol opened the fridge, and it was stocked with some Tupperware containing leftovers, a jug of milk, some eggs, and a dozen cans of beer.

She said, "It feels like Chad lives like a guest in his parents' house and just uses the kitchen. His room is somewhere else."

"I'll bet it's the basement."

"Like a man-child who never left home. Let's check it out."

The ground floor of the spacious house also contained a large living room and what might be called a library. The place was tastefully furnished, but all of these rooms were covered by a thick layer of dust and smelled musty. They obviously hadn't been used recently. Carol's attention was drawn to a wall of framed photos in the library. It appeared to be a collection of family portraits, going back generations.

"Look at this, Jake." He came over to see, and she pointed to an old tintype image in a well-worn frame. It pictured a man with a beard and mustache, and he was wearing a Confederate soldier uniform. He stood outdoors in front of a cannon, and a Confederate flag could be seen on a pole in the distance. "Great or Great-Great-Grandpa Quigg?" she suggested.

"If so, it explains a lot," Jake said. "No doubt the Quiggs owned a few slaves at one time."

They kept moving through the ground floor and eventually found a door in the foyer near the front door. Carol opened it to stairs leading down. She held the light steady, and they descended to the cellar.

It was a lived-in space, and it was huge. Carol found a light switch and turned it on, saying, "I think it's safe down here." The entire cavernous cellar lit up, revealing access to several spaces that made up Chad's basement apartment.

The sight of the "living room" was a shock. Draped on one of the walls was a large Confederate flag. Jake went to it and felt the cloth. "I think this is an antique. It's the real thing," he said.

"For the love of God … what a douchebag," Carol muttered.

The walls around it were covered with other forms of right-wing insignia—Nazi swastikas, Iron Crosses, and a gigantic "4/19" spread in red paint on a white wall.

"I'm moving this guy way up to the top on the Janet Blanco killer list," Carol said.

Jake emitted a low whistle and then said, "I think you might be right."

Unlike the upstairs, the basement living room was littered with empty beer cans and bottles, dirty glasses, and ashtrays full of butts. The place smelled of booze, tobacco, bong water, and unwashed clothes.

Carol went through an alcove and into a bedroom. There was an unmade king-size bed, and clothing was scattered about. Here, the walls were plastered with more hate symbols but also posters of nude women. Several of these belonged in the bondage and sadomasochistic niches of pornography.

"This guy seems like a nice date, huh," Carol said.

"Hannibal Lecter in training," Jake responded with an uneasy laugh.

Carol went over to the chest of drawers. "Look at this." She pointed to a baggie full of white powder sitting on top. Wide open. Ready for use. She licked an index finger, stuck it in the powder, and tasted it. "Yep, it's what you think it is."

They had seen enough of the bedroom. Jake pointed to a curtain on the other side of the living room. "What's back there?"

"His torture chamber?" Carol led the way.

It was a space in which the floor was unfinished—just the concrete slab of foundation. A stone ramp gently led up to mechanical doors. "That goes to the garage," Jake pointed. "He can pull up in his driveway, open the outside garage door, drive in or back in and then down this ramp and unload—or load—whatever, and drive back out. He's thought this through."

There were a variety of machine tools on the floor, including a lathe and a pneumatic press. Hand tools hung on a peg board. Stacked against the wall were sheets of copper plates. Close by was a pile of short metal pipes. Three concrete slabs of roadblocks called "Jersey barriers" sat nearby. Small chunks of concrete were evident on the floor, as if someone had been breaking up a slab into smaller pieces. Lying in that work space were truck body parts—a spare rear bumper, pieces of trim, tail light assemblies, reflector mounts, and paint.

"What, is he doing body shop work on the side?" Jake asked. Then he noticed a couple of crates the size of steamer trunks shoved against a wall. One was open, and he looked inside.

"Holy shit, Carol, take a look," Jake said. "Any doubt in your mind there's enough explosive material here to level this entire town?" He fingered the packages and noticed warnings written in Spanish. "This stuff is from south of the border and is military grade."

She went over to the machine tools and saw that copper filings littered the tops and the floor around them. "He's making EFPs in his basement."

"Carol, I'll bet he makes them at the trucking company warehouse, too. This is just his home office. The MWs import it all from South and Central America and Mexico. Not only drugs hidden in furniture, but explosives for their bombs."

"Look over here," she said. A plastic garbage bag sat near a work table. Inside were taped-up bricks of what appeared to be more cocaine. "It's all here, Jake. Bomb-making shit and drugs."

"Let's start taking pictures," Jake suggested, "and then get the hell out of here."

They both went around the cellar snapping photos with their phones and then hurried up the stairs to the ground floor. They went outside the way they came in, moved around the house, and made it back to their car in a quick minute.

"Get us the hell out of here," Carol said as she buckled her seat belt. Jake started the car and headed for the highway.

"What now?" Jake asked.

"It's the middle of the night. Deke is asleep, I hope, and so is Sarah. I imagine my FBI friend is in bed and so is our pal at the Plainsburg police station. We have to wait until morning to report all this."

"Go back to the hotel and get some shut-eye?"

"If we're able to. I guess we should try. This is early Thursday morning now, right? It's going to be a long day. As soon as we get back to the hotel, send me all the photos you took. I'll compile the best ones and send them to Deke and Sarah. Then I'll send them to Felicia and to Sheila. Felicia will get them to the TEDAC group at the FBI. I'll send them all my report material about the trucking company and everything else we've found. This is about to break wide open, Jake."

"Now we just need to find Michael."

Jake drove the car out of Struck Gold Estates, more than happy to leave behind Chad's little shop of horrors.

45

There were several emails and messages on Carol's phone when she woke up. When the buzz of being in Chad's dungeon of hate had worn off, she had slipped into an exhaustion-induced deep and dreamless sleep, one that even the incessant vibrations and chimes of her work phone could not penetrate. There were texts from Jake, Deke, Sarah, Felicia, and Sheila. She wiped the blur from her eyes and, without moving from her hotel bed, held the phone close to her face and sent a flurry of replies.

To Jake: *I'm up, give me a minute.*

To Deke and Sarah: *Talk to you in a few.*

To Felicia and Sheila: *I'll call you back.*

There was also a text from a number she didn't recognize. It read: *Messages received. Hang tight. Help is on the way. JH.*

"Oh my God!" she said aloud.

She immediately dialed Jake and told him to come to her room. She threw on clothes and then called Deke.

"Carol, what you found is over the top!" he said. "It's close to game-over material. However, right now I want to be sure you and Jake are playing it safe up there."

"Deke, don't worry, we're safe, but listen!" She told him about the text. "Could it be him?"

"Truthfully, Carol, I've been thinking that Joel is no longer alive and kicking. I hope you prove me wrong."

"Deke, I'm optimistic. Look, I hate to cut you off, but I need to call Felicia and Sheila. They may have some news for us. I'll get back to you."

Next, she dialed Felicia. Her text had said, *Call me ASAP.* Unfortunately, Carol reached voicemail. "Felicia, it's Carol, calling you back. Hope you liked the photos I sent. You have my number."

She then hung up and dialed Sheila, who answered.

"Carol! I'm glad you called. Incredible photos you took. Did you break into the house?"

"No, a door was wide open, and we thought we smelled smoke inside," Carol lied. "Jake and I walked right in and found what you see."

"I really don't know what you want me to do. Chief Wainwright would stomp all over this and never let it see the light of day."

"You've got to go over his head. Local DA maybe? Or maybe go to the police in the next county over."

"I'll lose my job."

"Sheila, some people might lose their lives, and you hate that job anyway!"

"Okay, okay, but listen. We found Michael's car."

"What, are you sure?"

"2022 white Hyundai Elantra." Sheila read off the license plate number. "That's it, right?"

"Yes."

"It was in a ditch off the side of the road outside of town. As if the driver had wrecked the car and walked away."

There was a knock on the hotel room door. "Just a second, Sheila." Carol went to it. "Yeah?"

"It's Jake."

She let him in. He looked a little worse for wear, too. "Sheila, what's your department doing about it?"

"Nothing. The car was towed. It'll likely stay in the impound yard until it's claimed by someone."

"Sweet Jesus, Sheila! Are you a real cop or a meter maid? It's your time to step up."

"Carol!"

"Sorry, sorry. We're under a lot of stress."

"Hold on a second..." There was a click and Carol was put on hold.

"What's going on?" Jake asked.

"Sheila says they found Michael's car. Oh, and look at this." She showed Jake the text from "JH." His eyes grew wide and his jaw dropped. She put the phone back to her ear. "When I asked—hello?"

"Carol!" Sheila was back on the line. "Get out of your hotel. Wainwright and Bostick are coming to arrest you."

"*What?*"

"I didn't know, but I just heard about it. They left twenty minutes ago."

"Shit. Talk to you later." Carol hung up and told Jake the news.

Wide-eyed, he spit, "Let's go, then!" and they got moving. Jake hurried back to his room to grab some things, Carol gathered her personal belongings, and they met in the hotel lobby.

It was too late.

As soon as they stepped outside to head for Jake's rental car, they were confronted by Chief Wainwright and Detective Bostick.

Wainwright pulled his weapon. "Get your damn hands up. You're under arrest."

Carol was unshaken. "On what charge?"

"Criminal mischief. We've had complaints. Detective Bostick, search these carpetbaggers and cuff 'em."

"Bad move. Really bad move, chief," Jake said.

The pair was forced to put their hands on the exterior hotel wall and spread their legs. Bostick immediately found Jake's concealed handgun. "Well, lookee here, chief."

"I'm licensed for it, and besides—I don't need a permit to carry in this state!" Jake protested.

"Tell it to the judge. Ken, take their cell phones, too. We'll come back and search the car."

Jake's lock picks were confiscated, too, and then the handcuffs were snapped on with their hands behind their backs. The investigators knew it was of no use to resist. It would just make things worse.

* * *

They were marched into the police station, where a sergeant was manning the front desk. Carol didn't see Sheila Denning.

Jake observed that his colleague was huffing and puffing, her face red with anger. She was about to explode, and he knew that wasn't going to be good.

Sure enough, Carol launched into it. "Let me tell you something, pal, this is one arrest you'd better get right!"

"You're in no position to tell us anything, lady," Bostick snarled.

She turned to Wainwright. "You've had a missing person report about one of our associates since Wednesday, and you've done exactly zero to follow up on it. You have a bunch of psycho Nazi bikers operating in plain sight, probably in the drug running business, and probably holding our partner as we speak with some lame-ass hostage plan in mind. Your own son appears to be involved—"

"*Hold it right there, you crazy bitch!*" the chief bellowed.

"No, *you* hold it! Either you get busy acting like a real police chief or this town is going to be crawling with real law enforcement professionals within about an hour—"

Wainwright drew his sidearm again and pointed it directly at Carol's face. "*Enough!*"

She quickly shut up, but she stared him down until he lowered the gun.

"We get a phone call," Carol said quietly.

"Right now, lady, you get what I give you," the chief said. "Lock 'em up, Ken. We'll book 'em later after they cool down."

Wainwright opened the gate in the barrier and the detective and sergeant trooped them through and toward the back. The station had exactly two cells. Jake was placed in one, and Carol in the other. The cops slammed the doors shut and locked them.

"You're going to leave the cuffs on?" Jake asked. "Oh, that's priceless."

"Best thing you can do is shut up," the sergeant said. He and the detective left the holding area. Jake and Carol were alone.

Carol paced back and forth. She was ready to explode and finally made a loud animalistic noise that was half a curse word and half a scream of sheer unadulterated anger.

"So, that went well," Jake said.

* * *

Richmond, Virginia—Thursday

It had been a long, frustrating, and worrisome day.

Deke had spent a lot of his time on the phone with Sarah talking about the revelations that had been uncovered in the past couple of days and reviewing with Dan Lawson all the evidence they possessed.

Now the big mystery Deke was confronted with was why there had been no communication from Carol or Jake since that morning. Those two were not known for remaining silent at times like this. No one in the small team with Deke had heard from them and all explanations for that pointed in the direction of bad news. By dinner time, everyone was beginning to think something may have happened to the pair. Sarah had called their Plainsburg hotel and confirmed that neither of them had checked out. Deke had to tell himself that they were busy chasing leads, but in his heart he knew they were in trouble.

Should they call someone? Who? Certainly not the Plainsburg police. And if they did inform another law enforcement entity, what would they say? *We haven't heard from a couple of colleagues for ten hours.* That wasn't going to motivate anyone with a badge.

Dinner with Bernie, Gina, and Dan had been quiet. Everyone was in a somber, anxious mood. They were due in court the next morning, and there was still no news about Michael, Joel, or Carol and Jake, for that matter.

Usually, Deke was strong and confident the night before a big hearing. Now, though, he simply felt helpless.

46

Somewhere in Kentucky—Thursday

"This is your last dinner with us," Rusty announced to Michael as they sat at the picnic table, scraping up the last of a plate of beans. Chad, sitting across from them, snickered. Rusty shot him a look and said, "Now, now, Chad. This is our guest's last night here."

Chad said, "Sorry we couldn't honor a request for a real last meal." He and some of the other MWs laughed at that.

They had kept Michael in the cabin all day, but he had been aware of a lot of activity going on outside. Much of the gear the MWs had brought to the site was being packed away. They were obviously preparing to vacate the premises. What they were going to do with Michael was unknown, except that a couple of the men had pounded a tall wooden stake in the ground about thirty feet away from the cabin.

Rusty told a couple of men with AR-15s in hand, "Please escort our guest to the outhouse. When he's done, take him to the throne. Use the tape."

Michael winced. They were going to make the night extremely uncomfortable for him.

They took away his plate and drink, and then they got him to stand and go to do his business before tucking him away for the night. When he was alone in the outhouse, Michael racked his brain trying to come up with a way to elude the guards and escape. Unfortunately, there was only one door to the antiquated facility, and the gunmen were standing right outside.

When Michael was finished, they moved him back to the cabin. Instead of zip tying his wrists and attaching the ankle leash, they made him sit in the chair that was bolted to the floor. The men then wrapped duct tape around his torso, securing it to the back of the chair. They taped his forearms to the arm rests, and his calves to the chair's front legs. Just as he had been when he had first awoken in the cabin on Tuesday. He couldn't move.

Rusty and Chad came in, and the leader told the two men, "Frank, Smitty, I'm leaving Wayne here with you two. Sometime tonight, after midnight I imagine, Johnny, Zach, and Stevie will show up and relieve you. But stick around until we get back tomorrow, y'hear?"

Frank and Smitty nodded and left the cabin.

Rusty then addressed Michael. "I guess you figured out that all that tough guy show you put on can be real painful. It can get a lot worse with these boys I'm leaving you with. So you be nice. We'll be back tomorrow afternoon … after the hearing. I sure hope your boss does what he's been told, for your sake."

"Right. You're not going to let me go," Michael said. "Quit bullshitting me. None of this has to do with what my boss decides. But after I'm gone, someone's going to figure all this out and you and your shithead friends are going to spend some dark hours on death row. So kiss my ass."

Rusty and Chad looked at each other. Chad then stepped forward and bent so that his face was close to Michael's. "All right. No more bullshit. This is your last night here, for sure. It's your last night, period. That stake we put in the ground today? It has your name on it. I want to leave you with a nice image in your head for you to think about all night until we return. And that's a picture of you, tied to it, burning like Joan of Arc." Chad patted Michael on the cheek, and then roughly slapped it. Next he took a black Sharpie out of his pocket, uncapped it, and scribbled something on Michael's forehead. "There. Now you're all pretty. Rusty, you got your phone? Show him my artwork."

Rusty pulled his phone out of his pocket, manipulated it to selfie mode, and showed the screen to Michael. Chad had written "4/19" on Michael's skin.

"It would have been my preference to tattoo it on your face, but our guy isn't here to do that. Well, so long, *lawyer*." He emphasized the last word as if it were the ugliest epithet in the books. As a final insult, the man spit in Michael's face.

The two MWs left him alone in the cabin.

Michael closed his eyes and tried to relax as the spittle ran down his nose and mouth, but he couldn't. The sun would be down soon, and then what many of his fellow soldiers in Iraq had called "the night terrors" would begin.

One more thing ... What was that one more thing he could pull off?

* * *

Plainsburg, Kentucky—Thursday

Carol and Jake sat in their respective cells, handcuffed, angry, and silent. Hours had passed. At one point, the sergeant brought them food from McDonald's, uncuffed them, and watched as they ate. Immediately after they had finished their Happy Meals, the sergeant reapplied the cuffs.

He said, "Chief said for you both to have a good night's sleep. It's time for us to go home. We're closing up the station till morning. All 911 calls get forwarded to us at home, y'know."

"You're leaving us here alone?" Jake asked. "At least uncuff us!"

The man started for the door.

"We're still owed a phone call!" Carol snapped. The sergeant gave an imbecilic laugh and was gone. Over the next few minutes, they could hear the officers saying "good night" to each other and doors slamming. Then it was quiet. Dead silence.

"They still haven't officially booked us! 'Criminal mischief' my ass. The lawsuit these guys are going to face will bankrupt this entire city for generations," Jake said.

"Well, the real question is what do they really plan to do with us, Jake? They know the law. Or, hell, maybe they don't. But what's their endgame, here? Are we both going to be found to have committed suicide, hanged in our cells, or maybe blown up along with this entire jail?"

"This is likely tied to the hearing in Virginia," Jake said. "They're waiting to see what happens tomorrow."

"And then what? If they let us go, they know we'll sue the shit out of 'em. If they don't let us go, then that means they have *other plans* for us."

"We've been in worse situations, Carol ... well, maybe not."

47

Somewhere in Kentucky—Friday

It was around one in the morning. The forest was pitch dark, and only the sounds of insects filled the cool air.

Joel Hartbeck, dressed in camouflage and his face painted in a green and black commando-style mask, slowly crawled forward through the brush to get a better look at the cabin.

Two armed MWs sat in folding chairs out in front. A lone pickup truck stood on the dirt road leading off the property. Joel knew that a third man was inside the cabin with Michael, likely sleeping on a bunk.

Joel had been on the premises for hours. He had seen Rusty Wainwright and the skinhead known as Chad leave in the white box truck, along with other members of the MWs. Now that enough time had passed since the others had left, Joel figured it was time for action. With one of the three guards off duty and presumably resting, the odds were better.

Joel had done what he could to improve his chances. Along with being decked out in full jungle combat gear, he carried a handgun, a silenced AR-15, a Fairbairn-Sykes military fighting knife, and night vision goggles.

He had been waiting a long time for this moment of payback. It just came a little sooner than expected, and it now required him to balance the need to save his friend with his thirst for vengeance.

* * *

Back when Joel had contacted Michael Carey about Bank Antriol's crimes, he had known he had a target on his back. What had happened to Janet was the writing on the wall, both figuratively and literally. The "4/19" that the killer had painted in her kitchen was the same MW signature found on his car. It had always been clear that if the MWs found him, he was a dead man.

At first he had moved around in Plainsburg, staying at the few fleabag motels and hotels that still existed. They'd found him at the Mountain Man Motel, so he'd moved to yet another remote seventy-year-old two-story dump. One night when he was in bed, he had been awakened by noise in the street. He peeked out and saw a pickup truck emblazoned with a Confederate flag on the side. Several MWs were coming toward the building. Joel had quickly dressed, gathered the small amount of things in his possession, and hustled down the stairs. He went out the back exit just as the men were entering the front. Joel scrambled to his car and made a run for his life. That was when he knew he could no longer stay in Plainsburg.

Joel spent the next block of days, weeks, and months living like a hermit. He avoided hotels and motels and instead resided in a succession of makeshift encampments in the woods and mountains all over southern Kentucky. He drove to North Carolina to trade in his car and buy a used junker of a Chevy Tracker. The North Carolina plates, he hoped, would help disguise his movements.

He rented a PO box in Pikeville, where he could store his important documents and keep a supply of burner cell phones, as well as the one good phone where people like Michael could leave messages. Since the box was accessible 24/7, Joel could visit it in the middle of the night, listen to his messages, and turn off the phone again so it couldn't be traced. He also stored all the important documents pertaining to the Antriol case there, including the material Janet had copied for him. The documents that had cost Janet her life.

Another important step was to move all of his savings out of his Plainsburg bank and operate solely with cash. He knew that tracing bank transactions would be child's play for Antriol.

And then he got sick, probably from sleeping in the forest. At the beginning he thought it might be the coronavirus again, but he was hesitant to find a place to test. Whatever it was developed into a serious case of pneumonia. Joel returned to North Carolina and went to an emergency room in Asheville. He was in the hospital for four weeks because a staph infection developed on top of the pneumonia. Death from illness instead of a shotgun blast to the face by MW psychopaths actually seemed to be comforting during the darkest times in his recovery.

The ordeal had left him weak, so he had to spend a month training again. He spent money on weapons and gear, and, ironically, started doing what the MWs were doing—he "played soldier" again, this time up in the mountains. Joel refamiliarized himself with everything he had learned during his time in the military all those years ago.

Then came the bombings. When Joel's image popped up in the media as a possible suspect, he knew that he had been framed. The MWs hadn't been able to find and kill him, so instead they had offered him up as the sacrificial lamb to law enforcement. There was no other way that the FBI could have obtained any information about him. This was further justification for Joel to live off the grid.

He then set about doing serious intel gathering on the MWs. He began to explore the woods and mountains in southern Kentucky and, by carefully surveilling dozens of properties well hidden in the deepest parts of the forest, he was able to determine over time the locations of most of the MW hideouts.

Through all these days, Joel periodically checked the messages on his phone hidden in the PO box. Finally, after months of disciplined retraining in the Kentucky mountain forests, he was reasonably prepared for what he knew lay ahead—he received Carol Morris's message about Michael being abducted. He knew the time for intel gathering was over.

Joel was never sure whether he chose a one-man rescue idea out of a need for vengeance, a subconscious urge for suicide, or a sincere belief that he was the only one best able to save Michael. Whatever the reason, he decided to take on the task himself rather than involve Michael's law firm or the authorities. He had always been a loner, even when he was an EOD tech in Iraq. Joel had never trusted "the Man."

It was just several hours earlier on Thursday afternoon that Joel set out to find someone who could tell him some things. He made his way to one of the MWs' cabins and came across a lone member who was gathering firewood. Just one blow with a log to the back of the head had Joel's prey unconscious on the ground. After a long drive to an isolated area and less than thirty minutes of unorthodox interrogation, Joel had learned not only where Michael was being held prisoner, but also as much as he needed to know about the MWs' relationship with a Colombian drug cartel. Unfortunately, the man didn't know a lot about the MWs' ultimate plans for Michael, but he did know a little bit about what was supposed to happen in Richmond, Virginia, on Friday morning. When Joel was finally satisfied that he'd extracted everything he could from his subject, he had no qualms about making sure that at least this one MW would never report back to his buddies. They were all killers in Joel's opinion. If one was going to live by the sword, then dying by a knife to the throat seemed appropriate. Rough justice. Joel left the body for the wildlife.

He immediately called Carol to warn her about what the MWs were planning in Richmond, but he got her voicemail. Joel left her a detailed message, hung up, and trusted fate that she would receive it.

As night fell on the forest, Joel knew what he needed to do.

* * *

Now, Joel slipped on the night vision goggles to get a better view of the cabin. Night turned to day, and he could now vividly pick up details of the structure. The MWs continued to sit quietly. One of the guards had a slight boyish build and in Joel's estimation could not have weighed more than 130 pounds. The other one appeared to be much more of a threat and could easily have made a living as a bouncer in any Kentucky honky-tonk. Joel considered just lowering his long rifle and shooting them both in the head. It would be an easy shot, but that would leave the guy inside with Michael. The MW might take it out on his friend if he became spooked. No, he needed to get inside the cabin as quickly and silently as possible to neutralize the primary threat to his friend.

It was only a matter of time before one of the guards had to go use the outhouse, and that moment finally arrived at 1:11. The Bouncer stood, threw his cigarette on the ground, stomped the butt out, and said something to his pal. He then walked around the cabin toward the back.

Joel moved as quietly and quickly as a leopard on the hunt. It didn't surprise Joel at all that the MW skipped using the outhouse itself, but rather went to a nearby tree to urinate.

Now.

Joel rushed toward the man's back. Before the MW could register the sound of boot steps growing louder, Joel flung an arm around the man's neck and used his other hand to put pressure on the back of his head. This choke hold immediately cut off the guard's air flow and also prevented him from calling out. The MW struggled, but Joel held fast, kneeing his prey between the legs as well. The man collapsed to the ground, allowing Joel to draw his Glock and slam the butt on the back of the MW's head. Lights out.

Joel searched the man's pockets. No keys. He left him there and snuck back to the side of the cabin. He peered around the corner at the front. The boyish man still sat in his chair.

"Hey, you have to look at this!" Joel called out. "Come here, quick!" He then ducked to the side and squatted behind the picnic table in the dark.

"What?" the other man responded. "Smitty?" Joel waited. Eventually the man came around to the side. "Smitty? Where are you?"

Boyish Man walked further toward the back of the cabin, allowing Joel the opportunity to rise, move quickly behind him, and slip a rope around his neck. With power driven by months of pent-up anger, Joel tightened the rope with a force that could possibly crush the man's windpipe before he passed out. It was an immediate mismatch of strength. Joel threw the man to the ground face down, put a knee in his back, and tightened the rope until the only movement was an irregular twitch coming from his legs. Alive, but barely.

A quick pat of his pockets revealed that this one had the keys to the cabin. Joel took them and moved to the front of the structure. There were only two keys on the ring, and the first one he tried unlocked the door. It was a heavy, thick door reinforced by steel strips. Joel opened it as quietly as he could, but it still creaked.

He stood for a moment, allowing the infrared goggles to do their work. A single oil lamp still burned with a tiny flame, casting a ghostly greenish light over the space.

Michael was sitting slumped, head down, affixed to a chair with tape. He had fallen asleep.

The third MW lay on one of the several cots in the room. He snored loudly and was dead to the world.

Joel silently moved to Michael and placed his hand over his friend's mouth. Michael jerked awake. Joel put the index finger of his other hand to his lips.

Michael's eyes widened at the sight of the man standing in front of him. The green and black war paint was startling at first, but then recognition set in. His miracle had come.

Joel shook his head to emphasize that Michael should remain quiet. He then released his hand from Michael's mouth and moved to the sleeping MW on the cot. Joel drew the Glock and stuck the barrel into the man's temple. The man snorted and jerked his head up.

"Oh, did I wake you?" Joel asked. "Well, go back to sleep." With that, he struck the MW hard with the gun butt. The guard still managed to move and fight back, so Joel hit him again directly in the temple. As blood gushed out of the wound, Joel was certain that he was out cold.

Joel turned to Michael and said, "Well, look who the bozo is now!"

"Joel, you mangy bastard, am I glad to see you!" Michael croaked.

Joel drew the knife and set about cutting the tape, but there were gobs of it. It took several minutes to do the job as they continued to speak softly.

"Joel," Michael said, "the MWs plan to detonate an EFP outside the courthouse to hit Deke and the team. We have to warn them."

"I know, I just found out *today* about it. I've learned a lot about their operations since we last spoke. Willis Lee—"

"Yeah, I figured out he's the key player, the go-between connecting the bank with the MWs and a Colombian drug cartel."

"He's a *member* of the MWs, working undercover as a banker. The MWs are the cartel's distributors in the US, and Willis uses Bank Antriol to launder the cartel's money. The bank vice presidents—" Joel grunted as he ripped off the final piece of tape.

"Dullea and Maher." Michael slowly stood and stretched to work out his soreness.

"*Those guys* allow the laundering to go through the bank's transaction system. Everyone makes money. When Dullea created that AML unit in Plainsburg, he appointed Willis, with his crazy savant brainpower, to be the bank's man on the ground."

Joel found the roll of duct tape on the table by the two oil lamps, and together they bound the still unconscious MW to the cot. The finishing touch was taping over the man's mouth.

"Dullea quickly promoted Willis to a supervisory position so he could be a watchdog for the bank. Not only was Willis watching over money laundering for drug cartels, but he also smoothed the way for the reverse laundering of illegal transactions that your law firm is interested in—the terrorist shit."

"But why the bombings?"

"I think that's Willis's doing with the VPs' blessing. He employed the MWs—with the bank's money—to throw shade on all the illegal transactions the bankers in New York are allowing. Some of the bombings were just deadly diversions, but the others were direct hits to take out obstacles like Beech and that vault in Tennessee."

Michael said, "The thing is, though, these idiots don't realize that all this chaos and destruction won't really stop the lawsuit from going forward. If you ask me, it's to cause delays."

"Delays for what?"

"So the kingpins can execute an escape plan."

The sound of a vehicle approaching got their attention. Bright lights swung over the front of the cabin and across the open door. "The fun begins." Joel said. He slammed the door shut and locked it from the inside.

A man shouted, "Give it up, boys! Come on out, and we can talk about your future!"

A gun fired and bullets hit the other side of the wooden door. Michael jumped back, but he was amazed that the rounds didn't perforate the wood. "That's a thick door!" he exclaimed, impressed.

Joel looked at Michael and said, "These old cabins are built like war bunkers. Those guys outside must be the relief crew. I screwed up. I should have punched the ticket for those two cretins I found standing guard. And now their gaggle of goons are out there with them. Sorry about that, pal."

48

Carol heard a noise somewhere in the police station.

She opened her eyes to see that she was still in the jail cell. After several hours of fitfully pacing in the small space, she eventually released her anger and lay on the bunk. She must have fallen into a light sleep. Jake had resigned himself early on that there was nothing they could do. Jake had dropped onto his bunk and immediately gone to sleep. Carol had envied his ability to do that.

Now, though, she sensed that someone had come into the station. What time was it? The chief and the sergeant had left hours earlier. It must have been after midnight.

Oh, my God ... it's Friday already...

Then the door out to the front of the station clanged and unlocked. Carol sat up, and Jake immediately woke up and bolted upright, too.

The door rattled and opened. Officer Sheila Denning stepped through.

"Sheila!" Carol said. "Are we glad to see you."

"Hey, Carol, hey Jake," Sheila said. She went to Carol's cell door. "I am *so* sorry this happened to you. When I heard they'd locked you up, I was livid. I couldn't believe it."

Sheila produced a set of keys and unlocked Carol's cell, and then she did the same for Jake. She then took a smaller key and unlocked both sets of handcuffs. The two investigators stepped out and were free.

"You're the only one here?" Carol asked.

"Yep. I had to wait until now just to be safe. I … I'll likely be fired for this. But you know what? I don't give a shit. You were right when you had to remind me that I'm a cop and, yes, I really do hate this place. What I've learned from you guys and from my own digging is that this place is a law enforcement organization in name only. They're as corrupt as they come. The chief is protecting the MWs, and I'll bet my police career that he's being bribed to do it. Not to mention his son is their ringleader. Come on; let's get you out of here. I suggest you leave Plainsburg now. If the chief or any of the others find you anywhere in the county, you may not make it out alive."

"We need our cell phones, and I had a purse," Carol said.

"Right. Follow me. I don't want to turn on the lights in there."

Sheila led them through the door and into the dark main station area. She used a flashlight to illuminate the path, went to a cabinet, and unlocked it. "Your personal belongings are here." Carol and Jake grabbed their phones, Jake's wallet and lock picks, and Carol's purse.

"I had a gun," Jake said.

"Oh," Sheila answered. "That's probably locked in the weapon storage safe, and I don't have a key or combo to that. Only the chief and deputy chief do. I can't get it for you. I'm sorry."

Jake shrugged. "Screw it. I can always get another one."

Carol added, "Jake, I'm pretty sure that by the time this is over, this police Boss Hog is going to be giving up a lot more than just your gun." Carol then saw the clock on the wall. "Damn, it's one thirty in the morning."

"Are our rental cars still at the hotel?" Jake asked.

Sheila looked confused. "Cars, plural? They impounded a Chevrolet Tahoe."

Jake winced. "Yeah, that's mine. Damn! That's *another* rental car I've managed to lose in this godforsaken place!"

"They didn't know about my car?" Carol asked.

"I don't think so," Sheila answered.

"Then mine is still at the hotel," Carol said. "At least it better be."

Sheila said, "I'll give you a ride. Come on."

Once they were out of the station and in Sheila's patrol car, Carol checked her phone messages. There were a half dozen from Deke and Sarah, wondering where the hell she was. Jake had the same on his own phone. There was also one on Carol's phone from a number she didn't know. She held the device to her ear and listened.

Jake watched Carol's jaw drop, and then her expression changed from surprise to elation, and then to one of abject terror.

She hung up and stared at Jake.

"What?" he asked. "What?"

"It was Joel Hartbeck. He says he knows where Michael is, and he's going to free him tonight. Says he has to do it alone, it's the only way, and for us not to worry. He's supposed to call again Friday morning, whatever that means. It's still several hours until sunrise. But there was something else he said, too." She turned to Sheila. "How far is it to Richmond?"

"About seven hours."

Carol looked at Jake and said, "I'll fill you in when we're on the road. This is serious. We'll get our stuff, check out of the hotel, and go. Sheila, thank you so much for helping us out. I know that this is going to cost you, and I'm sorry for that."

"Don't worry," Sheila said as she pulled into the hotel parking lot. "It's the chief who's going to wish he never pissed me off. My resignation's already written. There's also a draft of a letter to the district attorney and the FBI explaining all the details about the criminal enterprise that prick Wainwright runs around here."

"Well, then, I'll do what I can to help you find other law enforcement work," Carol said, "if that's still what you want."

"I don't know about being a cop, unless they put *me* in charge here," the officer replied. "But if you find any possibilities in the kind of work you two do, please give me a shout."

Carol and Jake got out of the car. Sheila Denning waved goodbye as she drove away.

"Time is wasting and we're already way behind, Jake," Carol said. "Now are you going to tell me what's going on?"

"We have to get to Richmond before dawn and in time for Deke's hearing. And I have to make a million phone calls."

She played him Joel's message, and Jake's jaw dropped, too.

* * *

Somewhere in Kentucky—Friday

"How many of them are out there?" Michael asked.

Joel went to the window with the black drapes. He peered out and shook his head. "This is the side of the cabin. Doesn't tell us anything. There was only one truck outside when I got here."

"I do remember Rusty saying three guys were coming as relief."

"If those two guys I worked over outside are functional again, then my best guess would be that we're dealing with five of these assholes."

Michael looked around in frustration. "Why is there only one damn window and one door in this place?"

"I don't know the answer to that," Joel said, "but you're going to need this when they come through that door." He drew his Glock and handed it to Michael. He then gave him four extra magazines. "I'll handle the AR."

The man taped to the cot had regained consciousness and attempted to communicate. Michael gave him another blow to the head with the butt of the Glock.

A loud voice hollered from outside. "Come out now or this is going to go real bad!"

Michael asked, "Do you have a cell phone?"

"Yeah, but I'm not sure how much good it's going to do us." Joel pulled it out and looked at it. "Inside here there isn't any reception. I had a bar or two at most coming into this area, and we'll need to be miles from here to get a reliable signal. We can't count on phone use." He looked at the ceiling. "Man, they made these things to last. It's a bunker."

"How far away from Plainsburg are we?"

"Hour and a half drive, as the crow flies. I left my car three miles from here and made my way on foot through the woods. If we can get out of here, we're talking a good two and a half hours, maybe, to get back to town."

A volley of bullets battered the door and front of the cabin. The two men instinctively ducked and got out of the way, but then they relaxed. The rounds were not penetrating the structure.

"What kind of firepower do these guys have access to?" Michael asked.

"From what I've seen tonight, just guns."

The window suddenly exploded in a hail of gunfire. Michael and Joel ducked again and moved to opposite sides of the cabin. When it stopped, the smell of cordite filled the cool air now wafting in from outside.

Joel held a finger to his lips. They could hear voices outside the window. The window opening was about five feet off the ground and easy for someone to crawl over. Michael pointed the Glock at the window, and Joel did the same with the rifle. As they expected, the head and shoulders of a man appeared. An arm and hand gripping a handgun thrust forward and started randomly shooting.

Joel and Michael let loose.

The man screamed and fell back into the darkness. They heard anguished cries and the other men jabbering in anger.

"That's one down. If we can punch the tickets of a few more, the others will run. These are cosplay soldiers we're dealing with. Aim to kill, Michael," Joel said.

"Roger that. Help me with this," Michael said. He had moved to the table, set the lit oil lamp on the floor, picked up the other one, and pitched it out the open window. Joel went to the other end, and they tipped the table over so that the top faced the window. They crouched behind the overturned furniture.

"Not sure how much protection this will give us," Michael said. "But it's better than nothing."

"Hey assholes!" someone outside called. "We want to know how long it takes lawyers to burn to death! It's time to find out! Either you walk out in the next five minutes, or you roast!"

Joel looked at Michael. "Brother, I'm pretty sure they mean it."

"I know they do. That stake in the ground outside was meant for me."

Joel raised and moved to the window. He carefully peered out. "Nobody out this way now. They're all in front."

"Can we slip out?"

A bullet ricocheted off the window sill. Joel ducked and moved back behind the table. "I guess that answers that."

Michael looked around again. Then he stared behind him. Joel followed his gaze.

The fireplace. It was large, old, and primitive like many of the hunting camp fireplaces designed to not only remove smoke in the winter but also circulate fresh air in the hot summer months.

Michael crawled over to it and examined the flue. It was closed, but he found the metal handle and pulled it. The exit space was larger than he expected. The open flue revealed a straight shot of brick ductwork covered in thick black soot ascending to the roof.

Joel said, "I'm a much better Santa than you and in much better condition right now. Let me at that chimney."

"Three minutes!" the MW yelled from outside. "Then you guys are crispy critters!"

Michael stood and eyed his friend. "No, brother, that's where you're wrong. You're a little bulkier than you were back in the day."

"You mean fatter? Is that what you're saying?"

Michael decided to buy a little more time and shouted out the window. "Light this place on fire, and your little friend in here burns up with us! But that's your call. Want me to ask him what he thinks about you burning him to death?"

There was a delay of a response, and then what sounded like an argument going on outside. Then: "He's a soldier! Soldiers make sacrifices!"

Michael knew he had them talking among themselves. There was no clear leader. He had bought more time.

Joel squatted and looked up the flue. He even maneuvered his body and attempted to stick his head and shoulders through. He got as far as his belly.

"Nope," he said, coming out and down. The top half of his body was now covered in black soot. "I hate it when you're right. See if you can do it, Mr. PJ."

Michael stooped and got beneath the flue. He exhaled, pushed all the air out of his lungs, pushed himself up, and then stood upright, half of him in the flue and half standing in the fireplace. "I can make it, Joel."

"All right then."

Michael slid back out. "How do we play it?"

They quickly laid out a plan of action, and then Joel said, "Take the AR, leave me the Glock."

"I can't climb the flue with the rifle."

The MWs were becoming impatient. "One minute! Come out *now!*"

Joel looked around the cabin and grabbed what was left of the duct tape. "Use this to lengthen the AR sling. You can pull the AR up behind you as you climb. This is strong enough. It will hold."

"Only one way to find out. Wish me luck," Michael said as he quickly rolled the tape into a crude rope and tucked one end into his belt. He handed the Glock and magazines back to Joel. He slithered into the fireplace and started his climb. Joel tied the tape rope to the AR sling and held the gun until the tape-rope tugged on it. He then helped guide it into the flue below Michael.

Without warning, a Molotov cocktail sailed through the window. It was poorly thrown and caught the top of the window frame, shattering the bottle and sending a cascade of flaming oil across the cabin. It landed next to where the MW member lay taped to the cot. His effort to scream through the tape-gag was barely audible over the whoosh of flames. He flailed wildly as the gasoline-fed fire engulfed his body. This was difficult even for Joel to process. He put an end to the man's suffering with two shots through the smoke to the MW's head.

Joel pulled the table to the fireplace opening and moved to escape the flames spreading around the cabin. He was able to create a temporary fire break with the table, which also afforded him some protection from bullets. The flue was still moving fresh air downward, but Joel knew it wouldn't last long.

Then he started to feel the heat.

49

Michael swallowed hard. It was becoming more difficult to breathe as smoke seeped through the gaps between his body and the claustrophobic chimney. He could feel cold air on his face and hot air on his legs, and any oxygen coming down from the crown above was waning.

The bastards have really done it. They're trying to burn us alive.

He had to climb the flue the same way one might ascend a rock chimney in a cliff face. It was something he had been taught during PJ training. You push with your legs and hands on the wall you're facing, and then slide your back up the wall you're leaning against. It was slow, grueling work. Michael had to use his kneecaps to find bricks jutting out enough to provide a hole. Luckily, the chimney was not a tall one.

Michael heard Joel call from below, "How are you doing?"

"Slow going and smoky!" he responded. "But I'm good."

The AR-15, dangling three feet below his bent legs, clattered against the bricks as it swayed on the tape-rope. There was nothing he could do about that now.

He heard more gunfire outside the cabin, followed by louder, single shots from the Glock below. Joel was returning random fire through the window. The overpressure of the gunfire in the cabin pushed more smoke into the chimney. Michael kept climbing.

Michael counted his progress by inches. His strength was diminished from the lack of real food over the past three days and from the brutal beating he had taken only hours before. Every fiber of his body was screaming in agony.

One more thing ... one more move ... one more thing ... one more move...

Don't look up. That makes it worse. Just keeping going...

"Michael?" Joel called. "You okay?"

He could barely grunt the reply. "Yeah!"

"I hate to rush you, man, but I'm almost out of time down here!"

Michael knew that was true, because the heat was increasing around him, too. The smoke was close to overwhelming him. He knew that if this happened, it was game over.

Precious seconds passed as he kept ascending ... Eventually he dared to look up to check his progress and saw that the opening was finally about three feet above his head.

Just a little more! Come on...! One more move ... one more thing...

And then he was there.

Michael's fingertips gripped the edges of the final bricks and thrust his torso out of the chimney, emerging into the dark, smoky air. Flames at the front of the cabin illuminated the immediate surroundings, but thankfully the roof was not ablaze. But it was getting close.

He pulled up the AR, duct tape intact, and set the selector switch to "fire." It was engaged and ready to deal with the problem at hand.

The roof was at a gentle incline. He moved to the edge and peered into the smoke and flames below him. He could see two MWs on the outside of the inferno, watching the door. They each held long rifles.

"Play with fire, you get burned," Michael muttered to himself. He raised the gun, got one man in his sight, breathed, and squeezed the trigger. The recoil against his shoulder brought back memories. He was once again fighting for survival. For himself and for his fellow soldier.

The man dropped. His buddy looked over at him, confused and panicked. In a continuous movement, Michael zeroed in on the second guy's head and squeezed the trigger.

Red mist. Two down.

Then, as was agreed with Joel, Michael pointed the rifle at the sky and let loose a pattern of two shots, one shot, two shots, one shot.

* * *

Inside the cabin, Joel heard the signal that he and Michael had chosen. His friend had made it!

He began to crawl on his stomach from his safe haven to the front door through narrow channels on the floor that still had not fully caught fire. It wasn't the flames that threatened Joel as much as it was the deadly smoke. He realized that there was a high probability that the carbon monoxide he had to fight his way through might take him out before he ever reached the door. Holding his breath was his only option, but there was no relief for his burning eyes that made navigating across the floor more difficult. It was sheer stupid luck that made his efforts pay off.

The door!

His brain commanded him to unlock and open the damn door as he fought to maintain consciousness. He grabbed the key from his pocket and forced his body up to his knees. He thrust the key in the hole and then grabbed the almost white hot door handle.

Joel succeeded in pulling the heavy door open.

Instincts again directed him. He dropped to his belly again, held the Glock in both hands, and began firing into the smoke and flames outside. He couldn't see anything beyond that.

Even the smoke outdoors was overpowering. The flames that had taken to the forest floor around the cabin leapt toward his body as he fought to extinguish the fire making its way up his right arm. He emptied the Glock and pulled most of his body through the door only seconds before he lost consciousness.

* * *

Michael heard shouting below. At least two MWs were still alive. It was not easy to see past the growing flames and smoke. However, he could barely make out through the haze the tree line beyond the clearing in front of the cabin where an SUV and a pickup truck were parked. There was movement there, and he realized two men were getting into the SUV. A few seconds later, it pulled out to the road. The cowards were running.

He aimed the rifle at the back of the car as it began to speed away. He could blow out the rear tires or choose the back windshield and maybe strike the driver or his passenger.

Michael, recalling what he had gone through at the hands of these men over the past few days, elected to go with the latter option.

He squeezed the trigger three times. At first the SUV kept going and he thought he'd missed … but the vehicle veered off the road and crashed into a tree. Only one man got out of the car and started to run down the road. Michael centered the figure in his sight and had no qualms with triple tapping the trigger, ending the man's attempt to escape.

Satisfied that no more MWs were in play, Michael threw the gun down to the ground out of the range of the flames. He then backed up, focused on the area of dirt and grass that was his target, and bolted forward. He made a broad jump off the roof. The ground came rushing toward him. He lightly touched the earth with the soles of his boots and immediately executed the forward body roll that he had practiced endlessly years ago during training.

Michael stood and eyed the flaming cabin. The fire had covered most of the front of the building and was now edging onto the roof.

"Joel!"

Silence.

"Joel, can you hear me?"

Michael quickly scanned the hellish scene before him, took a deep breath, and then he ran into the flames. He was at the door in seconds and found Joel semiconscious on the floor with half his body still inside the flame-filled cabin. Michael grabbed him under his arms and pulled hard, dragging him over the threshold, across the flames, and out onto safe ground. He then rolled his friend twice to make sure the man's charred camo clothing wasn't ablaze, and then he slapped Joel's cheeks.

"Take a breath, brother!" Another slap. "Wake up!"

Joel's eyes fluttered, and then he gasped and coughed. Michael helped him sit up on the ground. Joel continued to cough violently, nearly retching, but finally he was able to breathe.

"We made it, buddy," Michael said.

"Where ... are the ... shitheads?" Joel coughed again.

"They're gone, brother. They won't be marching in any more hate protests."

They sat there a few minutes watching the structure burn, grabbing a much needed rest and several breaths of air. Finally, they stood. Michael felt no pain in his legs or feet from the jump. Joel took a few wobbly steps with Michael's help, and they went to the remaining pickup truck. Michael opened the door. "Well, whadaya know," he said. "The valet was nice enough to leave the keys. What time is it?"

Joel looked at his wristwatch. "Two thirty-ish."

"All we need is to drive until we get some bars on that phone ... we still have some time."

50

It was an hour after dawn when the white box truck arrived in downtown Richmond. Rusty, Chad, and Willis sat in the back on jump seats. The driver and passenger were trusted MWs by the names of Don and Snake.

As they drove closer to the courthouse, Rusty made a call to one of the MWs back at the cabin. He got voicemail and yelled into the phone, "Why aren't you answering, jackass? There's gonna be hell to pay when I get back!" He hung up and cursed.

"What's going on?" Willis asked.

Rusty grumbled, "Everyone at the cabin is probably asleep. You can't depend on anyone these days."

"Well, I wouldn't worry about it. Not even God can find that cabin."

Chad added, "Pretty soon we'll know how long it takes to roast a lawyer. But first let's see how well they blow up!"

At six thirty in the morning, the streets of downtown Richmond were surprisingly quiet with barely any signs of life. An occasional truck or car drove by, but mostly they had the city to themselves. Don drove the white truck to Grace Street behind the courthouse, and then turned right again on 7th, a one-way street. The truck crossed over Broad Street and pulled over to the first parking spot on the left side. The corner building boasted a sign that read, "UR DOWNTOWN." The ground floor was a coffee shop that appeared dark and empty. A sign on the door read: CLOSED—WATER MAIN BREAK—SORRY FOR THE INCONVENIENCE.

Rusty, Chad, and Willis got out of the truck, went to the corner of 7th and Broad, and were satisfied that they had a good view. The courthouse and its main entrance were across Broad Street at an angle from their vantage point. There, parked in the far-right bus lane near the courthouse entrance, was the UPS truck. It appeared as if it had broken down. Orange traffic cones were set up in the back and left side to direct traffic around the truck. The two rear tires were flat, and the hazard lights were blinking. To anyone curious, the driver, who sat behind the wheel, was waiting on road service.

"Blue and the boys set it up just right," Chad said. "It's right where we wanted the truck."

Rusty asked, "Where's their getaway car?"

"On 8th Street," Chad answered. "A brown Honda Civic, parked at a meter. When you call him, Blue and his team will leave the truck, run around the corner to 8th Street, and disappear."

Willis, craning his neck to scan the buildings outside the vehicle, said, "This truck is probably all over security camera footage now."

"We know that, Willis," Chad said.

Rusty explained, "We told you we're ditching the truck once we get away. Remember? And there's been zilch on the police scanner."

Willis sheepishly shrugged. "I know, I know, just sayin'..."

Rusty squinted at Willis. "You okay, Willis? You're acting kind of like you don't want to be here."

"No, no, I just..." Willis waved an arm at the empty street. "Something doesn't feel right. My Spidey senses are telling me we should, I don't know, maybe step back and reevaluate the situation."

Chad growled, "Oh, come on. Willis, you helped us plan this thing. You're not wussing out now, are you?"

"No, no, I..." Willis shook his head and shrugged. "It's all good. Everything's going as we planned it. We're getting two million from the bank for this job. Let's do it!"

Rusty laughed a little. "We're already here. We *are* doing it." He pointed down Broad Street in the opposite direction of the courthouse.

"We've gone over this a dozen times but I'll say it again. The hearing is scheduled for eight thirty this morning. The Hilton Hotel is two blocks that way. According to the intel from the Antriol law team, Deketomis and his team are staying there, and they always walk from the hotel to the courthouse. They'll want to arrive at least an hour early. It's possible they might walk right here to this corner and then cross Broad to the other side to the courthouse. Or they might walk along Broad on the other side of the street. We don't know. But we have to watch for them on whatever side of Broad Street they're on between seven and seven-thirty. You've seen their pictures. As soon as we see them, I have to call Blue and tell him to get the hell out of the truck, so get it right. Then, Chad … you'll know what to do."

"Damn straight." He held up a cell phone. "When I make my call, you're gonna see our little baby blow the back doors off and shred anyone and anything on the sidewalk and street behind the truck."

They got back in the truck and Rusty addressed them all. "Okay, gents, everyone put on your workmen overalls. We now work for Quigg's. I'd say we have about an hour, so be calm, be cool, and let's do this. Recheck your firepower and have 'em close by just in case the bomb doesn't take everybody out completely. Remember, two quick shots to the head to everyone still moving, and then we're out."

* * *

As the sun rose over Richmond, traffic on Broad Street increased. The men became alert as they saw a police patrol car stopped behind the UPS truck. The MWs watched from their block and a half distance. The officer got out of the car and spoke to the driver, whom the MWs knew to be Blue. The cop shook his head as if the situation were out of his control, got back in the patrol car, and drove away. Not one time did he ask to look inside the truck.

Chad spoke in a high-pitched voice as if he were imitating Blue. "I'm so sorry, officer, but UPS promised me that they're sending road assistance as soon as possible. Should be within the hour, sir!" He then switched to his own voice. "Looks like Blue remembered what to say."

Rusty chuckled. "So far, so good, but stay focused."

Most employees of the courthouse used back entrances, but a few sometimes entered through the front. Oddly, it was seven o'clock and there was no sign of workers making entrances.

The MWs remained in the white truck until 7:10, and then Rusty got out, went around to the back of the truck, and opened the doors. Inside were pieces of furniture, carefully arranged to give the impression that the men were there for a reason. Don helped Rusty unload a couple of shelving units and placed them on the sidewalk. Again, it was for the sake of appearance. Anyone walking by would think they were delivering furniture.

* * *

Willis became increasingly concerned because there didn't seem to be much activity anywhere in front of the courthouse. He wondered if it was some kind of special courthouse holiday, but he kept his observations to himself. How many cameras covered the courthouse entrance? Did any parts of his careful planning with Rusty and Chad have holes? How could they? He was Willis Lee, the guy they all called the *wunderkind* for his smarts. Blake wouldn't trust him to oversee the MWs' part in the bank's undertakings if he didn't have the brains to do so.

Willis knew, though, that mistakes could be made. Chad was wound so tightly that he was always a threat. The man was a killer, and he had murdered many times for the MWs. Chad was also good at making bombs. He had somehow picked up that knowledge, and the MWs had arranged to buy explosives—along with drugs—from their business partners in Colombia. To Willis this seemed to be the ideal solution for the MWs'—and the bank's—problems. Unfortunately, though, Chad was a loose cannon. Unpredictable.

And these idiots seriously don't appreciate what I've done for them.

The more Willis thought about it, the angrier he became.

The lawsuit against the bank had put the MWs in an untenable position with the cartel. It had shone a light on the bank's corruption, which had always been a benefit to the drug lords needing to wash cash.

It was Willis's *ingenuity* that had convinced the New Yorkers that the MWs would provide the means by which the lawsuit could be delayed and made unwinnable. Removing Janet Blanco from the equation had briefly cooled the heads of the cartel, but Joel Hartbeck had been an unforeseen wrinkle, and then the Gold Star attorneys had been given more information than what Willis had thought possible. The cartel had made it clear that heads would roll if their laundromat was shut down. Now that the Gold Star attorneys had a magnifying glass on the bank's *other* transactions with the DOJ's sanctioned entities in the Middle East, everything was in jeopardy.

When Blake had suggested to Willis that it was time to take a final big payoff and leave the country, he'd jumped at the chance. Eliminating the Gold Star attorney and his team would cause further delays so that Willis and the New Yorkers could finish the money washing job and get the hell out of Dodge.

There was just this one final job to do.

* * *

At 7:20 a.m., a Coca-Cola delivery truck pulled onto 7th Street right beside Rusty's strategically parked white box vehicle. It was a tight squeeze for it because it was roughly the same size as the box truck. It pulled up to the curb in front of the MWs vehicle and stopped. The back end stuck out into the road such that only smaller cars would be able to get by and pass it. There was no way the MWs could make their escape when the bomb went off.

"What the hell?" Chad growled. "What are they doing?"

A man wearing a Coca-Cola company jumpsuit got out of his truck and went to the back. He opened it up, revealing stacks of Coke cartons. He removed a hand truck and began to stack cartons on it. The man was apparently delivering beverages to the coffee shop, even though it was closed.

Rusty stepped out and confronted the man. "Are you going to be long? We'll need to get out of here soon. *Very* soon."

The man shrugged. "Sorry, pal. I have a delivery to make. I won't be too long." He continued his work, slowly guiding the hand truck to the coffee shop's door. Someone inside unlocked and opened it for him, but Rusty couldn't see who it was. He spat on the street and turned back to his men.

Don, who was standing at the corner of 7th and Broad and peering northwest with small field glasses, ran to Rusty and said, "Deketomis is coming." Rusty joined him at the corner and saw that, sure enough, the lawyer was walking alone on the other side of Broad.

"Where's the rest of his team?" Rusty asked.

"No idea!" Don responded.

Rusty went back to the truck and told Chad, "Get ready. The lawyer will be in front of the courthouse in about two minutes, I reckon. He's just crossing 6th Street. I'm calling Blue."

Willis experienced a wave of panic. "How are we going to get out of here? The Coke guy is still in the coffee shop!"

"We run if we have to," Rusty answered with a shrug. He then pulled out his cell phone and spat, "Here goes!" He dialed Blue's number.

Nothing happened.

He looked at the phone. "What the hell?" He tried it again. "I don't have a signal. Shit, I'll restart the phone." He quickly did so.

"The lawyer is at 7th Street!" Don said. "In twenty seconds, he'll be at the courthouse entrance!"

Chad had his own cell phone out and was ready to dial the number to set off the EFP. "I'm doing this whether Blue is out of the truck or not!"

Rusty's phone finished restarting, and he dialed Blue's number again. When the call didn't go through, he panicked. "There's something wrong!"

"The lawyer is in front of the doors in ten, nine, eight, seven, six..."

Chad: "Here goes!" He dialed the vital number.

"five, four, three..."

Again, Chad's call didn't seem to connect. The line appeared to be ringing, but nothing happened. He screamed like a caged animal.

"two, one... and ... the lawyer entered the building!"

At that instant, the side doors of the Coca-Cola truck rolled up and ten men and women wearing FBI Swat Team jackets and decked out in Kevlar vests poured out. With an array of tactical rifles and handguns pointed at the white truck, several yelled, "Get out with your hands up! Throw down your weapons! Out of the vehicle, out of the vehicle, now!"

"Shit! Shit!" Rusty cried.

Chad yelled, "Screw this!" He grabbed an AR-15, jumped out the back of the truck, and ran into the intersection of Broad and 7th Streets. He then turned and started firing the weapon at the FBI agents. Bullets flew, breaking windows in the coffee shop. For the first time, Chad recognized that there was no one inside. It dawned on him why there were very few people walking on the street anywhere near the courthouse.

The agents took cover and returned fire. A female FBI agent zigzagged across 7th Street from the Coke truck and took aim with her M4 carbine.

Police cars suddenly zoomed across Broad Street from the other side of 7th Street, sirens and lights blazing. More poured out of 6th Street onto Broad and sped to the intersection. Things were moving so fast that Chad became disoriented. He was surrounded.

The female FBI agent fixed the MW in her sight and let loose a burst of fire from the M4. Chad violently jerked three times, spun around, and fell to the road in a heap. A half dozen FBI agents converged on the lifeless body with guns drawn and targeted.

Felicia Paul, the agent who had shot the bomber, then went back to the white truck to assist in making the arrests of the other MWs, who had surrendered in shock.

Willis Lee, however, jumped out of the back of the white truck and started running northwest on Broad. An agent shouted for him to halt, but he kept going.

Carol, who had been hidden safely the entire time in the coffee shop with Jake, burst out of the store and pursued Willis. Even though Carol was in her fifties, she was twice as fit as the younger man. She chased him to 6th Street and just beyond before she finally caught up to him. She leaped and tackled him. He cried out, saying, "I didn't do anything! I've been a prisoner! Help me!"

"I'll help you!" Carol said, and she kicked him in the face.

By then, two Richmond police officers also in pursuit caught up with them. They cuffed Willis and read him his rights.

Carol walked back and joined Felicia and the FBI team as they rounded up the MWs.

Rusty Wainwright's face was an expression of disbelief, anger, and confusion. He watched as Felicia took his cell phone and dropped it in an evidence bag. She asked him, "What, you dumb shits have never heard of a mobile phone jammer?" She nodded at the Coca-Cola truck. "That thing is full of jammers. Not that we needed them!"

Even more puzzled, Rusty gazed across the street, where men in UPS uniforms emerged from the disabled truck in front of the courthouse. He couldn't believe his eyes, because Blue was not among them. In fact, he didn't recognize any of them as MWs.

"Oh, are you looking for your pals?" Felicia asked. "Well, first of all, that's not your stolen UPS truck, dumbass. That truck's owned by your friendly neighborhood FBI. And your pal, Blue? He and his two buddies were arrested, and the bomb squad took away your toy. Blue's sitting in the same kind of holding cell we're about to throw you in. These guys next to me are your pals, now. They're going to read you something about what you can do next, and then they're going to haul your ass off in that big black wagon driving up now."

The police marched Willis over to the group of detainees, where he sat next to Rusty in stunned silence. Together they watched law enforcement personnel taking photos and stretching yellow tape around Chad's dead and bloody body in the middle of the street.

* * *

Across the street at the courthouse, Deke reemerged from the front doors and watched the excitement. The "pedestrians" all around the courthouse had dropped character and were now revealing that they were all part of the operation. An FBI agent approached him and asked, "Are you all right, sir?"

"I'm fine. I'm so glad no one got hurt," Deke answered.

"You were a very brave soul to volunteer to do this."

Deke shrugged. "All I had to do was show up." He saw Jake and Carol crossing Broad Street and coming toward him. Deke commented to the agent, "Those two will never fail me. It's always downright humbling."

"Every now and then the good guys win. Good luck to you, Mr. Deketomis." The agent went away and Deke joined his teammates.

"All good?" he asked.

"I'm fine," Carol said. She wiped her brow. "I guess I went a little batshit crazy there for a minute, but I couldn't help myself."

Jake said, "At least for now I'll take back all that bad stuff I always say about the FBI. They had this tightly wired from the word go. Carol and I insisted on hiding out in the coffee shop to watch it all go down, and they let us. And you know what? I'd say we earned that right."

"Where're Gina and Bernie?" Carol asked.

"They're already inside the courthouse. We arranged for them to arrive through the back entrance." Deke looked around. "I'm simply amazed how this was pulled together so quickly. I had no idea what was going to happen. An FBI agent asked me if I'd be willing to simply walk to the courthouse. He said there was a pretty real risk involved, but I'm sure it pales in comparison to what you two have been through in the last few days."

Carol said, "Thank you, Deke. It really did come together quickly. Joel had left a message on my phone saying he was going to rescue Michael. He also said there might be a bomb at the courthouse here, but he didn't know the exact details. It wasn't enough to give any law enforcement a ring. But then Jake and I were on the road to Richmond when I got Michael's call, and apparently *he* had worked it all out. He and Joel were already driving back to Plainsburg. I immediately got hold of Felicia in the middle of the night. She took the information and ran with it. She demanded that the Virginia office allow her to join the operation."

Jake continued, "Information came from different sources like puzzle pieces. Carol and I told them what we had discovered at the Quigg home, Joel Hartbeck had valuable data from his own intel gathering on the MWs, and Michael provided fragments of conversations he'd overheard at the cabin where he was being held."

"The FBI figured out from keywords like 'Blue,' 'driving,' 'coffee shop,' and 'corner' where the MWs would be parked to watch for you,"

Carol said. "They got the coffee shop management to close for the morning. A lot of folks were scrambling in the wee hours to get this done."

The FBI paddy wagons pulled away to transport the prisoners. Carol spotted Felicia Paul across the street and waved at her. Felicia gave her a thumbs up.

"Have you been able to talk to Michael?" Jake asked Deke.

"Yes," he answered. "He and Joel are recuperating in a hospital in Plainsburg. They'll be fine. Michael is worse for wear and was pretty badly beaten, and Joel suffered some smoke inhalation and a few minor burns across his body, but overall they're healthy. And alive. They should be good to go in a day."

Carol looked at her watch. "It's about time for the FBI to land on the other targets. Wish I could be there to watch!"

* * *

New York, New York—Friday

Karl Maher rushed into Blake Dullea's office at Bank Antriol.

"Are you ready? The car's waiting downstairs!" he said with urgency.

Blake was still downloading files to flash drives from his computer. He was on his third out of six.

"I'm almost done," he said, breathlessly.

"No, you're not. You're not even halfway. We gotta go, Blake. Seriously."

"Hold your damn horses. We're going to be okay. If we appear to be in too much of a hurry, then people might get suspicious."

"Damn it, Blake, don't you understand what's happened? Richmond was a bust! Those redneck rats are going to squeal. Maybe they already have! My cousin Ahmet has everything set up for us. We just have to get to JFK, get on the plane, and fly to Cairo, but we have to get the next flight, and it's in two hours! Get your ass moving!"

Blake gripped the edge of his desk and turned his head to gaze at his partner with venom in his eyes. "Don't. Rush. Me. I'm giving up my *life* here. What's my wife going to say? What are my two daughters going to say when they're older? 'Oh, our daddy left us without telling us good-bye.' That's what I'm going to have to live with, Karl. I don't know if I'll ever see my wife and children again! So shut the hell up!"

"This was *your* idea, Blake," Karl grunted. "You said, 'if we cause enough chaos then that'll give us time to take the money and run.' My family in Egypt was the escape hatch. Well, your whole chaos idea failed. It's time to run."

There was a knock on the door behind Karl. Both men turned to see Alicia, the receptionist of the tenth floor. She had a look of bewilderment on her face.

"Yes, Alicia?" Karl asked.

"Um, excuse me. There are some FBI agents here to see you both."

Before the bankers could react, two men and a woman wearing FBI jackets appeared behind Alicia. The woman gently moved Alicia out of the way, and the three agents stepped into the office.

The man who resembled Clark Kent spoke. "Blake Dullea? Karl Maher?"

"Y-yes?" Blake answered in a strangled voice.

"I am FBI Special Agent Kirk Turkel." He flashed his badge. "You both are wanted for questioning at the Federal Plaza building. We're here to escort you."

Karl and Blake looked at each other with wide eyes.

Karl asked, "Are we under arrest?"

The woman answered, "Not yet."

Turkel added, "If you need to call your attorneys and have them meet you at Federal Plaza, then you have sixty seconds to do so. If you resist in any way, then we *will* arrest you, and you will be escorted out of the building in handcuffs. Your call, gentlemen." He nodded to the other male agent, who stepped forward to give them each a search warrant for everything in their respective offices.

"We'll start by collecting those flash drives you're in such a hurry to load," the agent said.

Karl Maher's knees buckled, and Blake Dullea had to grab his partner to prevent him from collapsing.

51

The turmoil and disruption in front of the courthouse that morning delayed the Antriol case hearing to eleven in the morning. Deke, Carol, and Jake had spent a couple of hours with the FBI and Richmond police providing statements. They had also checked in with Michael again to see how he was doing. He expected to be released from the hospital that afternoon. Joel would have to remain an extra day for observation and possibly undergo new skin grafts down the road, but he was going to recover. Right before the hearing, Carol received a text from Sheila Denning in Plainsburg, saying that their mayor was "freaked" about her report regarding the police department's involvement with the MWs, and that the local district attorney "was all over Boss Hog's butt." Carol and Jake would be required to submit affidavits regarding their false arrest and imprisonment, which they were enthusiastically prepared to do.

At the appointed hour, Deke, Bernie, and Gina sat at the plaintiff's table in the courtroom. Carol, Jake, and Dan Lawson sat close by in the gallery directly behind the partition. George Mendel, Oliver Wrecker, and their battalion of support attorneys were in place at the defense table.

Judge Trackman entered the courtroom and the bailiff called the hearing to order. The judge took her time setting items in place at the bench, knowing full well that she was generating a bit of suspense. She then looked up at Deke and said, "Mr. Deketomis, I understand you were involved in a bit of excitement this morning."

Deke stood and answered, "Yes, your honor."

"I trust you're unharmed and able to proceed."

"Yes, your honor. Our team is in good shape. Thank you for your concern."

She nodded and Deke sat. The judge then addressed the defense. "Mr. Mendel, were you or any of your associates involved in this morning's unrest?"

George Mendel was surprised by the question. Obviously shaken, he stood and replied, "No, of course not, your honor."

With a hint of a smile on her face, Judge Trackman said softly, "I just had to ask. No need to take it personally."

Confused, Mendel sat.

"Before I announce my decision in this case, is there anything counsel would like to say first? I'll start with the plaintiffs. Mr. Deketomis?"

Deke stood again and said, "Your honor, the evidence is pouring in that Bank Antriol employees were behind the attempted bombing outside the courthouse this morning. Mr. Willis Lee, a Bank Antriol employee, was among those arrested. I understand he's already promised the FBI that he is willing to talk in an attempt to make a deal with the Justice Department. Frankly, I believe his crimes do not warrant dealmaking, but that's up to the DOJ. It is also my understanding that two executive vice presidents of the bank in New York are in custody there. My associate attorney, Michael Carey, was kidnapped on Monday and held against his will in the woods of Kentucky by known criminal accomplices of Bank Antriol employees. Our primary witness, Joel Hartbeck, has come out of hiding and was instrumental in freeing Mr. Carey. They will have plenty to say about what's been happening regarding the crimes committed against them. They will also be able to provide the court with overwhelming proof that Antriol as of this week was still in the banking business with terrorists and drug cartels. The information they will provide goes to the very heart of this case and, now more than ever, we must keep momentum behind our discovery efforts. As I have said before, lives are in the balance. Any delay would create more danger for innocent people who fall victim to the criminal organizations with whom Bank Antriol has done business."

Deke sat down. He could feel the electricity in the room. The attorneys at the defense table shifted uncomfortably in their seats.

The judge addressed them. "Mr. Mendel?"

George Mendel stood, cleared his throat, and boldly stated, "Your honor, Bank Antriol will vigorously defend these accusations. They are sensational lies that are attempting to connect bank employees with hardened criminals. There is absolutely no evidence to support charges like that. Moreover, any investigation into potential criminal conduct needs to be managed by the Department of Justice and should be separate and apart from what goes on in this civil case. We are still at the same place we were when all this nonsense began. We demand a stay in the case."

Jake couldn't help snorting loud enough for everyone to hear. The judge shot him a glance, but she didn't say anything. He bowed his head to suppress a laugh, and so did Carol.

"Is that all, Mr. Mendel?" the judge asked.

"Judge, if you don't grant this stay, I promise you'll run the risk of reversal on appeal."

Everyone in the room nearly gasped at George Mendel's audacity. The judge, however, merely stated, "That's a risk I'm willing to take. Now sit down, counselor."

"Yes, your honor." He sat and immediately began staring at the ceiling, obviously wishing he were anywhere but the courtroom.

"Very well. I deny Bank Antriol's request for a stay. Mr. Deketomis, please continue with the discovery schedule this court ordered and let's be ready for trial on the date set aside." She banged the gavel. "Good day."

She stood and exited the courtroom.

While Mendel and company grumbled and packed away their things for a hasty exit, Deke and his team stood and embraced each other. Congratulations went to everyone all around.

Bernie was near tears. He took Deke by the shoulders and said, "There are so many families and veterans who will think you're a hero."

Deke replied, "I'm not the hero here. My clients—the plaintiffs—are the real heroes, and it's my honor and pleasure to see that justice will be done for them. Their sacrifices and service to this country will never, *ever*, be forgotten."

Deke turned to gather his papers and slowly packed his briefcase. He knew that there was still much work to do and many sleepless nights ahead. Wall Street crimes would not stop here. The events over the past few weeks had simply been deadly diversions that took attention away from the real enemy—preexisting power structures and systems that had been in place for decades and allowed generations of greed to profit off the same crimes.

This was but one resounding victory in a battle of a larger war still being waged.

EPILOGUE

Pensacola Beach, Florida—Six Months Later

The turquoise waves of the Gulf of Mexico lapped onto the white sand in a meditative and leisurely rhythm. There were dozens of people present, mostly families with children, but Joel Hartbeck felt as if he had Pensacola Beach to himself. He consciously tuned out the noise of kids laughing and playing—not that he minded it—and concentrated on gazing at the vast horizon of blue in front of him. It was difficult to tell where the ocean ended and the sky began. Certainly different from the landscape he had grown up with in Kentucky.

Dressed in board shorts, a long-sleeved sun shirt to cover the burn scars on his arm, and sunglasses, he lay on one of two comfortable recliners, and, at that moment, didn't have a care in the world. The beverage in hand was iced tea, and it was cool and refreshing.

"Hey, brother," came a voice he knew well.

Joel turned to see Michael Carey walking toward him. He, too, was dressed for the beach. He carried a small cooler and a towel.

"I brought a little something to eat," Michael said.

"Oh, man, you just rescued me," Joel said. "I was dying here."

"You don't look like you were dying." Michael set his stuff down and stretched out on the recliner. "Ahh. This is great. Sorry I'm late."

"No problem."

"You got settled into the new place all right?"

"Yep, and I love it down here. Moving from Kentucky was the best decision I could have made," Joel said. "Thank you for encouraging me."

"You're welcome. And the new job?"

"Nicest place. Best people I've ever worked around in my life. What really surprises me is that my engineering skills are still pretty good."

"Glad to hear it."

"How are things with you?"

"Busy as always. You probably want to hear what's up with the Antriol thing."

"I do."

"Deke just finished testifying at a grand jury in New York that the DOJ was conducting. The criminal charges are coming down. Blake Dullea and Karl Maher are toast. They're going to be held responsible for the bombings, along with a bunch of other people."

Joel did a fist pump. "Yes!"

"And our lawsuit is bulldozing Antriol. No question about it. All the veterans and Gold Star families are going to benefit, big time."

"That's such good news, Michael. What happened in Plainsburg? Last I heard there hadn't been any charges yet."

"Well, you know the entire police force was replaced, right?"

"Uh huh."

"Well, all but one. They appointed that officer who helped us, Sheila Denning, to run the station. I'm sure the town was shocked when people heard a woman is their new police chief."

Joel laughed. "I hadn't heard that. That's good news, too."

"I'm pretty sure that with everything Willis Lee is spilling, the esteemed Chief Bert Wainwright is gonna go down. He'll be indicted, along with that entire MW gaggle. The MWs are out of business. With Willis telling everybody *everything*, it'll happen. After the feds cleared us for your little cabin search and destroy operation, the dominos really started to fall. You know, Willis has even pegged Chad for Janet's murder."

"I had heard that," Joel said.

"By the way, I guess I haven't said so before, but I'm sorry about Janet, Joel. I know she meant something to you."

Joel nodded and looked down. "Thanks. It just pisses me off that Chad is dead and won't suffer for what he's done. He got off the earth much too easily for all the evil he did on it."

"Hell, he's dead," Michael replied. "In my book, that qualifies as punishment. At the very least, it's one of the small victories."

They were quiet for a while, calmly sipping their drinks, watching the ocean, and soaking up the rays.

Memories of Kentucky would probably always be with Joel, and much of them were unpleasant ones. For years, his life had been a string of constantly unfolding nightmares. The war, the EFP on the bridge, his troubles post-discharge, Janet, the weeks of hiding in the woods, and the night he rescued Michael were on continuous replay in his head. But the sunshine, change of scenery, and presence of true friends in Florida were helping to transform him. He felt invigorated and alive for the first time in years.

Now, as he enjoyed the smells, sounds, and sights of the beach, Joel was as content as he possibly could be. He didn't know what the future was going to bring, but every sense in his being told him that smoother sailing was ahead.

Joel caught himself staring not at the sea and sky, but at Michael. He couldn't hide the big smile or control the belly laugh as he thought about how their friendship had run a full circle.

"What the hell are you laughing at?" Michael asked. "You're creeping me out."

Small victories, indeed.

THE END